IN HOT PURSUIT

They sat close together in the ancient Hidden City, jumping whenever there was a close thunderclap. As lightning illuminated the Mahali jungle, Joyce spoke at last. 'Faith, I'm – I'm sorry for being such a bitch to you.'

Faith chuckled. 'Isn't that supposed to be *my* line?'

Outside the storm continued erratically, like an air raid in some old war film. They faced each other. Feeling a hot wave pass through her, Joyce's eyes drifted down, catching at a moment of lightning her friend's groin, encased like her own in damp knickers. Joyce remembered how Faith had looked under the waterfall, at the water tower, in the London club, and Joyce felt her own dew escape and quickly gather in the gusset of her knickers. The air, and the tension soaked within it, hung heavily between them. They both knew where this could lead.

IN HOT PURSUIT

DELLA SHANNON

First published in 2000 by
Sapphire
Thames Wharf Studios,
Rainville Road, London W6 9HA

ISBN 0 352 33553 X

Typeset by SetSystems Ltd, Saffron Walden, Essex
Printed and bound in Great Britain by Mackays of Chatham PLC

For DC – for leading me to my banquet

ONE

She was lightning. She was quicksilver. She was Faith Ballard, the hottest desperado running and tonight she was running for her life.

Well, perhaps 'life' was an exaggeration; she couldn't be *absolutely* certain the Dobermann in hot pursuit would kill her – just make her look like a letter damaged by the Post Office. She'd probably end up in one of those plastic bags with the caption, 'While we try to ensure that every delicious young black woman is delivered to you in the condition received, this is not always possible . . .'

Enough babbling; the balcony was close. But the Dobermann was closer. With the odds rapidly approaching zero, she whispered a quick prayer to St Rita of Cascia, Patron Saint of Delicious Young Black Women (well, Impossible Cases, actually; but that would apply to Faith, too).

And in answer, the dog, a sable, forty-kilo meteor, leaped into the air – and was jerked back as it reached the end of its chain. She heard the noise, turned to see, tripped over her own boots and fell on her ass. The dog barked and snapped, mightily ticked off at being cheated of its prey; but the chain held from wherever in the flat it was anchored.

Faith rose, saluted the beast with a raucous laugh and her middle

1

finger, and made her way to the sliding balcony doors, feeling bruises forming on her cheeks already, despite her heavily padded all-black mask and bodysuit.

The flat's alarms continued to screech at her, as they had since she'd crashed in through the skylight. Guesstimations raced through her mind as she stepped outside: ten, fifteen seconds for the lobby guards to wake up and pinpoint the source of the alarm; maybe forty seconds for the lift to descend and pick them up, then to reach the fifteenth floor . . .

Close, boys, but not close enough.

The Manhattan midnight wind, slightly chilled for October, whipped about Faith as she glanced down below, uncaring of the height. It was an upmarket neighbourhood, and down below, clubs lined the street, with revellers lining the pavements in pairs and groups.

Revellers – and police! So soon? Probably already called in on some disturbance outside a club; this was getting better by the minute.

She glanced upwards, at the skeleton of a much taller building still under construction across the wide street. Moments before, she'd been up there, harnessed to a parachute as well as grief and self-pity. She was an Adventuress, a Daredevil, a Risk Taker living La Vida Loca – she'd been taught well – but now with her teacher gone, gone from her life for ever, she didn't quite care if she survived or not.

A dangerous mindset indeed.

So, when the crosswinds collapsed her primary chute moments after she'd leaped into the air, her first thought had been: OK. This is It. It was Time for Her to Die.

But her second thought had been: Oh No It Fricking Wasn't.

And she opened the secondary chute, just in time. However, it didn't prevent her from plummeting into the skylight of an adjacent building. Fortunately, there was no one in the flat. Unfortunately for Faith, there was the dog, which had prevented her from getting to the front door. How she managed to unharness herself from the chute and escape would have to be examined later. For now . . . she quickly hooked up the spare abseiling ropes she carried, and began her descent down the side of the building.

Then there were lights, cries from below – she'd been spotted! She'd stopped her descent around the sixth floor, then kicked herself away from the side of the building, then again, galvanising her momentum, until she twisted slightly, straightening – and crashed through an adjacent window. She landed on her ass – again – in a corridor: ouch.

The lift was ahead, but that was no good; they'll be watching it, and the adjacent staircase. Then again, she couldn't just sit there, waiting for the guards or a tenant investigating the noise. Quickly she unhooked herself from the ropes, rose and began checking doors, a desperate gamble to find one unlocked. Come on, St Rita, get it in gear –

One door opened: hallelujah! Quietly she stepped inside, locking it behind her; never could tell who else might drop in.

The interior, in the citylight from the open window, was all shadow and soft cushions. Pausing in the living room, she looked for the drinks cabinet; they'll search this floor, but not confine their efforts, in case she escaped to another –

'Master? Are you back?'

Faith froze at the voice from the bedroom. Damn, damn, *damn*, talk about the frying pan and the fricking fire –

'Master? Release me, please. I'll be obedient. I *promise.*'

A woman's voice. And those words . . . Faith's curiosity got the better of her, and she ventured forth, ready for anything –

– Or so she thought.

The bedroom was well lit, warm and furnished with the usual mod cons. Which nowadays apparently included chains, switches, belts and a naked woman suspended by her wrists near the bed: young-looking, tall, lean but fit, sweat glossing her skin, chestnut-haired, narrow-chinned. Her breasts were small, firm-looking, and the nipples neat and dark in colour, glistening with sweat, dripping down to collect like dew around her groin. Yes, Faith stared there, too: the woman's pubic hair was a tawny delta barely sheltering her slit.

She was manacled to ceiling chains, though there was just

3

enough give so she was on her feet rather than swinging by her wrists. She twisted, as if to display the fresh pink stripes across her firm cheeks, then opened her hazel eyes to Faith. 'Master, I – *Master*?'

Faith stood dumbstruck, feeling the heat flood her face. Well, at least the girl couldn't run for help. But if she cried out – or would the neighbours be used to hearing strange sounds from in here –

The woman drew breath, as if she would do just that, but then whispered with heavy, nervous expectancy, 'Has my Master sent you to punish me in his absence?'

What the hell was she talking about? Then Faith understood: her own outfit must make her look like a fetishist's poster girl. Smiling beneath her mask, reminding herself how aroused she always got when her adrenalin was pumped, she decided to test the waters, affecting a commanding voice. 'Yes, he did. What do they call you?'

'Daphne.'

'You will address me as "Mistress"!'

'Y-yes, Mistress. Forgive a slave.' Her voice grew moist and husky with desire. Faith became aware of how her own nipples were growing hard, almost aching. She'd never had a woman like this before; it was . . . intriguing.

Intriguing, hell; it was downright *horny*. 'And did your Master say when he would return?'

Daphne nodded. 'He said he would be back at one.'

In another two hours. Daphne's words suggested this wasn't a new situation, although Faith questioned the judgement of leaving someone manacled alone like this. What if there had been a fire? Then, on closer scrutiny, she saw that the ceiling manacles weren't fixed; Daphne could remove them at any time. And she *chose* to remain like this until her man returned?

That took commitment.

Or insanity. Faith hadn't decided which yet.

Maybe there was no difference. 'Look, I've got to be honest with you. I'm not who you think I am. Your master didn't send me.'

'My master said you would be deceptive. He said you would be mysterious and beautiful and puzzling and powerful.'

'No, really –'

'Whatever you say, Mistress.'

How far could Faith take this? How far did she *want* to take this? She moved closer, drew in the musk of Daphne's sweat (or was it her own, inside the mask?), before reaching out and taking Daphne's left breast in her gloved hand, squeezing and rolling it until the nipple hardened further. Faith's words purred, a cat toying with her prey. 'What *am* I going to do with you?'

The girl shuddered. 'Whatever you desire, Mistress. I am your slave tonight.'

Faith smiled, though every iota of common sense screamed at her to concentrate on escaping the building. But Faith also remembered something else her teacher had taught her: always take the opportunity to broaden one's horizons . . . She undid the chains, but left the woman's wrists manacled; Daphne fell to her knees, arms obviously aching, a ragged moan escaping her lips – a sight which made Faith moisten further with wanting. Faith sat on the edge of the bed, resting her chin on her hand, the Thinker in repose. 'Are you wet?'

'Yes, Mistress.'

'Prove it.'

'Yes, Mistress.' Daphne reached between her legs, cupping her mound, squeezing gently but firmly, before sliding one, then two fingers between the moist groove of her sex, disappearing, reappearing. Faith watched intently, imagined those were her fingers there, her tongue, making Daphne beg for mercy; her hand drifted between her own thighs. She drew off her mask, shaking the sweat from her shaven, coffee-coloured head, running a free hand across the scalp, then over her square jaw. She smiled; like a lot of things about her, Faith's smile seemed too big for her face, but somehow she managed to support it. 'Am I beautiful, slave?'

Daphne was deep in her role, her eyes as glossy as her skin. 'Oh, *yes*, Mistress. I love you.'

Faith slowly raised her right boot between Daphne's parted

thighs, until she was gently tapping at the entrance to the woman's sex. '*Prove it.*'

Daphne obliged, her hands now removing Faith's boots and socks, then lovingly kissing, licking, nibbling away at the toes, demonstrating a devotion Faith wasn't used to – but *could* get used to, very quickly. Faith tried to keep upright as electric tingles snaked through her, and she struggled to peel off her gloves and top, then her bra – what the hell was wrong with her fingers? Her breath was escaping in helpless staccato giggles now as she undid her trousers.

Unable to continue, she lay back with a grunt and let Daphne do the rest, noting to herself how the damp gusset of her panties had to be peeled from her body. Once free of the smothering clothes, Faith crawled backwards to the pillows as if in escape, Daphne following her in pursuit. She reached under to caress Faith's cheeks, stopping to ask, 'Does my Master punish you, too, Mistress?'

Faith winced at her touch there; it must have been tonight's bruises. She suppressed a grin. 'Never mind, girl; get to work.'

And she did, burying her face between Faith's spread thighs. Faith felt Daphne's lips, Daphne's tongue penetrate her damp pocket, giving Faith as much a chill as the metal of her bonds, brushing against her hot, sweaty skin.

Faith moaned, her hands curling into fists, drawing up bedsheet with them before moving on to her full, aching breasts, and she ground her crotch against the eager, expert mouth. She came once, then again, and again, like an echo – God, she was aching for it! – as Daphne continued her supplication, until Faith could tolerate no more, and cried out, 'Lie down – *now!*'

Moments later, Daphne's wrists and ankles were bound securely to the four bedposts, her mouth gagged with Faith's frilly red knickers, her right thigh being humped by Faith, even as Faith slid one, then two, then three fingers into Daphne's hot, wet, velvety channel. She moaned inside her makeshift gag, lifting her buttocks to meet Faith's penetration.

Faith, surrendering fully to the simple, potent pleasure of carnal lust, yelped like a bitch in heat, letting another climax spark and flood within her, making her tighten reflexively around Daphne's pale, creamy thigh. Maintaining a hard, merciless rhythm, the squeak of the bedsprings competing with her own, Faith let the waves pass through her like shivers, urging more to come forth, to be fruitful and multiply –

'*Freeze!*'

Both of them did, like statues, in the sudden, totally unexpected presence of policemen and building security guards. Faith felt her face turn seven shades of red; stupid, stupid *bitch*, she should've realised they might have keys to the flats here! She should have been listening!

She began wondering what the food would be like in prison.

Then the security guards relaxed, looked acutely embarrassed, though the policemen, who'd seen it all before, were smirking, even laughing. One of the guards, pass key in hand, gulped. 'Sorry, Mrs Parkinson; we heard noises in here and knocked, but –'

Daphne mumbled; Faith helpfully removed the knickers from her mouth. She wet her lips and demanded, 'What the hell's going on?'

The guard with the key seemed to turn as red as Faith felt now. 'Some man broke into one of the top flats! He crashed into a window on this floor –'

Hearing this, Daphne's eyes met Faith's, and in that instant, it all became clear to the girl.

But Daphne didn't scream, didn't call out or alert them to the truth, remained as nonchalant as she could, under the circumstances. 'Well, *I* haven't seen him.' She glanced up at Faith casually. 'Have you?'

Faith fought to keep a grin off her face as she folded her arms across her chest and shook her head wordlessly.

Daphne looked back at the guard. 'Then don't let the door hit you on the ass on the way out.'

'Yes, ma'am. Sorry, ma'am.' Everyone began filing away, politely waiting until they were out of sight before laughing.

As they finally departed, Daphne's head pounded the pillow in bold frustration. 'Damn, damn, *damn*! It'll be all over the fucking building by morning!'

Faith, fighting the shock, waited until she heard the front door slam shut before saying, 'Thanks.'

Daphne nodded, the role of slave temporarily shelved in her chagrin. 'I hope I haven't made a mistake, doing that.' Now she eyed Faith as if seeing her for the first time. 'Are you *really* a thief?'

'No, I'm a musician.' She grinned. 'But I have stolen a few hearts in my time.'

Daphne looked dubious. 'Then what were you doing up there?'

Faith sighed, wiped the sweat from her skin again, the grin fading. 'I thought I wanted to die tonight.'

Now Daphne looked concerned. 'What? But *why?*'

Faith's face grew sober. 'Someone very close to me died recently.'

'Oh. I'm sorry.'

'So was I. Mostly for myself. I didn't want to be alone. But I think I'm past that now.'

'Glad to hear it.' Daphne smiled. 'Why don't you untie me and we can talk about it?'

'Later,' Faith lied, catching the clock from the corner of her eye. Now that she was going to live again, she had a plane to catch to London in a few hours' time. 'I'm on a bit of a tight schedule.' She began moving upwards, drawing her crotch towards Daphne's waiting, eager mouth.

The bedroom air was scented with jasmine, the smoke from the burning joss sticks rising like grey strings severed from marionettes, marionettes now moving of their own free will on the low, wide bed. By lamplight filtered and rouged through a discarded blouse, the marionettes twisted and writhed about each other, their movements slow, as if underwater, or under the influence, or simply unsure. Limbs, pale and soft and alike, snaked about each other, the groan of mouths and bedsprings marking the gentle testing. Full eager lips moved to heaving breasts, anxious fingers to dark deltas, the urgency for release thick, heavy, like the air before a storm, the drumbeats of anxious hearts machine-gun-rapid. Then the voice again, merely a whisper: 'Come on, Joyce. Join us. Take a risk . . .' Then the scent of jasmine merged with something harsher − silk burning against naked bulb . . . water drenched the fire, now but not then . . .

★

As Faith Ballard found herself again in New York City, at the same time, halfway around the world in another bedroom, Joyce Butler Wilde awoke to the gentle patter of the rain outside her London flat. It was a lovely sound, a perfect coda to the erotic dream she'd just had. Stripes of grey morning light cast evanescent patterns through the venetian blinds on to her bed, shifting as she ran her hands over her nude body beneath the sheets, enjoying the sensual response, before she stretched her limbs in all directions. She woke fully and lay still beneath the sheets, recapturing the images played in her mind moments before.

Joyce knew why she'd dreamed it − again − recognised the unpleasant inspiration for it in her own memories. But the dream itself was different enough to be savoured in its own right, like an old song remixed for a new generation.

Joyce was gay. She wasn't very experienced at the practising side of it, partly because she'd been a late bloomer, partly because of her nature. She wasn't promiscuous, wasn't gregarious, had no current partner, or recent lovers. She was content to remain celibate; it helped avoid complications with the other aspects of her life. It gave her strength.

Between her legs, her pussy pulsed for attention once more, and more visceral thoughts returned. For a naughty moment, she brought her fingers to her nose, sniffed; she'd been touching herself in her sleep again. Lovely. As if no longer needing to skulk about by themselves now, Joyce's hands descended to her breasts, lying flat on her chest, shapeless as jellyfish. Gently her hands kneaded them, Joyce biting her lip in sympathy at the acute pleasures generated; it was like squeezing a sponge of water over her body.

Joyce tried to identify the women in the dream; they certainly weren't the original characters from her memory (which would have brought with it more serious psychological complications). She'd read once how dreams weren't symbolic or supernatural, but simply the brain's way of organising events and memories and wishes dredged up over recent days like the maintenance programs on her computer. It had nothing to do with magic, or even wish-fulfilment; the women could have been working in the corner paper shop or salon, or people she'd seen on television.

In the here and now, Joyce's fingers softly toyed with her nipples until they grew so stiff they felt as if they'd pierce the cotton sheets above them. Her vulva replied readily and immediately, and she brought her hand back to rediscover the strands of dew in the dark matted hair. How remarkable that a dream could arouse her so quickly.

Without realising it, Joyce's right hand dived further into the entwined hair. Her left leg rose, tenting her sheets until the foot was flat against the yielding mattress and the knee pointed straight upwards. Her thighs parted further, ever so slightly.

Her sex opened, gasping for air, for stimulation, and her fingers tentatively sought out the expectant nub of her clit. She gasped aloud, licking her lips, her body hot, fluid, no longer quite substantial. The movement of her arms, and her body's responses, were not sleep-stiff, unsure, but part of something ephemeral, like the bodies of the women in her dream. It wasn't a desire for a current lover, Joyce assured herself. It was just idle, curious daydreaming.

She would walk in on them; they would pause long enough to look up at her, appraise her – would she be worthy enough that they let her join in, or would they be selfish, dismissive? Of course, they would invite Joyce to undress and lie down. And of course, she would accept, gasping as their hands would run over her, worshipping her. She would take a chance.

She grunted and pressed her thighs together, the finger of one hand remaining insistently in her pubic hair. Joyce pretended to resist, as if her hand really belonged to one of the two women, seeking to pierce her, open her up to their inspection, their sweet torture. Her palm kept massaging her mound, grinding down on it, steadily eroding her token resistance, stopping only short of her throbbing clitoris; touching that now would be too much for her, she felt so sensitive.

But her pussy was as impatient and demanding as its bestial namesake was, and Joyce finally relented. She bit her lip, moaning, eyes clenched shut, head and body cambering back and jerking at the penetration of itself, and her vagina clamped down on her fingers in response, resisting further entry in order to augment her pleasure at its inevitable succumbing. She pictured that a tongue, a tongue lapping away with expertise, had replaced the woman's hand.

When her thumb inevitably swivelled upwards to massage her clitoris, it completed the circuit that finally brought Joyce to a long, strong, well-deserved climax, overflowing like the gutters outside, and bringing with it a ragged moan that echoed hollowly in the bedroom. Then she sighed and relaxed, drawing her exposed foot out of the cool air and back under the sheets' embrace. In her bedside table lay her vibrator; she enjoyed it, but somehow found her own touch more satisfying after a sexy dream.

In the afterwaves of orgasm, there came unwanted guilt. Joyce knew that dreams were just dreams, but still that hook pierced her flesh; she twisted in place, face down, as if to avoid the unwanted thoughts and feelings, sought the euphoric bliss. But it was gone, like the night.

In the distance came the clutter of post through the front door slot. She glanced at her clock, reluctantly cast off her sheets and rose to prepare for the day, first avoiding, then giving in to her masochistic nature by acknowledging the reflection cast in the full-length mirror by her wardrobe.

Joyce was small in stature, with what an ex-girlfriend in a moment of drunken candidness had once called 'a washed-out look': frizzled copper hair reaching her shoulder blades, pale, freckled skin, a woolly russet delta, prominent nose, cool blue eyes wide set and sharp with scrutiny, and a round chin between full cheeks. Her frame was compact, betrayed only by her ample breasts and a slight roll of fat around the waist.

She showered, dried and dressed, selecting her favourite scarlet oxford shirt, black wide-leg trousers, tights and lilac pumps: casual, but dressy enough, ideal for her customer-free office environment. As her tea and toast boiled and browned, she checked her e-mail: more messages from magazines and newspapers, asking for interviews, comments, anything. She deleted them. The snail mail at the door was little better. It had been weeks now, and they still wouldn't let her alone.

Then Joyce saw the plain brown envelope, with the familiar return address on the back – and promptly binned it. It was just those solicitors again, *that woman's* solicitors, still wanting to arrange a meeting.

But she didn't want to meet them. She wanted nothing from them. Her existence was complete in itself, pristine in its order and management: she had a career, a good friend, and a life that made her comfortable. And she'd *earned* it. She wanted nothing more. Especially not from *her*.

TWO

'I had that dream again.'

Joyce had waited until reaching the gym, changing and entering the brightly lit red and white racquetball court she'd reserved that morning, before mentioning it to Rhonda. Immediately she regretted mentioning it at all.

Rhonda Howlett paused, adjusting her T-shirt and shorts yet again, eyes alight with the amused promise of an interesting conversation. 'The two women?'

'Two different ones.'

'You're insatiable.'

Joyce was chagrined. She was probably mad to go revealing something like that to her, even if she was her best friend. Rhonda Howlett was a tall, friendly, tawny-haired woman of flat-faced prettiness and wide, challenging sea-green eyes, and who'd been close to Joyce these past few years. Somehow she managed to keep her job despite doing only a fraction of the work Joyce did, spending the rest of the time out shopping, taking coffee and cigarette breaks and checking on her appearance.

Still, she made Joyce laugh, and they'd shared much together, although Rhonda was straight – and from the many sordid stories she'd related to Joyce, she was eager to demonstrate that fact with every man – and their relationship would never go further than it was now. Which, sometimes, Joyce had to admit, was a shame. 'And they were still – '

'Yes.' Joyce glanced back at her reflection in the glass wall, as if to divine a vision. 'More or less. I think the lamp caught fire quicker this time. And water rained down on it from somewhere. Probably because it was raining outside at the time.'

'Analyst. So you still didn't get a chance to join in?'

'Rhonda!' Joyce glanced about needlessly, as if they weren't alone. The acoustics in here . . . 'I don't want to *join in*.'

'Why not? It's just a fantasy. The ultimate safe sex, guilt-free and non-fattening. Especially since you don't want a partner in real life –'

'It's just a variation on a memory, that's all,' Joyce reaffirmed, though even she had trouble believing herself. 'Because of the news about my mother. I keep getting mail.'

Rhonda shrugged. 'She *was* popular.'

'Notorious, you mean. And those solicitors sent another one of those letters this morning.'

Rhonda shrugged. 'They probably can't stop hassling you until you sign some release papers or something.'

'I suppose.' Joyce had to admit, the woman had a point.

And now, she sharpened it. 'Just take the money and run. Go buy yourself a boob job or a car.'

'I don't want her money. I received very little from her in life. I want even less from her in death.'

'Fine, fine.' The grin returned. 'Now, let's get back to those two women.'

'No, let's not.'

'Hey, *you* brought it up; it's your dirty, filthy little lesbian wet dream.'

Joyce sighed, bounced her blue rubber ball and gave it a whack, watched it ricochet off the front wall of the court. She should have known Rhonda wouldn't let something like that lie; the woman was like a cat toying with a half-dead mouse. 'I think you're reading too much into it. I just have a vivid imagination.' Rhonda returned the ball, and Joyce was ready for it, and the dubious reaction she no doubt wore now. 'A dream doesn't have to have any significance. Freud himself said that sometimes a cigar is just a cigar.'

'Not if you're with certain ex-Presidents.' Rhonda returned the shot. 'Are you saying that you're content to remain celibate, for the rest of your life?'

'Yes,' Joyce lied, through pursed lips and clenched teeth. 'I'm content.'

And Rhonda saw right through it. 'Bollocks. It's not about contentment. It's about *fear*. You don't have to be gay to fear risking opening your heart to another person, you know.'

'Are we hear to chat, or play?'

Rhonda flipped her the ball. 'You started it.'

Satisfied that the discussion was over, Joyce took up a position at the service line, halfway between the front wall and the back one. Bending her knees and back, she brought her racquet back with her right hand and bounced the ball low in front of her with the left, delivering a wicked blur of a line drive. She'd never been one for sports, but this waistline of hers had to be fought, and this, along with her twice-weekly swim, was better than being in a group for aerobics or other exercise. To her surprise, she found she was good at this.

To her greater surprise, she found Rhonda was just as good. Within a short time, both women's clothes were patched with sweat, their faces red.

Rhonda grinned through her fatigue. 'That's it, I've got to cut down on the scones at break time.'

Joyce frowned at the remark, knew the woman hardly had an ounce of fat on her, and never gained any, no matter how much she ate. Bitch. 'Well, since you're conceding victory to me –'

'As if we were keeping score!' Rhonda exclaimed, wiping perspiration from her brow with the back of her hand.

'– Then *you'll* be buying dinner.'

Suddenly, both women's attentions were drawn to a tapping on the back wall, at the door. Another woman was peering in at them, an attractive woman in her late twenties, with long, dark hair bound up in a sizeable braid. She was making a T-shape with her hands, signifying a time-out.

'I know what *I'd* like to have,' Rhonda suggested, as if cryptically, though Joyce, blushing seven shades of red, knew exactly what she meant. But before she could reply – assuming she would – Rhonda had opened the door. 'Hi, Leah! Didn't know you were into racquetball!'

The woman stepped inside, idly twirling the racquet in her hand. 'On and off.'

'That's the way I do lots of things, too,' Rhonda joked, glancing at Joyce. 'Look, Joyce, Leah plays racquetball, too. Maybe you two should go a few rounds together?'

It was all Joyce could do to keep her heart from leaping from her mouth along with her clumsy reply. 'Yes, sure, someday. Bit tired now. Hope you don't mind, been a long day and all, have to get going –'

Leah smiled – in pity, Joyce felt – and cut her off. 'That's OK. I'm waiting for someone anyway.'

'But perhaps another time?' Rhonda suggested, looking all innocent.

Leah nodded, still staring at Joyce. 'I'd like that.'

Joyce nodded, suddenly at a loss for words.

Steam from the prior users had beaded the pink-tiled walls and floors of the ladies' showers and changing alcove, but Joyce and Rhonda had the place to themselves. 'Bitch!'

Rhonda was the font of all guilelessness now. 'What?'

'You *know* what!'

'I don't! I –' Now came the false revelation. 'Don't tell me you *fancy* her?'

Joyce hissed as she tied up her hair, refusing to let the conversation continue.

Not that she needed to, with Rhonda around. Rhonda removed her T-shirt, mopping her brow with it once more, before dropping it on the bench and reaching behind to unclasp her sports bra. She leaned in closer, until her breasts brushed against Joyce's shoulders. 'Why don't you ask her out?'

Now Joyce sighed, ignoring the touch. 'It's not as simple as that when you're . . .' She glanced about, as if her voice might carry out into the locker room, before pulling her own shirt over her head.

'I think the word you're looking for is "gay",' Rhonda helped out. 'And in this case, it can't be *that* difficult. You obviously like her. She seems to like you . . . God knows why . . .' Quickly she dodged the flick of a towel from Joyce, pulled off her remaining clothes and grabbed her shower gel, before padding off into the shower room.

'Thanks,' Joyce called after her belatedly, sighing and closing her eyes as she continued undressing. There was one thing worse than having an obnoxious friend.

Having an obnoxious friend who was right all the time.

The showers were set into individual cubicles of baby blue, shoulder high; Joyce approved. She took the stall beside Rhonda's, catching some of the water from her friend's stall; it felt lovely and warm.

She closed and latched the door, announcing, 'She and I wouldn't get along.'

'You're just fishing for excuses. It's cowardice.'

'Really.' Joyce turned on the shower, immediately jumping back with a squeal at the icy blast which struck her body.

Rhonda still wore her innocent mask. 'Sorry; I should have warned you.'

Joyce scowled, holding out her hand until the water reached an acceptable temperature, before returning to stand below the stream. 'If you think she's so great, why don't *you* ask her out?'

'I just might do that.'

Joyce guffawed, until she saw the serious look in her friend's eyes, that unmistakable, no-nonsense gaze. Still, she had to ask, 'Are you serious?'

Rhonda deliberately took her time with her reply. 'Why not?'

'Because you're not gay!'

'What does that have to do with it? Can't I at least try it? Or do you have to have a licence before you can practise? Does an experienced lesbian have to be there with me in case I lose control?' She stared directly at Joyce. 'Would she *not* go to bed with me, if she knew I was straight?'

It seemed to be a straightforward question rather than a rhetorical one, so Joyce replied. 'Some women resent it. It makes their own lifestyles seem like choices or hobbies, rather than a part of what they are.'

Now Rhonda grinned. 'But not all? Some would give me a tumble, right?'

Joyce swallowed again. 'Yes.'

'Good. Then if you're not going to approach her, *I* will.'

Joyce continued staring, overwhelmed, at a woman she thought she knew inside and out – figuratively speaking, of course. Then she smiled slowly, assuredly, and reached for her own gel. 'No. You, with a woman?' She shook her head under the spray. 'No. You talk big, but not even *you* would do something as bold as that.'

Rhonda took a moment to look sober. 'You obviously don't know me as well as you might think.'

But Joyce was having none of it. 'You're lying.'

Rhonda started to reply, then paused, as if in fresh appraisal of her friend. 'Is it so hard to believe? Not everybody's as staid as you are.'

'You don't even know if you'd like it or not.'

'Well, I'll certainly never find out by not trying, will I?' Now it was Rhonda's turn to frown, and point over the stall in Joyce's direction. 'The opportunity for adventure is around us, all the time; we don't have to climb mountains and wrestle with bulls like your mum did.'

Joyce winced at the mention of her mother, but Rhonda pressed on regardless. 'You've never been on a boat or in a plane; you've never left the *country*, even on holiday. And you hardly ever get drunk, or eat foreign food, or wear outrageous clothes. And how many lovers have you had?'

Joyce glanced about, certain Rhonda's voice was loud enough to be heard outside. 'Let's not get into that *here*, OK?'

But Rhonda was on a roll. 'You should live a little. Put some colour to your cheeks. All of them.'

'Really?' Joyce cast a dry reply to that last observation. 'Erstwhile lesbian, lifestyle critic, agony aunt: is there no end to your surprises?'

Rhonda's reply was multi-layered as she turned off the water and exited her stall. 'You have *no* idea.'

Joyce was alone again, found herself standing there; the palmful of lavender gel she'd just patted on to her shoulder, now ignored, slid down her smooth, wet skin in long, slim fingers to cup her left breast. She squeezed out more gel, idly sculpting masses of white foam like seaweed, before applying it to her body. Her nipples were standing up from the physical contact.

Rhonda had been right, damn her; Joyce *was* attracted to Leah, who worked in another part of the same company as they did. And she knew Leah came here often; it was another unspoken reason to taking up these weekly after-hours workouts. And *yes*, she knew Leah was gay, too, though neither woman was officially Out among their colleagues; Joyce may not have been an active member of the Scene, but she wasn't totally oblivious, either. It wouldn't be the most difficult thing Joyce had ever done, approaching the woman, perhaps at lunch in the canteen. It could be totally innocent at first . . .

She started when her hand moved between her legs, lathering up her pubic hair, massaging her mound. She hadn't expected to feel that familiar twinge, especially not now, practically in public. She looked about again; she was still alone, and with the stall door closed, no one could see below her head.

Her hands were covered in gel, and it streamed from them with the water to run down her legs. She worked deft fingers through her bush to find her clitoris, engorged, hungry, hungry for her touch . . .

But she pulled back, unable, unwilling to do anything so daring as *that* in public. She finished her shower, trying to wash away her many levels of frustration with the gel. And barely succeeding.

Joyce finished up another cheque lodgement record, impatient for the call; what was taking him so long? It was nearly time for lunch!

Her desk was in a tiny enclosure, one among many on the office floor, throat-high dividers offering a scant measure of privacy for each desk and desk owner. And her desk was immaculate. There were no photos of loved ones or furry toys or funny signs about How You Didn't Have To Be Crazy To Work Here (But It Helps). This Spartan look was in line with her belief that outside orderliness was a visible manifestation of inner organisation. She also believed it made her workplace stand out from the anonymous clutter of those around her, a distinction part of her desperately craved, despite her overall need for the security to be found in an unchanging situation.

She reached for the next lodgement, her fingers dancing over the computer keyboard. She was good at her job; no, she was *great*, and she was doing something substantial, something she could be proud of. As a charity-based organisation, the World Children's Advancement Fund may not pay the salaries more commercial employers would have, but at least she could sleep soundly at night, knowing she'd done her part to help others.

Which was more than her scapegrace of a mother ever did in all her globetrotting larks.

Then the overhead intercom beeped, and she froze, awaiting the call to his office. Instead, it was an unfamiliar voice. 'Ms Wilde, you have guests at Reception.'

Joyce started at that; she *never* had visitors.

Reception was a wide, high area of glass and chrome and low-down black leather waiting couches; Joyce's heels clicked along the polished floors as she approached the desk, her eyes already fixed and scrutinising the three women rising from the couches to meet her.

The one in the middle was a posh-looking figure in her early to mid-forties, a tall, pale, striking Nordic beauty with bright blue eyes peeking out from under her dirty blonde fringe. She was clad all in white: white herringbone coat with a wide fur colour, over a white silk blouse, white pleated skirt and white pumps; Joyce wondered how she managed to get through an hour in the city without dirtying any of them somehow.

The one on the woman's right was olive-skinned, perhaps Mediterranean in feature, with classical, freckled cheekbones, tight black curly hair and an upturned nose. She wore a plain avocado longcoat, black top and matching trousers, a nice but not ostentatious ensemble; Joyce approved. The woman herself held her body still, relaxed but ready, Heaven only knew for what, her gaze alert, never focused on one person or direction or thing for long, but it was a mercurial quality borne from caution, not capriciousness.

The third, however, was the most striking, and it was more than just the colour of her skin, coffee with a hint of cream. It was more than the shaven head, reflecting the fluorescent lights above, or the square jaw. It was more than just the vivid colours and contrasts of her black leather jacket, apple-red T-shirt and baggy green trousers, like she'd wrapped herself in some Caribbean flag. No, it was the eyes. Each of the women radiated something from their eyes – the blonde one affability, the Mediterranean one a polite caution, as if constantly on the lookout for danger – but the third one held challenge, appraisal. It was startling in its boldness. Joyce suddenly felt as if she was on trial – and in danger of losing, without even knowing the charges.

The blonde woman took an extra step forward, proffering her hand, her smile genuine. 'Good morning, Miss Wilde.' It was an educated, proper 'jolly hockey-sticks' accent that immediately caught one's attention. 'My name is Philippa Sheringham.' She indicated first the Mediterranean, then the dark-skinned woman. 'These are my associates, Ruth Bat-Seraph and Faith Ballard. We were friends and colleagues of Constance Wilde.'

Joyce breathed audibly. She wasn't in the mood for this, not now. Not ever, really. 'Yes, and?'

'*And*, we need to discuss your mother's legacy. We've tried contacting you before now regarding it; perhaps the post has been misdirected.'

Joyce recognised the attempt to help her save face before the others. But Joyce didn't need her help. She felt her face grow taut, her voice drop an octave. 'They haven't been misdirected. There's simply nothing I want from her, or yourselves.'

'Perhaps if you understood what was at stake –'

'No, perhaps if *you* understood: I don't care. I didn't care when I was told she was dead, and I don't care now.'

The dark-skinned one – what was her name again? Faith? It seemed too fragile a name for such a tough-looking nut – appeared ready to reply, and not too politely, either, when Philippa figuratively stepped in ahead of her. 'All we ask is that you hear us out. Let's do lunch. My treat. Thirty minutes of your time, that's all. If you're still not interested, then you'll never hear from us again.' She smiled invitingly. 'Quite a bargain, either way.'

Joyce glanced at the other two, the swarthy woman deliberately guarded, carefully neutral, the black girl openly hostile. They were an unlikely trio, none of them looking like solicitors. What had her mother to do with them? Joyce had brought a lunch with her today as usual, and was waiting to hear the news about the promotions, but nevertheless was intrigued, recalling Rhonda's suggestion that they wouldn't stop pestering her until she signed some papers or something.

Then there was the woman Sheringham herself: a striking figure indeed. And her scent: like roses, freshly picked but still vibrant.

She sighed; better to get this over with, she reasoned, and then get them out of her life for good. 'I'll get my coat.'

THREE

The restaurant, La Pomme Rouge, an enclave of rubber plants, marble arches and snooty attitude, was considered *très chic*, and whenever Joyce had glanced inside while lunchtime window shopping with Rhonda or on her way to cheaper eateries, she always saw crowds of hopeful patrons waiting for tables. Today was no exception; Joyce was in some of her best gear, yet felt decidedly underdressed, but then noticed nothing was said about Faith Ballard's scruffier appearance. It turned out Philippa had a table for four booked ahead for them.

'Were you *that* certain I'd be here with you today?' Joyce asked dryly.

'Oh, we would have come anyway,' the woman assured her cheerfully. 'I always dine here when I'm in town; their veal escalope is to die for.'

They had a table in the far corner, small and cosy near the kitchen doors. It was not an ideal spot, suggesting Philippa's influence wasn't as great as she first assumed, until Joyce considered how it might have been chosen deliberately, from the way in which Ruth took a seat nearest the wall, facing Joyce and the rest of the interior. Faith sat to Joyce's left, also keeping an eye on the surroundings, though in her case her wariness seemed less motivated by caution than by discomfort. No, she definitely didn't

23

look the type who would dine here on a regular basis. Joyce knew how she felt.

Philippa, on the other hand – Joyce's right hand, to be precise – appeared in her element, greeting the waiter by name, as she ordered a soft drink for Ruth, a beer for Faith, and an expensive-sounding wine for Joyce and herself. 'You'll love the Chardonnay Enjôleur,' she promised, smiling. 'Wine this elegant mustn't be savoured alone.'

'Fine, fine.' Joyce shrugged, then shrugged again as Philippa ordered lunch for them all, without asking: shrimp salad for Ruth, a cheeseburger and chips, of all things, for Faith, and the aforementioned escalopes for Joyce and herself; luckily for the woman Joyce wasn't a vegetarian.

The waiter disappeared, leaving such a silence among the quartet that the man might have carried the sounds away with the order. Philippa took the lead, twisting in her chair and sitting forward. 'Ms Wilde, we're aware of the rift that existed between your mother and yourself –'

'It wasn't a rift,' Joyce corrected her. 'It was a *chasm*. One that took a lifetime for her to make.'

Philippa seemed to absorb this, perhaps choosing her subsequent words more carefully. 'Please believe me when I tell you we wouldn't be here today bothering you if it hadn't been at your mother's explicit request.'

'Why? What is it?' Joyce nodded to the other two women. 'And why does it take three of you to deliver it?'

Philippa indicated each of her colleagues in turn. 'We all played a part in your mother's life, in the last few years. Business interests, personal concerns . . .' Philippa paused, as if realising she was getting ahead of herself. 'When did you last see her?'

The question tugged at Joyce's mind, bringing her heart along for the ride. 'When I was thirteen.'

Philippa nodded. 'Seventeen years ago. A long time.'

'A long time to hate someone, don't you think?' Faith annexed curtly, almost accusingly. Her accent was American, perhaps New York.

'That depends on the someone,' Joyce shot back, matching the girl glare for glare and trying not to stare at her shaven head. If that was all the young woman had to say, it was little wonder that Philippa was doing all the talking.

Philippa raised a hand, as if to cut the tension between the two women. 'But you followed her activities since then.'

'How could I not?' Constance Wilde was, to quote from one magazine account, 'a colourful character', befitting her exotic upbringing in the former British African colony of Mahali: businesswoman, writer, lecturer, activist, daredevil, even politician. But no matter what she put her mind to, the adjectives 'outspoken' and 'adventurous' inevitably followed. 'She could never stay interested in any one thing for too long. She was good at starting things, not so good at seeing them through to the end.'

'What the hell would you know about it?' Faith snapped. 'You were never around. Who are you to judge her?'

'Her daughter,' Joyce replied flatly, both angered and amazed by the level of obvious loyalty displayed for her mother by the younger woman. 'The daughter she hardly knew, too busy was she making headlines. Why, who are *you*?'

Philippa raised a hand again for silence, though it may have been as much to do with the reappearance of the waiter, with their drinks. Once he departed again, she opened the wine to let it breathe, and continued. 'Excuse Ms Ballard; she just flew in from New York yesterday –'

'Yeah, and my arms are still aching,' the woman quipped dryly.

Philippa continued, regardless, pouring the wine. 'Of late, Constance had grown introspective. And she'd decided to write her memoirs.' The wine paradoxically added sobriety to Philippa's voice and expression. 'She wanted to leave something of her life behind.'

Joyce decided not to comment on that, instead looked into her own glass, saw the curved, distorted reflection of her fingers, reaching back. 'And what has this to do with the rest of you, or me?'

'Do you know what a tontine is?'

Joyce paused, considered the unexpected question. 'Yes. It's a sort of . . . agreement, isn't it?'

Philippa nodded. 'Sort of. As a gesture of friendship and appreciation to us, Constance set up a tontine, so that we all might benefit from the rather substantial publishing contract she had signed in New York for her memoirs. And although Constance has died, the tontine ensures that the proceeds are divided amongst the surviving members.'

'I'm happy for you,' Joyce remarked into her glass.

'Be happy for yourself, too. You're a part of it.'

Joyce nearly spilled her drink. '*What?*'

'Yeah,' Faith sneered. 'We were just as surprised.'

'Me?' Joyce muttered, only half-listening, both hands now cradling her glass for reassurance. 'So, is that why you're here, to try and give me my share?'

'No money's been exchanged – yet. She was on her way back to her birthplace in Mahali when the plane crashed. Sudden thermal inversions endemic to the area, or so I'm told. The bodies, some of the luggage and the flight recorder were returned to the capital, Patricksburg. But her diaries were not among her possessions, and we assumed, if they survived, that they're still in the wreckage, in an isolated part of the savannah. We're heading out to see if we can find them, retrieve them, and ensure their publication.'

'And what has this to do with me?'

'Part of the tontine requires that all who might benefit from it should also share in the responsibility for its fulfilment.'

'And that's *it*? Just drop everything in my life and take up hers?'

'Consider it an extended holiday, if you wish, a chance to visit where she grew up. The trek across the savannah would, ironically, parallel one she'd taken herself as a teenager; she'd called it "Her First Great Adventure".'

'And now she's had her Last. Dying in a plane crash seems almost too dull for the likes of her.'

Faith slammed her beer glass down, making the cutlery rattle and people at neighbouring tables stare. '*Goddammit!* At least she *lived* before she died!'

'Faith –' Philippa warned reprovingly.

With minimal effect. 'She didn't waste her days in some pissant little office job, and her nights defrosting the fridge. By the time she was *your* age, she'd already been around the world once, sailed the Indian Ocean, rode camels to Morocco, skied the Alps, partied with rock stars and politicians –'

'– You forgot having me, abandoning me to continue with her precious "living" –'

'But haven't you ever wanted to emulate her, even a little?' Philippa asked, leaning forward, trying to maintain control of the conversation. 'Haven't you ever dreamed of going somewhere you thought you never would? Doing something that would make your heart pound and your blood race?'

Joyce was halfway through a reply when she felt the hand on her knee.

She looked to her right; Philippa's hands were hidden under the table, and she had that intense look on her face. And suddenly Joyce found herself inexplicably suffused with a desire that melted her from the inside like a white-hot poker. Perhaps it was the residual effects of that dream of hers, or her unrequited attraction to Leah, or touching herself in the gym showers, but whatever the case, Joyce suddenly felt a profound longing for this beautiful woman.

Then Philippa sat back in her chair, and unless she had simian arms, she couldn't possibly still be holding on to Joyce's knee.

And yet, Joyce still felt the hand.

And finally noticed the cheeky grin on Faith's face; she, too, was leaning forward.

Joyce pulled back, making the table shake and tipping over the tall, narrow crystal vase in the centre, with a single white rose.

Philippa's brow furrowed. 'Something wrong?'

Joyce continued to glare at Faith, who ignored her to reach out, as if to set right the vase – but instead stealing the rose, snapping most of the stem away and sticking the flower in her lapel. The girl had obviously touched Joyce's knee to rattle her – and it worked, too, damn her.

Joyce finally looked to Philippa. 'No. Nothing wrong.'

'If I may speak,' Ruth suddenly voiced, her first words since meeting Joyce; and though quietly spoken, the request, carried by her musical Israeli lilt, had been enough to capture the other three's attention, at least temporarily. She fixed Joyce with an earnest expression. 'It would be presumptuous of me – of *any* of us, however close we were to Constance,' she added, glancing once at Faith, 'to judge you, or your feelings towards her. But I ask you to put aside your animosity long enough to appreciate the offer with a clear mind. Philippa's correct; it is an opportunity, an opportunity to see and do what so many, forced to lead confined, sterile lives, can only dream about. An opportunity that many women would give *anything* for.'

Joyce had to admit, at least to herself, the sincerity – and validity – of Ruth's argument. All the more pity it came too late to change Joyce's mind. 'Well, that's the trouble with the world, isn't it?' she asked, surprising even herself with the acerbity in her reply. 'Opportunities usually go to those who don't appreciate them. Or need them.' She pushed her chair back and rose to her feet. 'I don't see any point in staying any longer; enjoy the veal, and thanks for the wine.'

Philippa rose. 'Wait – you don't have to make your mind up now –'

Joyce raised a hand, cutting off the woman's entreaty. 'You're wasting your time. I'm content with what I have already.'

'*Cows* are content with what they have,' Faith sneered loudly as Joyce departed. 'And they produce a mountain of shit before they're led to the slaughterhouse.'

The meeting had unnerved Joyce; upon returning to her desk, she'd wolfed down her sandwiches and oranges, and now felt faintly sick. How *dare* they judge her like that? They were outsiders. They knew *nothing* about what had happened – or not happened – between Joyce and her mother! Still, she was glad they'd finally been told off. Now maybe they'd take the hint and leave her alone.

But before she could ponder it further, a voice, loud and masculine, this one hissing over the office intercom, shook her from her pensiveness. 'Ms Wilde, could you report to the supervisor's office, please?'

Joyce vainly tried to suppress a smile as she logged out of her computer and rose, straightening her blouse and skirt. This was it, her turn to prove to her mother – no, she meant *herself* – her own worth. Along the way, she stopped at Rhonda's divider. 'Well, here goes.'

The woman actually seemed to be hunkering down to do work; she never even glanced up. 'Joyce –'

'You're still coming over tonight for a celebratory dinner, aren't you?'

Now Rhonda looked up, appeared sober, even contrite. 'Don't raise your hopes too high, Joyce. It's not just Frank who decides on these things, you know.'

Joyce dismissed the warning. Rhonda was a good woman, but Joyce knew Rhonda had wasted her time with the board; her admonition was just sour grapes. Perhaps the supervisor had let Rhonda down while Joyce was out at lunchtime?

'Come in, Ms Wilde. Take a seat.'

He used her surname, though the office protocol was very casual, which confirmed he had something important to tell her. 'Yes, Mr Thomas.'

He smiled as he closed the door to the rest of the office floor, then proceeded to make a deliberately casual-seeming saunter around his office. Frank Thomas was a middle-aged, long-faced, snub-nosed man, with tanned skin and truculent black hair that hung forward in a comma over his forehead. He fitted well into his charcoal Armani suit, the jacket of which now hung casually over the back of his leather chair.

And his office matched his stark good looks: imitation oak panelling broken by a single Impressionist's painting, the view of drizzly grey metropolis outside superimposed by the charity logo frosted on the window glass, and the slim, glass-topped desk supporting a telephone/intercom, computer terminal and some papers. She liked it here; when she was promoted, she hoped to get an office like this. He stopped, hands clasped behind his back, as he affected studying his painting. 'Joyce, you've always been a

29

good, hard-working member here. It's been a pleasure having you here.'

Joyce let her smile blossom again, understood the routine by now. 'Thank you, Frank. This is about the board, isn't it?'

He turned to sit behind the desk, opened a drawer and withdrew a cigarette pack. He lit up and took a deep, disconcerting drag before echoing, 'The board.' Then his face turned a pale, wan shade that made Joyce's stomach churn. 'I'm sorry, Joyce. You didn't get it.'

She thought she had readied herself when she'd seen his expression; still, when it was actually said aloud, she found herself frozen with disbelief. 'Excuse me?'

Frank sighed at her, the sigh of a man forced by his authority into putting unpleasantness into words. 'You just missed it. By *that* much,' he added, bringing his thumb and forefinger together as if holding a needle between them.

Joyce listened, replayed it in her mind once, then again. Her heart began to thunder inside her, and she focused her eyes on Frank; what little bravery he may have possessed momentarily failed him, and he found himself studying the painting on the wall again just to have somewhere else to look as he continued. 'It wasn't that your interview had been bad –'

'Oh, I'm *sure*.'

Now he glanced back at her. 'Another just happened to be more favourable to the board at this time.'

'Like who? Rhonda?'

Frank rose to his feet again, reached up needlessly to straighten his tie – it was the office joke that he probably never stopped fidgeting even when he was asleep – before turning to the window. 'I really shouldn't say until it's formally announced.'

Joyce turned away herself from his back, too stunned to do much else. Oh God. She'd said it as a joke. It couldn't actually be *true*. 'Rhonda? You're not serious! She does *nothing* around the office!'

'You're exaggerating; you should see her performance rating. In addition, she has good presence. She's friendly, open –'

'– Open to all invitations, you mean. For her, a laptop means something beside computers.'

He took a step further away, still not facing her. 'You may be better with the computers than Rhonda, but you're also more . . . reserved. Which isn't a bad thing in itself,' he added, obviously responding to her expression. 'I consider you very . . . dependable.'

'*Dependable?*' She let out an exclamation of air from her mouth. 'Thanks a lot. You make me sound like a family car.'

'Joyce, the promotion requires you to be public-friendly, out-going, audacious, even. Especially when the company is a charity dependent upon donations. But you just don't give people that impression. You seem happier being on your own, where you are.'

'Yes. Happy. Content.'

'Content. Exactly.'

Was the entire world out to criticise her attitude? Yes, she'd used more or less the same wording in her defence of her lifestyle against those women, but to hear it from someone else, used against her . . .

'You wouldn't have liked the new responsibilities, Joyce –'

'Well, I'll never know, will I?' Galvanised by anger, she rose, turned and bolted from the office; to his credit or criticism, he didn't call after her or follow her outside.

When Rhonda wasn't in her cubicle – which was often – she was in the food court, which was shared by all the different companies in the building. It was a spacious atrium of tall greenery and a gurgling fountain, with plenty of secluded areas for people to relax from work, or escape from it, especially outside the usual serving hours, like now.

Joyce's eyes darted about, until she found Rhonda.

With Leah.

They sat facing each other at a small table, leaning close until their foreheads touched, chatting quietly and smiling at each other. So, Rhonda was trying to set up Joyce with her, to make up for –

Then she saw them kiss. It was quick, light, tentative. A first

31

kiss. Joyce recognised it as such. But it wouldn't remain their only kiss; she recognised that, too.

Joyce's heart raced. She watched as their hands reached out, encircled each other, squeezed each other, a further bridge. Despite her anger, Joyce was aroused by the scene. She'd seen other women kiss in the open, in those few times when ex-girlfriends had dragged her to gay discos, though she'd never dared do the same thing herself, even in the heady throes of passion. But to see her supposedly straight friend doing the same was –

Then they looked up together and saw Joyce. Joyce watched Rhonda pull back – slowly, reluctantly, Joyce noted – and her expression sober, caught out. It was the trigger that awoke Joyce, and fuelled her into drawing closer.

Rhonda glanced at Leah. 'Could you give us a few minutes?'

'Sure.' Leah shot Joyce a glance as she departed, a glance quickly withered with a returning dismissive glare.

The court was silent, empty but for them.

'*Why?*' Joyce asked Rhonda, her voice taut.

It was amazing, how such a seemingly simple question could carry so much weight. Or perhaps Rhonda was simply confused as to which betrayal Joyce wanted explained first. Silence hung between them, taunted rather than filled by the distant gurgling of the fountain. They could have been in some greenhouse, or even the jungle in Joyce's mother's homeland.

Rhonda reached out and took Joyce by the elbow, pulling her further into seclusion, looking surprised that Joyce hadn't lashed out at the physical touch. 'I said if you didn't ask her out, I would –'

'I mean the promotion!' And to her initial surprise, she did. Perhaps because she knew, deep down, as much as she was hurting as well from Rhonda being with the woman Joyce desired, Joyce knew she would never have approached her anyway.

'I also said you didn't know me as well as you might have thought.'

'That's not an answer!' Joyce's stomach churned. 'There I was, strutting about, sure of my success. And you knew beforehand. Why didn't you warn me?'

'I tried –'

'Did you enjoy how I would have felt? Did you *want* to hurt me?'

'No!' The answer was immediate, unequivocal, convincing. Then with it came a new expression, one burning away the initial remorse to match the hostility Joyce felt radiating from her own. 'I'm sorry you feel hurt. Whether you believe me or not, I *am* sorry. But you know, I'm *not* sorry I got the promotion. You're acting like I stole it from you, but I didn't. I *earned* it.'

'How? By fucking him? Is that why I didn't get it? Maybe if I'd been straight –'

Rhonda's eyes showed mixtures of disbelief and exasperation. Her reply came slow and taut, but still succeeded in cutting Joyce off in mid-protest. 'Believe it or not, Joyce, you don't have to be gay to miss out on promotions, or other things in life, for that matter. And I don't have to fuck the boss to get them, either. You failed – and I succeeded – because I take risks. Risks like dealing with people, with challenges, with *life*, instead of hiding in my cubicle, in my flat. You told me several times you were offered the opportunity to go to other countries as part of Frank's team, but you turned them down. Why? Because you were afraid.'

Joyce swallowed. 'I don't want to hear this.'

'No, you don't ever want anything that might challenge your complacency. You'd rather sequester yourself in your flat, deluding yourself into thinking that everyone lives lives as boring as yours!'

'Shut up.'

'You'd never get that promotion with your timidity. And you'd never get together with Leah, either. You'd rather spend your evenings alone, playing with yourself –'

'*Shut up!*' Joyce's hand struck Rhonda across the face. It had been a spontaneous, yet completely natural act.

As was the kiss which followed in reply.

It silenced her, froze her in place. Then melted her. Joyce's nipples tightened, sending potent flares of sensation downwards to her receptive, approving groin, as her lips pressed against Rhonda's: hot, sweet, soft yet unyielding. Their breasts also pressed against each other as if in imitation, and Joyce could swear her heart had stopped, just as Rhonda's tongue slipped between her parted lips and thrust into Joyce's mouth.

Shards of pleasure spread through Joyce, causing her to push forward, hoping Rhonda would push back, their bodies grinding as their mouths did. Joyce relished Rhonda's taste, sent her tongue into Rhonda's mouth to see what could be found, gasping inwardly as Rhonda began sucking on it. Their arms clasped each other, refusing to let go, nevertheless acknowledging that their pleasure would not last long, at least in this incarnation.

Joyce opened her eyes and looked up into Rhonda's, twin fires which mirrored her own unanticipated excitement; she could still feel the intensity of their kiss, an intensity echoed in the taut, puffy flesh of her sex below. She wanted more.

But then Rhonda pulled away, as if sensing that awakening hunger. She turned away, before sparing a final glance at Joyce. But what really gripped Joyce was the look in Rhonda's eyes. She pitied Joyce. Really *pitied* her. That was so far worse than hatred. 'I said I'd wanted to try sex with another woman. I'd have loved to have tried it with *you*.'

And that was how she left Joyce, alone with her anger and confusion and arousal and frustration. She'd started back towards the office area, but abruptly stopped and entered the ladies' lavatory, empty now. Quickly her body moved her into one of the cubicles, her hands shaking as she fumbled with the lock. There was precious little room here – they were obviously designed by men – but it would be sufficient.

She desperately groped for the hem of her skirt, lifting it up and sending her other hand down the front of her knickers, working deft fingers through her bush to find her clit, engorged, hungry, hungry for her touch. Her orgasm came quickly, easily; after the stimulation she'd just received, she'd hardly needed to touch herself. And she wasted little time in straightening herself out, to return to the sinks and mirrors, washing her hands, feeling relieved and ashamed and uncaring.

A wave of convulsive shivering overcame her, and she wrapped her arms about herself, hoping that no one else would walk in now. But then the shivering eased, and she was content to stand there a moment longer, gazing in disbelief at nothing in particular. Her eyes felt hollowed, as if she'd just had a good long cry, and her face felt haggard, worn.

That kiss . . .

After a while, she returned to her desk – feeling the eyes on her back, the whispers raising her hackles; office gossip moved faster than e-mail. Of course, she now had what she'd desired. She was the talk of the office – just not for the reasons she'd wanted.

But none of that would matter in five minutes' time.

She rebooted her computer and called up a blank page, one that would encompass her resignation.

But it sat there, a pale, taunting door to the unknown. The desire to quit was one thing; the drive to motivate her fingers to put words to her feelings was another. It was too big a step, too unexpected.

Rhonda had been painfully correct; Joyce never liked the unexpected. Her life was an orderly progression of dates and schedules and habits, a clockwork mechanism that others could only dream of. After work, for instance, she would go food shopping, then prepare a vegetarian dish for herself and Rhonda –

Well, that last was written off now.

That kiss . . .

To quit, now, a good, steady job in this uncertain economy, would be financial suicide. It was too big a step, and Joyce didn't like big steps.

Her attention returned to her work. More or less.

FOUR

Her encounter with the women, Rhonda's betrayal . . . that
kiss, and Joyce's response afterwards . . . it all conspired to
gnaw at her insides for the rest of the day, and on the way home;
the rain had paused, and the sky was a porridge of milky clouds
and salmon-pink light, promising more warmth than it could
provide.

She'd left the shopping for another night, heading straight home.
Her building's lift looked like something out of the nineteenth
century, a tiny brass cage wrapped by a helter-skelter staircase that
was far too imposing for her to climb that afternoon – or any
other time, for that matter.

But then, the lift always took for ever, too.

I'm content with what I have. Her words to that woman Faith
returned unbidden to her mind. Given what had subsequently
happened, it sounded like a joke now. In fact, standing here in the
lift, a sequestered place, like a confessional, leaving the earth to
ascend to the heavens, she could only admit to herself then and
there just how badly she'd been deluding herself all this time. It
was one of the rare introspective moments in her life, and the pain
she felt, like the reopening of an old wound, reminded her of the
futility in indulging in such recollections. But still, they came.

Joyce had learned of Constance's death through the newspapers;

even accounting for a slow news week, the story had been prevalent in several tabloids and broadsheets, and on television and radio. But there was no shock, no tears, no wailing or gnashing of teeth in response. Any feelings she might have had for her mother were deeply submerged, or stillborn, or burned away entirely. It didn't really matter, she supposed.

From what Joyce had learned from the aunt who had raised her, and her mother's infrequent letters, Constance Wilde had been the original free spirit, the cocky rebel with the infectious smile and laugh. And, like Hemingway, she'd led a never-ending rebellion against her origins, with its trappings and promises of bourgeois boredom, taking on and meeting all dares.

She'd been born to middle-class parents in Mahali, back when it was still under British rule and known as East Africa, and upon becoming an adult travelled to Australia, earning a doctorate in Literature, before spending the Sixties travelling the world, doing everything Faith had said, and more: sailed, skied, desert trekked, skydived, founded magazines, met – and screwed – the rich and famous.

At the end of the Sixties, like a postscript to the decade, she gave birth to Joyce. Constance revealed nothing about the identity of the father, though given the manner in which the infant Joyce was deposited with a relative soon after her birth, Joyce doubted if she'd been a love child. Later on, when Joyce understood what the word 'lesbian' meant, and how it applied to her mother – and herself – she could only guess as to the circumstances involved with her conception. At any rate, Joyce had no exigent desire to learn who her father was; she had little opportunity or motivation to grow closer to the parent she already knew.

Joyce had been put in the care of Susan, one of her childless maternal great-aunts living in London, while Constance went off to lecture and write, before disappearing for most of the decade to the Far East. Susan had been a good woman, who did her best to raise Joyce to be less like her itinerant scapegrace mother. And for the most part, Joyce thought she had succeeded; during her infrequent visits, the young Joyce referred to Constance as 'Auntie Mommy'.

Constance had returned to Britain on a seemingly permanent basis in the mid-Eighties, as if swept in by the wave of Thatcherite *zeitgeist*. But she'd soon turned her ardour, her talents, and the fortune she'd somehow amassed in the East, towards – or rather, against – the government.

There was a scandal, involving contracts in the Far East, and as she never obtained British citizenship, the government was able to deport her as an undesirable alien. For reasons known only to herself, Constance never fought the deportation proceedings.

Joyce had barely entered her teens the last time her mother stood before her. The woman had wanted the child to leave with her, travel with her; perhaps it was her way of making amends for abandoning Joyce as an infant. But it was too late, at least in Joyce's eyes. The girl had been mortified enough at school by the publicity surrounding her mother's antics, and told her so to her face.

There were letters after that, of course, but as Joyce stopped answering them, or even opening them, they grew more infrequent by the year, before stopping entirely. Joyce didn't care; she'd gone on to believe she'd made the right choices, by staying on the Straight and Narrow (no joke intended), the Safe and Sure. Except, of course, today had proven her wrong. The Safe and Sure pillars of her life – her job, her ambitions, her desires, her best friend – proved to be soufflé surety: firm-looking, pretty, but crumbling at the slightest disturbance.

Had Constance finally had the last laugh?

Joyce suddenly awoke from her reverie to find that she'd missed her floor and the lift was on its way down again. Dozy bitch.

The flat seemed cold, quiet, empty; the returning rain pattered on the windows incessantly once more. The only item from the afternoon post proved to have been hand-delivered, a videotape, with a note from Philippa attached: 'It's not too late. Watch this soon. Please.' A contact number followed. Joyce set it aside, though admittedly with less vehemence than she had the letter that morning.

Her vegetarian casserole sat on the table, untouched, cold, like her life. She couldn't help but keep glancing at the videotape sitting on the kitchen counter, as she searched for the remainder of that vodka and coke kept under the sink for when Rhonda came over. She'd never imbibed alone before, but tonight she was ready to break that little self-imposed restriction. She wished she could invite someone over for a drink and a cry, but all her other supposed friends were in fact friends of Rhonda beforehand, and it would probably be both uncomfortable and embarrassing for all concerned to involve them in this. Perhaps an ex-girlfriend? But then, she'd lost track of them. Damn.

That kiss . . .

She briefly surfed the Net. But only briefly, unwilling to trust that those alleged gay women out there weren't just teenage boys or dirty old men; she was unwilling to take risks even via Cyberspace. She changed into her plain blue cotton night-shirt.

That kiss . . .

She lifted the dog-eared paperback from her bedside table and carried it into the living room, curling up on to the low, plush slate-grey two-seater, hoping to escape from the desires gnawing relentlessly within her.

Of course, if she really had wanted to escape, she shouldn't have picked up an erotic novel. And the vibrator she took along as well was probably a dead give-away, too.

' "My hands were shaking as I pulled my dress over my head and shed my white cotton panties and bra," ' she read aloud, her voice cracked, Joyce not bothering to clear her throat for an audience of none.

But cracked or not, there was something undeniably comforting – and undeniably sexy – about hearing the words spoken aloud. ' "Karen, completely naked now, pulled me into her arms again and kissed me. The sensation of her breasts against mine, our stomachs pressed together, her tongue in my mouth, made me so hot I could barely stand. I offered no resistance as she pushed me towards the bed and on to my back.

' "She gently lowered herself on top of me, our lips still together. There was the incredible sensation of her pubic hair merging with my own, her lips sliding down my neck until her tongue found

39

my nipple. Moaning softly as she sucked at my breast, I felt her hand slide in between my legs. A gasp of pure pleasure escaped me as she smoothly inserted two fingers into the damp wetness of my pussy." '

'So hot I could barely stand'. Joyce remembered what that felt like. The narrator's seducer reminded her so much of Paddi. Paddi had been her first lover, when Joyce had been twenty-two, and Paddi an incredible five years younger, but with far more experience under her belt. Joyce's mother had been out of her life for nearly a decade at that stage, though she still made brief secret public appearances in Britain from time to time despite the exclusion order, just to embarrass the government – and Joyce. But Joyce struggled to get on with her life.

Paddi had been a student nurse, living with three others in the flat next door. It ended up like one of those stupid coffee adverts, with Paddi the spokesperson for her flatmates, coming round nearly every day to borrow sugar, tea bags, soap. Of course, it took Joyce for ever to realise she was being seduced by the younger woman – about three seconds after Paddi had started kissing her in the kitchen.

Paddi. That burr of honey-blonde hair, those icy-grey eyes, the pink cheeks and wicked laugh . . . those breasts, full but firm . . . her taste . . . and for one so young, she was remarkably patient with Joyce, too.

Which Joyce badly needed. She hadn't exactly been raised in a cloister, more or less grew into the conclusion that she was attracted to women rather than men. But until then, she hadn't done anything about it, the risk of public exposure being only one of the reasons. Suddenly Paddi had awakened something within her, something she could no longer deny.

Then, six weeks later, Paddi had moved away to continue her training in another city; she'd given Joyce no warning. Letters followed, dying out in frequency after a few months. Joyce was hurt, but didn't blame her; she'd probably bored the stuffing out of Paddi, always refusing to go out to the clubs with her and her flatmates.

In the eight years since then, there had been two others, one a chance meeting through the Internet, before Joyce had grown wise as to how risky this method of meeting people really was. Neither was particularly satisfying or long-lasting. But though Joyce may have since chosen celibacy as part of her lifestyle, she never forgot Paddi.

Thinking about the girl now, Joyce only realised then how much Rhonda had reminded her of Paddi, her drive, her vivacity. Her beauty. She blinked to realise she was squeezing her thighs together, feeling the wetness in between.

She twisted to lie on her back, letting her right leg drop until her foot rested flat on the carpet, and her thighs were parted. She continued to read aloud, as her hand snaked down a well-worn path. '"As I squirmed my hips in rhythm with her hand and fingers, her lips slid away from my breast. Her tongue left a silver trail of saliva as it licked its way down over the rise of my stomach. I shivered as her teeth lightly nibbled in the bush of my pubic hair, and then her tongue continued its journey and I felt like I was floating as her lips found the sensitive nub of my clit. Reaching down to clasp her head with my hands, I forced her face even deeper into my crotch. 'Ohhh, baby . . . don't stop . . . please don't stop . . . please . . .' I moaned hoarsely as I washed her face with my pussy."'

The flat no longer felt cold. She lifted her left leg up until the sole of the foot sank into the cushion, and her thighs parted further, revealing her copper bush, now cupped by her right hand, tentatively exploring as if for the first time. She was damp, and as she drew forth her clitoris and massaged it delicately, but insistently, as Paddi had first done to her, in this very room, she was working on making herself even wetter, if such a thing was possible. She nearly clamped her thighs together, such was the potency of the memory of the woman's head, the velvety tongue and strong lips piercing Joyce.

'"Karen rolled over on to her back and spread her legs wide in invitation. My heart hammering, I awkwardly scooted down on the bed until I was able to lean down and insert my head in between her thighs. My nostrils flared at the pungent woman smell of her, and then I closed my eyes and touched my lips to the

41

swollen lips of her pussy. My tongue snaked out and I began to lick her gently, but my lips soon discovered her sensitive clit. Sucking and nibbling lightly at first, I soon found myself trying to suck her insides out and I could hear her mews of pleasure somewhere far above my head . . ."'

Reluctantly Joyce drew her free hand away, reached down to the carpet for the vibrator left there, expectant. It was a narrow, silver model, seven inches sleek, and different enough in appearance from a man's phallus to avoid raising any doubts or old, bad jokes about lesbians needing the real thing (not that anyone, not even Rhonda, knew about this device, Joyce having ordered it over the Internet). The control at the battery end was easy enough to operate with the same hand that held it; it buzzed to life with a twist.

Then her hand, now wielding the sweet weapon, drew it along her stomach, feeling the hairs on her neck rise at the humming through her nightshirt to her stomach, then over bare skin to her damp pubic thatch. She bit her lip, feeling the tip of the vibrator as it brushed against her inner thighs, as if seeking its own way into her.

Joyce shifted slightly, aware of the beads of sweat beneath her now, as the lips of her sex swallowed first the cooler head of the vibrator, then, when she braced herself, almost the full stem as she pressed into her, enveloping it totally, literal fulfilment. She withdrew it and pressed it against her clit. Then pushed it inside her again. In and out. Delicious!! Her mind and body was awash with the sensations invoked, and she dropped her book and turned her full attention towards her release.

It was no slow canter tonight, rather a more urgent gallop, one threatening to drive her into the tight spaces between the two-seater's pillows like a lost penny from a pocket. Joyce was so aroused, spiralling over the edge into the blinding/deafening light/sound burst –

She clutched her thighs and let out a cry as she came, a cry from deep within. It was not especially loud in itself, but it left her already dry mouth and lungs feeling raw; she felt the vibrator withdraw from within her, but only as a distant afterthought.

I said I'd wanted to try sex with another woman. I'd have loved to try it with you.

It was not a new thought to Joyce. But she hadn't wanted to risk their friendship. So, another opportunity slipped from her grasp.

When she'd calmed down, quenched her thirst and cooled off, she took notice of the videotape again where she'd left it. This time, however, she lifted it up and carried it with her to the living room. Minutes later, Joyce found herself crouched like a Neanderthal before a fire, inches away from the television, watching the tape playback.

A twisted, wobbly close-up of Constance Wilde suddenly filled the screen, making Joyce fall back, as a sudden, unanticipated squeeze of poignancy gripped her insides, making her jaw drop in shock, then sigh, her eyes widening. It was as if the death had been a mistake, that her mother was still alive and trapped inside the television; it took only a heartbeat of embarrassment to acknowledge that the shot was due to Constance holding the camcorder in her hands, recording herself in extreme close-up. 'Hello, Joyce.'

Joyce hit the pause button and indulged in a good long stare. It first looked as if seventeen years hadn't changed Constance much. But then she saw the grey in the mass of light curly hair, and the lines on the tanned, square, happy-looking face, lines deepened with every smile on the wide, full, distinctive lips and those high, firm cheekbones, cheekbones demanding others to share in her enjoyment. No, what had fooled Joyce at first had been seeing the same vitality she recalled from nearly two decades before, a burning radiance within the woman, the vitality of a woman half – no, a third her age.

Chagrined by her initial response, Joyce breathed in once, then again, before hitting the play button and proceeding.

Constance returned to an electronic simulacrum of life, setting the camera down on what appeared to be a rock on a white expanse of beach. She was reclining on a chair beneath a large umbrella, while a brilliant sun made its presence felt just above the view of the camera lens, with fingers of piercing light. Her expression was relaxed as she pointed off-camera. 'This is Sydney Beach. I was here with a few hundred of my closest friends a year or so ago, at the Millennium, dancing naked until the dawn.' She laughed awkwardly. 'I hope you had just as good a time.'

Joyce recalled how she'd spent the time at home watching TV and rechecking the clerical Y2K Bug contingencies for the charity, and suddenly she hated her mother for inadvertently opening up a recent wound as well as the older ones.

Constance hesitated again, before laughing uneasily at herself. 'I had a script for this worked out, rehearsed it for days. Tried to find the right words to start this. It took for ever, and now, when I'm actually filming it, the words have escaped. Typical of me. I've never known what to say to you, have I?'

'No,' Joyce whispered to herself. 'You never have.'

Then Constance adopted a sober expression, as if she'd heard her daughter's reply. 'Look, I'll come straight to the point: I know I've fucked up as a mother to you. I'm proud of how well you've turned out, and I don't blame you for not answering my letters; I only wish I could work up the courage to visit you in person, instead of sending this tape.' Now she looked away. 'Maybe it's better this way. We don't have to look into each other's eyes.'

Her gaze returned to the camera, earnest and hopeful. 'I want to make it up to you. Hopefully, we'll both have grown up some since we last saw each other. I've not given you much, and I wouldn't insult your intelligence by offering you money now. But I *can* offer you my time, and a chance, a chance at doing things few others have done. I've decided to write my memoirs. I'll be revisiting all the places I've been to, maybe doing some of the same things which first brought me there. Walk with me, Joyce.'

Joyce frowned, confused.

Then it came to her: she'd received a copy of this tape once before, months ago, a plain brown package.

But she'd recognised the handwriting on the address. And binned it.

'There are things I want to tell you,' Constance informed her, 'but they wouldn't sound sincere or believable now. If you accept my offer, even if you decide not to see me again, maybe we'll still have forged some entente between us.'

Now her liveliness dropped another few degrees, replaced by an earnestness, an earnestness Joyce had seen many times before – in her own reflection. 'I'm not looking for forgiveness. Just . . . understanding. Understanding about the things I've done, the way I've felt. I hope it's not too late.' She looked away once again; true vulnerability dimmed her expression. 'Think about it, Joyce. I – I love you.'

Constance reached for the camcorder. All that followed was the silent snowstorm of blank tape.

Joyce stared at it a moment longer, as if hypnotised, before stopping and rewinding it. She sat on the carpet, her mind racing, trying to sort out her feelings. Sadness, yes, that was there. Regret. Anger at Constance, at the reopened wounds, and the reawakened resentment. Anger at herself, without knowing why; she was the injured party, after all.

But she was determined to change that.

Joyce found herself holding her breath to the sound of the ringing tone. Amazing.

Then came the voice, clear, unfamiliar. 'Do you wish to leave a message?'

Joyce blinked, having expected a direct line. 'Hello? I think I may have the wrong number.'

Rather than just agree and hang up, the woman on the line asked, 'With whom did you wish to speak?'

'Philippa Sheringham.'

'Ms Sheringham is out of the country. To whom am I speaking?' She paused. 'Joyce Wilde.'

'Ms Wilde, I have instructions that I should direct any messages from you to Ms Ballard.'

'Is she there?'

'I'm afraid not. Do you wish to leave a message for her?'

Joyce paused again. With the more sympathetic Philippa out of contact, could she trust that a message left for someone like Faith

Ballard would be accepted, let alone acknowledged? Suppose it was too late for Joyce to accept the deal?

'Ms Wilde? Are you still there?'

Joyce cleared her throat. 'This is very important. Can you please tell me where I might find Ms Ballard?'

FIVE

The woman could, and did, and a taxi ride later, Joyce reached the location given, a dance club in the outer centre of the city. It was only Thursday night, and the rain was intermittent, but there were plenty of punters out on the streets, though Joyce had no trouble getting into the club, a post-millennial retro-industrial establishment called the Stomping Grounds. It was all hard, metallic, angular lines and planes, like some child's Meccano set. The wire mesh, chrome and plate-glass look of the façade extended into the main room, where girder work criss-crossed the ceiling, leading to the long metal bar with its silvery sheen.

The music could be heard from outside, and once within, became a palpable force, rolling in waves across her face. Even without the vodka in her system, she would have felt submerged by the sounds; she preferred the more controlled and controllable aspects of tapes and CDs to live music (putting aside the cliché about if the music was too loud, then she was too old).

What surprised her, though, was the source of the music. Not that it was a band, but that the lead singer was Faith Ballard herself. Decked out in a tight black vest, leather wrist bands, baggy army camouflage trousers and Doc Marten boots, she clutched the long, thin chrome microphone stand, twisting it in place as she moved about the stage, like a farmer struggling with a particularly stubborn weed – but fully in her element.

The woman's voice was loud, strong, in-your-face, yet undeniably feminine, driving and enticing the throng of shifting, billowing bodies on the dance floor before the stage. It was a sea of humanity, bobbing and crashing, kissing and touching, petting and caressing and vanishing and never meeting again. The coloured strobe lights overhead turned the frenzied movements of the men and women – though mostly women, it seemed – into a thing more sensed than seen, floating and undulating like a fever dream. And they mostly appeared ten years younger than Joyce, as if she wasn't having enough trouble already accepting her current age.

A hand clamping on her shoulder made her start and spin in place. A man stood close behind her – tall, sweaty, broad in shoulder and chest, his pink face lined and bruised and topped with a military buzzcut. He was about Joyce's age, soaked in lager and attitude like a barman's cloth, and ill-fitting in his wrinkled suit. Nearby stood or sat clones and near-clones of him at the bar, watching, cheering him on, albeit barely heard over the music. Soldiers, or rugby players, no doubt, looking even more out of place here than Joyce felt. But unlike Joyce, they were too drunk to notice, or at least care.

His vice of a hand had slid down the sleeve of her denim jacket until it clamped upon her wrist, and he was now leading her into the sea of dancers. When she tried to pull away from him, his grip tightened until pain shot along the length of her arm and she cried out, unheard. Angry and afraid, Joyce glanced around her, at all the people pretending not to notice the scene and thus be obligated to try and intervene, and end up facing the drunk and his brick-shithouse-built mates.

Into the dancing throng but still within sight of his friends, as if to display his subtle seduction skills, the drunk pressed her close, twisting her captured arm behind her until she cried out again, once more the sound lost. Closer now, his aftershave – some noxious substance most men somehow associated with machismo – was overwhelming. As was the tongue he jabbed like a spear into her ear, letting it rummage around like a finger extracting lint from his navel. Further below, his erection pressed into the crotch of her jeans, making no direct contact but threatening a worse intimacy. She struggled, swore, stamped on his feet, all to no avail.

Joyce's stomach was churning, and her bladder was threatening to give way to her alarm. How far was he going to take this? Would he force her to go outside? Perhaps even with his mates along? How much more would she have to endure?

Not much at all, it turned out; he released her arm and seemingly pulled away from her, though it turned out not of his own accord, shock and surprise saucering his eyes, and a forearm around his throat rapidly turning his face purple. He struggled with the owner of the arm, a figure behind him, a figure of a woman deftly bringing him to his knees by cutting off the oxygen supply to what he laughingly considered his brain.

A woman Joyce immediately recognised as Ruth.

The Israeli's body and face were taut, focused, determined, ignoring her prey's feeble attempts to break free of her armlock, holding firm until he was fully on his knees and near-unconscious, before finally releasing him.

Joyce watched with unadulterated amazement, feeling the crowds instinctively back away around them, as the man collapsed, struggling to deal with the after-effects of the expert embargo of oxygen to his brain, clutching his throat, choking. Then motion to her left caught attention – the man's mates, moving *en masse* towards Ruth. Joyce tried to catch her attention over the continuing music, tried to warn her.

She needn't have bothered trying; Ruth saw them too, and half-turned to face them, driving the closest to his knees with a textbook-perfect toe kick to the groin – delivering pain that even Joyce felt sympathetically – then just as deftly using the second one's momentum, and drunken state, against him, sending him tumbling over the first with an arm twist. The third received a powerhouse blow to the face; he stumbled backwards, his hands covering his face and preventing Joyce from seeing the extent of the damage.

It was a display of balletic ferocity, like one of those ultra-violent Hong Kong videos Rhonda used to make Joyce watch.

Unlike those, however, she loved every second of what she saw tonight.

The burly, white-shirted bouncers from the front door appeared in view; Ruth nodded in a businesslike fashion to one of them, receiving an identical nod in return – they obviously knew each other, since they concentrated on removing the drunks. Then Ruth appeared by Joyce, leading her quickly and firmly in the opposite direction.

Through a door and into a narrow hallway further constricted with plastic crates of bottles and cardboard boxes, Joyce had to make herself breathe again, as if Ruth had locked an arm around her throat, too. She fell against the nearest wall, her head spinning, her heart pounding. But at least here the music and crowds and heat were muffled; Joyce's ears stopped thumping in time to hear Ruth ask, 'Are you OK?'

Joyce managed a nod, and a weak, 'Thanks. You were – you were *amazing*.'

Ruth nodded, displaying neither pride nor false humility, as if the threat of physical violence was a long-since established unpleasantness in her life. 'I try to avoid confrontation whenever I can – pride heals quicker than scars and broken bones – but those *shickers* had been trouble for the last hour anyway.'

'Trouble,' Joyce repeated.

'Faith's band doesn't usually attract their type, but given the weather tonight, the club's management weren't too selective about their clientele.'

Joyce nodded back, feeling both numbed by and acutely conscious of every word Ruth said. 'Thank you.'

Ruth allowed the corners of her mouth to rise. 'You thanked me already. Come on, you can wait for Faith in the dressing room. You won't be disturbed there.'

Joyce followed her slowly down the hallway. 'Where did – can I ask –'

'Israeli Army. After that, several private security firms.' She didn't explain further, or felt the need to do so. And certainly Joyce wasn't of a mind to press for details.

The woman opened a door into a windowless room more suited

to storage than changing clothes. Esoteric electrical equipment was stacked haphazardly in one corner, lumber and paint tins and broom handles sat or stood in another. More boxes and crates of empty bottles had been turned into makeshift chairs and tables. A filthy, cracked cheval-glass mirror stood like an ageing attendant by a Spartan toilet and sink, half-hidden behind a shower-like plastic curtain on a rusted wraparound bar overhead. The air within smelled of things Joyce preferred not to guess at.

'Did they tell you I was coming?' Joyce asked, for no other reason than to break the silence.

'Yes, they paged me. My apologies, I should have been at the door.'

Joyce brushed off the apology. 'At least you were there when I needed you most.'

The woman drew a chair from under a proper table and set it down, testing it. 'Faith shouldn't be long. I have to leave now.'

'OK. Thanks again.' Joyce couldn't help but giggle like a child.

To her credit, the Israeli just smiled in sympathy before departing, and Joyce sat down, gathering her strength and her wits again. She let the shivers just beneath her surface rise and pass through her like an electric charge. Had it not been for Ruth's presence in the club now, she doubted if she'd summon up the courage to leave this room tonight. Her cloistered lifestyle certainly hadn't prepared her for such trauma; was that the life experience Rhonda, and seemingly everyone else in the world, had wanted for her? If so, they could keep it!

Joyce found her hands had balled themselves into trembling fists, and on impulse she swung them out into the air before her, as if emulating Ruth's moves against those bastards. Yes! She rose to her feet again, kicking at the air, replaying the previous five minutes, only with her in Ruth's place, breaking bones, smashing heads in. Yes! *Yes!* That's it! If she'd had the skills – and the courage – none of them would have left the club alive!

Then common sense – or her earlier vodkas – took hold, and she stopped and held her head. Something colourful caught her eye at the table, and she moved closer to investigate. Nestled among the collection of carrybags and hardback luggage was a bright fluorescent pink handbill, identical to the ones plastered outside the Stomping Grounds, handbills featuring a picture of a scowling Faith; why hadn't she made the connection before seeing the younger woman onstage? The name of her band was apparently Skunk Another – what the hell kind of name was *that*?

Suddenly her kidneys demanded attention, reminding her of how little alcohol and heat and fear she could handle at once, and she made her way to the toilet behind the curtain. There were no words she could muster to describe the fetor of the facilities, and she endeavoured to be as quick as possible.

She was about to rise and draw up her jeans and knickers, when the dressing-room door suddenly swung open; Joyce instinctively reached out and drew the curtains fully across, feeling her face flush and boil with chagrin. Damn, this always happened at her flat, too, but at least there it was just the phone ringing or the doorbell chiming.

Afterwards she rose to her feet and quickly, quietly, drew up her clothes, ready to flush the toilet and alert the giggles beyond the curtain that she was present – when something made her first peer through one of the cigarette burns in the curtain itself. It was Faith, her dark skin glistening with sweat, passionately kissing a shorter, younger girl with a bouncy, leonine blonde mane. They were locked in a fervent, intense embrace, the blonde's longer, slender fingers, tipped with glossy, apple-red nails, impaling Faith's back through her damp black vest, provoking only a grunt or two from the woman.

The women's lips drew apart, as if for the breath which now raced in and out of their mouths, even as their eyes burned into each other, and their hands drifted down to clumsily work at the buttons and belts at the fronts of their trousers. Faith dipped her forehead to rest against the blonde's, and asked, 'You don't take much seduction, do you?' Her voice sounded throaty, masculine, from her singing.

The girl – a beauty with high cheekbones, full, slutty lips and an ample bosom unharnessed beneath her pink T-shirt – stared back with raw hunger. 'You've been seducing me all night. Your music.'

'Fair enough. Thank you, Cecilia.'

'My name's not Cecilia!' The blonde giggled.

'*Saint* Cecilia. Patron saint of music and musicians.' Faith grinned. 'I'm a good Catholic girl, donchyaknow.' And with that, she dived for the girl's neck, pushing her back against the table with the luggage.

Behind the curtain, ashamed and excited, Joyce knew – or at least convinced herself – that it was too late to say anything now. It was wrong to be watching this. And yet, she easily justified her continued silence. This was hardly a private place, was it? Wouldn't Faith be even more angry if she was interrupted now?

Yes, keep telling yourself that, Joyce. Meanwhile, her hand drifted to the front of her jeans, to the unzipped opening, stroking the white cotton of her knickers within, finding the upper groove of her pussy.

Faith was making the blonde arch backwards, taking the opportunity to draw the girl's T-shirt up to her armpits, exposing full, pale, round breasts with salmon pink nipples now creased and hard with excitement. Faith's mouth dived for one of them; behind the curtain, Joyce had to move to another hole to continue watching, all guilty notions filed away for later scrutiny, to make room for her current curiosity and concupiscence.

The blonde was crying out, biting her lip, begging Faith to stop and keep going, while helping to further undo the buttons of her jeans, letting Faith's hand dive down inside the waistband of black knickers beneath. The blonde supported herself fully on the rickety table now; Joyce winced, expecting it to collapse at any second, but unwilling to warn them. The scent of sweat and sex mingled in the air.

Suddenly Faith reached underneath Blondie and lifted her up from the table, her cargo wrapping her legs around Faith's lower back for support as Faith set her down on the thin, dirty carpet with a whoosh that rustled the curtain. Joyce held her breath and stepped back, fearful of being seen now, at this stage. Once the curtain settled again, Joyce took a tentative step forward, crouching to yet another hole to view the couple.

Faith was straddled upon Blondie, helping her remove and

discard her vest, sending it to join Blondie's own, which must have been removed when Joyce hadn't been looking. Faith's back was a smooth plane bisected by the slight rise of her spine, and intersected by sharp shoulder blades at the top, and her breasts were round and full with only the thinnest band of areola around the nipples, that the lovemaking had made erect. Her breasts swung lazily beneath her as she bent forward to suckle Blondie again. She must have bitten the girl, because Blondie yelped and cursed, playfully slapping Faith on the bum, before reaching between Faith's legs, rubbing through the coarse material of the camouflage trousers.

To little surprise, Joyce found her own hand copying the last action with herself, trying vainly to get inside her own knickers, without snapping the tab of her jeans. But no, as much as she wanted to relieve herself now – and so soon from her time in the flat! – it would be too great a risk that she would be heard. She needed to see it to the end, feeling an inexpressible kinship with the women, all sense of propriety and sordidness forgotten. She forced her breathing to remain slow and silent.

Beyond the curtain, Blondie had fully undone Faith's trousers, and with a little help on the owner's part, had drawn them down enough to reveal firm, brown, sweaty cheeks. Blondie's hand returned to Faith's pussy, continued to work away at it, though damnably out of sight from Joyce. Faith's back cambered at this more intimate contact, her eyes closed, her mouth opened, her teeth clenched, breath shooshing from her in hot gasps of delight.

Joyce could almost feel the waves of bliss radiating from the woman; with a twinge of guilt and excitement, she also acknowledged how easily she could smell her, a heady scent like Joyce's own. Feelings she thought sated tonight had returned with a vengeance.

Damn. It really *had* been a long time since she'd had a lover.

Suddenly Faith went into an instantly recognisable rhythmic spasm, bucking and writhing, and she moaned and collapsed on top of Blondie, panting, cursing, licking her lips, satisfied yet hungry for more. Joyce remembered such feelings, too. She watched again as Faith and Blondie kissed once more, before Faith halted and, with visible reluctance, checked Blondie's watch, before rolling off the girl. 'Aaw, shit.' She reached for her vest.

Blondie sat up on her elbows. 'What's wrong?'

Faith slipped into her top. 'Sorry. I have a plane to catch, double quick.' She paused, looking genuinely contrite. 'I *am* sorry.' She offered a smile. 'Don't think I'm just being selfish.'

But Blondie just shrugged and reached for her own top. 'S'OK. Probably wouldn't have gotten this far with the real Skin anyway.'

Faith grinned at the remark, which remained cryptic to Joyce, but to judge from Faith's response, carried with it no hard feelings. 'Do you think I'm as good as her?'

Blondie grinned back. 'Well, I haven't had her – *yet* – but as for your singing, you're just as good. And streets better than Letitia.'

Joyce frowned to herself and stepped back, listened to them straighten themselves out, then give each other a big sloppy kiss, before the door opened and closed, with one of the women remaining, and Joyce pondered how to gracefully announce her presence.

As it turned out, she didn't have to. 'You can come out now.'

Joyce almost didn't hear it. Even when she did acknowledge the invitation, she didn't react, not until Faith pulled the curtain across; a smile lifted the cigarette now dangling between her thick, dark lips. 'Show's over. Please deposit your candy wrappers and empty popcorn tubs in the nearest receptacle on your way out of the building.'

When Joyce started breathing again, she sounded as if she'd just sprinted a hundred metres. 'How – how did –'

'I saw the disturbance on the dance floor; Ruth told me afterwards what happened, and that you were in here.'

Confusion flared in her mind. 'Then why –' She couldn't quite put the rest into words.

Nor did she need to. Faith lit up. 'I was horny. And I *am* a performer.' She nodded towards Joyce's crotch. 'I suppose if you'd been a man, I'd have got a standing ovation.'

Confusion was rapidly replaced by anger, and Joyce discarded her earlier guilt at being a voyeur; now she felt as if *she'd* been watched. Been used. And she didn't like it. But she suppressed her anger, zipping up her jeans, turning and flushing the toilet, and washing her hands in the adjacent sink. 'I didn't come here to play Peeping Tom, I can assure you.'

Behind her, Faith blew a lungful of grey smoke in Joyce's direction, carrying her question with it. 'What did you think of my show?'

Joyce felt her embarrassment grow more acute, then with a start realised what the woman meant. 'I liked your singing. It was very . . . well, you looked like you enjoyed it.'

Faith accepted the towel, and the compliment. 'Thanks. I thought I might have lost my touch.'

'Your touch?'

She wiped the towel over her sweaty arms and head. 'I haven't sung in a while.'

'I thought that was your band out there. The handbills and all –'

'It *was* my band, but I'd left them after a fight. And then Constance died, and that took up more of my time. They'd got a replacement for me, but seeing as how they were in town tonight, they let me come back and do a set. Nice to know people still think of me as the best Skin.' At Joyce's expression, she sneered. 'You have no idea who Skin is, have you? Or Skunk Anansie? I bet your CD shelves are filled with Barry Manilow and John Denver.'

Joyce bristled, any burgeoning positive feeling for the younger woman flying out the proverbial window. 'David Bowie and Madonna, actually.' Then she wondered why she needed to justify her tastes to the likes of Faith. 'I've reconsidered the offer made today. I want to try it.'

If the announcement surprised Faith in any way, she didn't show it. 'And suppose *we've* reconsidered? Suppose you no longer have any say in the matter?'

The idea had crossed Joyce's mind, but she remained resolute in the face of the enemy. 'Then I'll want to hear that confirmed from Philippa or Ruth.'

'Don't you trust me?'

'No.' Joyce had almost answered before being asked.

'Good. At least you're honest.' Faith sucked in her cheeks, as if to get the most out of the last drag on her cigarette. 'I'm leaving tonight. We're meeting in Berlin early tomorrow morning, and flying out a day later.' She let the remains of her cigarette drop to the floor, quickly stamped out with the toe of a boot. 'My plane leaves at midnight; there should be an extra seat on it.'

'Tonight?' Joyce felt herself blanch. 'Maybe you could arrange a seat on a later flight, tomorrow, give me time to prepare –'

'You know, all that your mother had ever needed to go anywhere in the world was her passport and toothbrush. And sometimes, without even those. But then, I'm sure she didn't have a life as full as *yours*.'

It was an obvious, childish taunt, a dare to do something rash, something that Constance would have done; the younger woman was the epitome of arrogance.

And worst of all, it had the desired effect. 'Book me on your flight, bitch. I'll go and get my passport and toothbrush.'

Joyce almost didn't make it to the airport in time; though in truth she had precious little to do other than pack a small bag and change into her black skirt suit, an outfit she considered more suitable for air travel. She'd left an e-mail with Frank, requesting – demanding, really – to use up all her accumulated leave now, and the money in the bank would cover the upcoming rent and bills for months, if necessary, via direct debit. Luckily she had a valid passport, albeit until now used only for identification purposes.

Faith had changed from her stage outfit back into the earlier outfit, and said little as she handed Joyce her ticket and led her through what must have been, for the younger woman, a tedious procedure by now, judging from the number of stamps Joyce saw in Faith's passport. The younger woman was curt, and what little conversation was made stopped altogether when Joyce found their plane seats weren't even together. Her isolation complete, Joyce's paranoia began festering, and she wondered if Faith might be playing some cruel prank.

The flight itself wasn't as bad as Joyce had expected, once she'd learned to swallow to adjust her internal pressure, and ignore the dryness of the air. The meal was atrocious – she'd suspected they were served in plastic trays so the plastic might rub off and add some flavour – but she devoured it greedily, her stomach reminding her how she'd hardly touched her dinner hours earlier. Then she caught some sleep, somehow putting aside her excitement at suddenly taking off in the middle of the night to some exotic city, like a James Bond adventure.

They arrived at Tegal airport sooner than she'd expected, and as they hadn't checked their meagre luggage, their trip through the terminal to get a taxi into the city was also quick.

The silence between the two women had grown thick, uncomfortable, as they no longer had distance or commuter haste to fall back on for an excuse. Joyce didn't like it. She didn't like Faith, but she didn't like the silence much either. She sought a legitimate excuse to speak, settling for, 'How long did you know my mother?'

There was a pause and, for a painful moment, Joyce feared the other woman was going to be openly rude. But finally she breathed out, 'Most of my life. She sponsored my education after my parents died.'

'Really? That was nice of her.'

'Yes.'

That killed the conversation. The autobahn snaked into a city of light and beacon in the darkness, a city that could have been anywhere in England, at least until she started seeing the signs: familiar corporate logos tagged with German spelling gave her a dyslexic feeling. Then they reached what must have been their hotel, an elegant building in a quiet square. Suddenly Faith became animated, speaking to the driver in German before lifting both carrier bags sitting between Joyce and herself. 'Wait here.'

'Wait for what?'

'I'll be right back.'

'But I want to go in –'

'*Wait here.*'

For a minute, Joyce sat there, perplexed, shrugging at the taxi driver as he said something in German.

Then Faith hopped back into the taxi. '*Kurfürstendamm, bitte.*'

'*Ku'Dam, ja.*'

The taxi was on its way again, and Joyce was beginning to lose her patience. 'Where are you taking me?'

'To visit one of your mother's favourite Berlin haunts.'

'*Now?* It's after midnight!'

'The perfect time.'

'No, thanks – I'd just as soon go to bed.'

Now Faith fixed her with an accusing gaze, lit and shrouded by the streetlights passed outside. 'Constance Wilde could stay on her feet for seventy-two hours, dancing, drinking, partying, and without the use of drugs. And she was more than double my age. Don't you think you can stay awake another hour?'

Another taunt, another challenge. And like some Pavlovian dog, hearing a bell, Joyce found herself responding in textbook fashion. 'An hour?'

Faith's grin showed pearly. 'Maybe two.'

The *Kurfürstendamm*, or *Ku'Dam* for short, turned out to be a thoroughfare of pubs, nightclubs, fast-food takeaways and other shops, with runaway neon signs fighting for attention on the roofs. And like similar places back home, the area was lively with revellers, while man-boys cruised the streets like peacocks, in colourful, sleek cars.

Faith's enthusiasm was undiminished; she had stores of energy, despite having been on stage singing – and backstage screwing. Joyce had been curious about that last aspect, having expected such behaviour only from male performers, at least, judging from the tabloid stories she'd read. Not that she was very curious.

'Is it anywhere in particular, or did my mother just like to hang out on the street?'

Faith was bopping to music heard either outside, or to her own excitement. 'The Schattenseite.'

The driver seemed to recognise the name immediately. 'Schattenseite, *ja*.'

Joyce was less perceptive. 'What's that?'

'A nightclub,' the American replied. 'A special nightclub.'

Joyce turned away and stared outside, at the other cream-coloured taxis and articulated buses. 'We're only going in for one drink.'

She felt more than saw the grin on the other face. 'If you say so.'

SIX

The exterior surprised Joyce: an old-fashioned, elegant town-house surrounded by an ornate iron gate; it looked like a Cold War embassy, especially at night. Only the packed car park offered any hint of life within.

And within, the difference between the Stomping Grounds and the Schattenseite was the difference between a plastic bottle of supermarket cider and a magnum of Beaujolais, or perhaps more accurately, a haulage van and a Jaguar. Both took you to where you wanted to go, but the latter did it with a little class and style.

At least, as far as Joyce could tell, given the interior lighting – or rather, the lack of it. It was all indirect fluorescent UV strips, along the floor or behind the bar, just enough to stay within whatever safety regulations governed Berlin. If any.

And it was obviously designed to draw one's attention to the catwalk jutting like a pier into the heart of the club, and the dancers upon it: voluptuous, sultry, limber, scantily clad women, slowly moving, twisting, gyrating to the music, to the men and women seated along the perimeter of the catwalk, eager to insert notes of varying currencies into G-strings and cleavages.

A strip joint. One in classy surroundings, perhaps, but still a strip joint. Joyce was disappointed, though whether it was more in Faith or Constance was debatable. She remained silent as the hostess escorted Faith and her through the maze of tables and towards a booth thankfully away from the catwalk and the speakers. Faith whispered something to the hostess before turning her attention towards the dancers.

Joyce regarded her; the younger woman looked eager to join the catwalk devotees. 'Enjoying yourself?'

Faith grinned at her, her teeth pearly in the minimal light, oblivious or uncaring of the accusing tone in her companion's question. 'As a fellow artist, I appreciate subtle terpsichorean performances.' Then she laughed and raised her glass. 'Here's to La Vida Loca!'

Joyce didn't join her in salute, but tasted her own drink, quickly drawing the glass away; her face screwed up in disgust. 'What's *this*?'

Faith smacked her lips. 'Constance's favourite: a Between the Sheets.'

'What's in it?'

Faith pretended to think about it. 'Let's see: brandy, rum, Cointreau, lemon juice, paint thinner, nitro-glycerine –' She stopped at Joyce's expression. 'Puts hair on your chest and your ass in a sling. Only served after the cheque has been paid.'

Joyce set down her glass. 'And my mother *liked* this sort of thing?'

'She could put it away, all right.'

'I mean . . .' She reached out to indicate the dancers.

'Sure. Why should men have all the fun?'

'Maybe because it's all exploitative.'

'Hah!' She pointed to the dancers. 'We don't exploit them! They exploit *us*! Got us wrapped around their little fingers! I loved coming here with Constance. The girls loved her, too; she was a great tipper.'

Joyce's mind was reeling. There were women that really *paid* to come here? But then, she could see it herself now. Joyce would be the first to admit that perhaps she wasn't the most out and street-smart lesbian herself, but she'd never heard of anything like it before. It went against every instinct for discretion she had; she didn't go to clubs, especially not like this, and knew that her previous encounters had all been by chance or good fortune.

'Don't knock it,' Faith assured her. 'For many travelling dykes, it's the safest way to meet others for sex.' She leered. 'You know, you *can* be a feminist, and still enjoying looking at a nice body.'

'Really.'

Faith stared at her a moment longer. 'You're gay, too, aren't you?'

It sounded more of a statement than a question. But after another moment, Joyce replied, 'Yes.'

'But you haven't had any in a while.'

'That's none of your damn business!' She was fed up by the whole evening, and unwilling to pander to this woman. 'I'm going back to the hotel.'

'OK. Which one was it?' She leaned closer, elaborating, 'You should have been more attentive. Of course, you could always go back to the airport. But then, didn't I see you put your passport in your carrier bag?'

Joyce growled. Damn it, the woman was right! What could she do, wander the streets of Berlin after midnight, on the off-chance that she'd spot the hotel? She lifted her glass again and downed a mouthful, enduring the liquid fire, allowing it to fuel and temper her anger. 'Bitch.'

'Tell you what: if you agree to let me introduce you to one of these dancers privately, we'll leave immediately afterwards, OK? You have my word.'

'Fine, fine!' Anything to get out of here.

They'd adjourned to another, smaller room, where the walls were covered in black velvet curtain, even over the door where they'd entered; perhaps the liquor helped, but Joyce found it somewhat disorientating. There were armless brass chairs with black leather seats and backs. Two chairs were placed in the centre, with a metre between them. Suddenly Joyce felt vulnerable, the centre of attention; just get this over with, she assured herself, and she can return to the hotel.

'I've arranged for Esta,' Faith informed her. 'Constance's favourite.'

'But why am I sitting like this, if she's just going to meet me?'

Now Faith put on a totally unconvincing look of bemusement. 'Did I say she was just going to *meet* you?'

Before she could explain further – assuming she would – from hidden speakers came music, raunchy music thick with guitar riffs and primal drumbeats – Bowie's *Jeangenie*, Joyce recognised – and from behind another curtained wall emerged a young woman.

She was perhaps even younger than Faith and, if she wasn't near naked, would have looked as if she should have been home baking apple tarts rather than dancing in a Berlin club. Her frizzled blonde hair was a wild leonine mane, and the apple cheeks of her baby face were rouged almost to the point of tartiness, but not enough. She wore a lacy black bra that uplifted her small, pale breasts, matching black lace knickers that left little to the imagination, stockings and shoes; around her neck hung a leather collar, like for a dog, and leather bands with studs were clasped to her wrists.

Joyce sought the righteous indignation appropriate to witnessing such exploitation – until the girl began gyrating to the music, and Faith began cheering and wolf-whistling like a Marine on shore leave. And it quickly became obvious that Faith had been correct, that not only was Esta *not* being exploited here, but that she enjoyed her work, too, investing thought and effort into her routine.

And it *was* erotic, a raw, primeval offering to the gods of erotica. Esta's hands reached behind to her bra clasps.

'Take it off, baby! Take it all off!' Faith crooned over the music.

Smiling at her, Esta let her bra straps glide down her arms into one hand; she flung it to Faith, who laughed hysterically as she caught it, wrapping it like a stole around her neck. Then Esta undulated slowly, caressing her small, upturned breasts, massaging and squeezing until her nipples, large and pink, hardened and jutted. Then she moved to her knickers.

'Yeah! Yeah!' yelled Faith, fully immersed in the action. She probably would have paid for this sort of show even if Joyce hadn't been here.

Esta peeled down her knickers and tossed them to Faith, who caught them and brought them to her face, breathing in deeply, shamelessly. Clad only in stockings and shoes, collar and bracelets now, but undeniably in charge of the business at hand, Esta spread her long, slim legs and arched her pelvis, shimmying her hips slowly and deliberately, as if impaled on to some invisible presence. Her pubic hair had been shaved at the sides until only a line of tawny floss remained to mask the division of her sex.

Her arms outstretched as if bound, Esta was 'led' towards Faith, playfully slapping the black woman's hands away when she tried to touch her. She ran her tongue lightly down from Faith's shaven scalp to her forehead, her nose, to almost reach her lips – then backed away, leaving Faith shuddering and moaning, begging for more.

She moved on to Faith, literally. Supporting a breast in each hand, she nuzzled the black woman's face between them; beads of sweat mingled, exchanged. Adjacent to all of this, Joyce fought to keep the trepidation, the excitement off her face, aware of Faith's eyes glancing over to her at times, gauging her reactions.

Then Esta moved on to *Joyce's* lap. She held Joyce by the shoulders, as if the latter woman might panic and bolt – which, Joyce admitted inwardly, would have been a possibility, if she wasn't also enraptured by the performance. She felt dizzy, swamped by the scent of Esta's sweat, and further below, her arousal, mingling like heady perfume. Joyce's face now sat where Faith's had moments before, between Esta's breasts, the woman's nipples erect, and she felt the urge to send out her tongue, for a taste.

But Esta pulled back, teasing, tantalising. Joyce wanted to will her body to rise, to push the dancer away, run off, do something – maybe, even . . . no! She wouldn't succumb to this! Then with a start Joyce realised that Esta was straddling her thigh fully now; Esta's pussy was furnace-hot through Joyce's tights, wet – like her own. Then Esta began rocking back and forth, rubbing her clit against Joyce's thigh, a wanton bitch in heat.

Joyce barely heard the almost frenzied cheers from Faith beside her, swallowed up as she was by the unabashedly carnal act performed literally upon her. Esta's back arched, her hands roughly kneading her own breasts, eyes closed, mouth growling in a raw, feral manner – letting out a yelp as she climaxed, shuddering, not all of it a show for her audience, her thighs squeezing Joyce's own.

The music stopped. Esta, still reeling from the afterwaves of her orgasm, leaned against Joyce for support. Joyce held her, reeling, too, in her own way; she stole a glance below, to see the moist patch left on her tights. She wondered what it would taste like. Esta then kissed her full on the lips, a hot, strong kiss Joyce responded to, before rising again.

'*Danke. Das war, Esta sehr gut. Sie führen sehr gut durch,*' Faith announced, breaking the spell, and slapping the departing girl on the bum as she passed.

Faith rose and stood before Joyce, slapping her shoulder like a hyper-hormonal teenage boy. 'Well, did you like her? She make you wet?'

'No,' was all she could weakly manage.

'Liar.' And with that she reached out and unceremoniously parted Joyce's knees, drawing the hem of her dress up. Joyce could have called out, could have pushed her away, and could have stopped her in any number of ways. Instead, she found herself looking down, to see what her body and mind had already confirmed: the dark wet patch of arousal in the gusset of her knickers. She'd never seeped like that before.

Faith straightened up and raised an imaginary glass in salute. 'Like I said, here's to La Vida Loca, baby.'

The conference room was in a tall building overlooking the Spree river, which wound like the autobahn through the cobbled streets and low, ancient houses of Old Berlin, while in the distance, the East Berlin Television Tower with its revolving restaurant winked red.

But apart from the view, the room – all polished hardwood and burgundy fittings – was starkly functional, serving its purpose of providing quiet and security for the four woman seated about the table. Not that Joyce noticed much, being preoccupied with this stabbing mother of all hangovers behind her eyes, and rummaging through it to find the connecting memory between the club and Faith returning her to the hotel was like wading through molasses. No, still hadn't found it.

Her mnemonic quest must have been like a beacon; Philippa, sitting closest to her at her left hand, poured a cup of coffee from a brass jug, sliding the cup and saucer gently towards her. 'Before we begin, I believe Faith has something to say to you.' Now the Englishwoman looked across the table. '*Don't you?*'

Faith sat at Joyce's right hand. The American hid her hangover behind black sunglasses, and cradled a tumbler of whisky – an obvious believer in the hair of the dog – staring into the contents of the glass. Her subsequent deadpan words seemed to be wrung from her like blood from a stone. 'I'm . . . I'm sorry for putting you through last night. It was . . . immature and irresponsible. I'm really *dreadfully* sorry.'

As apologies went, it was among the more pathetic Joyce had ever heard. But she was in too much discomfort herself at that point to do more than nod and mumble, 'Forget it.'

Joyce reached for the coffee, as Philippa proceeded. 'We'll not be long, just a few legal preliminaries, and an overview of the coming fortnight. We'll land in Mahali's capital, Patricksburg, tomorrow night. The next morning, there's an additional plane ride to Mzuri, Constance's hometown. There's a game reserve near the town, where Ruth and a guide will show us the ropes of wilderness survival for a day. After that, it's a week's journey through some isolated terrain, to the crash site.'

'Sorry,' Joyce had to ask, for some reason, 'why don't we just fly straight to the crash site? Or is that a stupid question?'

'No, it's a valid one. The area's thermal inversions make flying hazardous – Constance's own accident only confirmed that. Also, Mahali's maintained strict military control over the region for decades, particularly in its border disputes with Bahaska; ironically, it's that control which has allowed the savannah to have remained relatively free of poachers and tourists. During the course of the trek, we may be met by army or air patrols, but we'll have all the necessary travel permits. Oh, and we have a private doctor ready tomorrow morning to provide the necessary inoculations. Ruth's made all the necessary checks regarding local trouble . . .'

The talk continued, but Joyce's mind had begun to wander. Perhaps it was the remnants of the alcohol in her blood, the memories of last night, or the amount of information being fed her, but her head was spinning.

When it was over, she was still sitting there, when Philippa looked between Joyce and Faith, and announced, 'Joyce will stay with me tonight.'

She glanced questioningly at Joyce, but Joyce shrugged, though inwardly she was delighted, finishing her coffee. The less she saw of Faith Ballard, the better.

As if she'd read Joyce's mind, Faith rose, somewhat indignant despite her attempts at nonchalance. 'I think I'll go somewhere and quietly die.'

Philippa's eyes followed Faith's departure, then turned to Joyce and offered her a warm, confident smile. 'If she gives you any bother during this little adventure of ours, let me know.'

'Thank you.' Joyce nodded, then found herself following up with a yawn she couldn't stifle.

Philippa obviously couldn't ignore it. 'You probably would like to go to bed now and sleep through the next twenty-four hours. But you'd regret it later. Berlin's a lovely city to visit when the weather's as clement as today. And it's an even better place to go shopping.'

The woman's quiet enthusiasm was infectious, and despite her fatigue, Joyce wanted to see more of the city, her first foreign city. But still, the last day had seemed the textbook definition of the adjective 'whirlwind'. 'Nothing too taxing, I hope?'

Philippa's smile broadened. 'Of *course* not.'

She didn't exactly keep her word, but she kept Joyce too entertained to complain about it. After stopping for money from the nearest machine, they perused various open-air flea markets, admiring but not purchasing anything of note. 'It's better on the weekends,' Philippa had explained, 'when most antiques and second-hand dealers have stalls out. Oh, and whatever you do, don't buy any so-called "authentic" pieces of the Berlin Wall.'

Joyce smiled and nodded at that, more absorbed was she by the saxophone-playing buskers, and the groups of lovers strolling amongst the stalls, with the ancient buildings behind them. The first thing that struck Joyce was how old many of the sites were; a childhood of English and American war films had prepared her to see a city almost completely rebuilt into an anonymous metropole after the war, but there seemed so little that had actually been destroyed. The second thing was that this was her first view of ordinary Berliners, and she realised how much her reluctance to go out today had been shaped by her initial experience last night.

From the flea market they found themselves in a park, where patchworks of luxuriant flowers were in full bloom. The scent of them and the furrowed earth filled Joyce's nostrils; it was an invigorating experience.

Philippa's heels clicked on the cobblestone path, her hands jammed unnecessarily into the pockets of her white longcoat. She looked up into the sky through fashionable round sunglasses. 'I hope we have as lovely weather in Africa.'

'Yes,' Joyce replied absently. It seemed such a far-off event. Or was it that she was merely more focused on walking beside this beautiful woman? 'Have you lived here long?'

'Since before the Wall fell. It's a good place to deal in art.'

'Is that your job?'

'More like a hobby now. I do liaison work for Advanced Idea Mechanics.'

Joyce started in recognition. 'I know them! My company has had dealing with them.'

Philippa nodded in acknowledgement. 'My work mostly involves making the outside world aware of the continuing slave trade in the region, identifying the ringleaders and so forth.'

'You do good work.'

'Thank Constance for that.'

Joyce took this in, absently stepping around a family of grey pigeons working diligently at the discarded remains of some crusty bread roll. 'Why her?'

She stopped in her tracks, prompting Philippa to stop as well. Philippa seemed to regard her, before turning to the edge of the footpath, as if admiring the rhododendrons. 'I owe her. A great deal. I'd grown up privileged, silver spoon and all that – I know my working-class accent fools everyone.' She didn't manage more than a smirk at her own joke. 'I used my family connections to enter the world of art. I was on top of the world, and quite proud of myself.'

She half-kneeled now, reaching out to cup one of the flowers, but being careful not to pluck it, or even disturb it. 'Then I met your mother. There's no need to go into details. But through her, I saw women who needed my help. And women who'd made *real* achievements, starting out from nothing, to get where I am today. They deserved the pride I was draping myself with.'

Joyce frowned, moved closer. 'You *should* be proud of yourself. You're a remarkable woman in your own right.'

Philippa looked up at her, genuinely grateful. 'Thank you.' Now she rose to her feet again, once more exuberant. 'There's money burning ulcers in my purse, and there's only one cure: shopping. And since we need to do some *serious* shopping, there's only one place in this city to go.'

Philippa had been right. It was called the Kaufhaus de Westens, or KaDeWe for short. But that was the only thing short about it. From the outside, it could have been one of those massive Cold War-era civil service buildings. The inside, however, revealed it to be a seven-floor department store, the largest in Europe according to Philippa: an elegant twenty-first-century rabbit warren of square glass lifts, escalators and walkways, a fabulous shrine to consumerism. Joyce imagined that if a modern-day pharaoh had to be entombed, with all his treasures and attendants, then *this* would be the place for him.

The KaDeWe had everything, from buttons to bread, from Wedgwood china to Escada overcoats, from fresh wild boar to Moroccan mushrooms. And by the time they'd reached the seventh floor, where the food was displayed, they were laden down with shopping bags filled with outdoor wear, boots, and a dozen things Joyce would never have thought of purchasing.

They finally settled at a café table with a gorgeous view of the previous floors. Joyce cradled her mug of Swiss mocha coffee. 'I feel guilty, you buying me all of this – you should have let me pay for it –'

'Nonsense.' Philippa's eyes brightened beneath her blonde fringe; she still seemed alert, even after over six hours of perusing the many shops within the building. 'It's all being written off as business expenses.' Philippa reached across and patted her hand. 'Drink up, we still have a few more places to go before we return to my flat. There's a lovely restaurant overlooking the Spree, and a fine jazz club.'

'You like jazz?'

Philippa nodded. 'Every kind, except Dixieland.' She leaned closer, as if to impart a deep secret. 'You can't dance to Dixieland.'

Joyce laughed. The uncertainties of the past two days had somehow melted in this woman's company.

Philippa's flat, a plush expanse of luxurious leather and dark wood panelling, was dominated by sets of paintings and etchings on most of the walls: brilliant, vibrant landscapes, street scenes and slices of everyday life. In the background, classical Spanish guitar played on the CD, lending to the civilised atmosphere.

They sat a space apart on the low, soft, white leather couch, facing each other, Joyce cradling her wineglass, careful not to spill it. It was late when they'd returned, and Philippa had changed into a white silk knee-high kimono, slackly tied at the front; ample, creamy cleavage peeked out from the folds, and long, smooth legs tucked themselves comfortably beneath her.

Philippa was obviously proud of her collection, her tones hushed, almost reverential. 'I deal with all manner of art, but my heart belongs to Impressionism. Degas, Morisot, Sickert, Pisarro, Renoir – they're my true loves. When I was twelve, my class was dragged kicking and screaming to an exhibition. The others spent their time tittering over the nudes, but I'd fallen in love with everything I saw. I spent my luncheon money and weekly stipend on buying reproductions from the souvenir shop. I had a large allowance. By the age of sixteen, I'd saved enough to purchase my first original. And the rest . . .' Her hand slowly reached out, as to encompass her collection.

'They're magnificent,' Joyce echoed. She wasn't an expert. But the old cliché was true: she didn't know much about art, but she knew what she liked. And she certainly preferred these vibrant portraits over what now seemed to win the prizes. 'Which ones are your favourite?'

'The Renoirs.' She pointed towards the far end of the room.

'Why those?'

Now Philippa seemed to blush in the low, intimate light. 'He preferred painting women. And I admired his drive; even in his final years, when he was crippled by arthritis, he continued to paint, strapping the brush into his hand.' She turned her head towards Joyce. 'I've never been this intimate with anyone – about my art, that is. I'm usually quite selfish.'

'I think you've been very generous. And it's appreciated.'

Philippa waved off the compliment. 'You're a worthwhile investment.' She tilted her head in mock conspiratorial fashion. 'And it never hurts to keep a business partner sweet.'

Both women laughed quietly, Joyce's laughter reluctantly diminishing. 'If I survive the next few weeks.'

'You will. With my help.' Philippa's voice adopted a wistful quality. 'And Ruth's.'

'I notice you left Faith out?' Joyce ventured.

'Yes.' The word hissed out slowly. 'Oh, I like her well enough. I merely consider her . . . flighty. Immature.'

Joyce couldn't help but agree. 'How *did* my mother get to know her?'

Now Philippa's ebullience dimmed, with hidden obligation. 'I'm . . . not at liberty to say.'

Joyce stared, bemused, before the penny dropped: *Constance and Faith had been lovers*. That explained so much now. Her mind made comparisons with all those sleazy jokes about older rich men with younger, gold-digging women, waiting for them to die in order to inherit wealth and power, and Joyce's stomach churned. This was all about her getting a portion of the money Constance promised through the publication of the memoirs. Damn her.

A smile and a remark from Philippa caught her attention again. 'I can almost see the wheels turning in your head.'

Joyce couldn't help but smile back. 'I think I understand a little more now than I did before.'

'As long as I don't bore you.'

'You couldn't do that.'

A heady silence settled between them, carpeted only by the background music. Philippa stared intensely; Joyce found herself breathing heavily and, somehow, becoming very passive under the other woman's gaze, her subsequent voice. 'You know I'm a lesbian, don't you?'

'I . . . I sort of guessed. I didn't want to ask.'

Philippa shrugged, then breathed audibly, as if gauging her next question. 'May I ask about *your* preferences?'

Joyce didn't answer, not out of reluctance or that Philippa had most likely guessed already. Tonight, her head was feeling very light, and the room suddenly seemed warmer than before, the distance between Philippa and herself much shorter. Her immediate instinct was to leave, to run and return to her safe, predictable . . . boring life.

Except, of course, yesterday had proved that it wasn't safe or predictable. Just boring.

'I'm asking,' Philippa continued, reaching out and taking Joyce's glass, setting it and her own aside; Joyce shuddered as their hands briefly touched. 'Because of what I might do now . . .'

She didn't wait for an answer, pulling Joyce into a kiss before Joyce realised it. She recovered to open wide, allowing Philippa to snake her tongue within, exploring her inner cheeks. Joyce's heart threatened to leap into her mouth to meet the invader, and she half-struggled to pull away, a token gesture, before she felt herself melting.

It was Philippa who finally pulled back, still clinging on to Joyce with both hands. Joyce felt lost as the other woman fixed an inescapable magnetic gaze upon her, her words husky, laced with wanton passion. 'I'm sorry. I've wanted to do that since . . .'

'It's OK,' Joyce found herself whispering, Philippa's words and actions helter-skeltering through her head. She was aware that she was shivering, and she began to admit to herself the level of her own passion. She felt as if she'd just been pushed off a great height. No, not pushed – jumped, of her own free will.

Philippa drew at Joyce's blouse, pulling it up, raising it to expose Joyce's belly, her breasts, encased in her sensible white bra. Philippa feasted upon them with her eyes, then with a half-leap she was on top of Joyce, nipping and licking the skin just above the cups. Joyce moaned aloud, then again when Philippa lifted the woman's breasts out from under the bra, rolling her tongue around each erect nipple. Joyce pulled Philippa's head closer, cursing the feelings running juggernaut through her, bucking as Philippa's hand reached under her skirt, threatening to pierce Joyce's tights and soaking knickers with her fingertips.

But suddenly Philippa seemed to catch herself, drawing back to rest at one end of the couch. 'I'm – I'm sorry –'

'Don't be,' Joyce replied, confused, aroused. 'I want it too –'

'No – that's not what I mean.' She reached for her glass, seemingly unable to look Joyce in the eyes. 'I'm not usually that forward. I'm not into casual sex.'

'What?' Seeing Philippa reach for her glass made Joyce fix her blouse again.

'I'm sorry. But I've been burned before. If I make love with someone, I have to know them very well. I have to know if they're willing to commit themselves fully to me.' Her gaze dropped into her drink. 'I'm a very possessive woman. I give a hundred and ten per cent to my lovers. And I expect the same in return.' She breathed. 'I'm sorry.'

'Please, let's forget it.' Joyce realised that didn't come out the way she'd wanted to express the storm of feelings rushing within her. The spell was broken. She rose to her feet. 'I think I'll go to bed. It's late.'

'Yes.' Philippa sipped at her glass, before shrugging and finishing the contents. '*Gute Nacht.*'

'Yes, good night.'

Joyce was at the doorway to the living room before she stopped at Philippa's final words. 'I won't bring this up again, if you don't. And I hope it doesn't affect our relationship. I'd really like you as a friend, if nothing else.'

Joyce glanced back. Philippa had shifted in place and her kimono had parted slightly from the waist down, revealing an expanse of milky thigh. Joyce's gaze had dropped, for an unsalvageable instant, and met Philippa's on her return. It had been a corny line, but Joyce didn't take it as such. 'Don't worry. We're friends. If nothing else.'

SEVEN

It was only her second flight, but already Joyce felt like a veteran globetrotter; she suspected she'd been given a mood enhancer among her noxious cocktail of vaccinations that morning for yellow fever, typhoid, malaria, hepatitis, *et cetera*.

Then again, perhaps it was just the company she was keeping now as opposed to her first flight: Philippa sat beside her, keeping her amused through nearly the entire eleven-hour flight to Mahali's capital Patricksburg. She had an endless number of stories of the art world, and the plethora of celebrities, eccentrics and dilettantes who inhabited, orbited and frequented it.

Without ever bringing up the touchy subject of the night before, she remained an engaging raconteur, one who entertained Joyce without making her, a neophyte on the subject, feel out of her depth. She'd even taken Joyce's mind off her initial disappointment at not having a window seat, something she'd wished she'd had the presence of mind to ask for when the arrangements were being made.

Faith had the window seat, but Joyce decided to let her keep it. Ruth and she had kept mostly to themselves during the flight, though Joyce, feeling more empathy with Ruth, and kept more occupied by Philippa, didn't take it personally this time. Still, Joyce couldn't help but feel she hadn't been told the full story about . . .

well, about *something*. Or was that just latent paranoia from Faith's manipulation of her in Berlin? Yes, that had to be it; with Philippa – and Ruth – around, Joyce knew she was in safe hands this time.

It was evening when they arrived at Patricksburg's airport and, as with Berlin, Joyce could only tell she was in a foreign country by the languages she heard and read. Then she stepped outside and felt the heat, a dry flannel whip across the face that, combined with the ambient smell of jet fuel and the hours of travel, enervated her. 'I think I could sleep for ever,' she confessed, as they retrieved their bags.

'Don't expect me to carry you through the savannah,' Philippa joked.

'*Ruthie!*'

The quadrumvirate turned as one to the loud foreign voice carrying through the baggage claims area of the terminal. At first Joyce thought the obvious caller was a man, short, stocky, with slicked-back black hair and pale face, and wearing scruffy jeans, cowboy boots and a sleeveless black T-shirt that displayed massive arms. Then she saw the obvious breasts, recalled those few times she'd watched popular television, and Joyce turned to Philippa and asked, 'That looks like –'

'It is.' But Philippa looked neither surprised, nor pleased. But she put on an affable smile. 'Nina!'

The new woman's face widened as she approached the quartet, as if to swallow them with her mouth as well as her arms. As it was, she turned first to embrace Ruth, lifting the taller woman up and spinning her around, before laying kisses on her cheeks. Then she set down Ruth to reclaim her dignity, and moved on to a more enthusiastic Faith. As she reached Philippa, her Cockney-American accent revved like a motorbike. 'Phil-er-up! About freaking time you got here! So how are you, you big muff diver?' She reached down to cup one of Philippa's cheeks. 'Putting on weight, I think – but it suits you!'

Joyce was shocked by the open coarseness of the greeting, though no one else seemed put off by it, at least not visibly. Joyce had to remind herself that, if she was correct about the woman's identity, then she already had a reputation for outspoken behaviour – in fact, revelled in it.

Philippa broke the embrace to introduce Joyce. 'Nina, this is Constance's daughter, Joyce. Joyce, this is Nina Hoskins.'

'Yes.' Joyce couldn't help knowing her: an East End comic actress on stage and the BBC, who struck it big in Hollywood in one of America's most popular sitcoms, and was seemingly destined to repeat her success on the big screen.

Until she'd been outed.

'A pleasure to meet you, Ms Hoskins. I admire your work.'

Joyce held out her hand, but instinctively knew that wouldn't be enough for the woman. And she was right: Nina gave her a massive, ebullient bear hug, before correcting her. 'I don't stand on ceremony, it never stood on me: just Nina, please. Or El Niño. Or Sexy Knickers.' She gave Joyce's bum a quick squeeze before releasing her, looking her over again, eyes dancing like those of a mischievous child finally given playmates to share in her naughtiness. Then she hugged Joyce again as if they'd known each other for years, before returning to Ruth and hugging her again.

Joyce leaned close to Philippa again. 'It's really her! I didn't know you knew her.'

Philippa nodded, almost as if distracted, unable to take her – was it disapproving? – glare from the woman. 'Ruth knew her better; they'd met when Ruth was bodyguarding Hollywood celebrities.'

'Has she come to see us off, then?'

'If only it were that easy,' Philippa replied cryptically. She sighed as she added, 'She's part of the tontine. But she'd been given special dispensation out of going on the trek because she was supposed to be filming in New Zealand now.' Then she announced aloud, 'Nina, you're quite a surprise; we hadn't expected you here.'

The woman left an arm across the shoulder of a clearly uncomfortable-looking Ruth, and declared, 'You don't get rid of me that easily, Philadelphia.'

There was just enough bite in the reply to suggest it wasn't entirely jovial.

There was an obvious measure of tension with Nina's appearance – tightened further when she announced she was coming along for the 'party', despite Philippa's quiet insistence about the inconvenience of adding her to the travel permits, equipping her and so forth.

'I'll pull my weight!' Nina mock-pleaded in the rented mini-van. 'I'll carry the beer! As for the permits, it'll be a piece of piss – everybody knows and loves me!'

Even in the half-darkness of the van, Joyce caught Philippa's eyes rolling. But despite this, Joyce found herself warming to the woman.

And the city. Above and around them, the lights of Patricksburg dazzled her. It didn't have the stately charm of London – or Berlin for that matter – but it was young, with the golden beckoning sparkle of Vegas, the skyscrapers and bustling kinetic energy of Manhattan, and the exotic spice of Hong Kong.

At the hotel, Philippa stopped them all, herded them together and began taking pictures – 'for posterity', she called it. They'd barely checked their luggage into the hotel when Nina bounced around again like a demented puppy. 'Right, right, now let's go celebrate! And I found just the place.'

Faith bared her canines too, as if she hadn't just endured an eleven-hour flight, and punched the air. 'Yeah! Party till you drop, baby!'

'You two go on,' Ruth urged soberly.

'*No!*' Now Nina puppy-dogged Ruth. 'You've *got* to be there! I came halfway around the world to be with you, pudding!'

'It wasn't halfway round the world, and I have work to do,' Ruth declared wearily.

'Work tomorrow! Party tonight!'

'*Tomorrow* we leave for Mzuri,' Philippa reminded her. 'We'll need to ready additional permits in the capital. *And* pay to get them quickly processed.'

Nina stuck out a defiant tongue at her. 'Fine. The three of us will manage without you two old farts.'

Joyce tried not to laugh. And she tried not to yelp as Nina

grabbed her by the wrist and dragged her back outside with Faith, feeling swept along by the storm of personality that was El Niño.

It looked like a church from the outside. The radiation-red glow of a neon sign fell on her: Fallen Angels. A popular club, too, to judge from the parked cars littering the grounds and the queue of patrons at the front door, bopping in place to the strobe light and thunder and chaos seeping through the vibrating house windows.

Nina dragged them both past the queue; Joyce felt no surprise that they were allowed entry by the doorman and past the ticket booth – no doubt Nina had cased the place before the quartet's arrival. The waves of heat she felt as she entered were almost staggering, even when compared to the tropical heat outside.

And what was once filled with the silent and devout in prayer and contemplation, now accommodated a writhing sea of humanity, cavorting and swaying to the steel-edged siren spell of the heavy metal music and the hypnotic strobing flashes of the rainbow light above. Despite the addition of the long bar and the tables and chairs, the owners had maintained the stark, medieval decor of the church, all black iron mesh and wood and stone; even the Millvine cross and circles remained on the wall above the bar, albeit in neon.

A minute after entering the Fallen Angels, Joyce was reminded of why she didn't like the club scene. She'd almost forgotten her experiences of several nights before, in the Stomping Grounds in London, forgotten about the heat of the place, the claustrophobia, the throbbing assault of the speakers on her ears and solar plexus, the incessant insistence of complete strangers informing her that she has in fact pulled ... If it weren't for Nina, she certainly wouldn't have come out – so to speak – with the detestable Faith alone. But even so, her third visit to a club in forty-eight hours made her feel like she was more than making up for lost time.

She was content to spend the majority of her time minding the tiny round steel table they'd secured in the shadowy far corner of the club, where other patrons used the relative seclusion to kiss and cuddle. Joyce tried not to look. Really.

It took a while for her to acknowledge that one of the reasons for her being here now was to give Philippa a chance to get to sleep before Joyce returned to their room. The rooms with twin beds had been reserved before Joyce and Philippa's encounter in Berlin last night, but the woman had graciously offered to arrange a trade for Joyce with Ruth, or more preferably Faith, or even get a separate room for Joyce entirely. But Joyce refused, citing the pointlessness of it. They were adults, after all.

Which didn't really address the dilemma. She could admit to being attracted to Philippa. Who wouldn't be? She was beautiful, intelligent, witty, urbane, voluptuous . . . and from the way she'd kissed and fondled Joyce last night, the woman felt something for Joyce, too.

So why hadn't Joyce gone to the woman's room afterwards? Was it really as simple as she'd said, that she wasn't into nonchalant, insouciant, casual sex, like Faith? Well, what's wrong with that? Joyce felt the same way!

Every so often, Nina would bounce back, dropping Faith off at the table to order more drinks, before grabbing Joyce and dragging her to her feet. Joyce was no dancer, but fortunately the dance floor was so crowded that she could employ her pathetic three-step moves in place without making an utter fool of herself.

Unfortunately, it meant that Nina was pressed close to her, her larger breasts frequently bumping against Joyce's every so often. Not that Joyce was afraid they would be spotted for being gay – pointless, really, under the circumstances – but it was the proximity to the woman. And there was that killer smile . . . Nina was attractive in her own way, of course, though Joyce preferred femmes. She smiled back weakly. As the music paused, Nina noted, 'You're a quiet one. Are you sure you're Constance's kid?'

The mention of her mother furrowed Joyce's brow. Obviously none of the others had informed Nina of the animosity that had arisen between Constance and herself. But this was hardly the time and place to go into details about it. 'I'm just the quiet type.'

The music started up again, but Nina had to respond to that, holding Joyce by the shoulders, leaning close and nearly shouting, 'That's OK. I'm turned on by the quiet ones!'

Joyce nodded, not hearing her properly.

It was an hour later, when Joyce was back at the table, having finished off another bottle of water and visited the overcrowded toilets for a second time, when Nina unexpectedly approached and said, 'Let's go. I have to get something for Ruthie, then we can head back to the hotel.'

Joyce glanced at her watch – unless shops here remained open all hours, surely it was far too late to buy anything? – but instead of questioning it, asked, 'What about Faith?'

Nina grinned and thumbed in the direction of the crowds. 'I think she's pulled. Come on, I gotta make it up to my Ruthie tonight.'

Joyce nodded, glad to be out of the company of Faith for a while, feeling the muscles in her legs weak, as if drunk; she didn't mind letting Nina slink an arm around her waist to support her as they drifted outside to the relatively cooler night air. Her throat was dry, and she wished she'd had another bottle of water before leaving. 'What was it you were going to get for Ruthie?'

Now Nina grinned. 'Well, it's really for her and me. Something we talked about before. And I know just where to get it, too. Come on.'

The air sobered Joyce up a little, and the company animated her. Both emboldened her to want to satisfy her curiosity on other things. 'Nina, how did you feel when you were outed?'

'Outed?' Now she looked about her in apparent alarm. 'Are you saying people *know* I'm a bull-dyke?' She laughed at her own joke – then stopped when she realised Joyce wasn't joining in this time. 'To be honest, I thought everybody would have already figured it out for themselves before those pictures appeared in the tabloids. I never hid it, but I never flaunted it, either; I saw myself as a performer who was a dyke, not as a dyke performer.

'And I sure as hell didn't think it would hurt my career as much as it did. I was a comic actress, for fuck's sake, not a sex symbol; I had no illusions that teenage boys were wanking to posters of me in their bedrooms.' Now she shrugged philosophically. 'Hey, it's their loss, not mine. The Aussies love me now; they even gave me my own talk show in Sydney. And while I was in Hollywood, I met Ruthie. One door closes, another opens, all that bollocks.'

Joyce nodded at that; the woman seemed to have handled the scandal with exemplary maturity, despite her ostensibly outrageous demeanour; Joyce doubted if she would have fared as well, seeing a promising career shot down simply because of her sexual preferences.

Suddenly Nina was off again, as if having just realised that her mask had slipped, and joked for another minute about various other women she'd shagged, or wanted to shag. Joyce let her carry on until she was spent, before asking, 'Did you ever meet my mother?'

Silence, followed by, 'Once. A good woman.'

As short and incomplete an answer as Joyce had ever heard from the woman. It spoke volumes, but unfortunately all in a language Joyce couldn't decipher. 'What did you think of her? How did –'

Suddenly Nina exploded in a flurry of energy, as if electrified by the neon sign ahead of them. 'That's what I'm looking for!'

More evasion, but Joyce didn't press the issue further; they had another two weeks or so together. Instead she looked to where Nina was leading her.

The tattooist and her parlour was one surprise after another for Joyce. First, she was struck by how tidy and organised it was, compared with what she'd expected. Then there was the tattooist, or 'skin artist' herself, a striking, well-spoken, jut-jawed Nordic beauty, tall and clean and elegant like a retired ballet dancer, her tattoos appearing only on her arms (as far as Joyce could tell). Then there was the general lack of business she had that night, until the artist explained she never worked on people when they're very intoxicated.

Joyce's final surprise was that Nina was not looking for a tattoo, but the woman's other offered service: body piercings. Nina drew Joyce over to a glass display case with trays of rings and studs and chains; the woman's eyes were alight with excitement, a child in a sweet shop. 'C'mon, Joy-Ride, what d'ya say? Nose, nipple, belly button, labia? Where do you want yours?'

'I'll stick to just my lobes, thank you.' Joyce felt her breath quicken, her heart thumping. The idea felt impulsive, dangerous. And yet, running parallel with her negative thoughts were positive ones. She was aroused, aroused at the thought of having some permanent physical display of her changed nature – though she questioned why she would warm to a piercing when she'd drawn a line at a tattoo.

When she looked up again, Nina was still staring, eyebrows dancing, teasing. 'Tell you what, I'll go first, OK? And if you decide to get one, I'll pay for yours. Well? Well, well, *well*?'

Joyce smiled. The actress was incorrigible – and yes, still attractive, too. Especially after that moment of vulnerability. 'OK.'

The back room was close, a tiny fan whirring in a far upper corner, the doorway closed off from the front of the shop by only a curtain, the floor dominated by an adjustable chair, like in a dentist's office.

Nina had quickly selected a smooth gold stud, and was now eagerly removing her shoes and trousers. As Joyce watched, she asked, 'Are you sure you don't want me to wait outside?'

Nina blew a raspberry. 'I've done nude scenes from the start of my career, BBC productions and all that. Nothing you can have a crafty wank over, 'course. Stare all you want.'

'I'm not going to stare.'

'No?' She almost sounded disappointed, throwing her trousers to Joyce, followed by her white cotton knickers, before hopping on to the chair and lying back, her exposed skin sticking to the paper lining the artist had placed there beforehand.

Forgetting her statement of a heartbeat before, Joyce did stare, stare at the mat of black hair between the woman's broad alabaster thighs. But she stood in place, unmoving, even when the artist appeared with gloves and piercing gun and blocked her view. Joyce's mind wandered to lewd thoughts, of those hands at the entrance to Nina's sex, opening them, perhaps releasing the dew and aroma of arousal. The woman must have done these scores of times; perhaps she was gay, too, and got off on it?

It was quick, as quick as the artist had promised when she'd explained the procedure to them both. Nina was laughing. 'Hey, Joy-Joy, come have a look.'

Joyce did. The artist, used to seeing bared pussies by now, had departed to clean her gloves and gun, leaving Nina unabashed at being naked from the waist down, her legs spread, her pussy open, rubbing herself with delight. Joyce kept a respectable distance, despite her mounting curiosity, and stared, spying the stud attached to Nina's outer labia, amidst her crinkled pubic hair.

Nina couldn't lose the grin plastered on her face. Her chest was heaving with excitement, and her voice was ragged. 'I didn't feel a thing, girl. Except horny.'

Joyce fought to catch her own breath, as if she'd just undergone the procedure as well. 'You hide it well —'

With a swiftness belying the woman's size, Nina reached out, grasped Joyce's hand, and brought it just as swiftly to her pussy. Joyce froze, her body, her mind on hold, as somehow Nina straightened Joyce's fingers out to help invade the deep cleft they found, the labia easily sliding open, slick with warm, milky fluids, the channel tight, velvety; her thumb firm on Nina's clit.

Their eyes locked together, Nina's filled with a frightening intensity of purpose, Joyce's with shock rapidly suffused with desire, desire to please this woman, to bring her off. Nina's pubic bone gyrated frantically against Joyce's hand, and she moaned in sublime ecstasy, soft rushes of breath escaping through clenched teeth. Joyce glanced away once, at the curtain, expecting the artist to reappear, perhaps wondering what the noise was all about. Then again, she was probably used to *this* sort of behaviour, too.

Finally, Nina shuddered and twitched as her long-awaited climax washed over her, sending her hips jerking in time to the crest of each wave, her swollen bud yielding to the force of Joyce's rough, rapid manipulation. Joyce felt hot and moist and wanting between her own legs. She was pulled down to get a hard, open, demanding kiss ground on to her lips, their tongues twisting, dancing, before Nina parted from her, gasping for breath.

Joyce backed away, suddenly aware again of where they were, who they were, who was awaiting them back at the hotel. She lifted up her hand, stared at the glistening juices coating her fingers like varnish, smelled Nina on them, smelled the betrayal. Suddenly, inexplicably, Joyce felt like an adulterer, and headed towards the entrance.

'Joy-ful?' Nina called after her.

'I'll meet you outside,' Joyce called back over her shoulder.

The outside had grown darker somehow, a little cooler. The city was still alive with the sounds of revelry.

Joyce leaned against a shopfront, her stomach churning, her pussy still awake and hungry; she fought to ignore both distractions. Though there had been no declarations, no real intimacy between Philippa and herself – yet – Joyce felt like she'd been unfaithful to Philippa, allowed her libido, her curiosity and attraction to Nina Hoskins, to direct her body into behaving no less shamefully than Faith.

Nina emerged, dressed again, plopped herself beside her. 'Are you OK?'

Joyce nodded absently. 'I don't blame you. It's my fault.'

'If you say so.'

Now Joyce stared angrily at her. Didn't the woman take anything seriously, even her own commitment to Ruth? 'What is *that* supposed to mean?'

The woman lit up a cigarette. 'I thought I had a hand in the proceedings – so to speak.'

'Does everything have to be a joke with you?'

Nina blew smoke from her nostrils. 'Most things in life already *are* a joke; comics like me just happen to notice it more than most, and talk about it. Timing and pain, that's what comedy is all about.' She patted Joyce on the shoulder. 'Let's get back.'

As they strolled in darkness broken by amber streetlamps, and silence broken by taxis and punters, Joyce's initial guilt and upset was evaporating. She regarded Nina. 'I'm sorry I snapped at you.'

The woman blew another raspberry. 'Forget it. I'm sorry you didn't stick around to get your pussy done.'

Joyce sighed, putting her arm around Nina as they kept walking. 'I'm sure I can get pierced another time.'

'I wasn't talking about the piercing.'

Now Joyce felt wicked, smiled wickedly, and looked about her before letting her hand drift down to squeeze Nina's ample rear end, amazed at how quickly her feelings could assume control once more, overcome her guilt and trepidation. 'We're not back at the rooms yet.'

Nina stopped in place, stared as best she could at Joyce in the half-light from the closed shops around them. Then, with a roughness that shocked and aroused Joyce, drew her into an alley between two buildings, their mouths, their tongues connecting once more. Joyce wanted her again, wanted her breasts suckled and her pussy penetrated.

Nina reached under Joyce's T-shirt, squeezing and stroking her aching breasts through the material of her bra. Sensations rushing and building around her body with her blood, Joyce helped her lift the bra upwards, allowing her breasts to hang free. Nina drew up the shirt to Joyce's armpits, cupping each breast, squeezing each nipple between thumb and forefinger, before bending down and taking one nipple in her mouth. Joyce moaned, pressing the woman closer, wanting more – now!

As if reading Joyce's thoughts, one hand dived down to the front of her jeans, cupping and squeezing the hot puffy mound between Joyce's parted thighs. Joyce dug her fingernails into Nina's cheeks, the concupiscence of a hot summer night and unsated passions having assaulted her senses. Nina fumbled with the catches and zip, before finally diving in, Joyce hearing and feeling the sound of stitches tearing as Nina's hand forced its way past Joyce's knickers, diving into her pubic thatch and the tense, moist sex waiting for her. Joyce cursed as Nina's thick, long fingers entered her, gathering her dew like a bee collecting pollen.

Joyce's pussy reflexively closed against Nina's fingers; she was impotent to fight the exquisite sensations running through her like wires. 'Come on, come on,' she found herself panting hungrily.

Nina graciously obliged. The world was set aside as Joyce's climaxes burst from her, one after the other, her body trembling in the other woman's grasp, cherishing every moment.

EIGHT

Philippa was drifting to sleep in one of the twin beds, when Joyce entered the room. She stirred enough to mumble, 'Hello. Everything OK?'

'Yes,' Joyce lied, slumping on to her own bed, staring at the dust strands waving like reeds in the near corner of the white stucco ceiling. Philippa rolled to her side to face her, propping herself up on one elbow. Her eyes remained half-closed, but she sounded more awake. 'Are you sure?'

Joyce almost replied. What had happened between Nina and herself had felt both unexpected and inevitable. She wasn't into casual sex with people she hardly knew; that was Faith's style, but not hers. And certainly not Philippa's. How would the woman react? If the position was reserved, Joyce thought she might be turned off by Joyce's behaviour tonight. Joyce could blame it on the drink, or the fatigue, or even the feelings stirred up by Philippa herself the night before.

She stared at the webstrands a moment longer, watched them shimmy to the unseen current from the air-conditioning unit over the beds, then turned and glanced at her companion. 'Yes. Go back to sleep.'

Philippa smiled and nodded, as if aware of Joyce's attempt to keep the truth back. But she lay down again. Joyce rose, stripped off and padded into the bathroom for a quick shower. The afterwaves of her orgasm – reached while out in the open, too! She thought only het couples and gay men did that sort of thing! – continued to echo within her. The sweat of a day's travel and an evening's revelry was washed away, but the memory remained, and with unwanted, unneeded guilt.

She dried off and slipped into a T-shirt and bikini pants, and lay on her bed once more, her mind racing with the events of tonight, and their implications for the rest of her so-called Adventure. The possibilities, good and bad, floated before her, like one of those dust strands set adrift by the air conditioner. They seemed to hang there, long after she'd closed her eyes . . .

The plane taking them north-west to the inland town by Lake Mzuri was a two-prop model, a smaller, noisier craft than the jet that had carried them from Berlin to Patricksburg, and the ride was punctuated with turbulence that worked on Joyce's stomach.

But the view was a feast for her eyes and camera: patchwork quilts of cultivated fields on undulating hills, broken by patches of village and bare rock; savannahs of flat-topped acacia and broccoli-shaped baobab trees and stunted thorn bushes; bands of olive and evergreen, sand pictures which mocked man's feeble attempts to set borders on Mother Earth . . . At one point, she glimpsed what appeared to be a band of pink-white beach nestled in the inner curve of a dark blue kidney-shaped lake. Suddenly, the beach became a *cloud*: flamingos, hundreds, perhaps thousands of them. Breathtaking. To have grown up here, amidst this beauty . . . For the first time, she envied her mother.

Ignoring Faith in the forwardmost seats, and Philippa and Ruth in the seats behind Faith, who'd offered little more than the minimal pleasantries to Joyce that morning, Joyce looked at Nina beside her, who was just as enchanted by the sights.

Nina looked at Joyce and smiled. Then she put her hand between Joyce's legs.

Joyce looked back at her, tried to move the hand away, nodding to the others in the front seats, though with the additional luggage packed in the space between theirs and the others' seats, the others couldn't see behind them unless they made a significant effort to do so. But Nina smiled back, and silently but firmly moved her hand upwards, until Joyce surrendered to the assault, the wind knocked out of her sails by the totally unexpected manoeuvre on Nina's part. Nina, an obvious expert in such matters, shifted in place, but kept her composure, calling out over the buzz of the engines, 'Faith, tell me a bit about this Kimya bird.'

'Kimya Upara,' Faith called back. 'She's part of the tontine. Helped Constance set up the Mahali Reserves, where she works. Good guide, good tracker.'

'Really?' Nina's hand was rough, even through the thick material of Joyce's jeans and knickers underneath. Then her fingers moved to the zipper.

'No, not –' Joyce whispered, fought to remove Nina's hand, to regain control once more, but she was undone by a lack of leverage and willpower, by her desire not to alert the others, and she ended up using all her energy not to show her true feelings.

'Yeah,' Faith continued, oblivious to the seduction occurring behind her. 'Her family knew Constance's parents. In fact, Kimya's uncle and father were part of the search parties sent out during Constance's First Great Adventure.'

'And what were her folks like?' Nina asked innocently, her fingers sliding under the waistband of Joyce's damp knickers, to Joyce's equally damp labia, damp with the warm fluids produced under the work of Nina's fingers. Nina grinned as Joyce's pubic bone began gyrating frantically against her hand.

'The Wildes?' Faith paused. 'Martin Wilde ran a successful transport company here. Patricia Wilde was a noted minister's aide. They both died in the same train accident outside Patricksburg in 1970.'

The information was interesting – particularly in that Faith knew more about her lover's past, than her lover's daughter – but Joyce had stopped listening, too preoccupied was she on what was being generated between her legs. Finally, Joyce shuddered and twitched as her climax washed over her, sending her hips jerking in time to the crest of each wave, her swollen bud yielding to the force of Nina's touch.

She slumped against the door – how wonderful!! – feeling the vibrations of the plane run through her body, a mere shadow of her own internal oscillations. And she found herself grinning beatifically at Nina, as the woman withdrew her hand and licked her moist, glistening fingers, one by one. Joyce could smell her own arousal, but was too blissed out to care if the others did.

Mzuri seemed almost as expansive as the bay which gave it its name (or was it the other way around?). The outskirts of the town consisted of simple mud huts bordering the surrounding fields. Closer to the bay – a deep blue dream framed by thickets of delicate, feathery papyrus clumped together in rafts – large weather-blasted stone buildings a century old dominated the view, eclipsed only by the higher minarets of the mosques.

'This was a Muslim trading route for centuries,' Philippa noted, giving herself another spray of insect repellent for luck. 'Until the British moved in a century ago. But the Mohammedan influence remains; you'll only be allowed to get liquor in the hotel, for instance.'

Joyce took her mind off the descending plane with its concurrent agitation in speed and altitude – and what Nina had just done to her! – by reapplying more sunscreen to her exposed areas. 'Fine by me; I've had more alcohol in my system these last two days than in the previous two months.' She peered down, saw bobbing and parked rowboats. 'If it was a trading route, I'd have expected a larger port.'

'The reefs and rocks are treacherous down there,' Faith contributed suddenly. 'And only small boats have ever made it. "Mzuri" means "narrow" in the local language.'

Joyce made an impressed sound. 'Not bad for a New Yorker.'

Faith made no further comment.

A van awaited them. Along the way, Joyce viewed the people, sitting on stone benches outside the terraced entrances to houses and shops, or strolling to the closed-canopy bazaar they glimpsed near the centre of town. Not many white faces in view; Joyce wondered how different it might have been, if it had been different at all, when her mother was a child in the Fifties and Sixties, before independence.

The van pulled up at the graveyard, rows of generously spaced grey and white markers surrounded by an old-fashioned iron-spiked wall, rusted and twisted in places. With the wind whipping the dust into devils at her feet, Joyce was reminded of those old Western films, those scenes set at – what was it called? – Boot Hill, just outside of the ghost towns. She started reading the markers, looking for Constance's.

To her surprise, she didn't have to – Faith led them to it, a site of earth more fresh than the others, headed by a simple marker in white marble, with Constance's name, dates, and a strange quote: 'I won't forget you'.

The others had bowed their heads, remained silent. Joyce followed suit, though in truth she felt nothing, except a strange, oppressive emptiness, as if suddenly discovering an incomplete part of herself. Which was obvious, of course.

So this was it, the final resting place of Constance Wilde, activist, adventuress – and bad mother: a nondescript plot in a small town in eastern Africa. Given the amount of deserved notoriety and undeserved loyalty the woman had generated in life, it seemed odd that she would end up in such a place, even if it was where it – and she – had all started. And despite all that had occurred in the past, all the bad blood, Joyce couldn't help but be moved. Her mother was here, or at least her body, and for good or bad, they would never see, never hear each other again. It was so . . . conclusive.

Afterwards, as they walked back to the van, Joyce risked moving closer to Faith. 'May I ask a question?'

The black woman shrugged, hands tucked into her trouser pockets.

'Shouldn't that have read: "*We* won't forget you"?'

Joyce waited for the inevitable smart-alec quip. Which never came. 'Among the Mahali people, it's believed that what we'd call the afterlife is the Real Life, and that all this –' she nodded towards nothing in particular '– is just a dream we have before we're truly born. We don't assure the dead that we'll remember them; we ask that *they* remember *us*.'

'Oh. Thank you.'

Faith shrugged again.

The hotel room awaiting them was even starker than the one in Patricksburg, but it compensated with its ornately carved Lamu furniture, and a balcony overlooking an interior courtyard overgrown with rich, vibrant rose-purple bougainvilleas. Ephemeral mosquito netting hung over the double bed. The one double bed.

Philippa was chattering away to Joyce, pausing at her expression to note, 'It's best to keep the netting up; the bugs somehow always get in.' Then her grin dropped with understanding, and for the first time in Joyce's experience, Philippa blushed. 'I, ah, didn't plan it this way. Really. I didn't even think to check if there'd be two beds.'

'I know.'

'I'll go and get another room booked –'

'No!' Joyce recovered, reminded of a similar argument in the capital city the night before, continuing with a less forceful tone, 'There's no need. We're only staying two nights after all. Right?' She was vaguely ashamed by her initial reaction, and by her subsequent words – methinks she doth protest too much, indeed. 'What now?'

There was a knock on the door.

Philippa looked up, her smile returning. 'You answer that, for starters.'

Joyce did. Nina was there, grinning. 'Come on, sexy. Let's go for a swim.'

Joyce glanced back at Philippa, who said, 'We're supposed to be meeting Kimya shortly.'

'And we'll be back . . . shortly.' Nina reached inside, clasped Joyce's wrist and tugged. 'Come on, girl, forget about Auntie Phillabuster and let's go out and play!'

Joyce felt herself blushing – then wondered why. Yes, Philippa no doubt disapproved, but so what? If Nina hadn't shown interest in Joyce, distracted her from the feelings she had for Philippa, then she'd be still here, aching for the woman . . .

Nina drove the minibus. Mzuri wasn't a typical English town of similar size and population. For one thing, there was the dust, gathering everywhere, occasionally pirouetting from the winds, sometimes even attacking travellers. Then there was the friendliness of the locals themselves; Joyce doubted if the same openness would be extended to Mahali visitors – at least, the black population – in Britain.

'Do you know where we're going?'

'Yeah, sure, Joy-Toy. I know this place like the back of my hand.' She then released one hand from the steering wheel and stared comically at it, as if for the first time.

The minibus was left at the road's end, and the pair sauntered to the rocky shoreline, overlooking the southern Indian Ocean. Their appearance scattered colonies of birds nesting or foraging; they protested, none more loudly than the gannets, which despite their cute appearances, sounded like shrill harpies. Occasionally Joyce would glance behind her, as if expecting to be followed, seeing no one. Rocks, white with guano, rose as if to rival the inland buildings, remaining unwashed by the rolling waves crashing upon them; the duo were struck with bullets of seaspray.

'Wild,' Nina said over the waves.

Joyce nodded as if the woman was addressing her, then started as she saw an antelope or some such creature, standing there at the edge of the treeline, in the mouth of some natural pathway through the trees. She froze, staring back with amazement; she'd never seen such creatures out in the open like this. For a moment, she realised that she was the intruder in their world, and felt the absurd urge to ask their permission to remain. But then something made it shy away back into the woods.

A laughter of delight escaped her lips, as did Nina's, and Joyce was glad the woman was there to share it with her. It was all so pristine, so primitive! And it was all theirs, at least for a short time!

Nina kneeled and removed her shoes and socks, and cast them aside. 'Come on!'

'What?'

'Swimming!'

'But – but I didn't bring a suit with me –'

'Neither did I!' The woman laughed.

'But . . . is it safe?'

'Let's find out!'

Shaking her head in wonderment, Joyce followed suit, removing her shoes and socks and squeezing her toes into the soft silt carpet beneath, filled with a sudden urge to run, to drive the muscles in her legs to their limits. And she did, balling her hands into fists as she kicked up spurts of shallow, wet sand behind her, hoping, knowing, Nina would follow.

After a short while, though, she slowed, then finally stopped, wiping the sweat from her reddened face. This stretch of beach was more to her expectations: a wider crescent of white sand, striped with lines of shattered seashells and larger families of rocks extending outwards, almost constantly sprayed with white by the large, ferocious waves. And she could see what Faith meant about the difficulty in arriving here by boat, unless your boat was small, and you knew the right way.

Suddenly Nina bypassed her – she had shed her shirt and trousers, and now ran in just her knickers! Joyce felt her teeth sink into her lower lip in surprise, looking behind them again, seeing no one (and knowing Nina wouldn't care if there was). Then Nina skidded to a halt, and began removing what little she had on her now, grinning madly. 'Come on, girl! Don't keep me waiting!'

The infection was spreading and Joyce succumbed to it, immediately shucking off the rest of her clothes – pausing only once, in a moment of vestigial inhibition, to glance about before lowering her knickers – and standing naked, out in the open air, for the first time.

Then she cast aside her regrets with her clothes and followed Nina into the water, avoiding the rocks and other suspicious-looking areas. It was so bloody *freezing* – but so bloody glorious, too! – and by the time she'd reached the point where the water was up to her waist, she'd grown accustomed to the temperature, and she lay back and closed her eyes, allowing the waves to gently lift and lower her. Above her, the gulls circled, occasionally cawing as if to protest her presence in their feeding grounds.

It seemed so natural to Nina, playfully splashing Joyce, making her squeal and splash back. The beachbed underneath her feet was a ticklish silt carpet, and the water a constant pull back and forth. She kept moving, invigorated now, accustomed to Nina seeing her breasts, or other parts of her, as she swam about.

After a time, Nina made a show of pursuing her, and Joyce half-stumbled to escape her clutches, shrieking and giggling as she was chased out of the water and back on to the beach, both of them collapsing, rolling over each other, battering themselves with sand.

Nina was suddenly on top of her, pressing closely. 'Kiss me.'

Joyce obeyed, her stomach somersaulting, their tongues dancing as the waves reached up and lapped about them. Joyce's breath caught as the other woman's eyes and hands roamed over her; cupping one of her breasts, squeezing appreciatively, before bowing and engulfing the nipple, sucking gently, then fiercely, biting. Joyce moaned, biting her own lip under the attendance.

Joyce was conscious of Nina's other hand descending along her belly; Joyce opened her legs in anticipation. Nina paused to stroke her mound, before delving into her hot, puffy sex. Joyce cried out, and pushed her pussy up to meet her thrusts. Her back cambered as Nina continued this delicious torture, sensations running through Joyce like current.

Nina drew from her breast to grin. 'Are you going to be selfish?'

Joyce couldn't speak, knew what was expected and, with her excitement mounting, shook her head weakly. Nina quickly flipped over and on top of Joyce, her thighs on either side of her head.

Then Nina's tongue continued where her fingers had started; Joyce thought she'd reached the heights of ecstasy before, but it'd been nothing compared with what Joyce felt now. Joyce opened her eyes and looked up into Nina's sex, a delicious pocket of frilled flesh with a deep pink inner lining, moist with milky dew, her clitoris protruding from the folds of flesh encasing it.

Joyce raised her head, drinking in the woman's musk, then buried her face into Nina, darting her tongue into her wet channel, licking, sucking, finally fastening on to her clit, as Nina had just done to hers. They both squirmed and sighed into each other as their climaxes finally arrived, the circuit complete.

Once over, though, Joyce felt her senses return, and she struggled to return to her feet and collect their clothes. What had happened? she asked herself, feeling rather foolish by her asking at all. Silly bitch, she *knew* what had happened! The real question was how could she do it, out in the open, in daylight?

The song of the muezzin, the Muslim official who called the faithful to prayer, floated via loudspeaker over the pastel jumble of houses and hotels at twilight, a modern concession for an ancient custom. Nina and she had returned to the hotel to find Philippa, Faith and Ruth with Kimya Upara in the dining room.

Their escort and guide for the following fortnight was dark-skinned, darker than Faith, clad in stone beige like Philippa but less new-looking. Kimya was a lithe gazelle of a woman, tight curly black hair extending almost to her shoulders, and gleaming blue eyes with the promise of adventure. She seemed perfectly suited to the wilderness and rugged terrain she crossed. And her handshake was as broad and warm as her voice. 'At *last*, they've arrived! And I was starting to think I'd have to get drunk with just these three!'

She was accompanied by a huge copper-black Alsatian, named Zebaki, who liked to plant his considerable weight on to people's laps, as if he was still a pup. Joyce had never liked dogs, but this one was so lovable . . .

They sat together to a lovely dinner of fried tigerfish in coconut sauce and locally bottled tamarind-based wine with a mule's kick that limited Joyce to one glass, while Kimya gave an overview of the itinerary. 'We're cutting it fine. It's almost *kunyesha mvua* – the rainy season.'

'Rain?' Philippa echoed.

'Lots of it,' Faith added, her words laced with the world-weary sigh of a farmer discussing locusts. 'It should hit us by the time we reach the encampment at the foot of the mountain.'

'Rain?' Joyce's question came out in a high-pitched, alcohol-induced squeak of curiosity. 'Maybe we should leave early.'

Kimya shook her head. 'No. You need time to get accustomed to the climate and to receive basic training.'

Nina fought to keep from looking bored. 'Yeah, well, maybe we should wait until your fricking rainy season's over?'

'No,' Faith replied categorically. 'That'll be months away. The diaries could be ruined, wherever they are.'

'Or found by poachers,' Kimya offered. 'Maybe unwittingly burned for kindling.'

'And there's the publishing contract to be considered,' Philippa finished. 'They can't wait for ever –'

'All right, all right!' Nina slammed the table with her open palm, looking thoroughly annoyed. Now she looked to Joyce, as if the woman might add her own voice to the others'. Joyce suddenly felt all eyes on her, and she made a feeble escape attempt by taking another sip of wine.

The talk continued, progressing into the bar/lounge, where they relaxed on low, plush, cushioned furniture. Music played from the stereo system behind the bar, and more than once Nina tried to get Joyce up on the dance floor. But while dancing in a crowded, anonymous club in Patricksburg was one thing, here, in a sparsely occupied hotel, with their companions and the hotel staff watching, was another. So Nina grabbed Isaac, the young, beaming barman, drawing him out on to the maroon-tiled floor. She made Isaac and Joyce laugh, but Joyce was also acutely aware of the looks the others were giving the woman. Especially Ruth.

Joyce rose to her feet, no longer comfortable in their presence. 'I'm going to bed.'

She was almost outside her door when Nina bounded up the stairs and slid to a halt beside her. 'Joystick! Where are you going?'

'Bed, we have an early start tomorrow –'

She dropped her keys when Nina's hands slid around her waist. 'Bed! The best invite I've had all day . . .'

Joyce's head spun, and her face felt flushed; she shouldn't, but

98

she turned to face Nina anyway, turned to let Nina push her up against the wall behind her, to let their breasts squash together as they kissed, mouths grinding, tongues sliding about, tasting their earlier meals and drinks. But then she pulled back, raised a hand between their mouths to keep Nina from re-attacking her, until she was able to ask, 'What happened between you and Ruth?'

Nina still held on to Joyce, but the woman seemed to sober up a bit, sighing theatrically. 'We were an item once. But she got clingy, possessive. Forget about her.'

'How can I?' It was only two nights before in London when the Israeli woman had saved Joyce from that drunken man in the Stomping Grounds. It didn't feel right. 'Why are you staying in her rooms, then?'

Nina looked down between them, now completely sober. 'She's . . . emotionally fragile. She once . . . tried to kill herself.'

Joyce's own face grew taut with the news. It was the last thing she had expected to hear. 'I – I didn't know.'

It seemed a foolish thing to say, but Nina shrugged. 'Not many people know about it. We may have broken up, but I still feel responsible for her. We still talk.' Now Nina looked up into Joyce's eyes. 'Is that stupid of me, or what?'

A rush of feeling welled up inside Joyce, and she reached up to stroke Nina's broad face. 'No, it's not.' Despite all her own problems, for Nina to show such consideration and affection for an ex-lover was laudable. They drew into another embrace – with Nina's hands descending to Joyce's bum.

It felt lovely, made Joyce melt, but something told her to pull back. Perhaps it was the additional information, knowing how much more complicated travelling with Nina and Ruth on the savannah would be now. Whatever the reason, she extricated herself from Nina's embrace and opened her door, sliding behind it. 'I'll see you tomorrow.'

She was closing the door, but Nina stuck her foot in the gap, leaning forward and noting her with an intense stare. 'I don't usually take No for an answer.'

There was something about the statement that made Joyce freeze.

A heartbeat later after she withdrew her foot, Nina's stare broke out into a patented wide grin. 'Night, night, Joy-Ride.' And she walked towards hers – and Ruth's – room.

Joyce closed the door and leaned against it, the feelings rushing through her. Her nipples were erect, sending potent flares of sensation downwards to her receptive, approving groin, as her fingers brushed over her lips, where Nina's had been moments before; she could still feel the woman's strength and passion on them. She could still taste the woman's pussy from the afternoon on the beach.

She stripped off haphazardly, needing a cooling shower. But even as she stepped under the water, her hand was between her legs, the intensity of the touch echoed in the taut, puffy flesh of her sex. She worked fumbling fingers through her bush to find her clitoris, engorged, hungry, hungry for her touch. Her orgasm came quickly, easily; after the stimulation she'd just received, she'd hardly needed to touch herself. And afterwards she supported herself against the shower walls, letting the water flow down her back and between her cheeks.

NINE

The day of training began at dawn.

After dressing in rough but sturdy and functional stone-coloured shirts, trousers, hats and black boots, they feasted on a breakfast of tea and coffee, various fruits, bread and honey. Afterwards, Kimya picked up the quintet in a large battered olive-drab Land Rover, loaded in the rear with much of the gear they'd be employing for the journey. No one spoke, either because they were hardly awake, or because of nerves, or because of the tension that hung like the morning mist.

They didn't travel far, just west outside of town, where the skeletons of abandoned round mud huts sat near a modern, low ranch house on a property wooden-fenced into an uneven shape.

'We'll get the more demanding tasks out of the way first,' Kimya instructed, signalling to some young children by the building, who disappeared into a wide open doorway. 'It'll help warm and limber you up. Then later on, things like setting up the tent, firing the guns and identifying hazards won't seem too difficult.'

Joyce drew up the zipper on her jacket – it was colder than she'd expected, even with the sun just appearing into view over Mzuri – and watched as the children brought out a half-dozen horses of varying colours, from coal-black to spotted grey, clip-clopping on the flat, dewy ground.

'These will be your best friends,' Kimya explained, approaching the steeds, fully expecting the other women to follow. 'Your guides, your protectors, your transport. You do not *own* a horse. You may hold the reins, but you are not its mistress. You and your horse make an unwritten agreement: you agree to treat it right, and it agrees to carry you and your provisions where you want to go. '

'How about Mister Ed agrees to go where I want it to go, and I agree not to beat the hell out of it?' Nina joked.

Kimya shot her a withering look. '*Anyone* can break a horse, Ms Hoskins. Just don't try it while I'm around.'

Philippa caught Joyce's eye, offering something Joyce couldn't quite identify. Was it empathy, an attempt to share whatever feelings Philippa might have regarding Nina, with Joyce? Or was it some sort of censure, as if it was already accepted knowledge that Joyce and Nina were lovers, and that now Joyce was somehow responsible for Nina's conduct?

Joyce rejected that notion – and also rejected the notion that Nina and she were lovers now. Well, they *had* been. But would that still be applicable when they were on the savannah?

Joyce found herself staring back at Philippa, seeking to find if there was still something there between them.

But then Kimya caught her attention again. 'Miss Wilde, it's best if you pay attention. Your life may depend on what you learn today.'

'What? Oh, sorry.'

Kimya was standing by one coal-black horse. 'I want you all to go to each of the horses, get to know them in turn. Then once they tell us which rider they like most – or dislike the least – we'll begin showing you saddling and unsaddling, feeding, watering and general care. And then you'll learn to properly ride.'

Joyce found herself beside a tall, chestnut-coloured horse; she enjoyed the smell of the creature, reached out and gingerly touched it, surprised at the warmth and softness of the coat, and by the harshness of the mane. It whinnied and harrumphed, breath clouding before it, before nuzzling against the side of her face.

Joyce laughed with delight. She'd made a friend.

The sun was climbing into a mid-morning arc by the time they were allowed to mount the horses. It was far easier than Joyce thought it would be, and once she grew accustomed to the height and the feel of the saddle beneath her, and acknowledged that every little twitch and sound her chestnut mare Shohan made wasn't a precursor to her bolting, Joyce was enjoying herself.

And Kimya had been right; compared with that, learning how to set up the tents, identifying edible and poisonous vegetation, reading a compass and map, using the right calls for Zebaki, even firing the long, loud, heavy rifles, was practically effortless.

It was late afternoon, when they were winding down, that Nina finally approached Joyce, grabbing her by the waist and tickling her, before nuzzling into her neck and whispering, 'Come on, let's go back to the beach. I'm aching for you.'

Joyce laughed, turned and looked to the others to see if they had indeed finished – and saw the look in Ruth's eyes before the other woman turned away and made a deliberate show of packing away some gear.

'Maybe you'd like me to do you here,' Nina taunted in her ear.

Joyce wasn't listening, her attention focused on Faith, striding up to her and grabbing Joyce by the elbow, pulling her from Nina and the others and guiding her around the corner of the building. Joyce pulled herself from the younger woman's grasp. 'Do you mind –'

'Do *you* mind? You and her are gonna be fucking up this trip big time!'

'What are you talking about?'

'We need everybody's mind on the job at hand. Can't you see how it's tearing Ruth up?'

She did. And it did hurt. But Joyce was determined to stand her ground against this interfering ex-lover of her mother's. 'Look, it's been over between them for a long time –'

'*What?*' Faith's frown confused and frightened Joyce, dredging up suspicions that, until now, had remained half-considered. The American woman's subsequent words edified those suspicions. 'It's *never* been over between them, you stupid bitch!' Now the woman chuckled harshly. 'She's been using you. She likes to torment

Ruth, drag her along like a . . . like a horse on a rein or something. Tease her by fucking with the likes of you. Practically under the poor woman's nose.'

Joyce was certain she'd felt worse than she did now.

Damned if she could recall when, though.

She turned and glanced back at the others by the vehicle. Nina moved and chatted and laughed with a silent, unlaughing Ruth, as if nothing untoward had been happening. As if Nina hadn't used Joyce so casually. But why did Ruth allow it? She seemed so strong, so self-assured.

How could Joyce face either woman again now?

'Well,' Faith was saying, lighting up a cigar, 'at least you're not malicious. Just half-witted.'

'Why didn't you or Philippa tell me before now?'

Faith blew grey streamers of smoke through clenched teeth before replying. 'Make it easier on yourself: go back to London. Leave this to the Big Girls.'

Joyce felt her face grow taut. Normally she tried to avoid confrontations of any kind, but she'd been through too much already, and had too much ahead of her, to let this continue. 'Look, I know you were close to my mother –'

'Closer than *you* ever were.'

Joyce continued regardless. 'And I can understand your resentment –'

Now Faith's face blushed with unanticipated outrage. 'You don't know *shit*!'

She turned away. Joyce, startled by the outburst, stood her ground nevertheless. 'I know that you've been against me from the very start, that you think I'm just some ungrateful cow –'

'Now that's the rightest thing you've said since we've met.' Cigar clenched between her teeth, she held up an equally clenched fist, counting each subsequent word with her fingers. 'Ungrateful, unappreciative, unthinking, un*everything*!' She gripped her cigar again. 'Constance Wilde was such a *remarkable* human being; I'd be proud to do a *tenth* of what she's done. She was a business-woman, a reformer, an explorer, a sailor, a lover, a pioneer –'

Now she stopped, then discarded her barely smoked cigar in

disgust. Her verbal bile was seemingly spent, leaving behind only a bewilderment, a vulnerability that struck Joyce despite their hostility seconds before. When the younger woman spoke again, her voice sounded lost, seeking answers. 'She'd done so much with her life. Why do you have to hate her?'

Hate. Such an appropriately ugly word for an ugly emotion.

But not one that Joyce would have applied to her feelings for her mother. 'I didn't hate her.'

'Why didn't you *love* her, then?'

When Joyce replied, she found her words matched the bleak melancholy her adversary radiated. 'Maybe because I didn't want her to be a businesswoman, or a reformer, or a pioneer, or any of that. Maybe because I didn't want her to be anything to me but a mother. And she couldn't even manage *that*.'

Sorrow hung in the air between them; even the birds in the nearby trees seemed to have grown quiet. But then sorrow just as quickly boiled into anger again. 'You had your chance to be with her when she was deported from Britain. You could have left with her. *Why didn't you?*'

For a moment, Joyce almost answered her. Certainly she felt as if her original reasons as a teenager – her acute embarrassment over her mother's antics, and her sexuality – were still valid. But her mind was now making comparisons between her stance then, and her mother's escapades at the same age. Now Joyce's chagrin seemed less legitimate, more overblown and exaggerated.

Suddenly she was tired, tired of being on the defensive against her mother's girlfriend, of all people. Did Faith believe her relationship – or even what happened last night? – gave her the right to question Joyce's decisions?

All she ended up saying was, 'Leave me alone. I'll walk back to town.'

To her credit, Faith complied without comment.

It was a couple of hours before Joyce had found herself back in town – stopping at her mother's grave. Her mind had gone into neutral during the walk and her feet ached in her boots. But now she sank to her knees in the soft earth before the grave, and wept.

Wept for unanswered questions, irreparable regrets, lost opportunities.

The sky had bled into salmon and roseate when she returned to the hotel, her mind made up. She found Philippa in their room, or rather sitting out on a wicker chair on the balcony overlooking the atrium, though her eyes appeared fixed on the sun setting in the west, in the direction where they'd be travelling tomorrow. She had stripped off her day's clothes, showered and looked far more refreshed in a lovely diaphanous evening camisole that teased with the lines and curves of her tall, voluptuous body. Now she sat there and raised a glass to her lips as Joyce moved to stand by the balcony doorway. The scent of bougainvilleas and perfume hung in the air, and there was a buzz from bold insects around them.

Neither woman spoke, until Philippa offered, 'Faith says you might be returning to England.'

Joyce fought back her anger; it wouldn't do to show that now; it would open up the floodgate to all the other emotions she didn't want to display to Philippa. 'She was wrong. I'm going with you tomorrow.'

'Are you?' It sounded more statement than question. She sipped at her drink, never looking up at Joyce. 'Then there's things you should know –'

'No wait –' Joyce breathed in deeply, hoping she wasn't going to get into deeper shit with her next gamble. 'I have some things to tell you first. I . . . I love you. I've loved you from the moment I first laid eyes on you.'

'Have you?' It was that seeming casual disinterest that stung Joyce. And deliberately so, Joyce knew. 'What of Nina?'

'That was a mistake. A dreadful mistake. I'm so sorry. I should never have got involved with her. And not just because of Ruth.'

'I see.'

Damn it, this was *gut-wrenching*! Her heart racing, her stomach churning, Joyce reached out and rested a hand on Philippa's shoulder. 'I want you. I *need* you. Tell me the feelings I felt from you in Berlin are gone now, and I'll shut up.'

She looked down to see Philippa stare at Joyce's hand from the corner of her eye. The woman sounded less determined and angry now, more skittish, like a puppy smacked on the nose and afraid of a repeat chastisement. 'My feelings *haven't* changed. But neither have my standards.

'I'm selfish. I don't do things in half-measures. And I don't take casual partners. If we *did* become lovers, I'd possess you. Just as you'd possess me. Just as you've been possessing me since I first saw you.' Now she tilted her head and kissed Joyce's hand on her shoulder. Joyce lifted her hand and rested her palm on Philippa's cheek, relishing the soft, warm skin. Then the woman asked, 'Could you live – love – under such conditions? It can be . . . overwhelming. Or so I'm told.'

Joyce moved closer, let the hand on Philippa's cheek drift to the woman's lips, felt them kiss her palm. Yes. Yes, she wanted it. She wanted to make love with this woman, be with this woman. Be possessed by her. Her stomach did somersaults inside her.

'Why don't you go and shower the day's dust off you?' Philippa suggested abruptly. 'I need to think. But I promise you an answer when you're done.'

Reluctantly Joyce nodded – to herself, now that Philippa returned to staring at the sunset – and said, 'OK,' before departing.

It was the quickest shower she had ever taken. And the longest. And when she emerged to stand before the sink and mirror, she found herself drying herself there, rather than in the main room, out of nerves, not modesty. She shivered, and not from the cool water she'd just stood under. She was genuinely afraid of the answer she'd receive.

She froze when she heard Philippa's voice. 'Come in here, Joyce.'

Joyce's heart beat in her chest like a trapped bird caught in the clutches of a cat. Her fingers fumbled as she wrapped the thick, plush white terry towel once, then twice around her body, before emerging, dripping residual water in her trail.

The sun had set further, and now rafters of mote-freckled carmine stretched through the open balcony doorway. Philippa stood there, one arm across her midriff and clutching the wrist of the other arm, which was straight against her side. Her head was tilted, and she was staring straight at Joyce; with the light on her like that, Philippa's nude body was clearly visible through her camisole. It made Joyce gasp.

Philippa's platinum blonde hair danced with the hem of her camisole at a slight breeze, as she asked, in a voice that was almost fragile, 'Will you promise to love me, Joyce?'

Joyce's answer was immediate, and as assured as if she'd been asked if the sun would rise tomorrow. 'Yes.'

But Philippa shook her head again slightly, and continued with, 'No, I mean it. Promise me.'

Joyce breathed in, took another step forward. 'I promise.' She wanted her words, her expression, to be saturated with certainty, with conviction. She wanted Philippa to believe her.

When Philippa hesitated, Joyce was prepared to repeat it. But then the woman said, 'Take off that towel.'

It seemed to have grown deathly quiet throughout the world – all that Joyce could hear was the rush of blood in her own body – and her eyes remained locked on Philippa's as her hands reached up and tugged at the folds of towel maintaining her modesty. It dropped to her feet, and she reined in her gasps, her arms instinctively crossing her stomach below her breasts, wanting to cover herself up again. Keeping her eyes towards Philippa's was the hardest part, feeling her vulnerability – and her excitement – grow more acute.

Then Philippa started forward, slowly drawing the camisole over her head.

Joyce took the moment when Philippa's gaze was hidden by the camisole to breathe in sharply, taking in the long, slim, alabaster legs, the sharp curves of hipbone, the enviable stomach over the wispy flaxen fleece on the woman's sex, the breasts, full and firm and jutting . . . beautiful. It made Joyce weep with delight inside at the sight of such beauty.

Philippa cast aside the camisole when Joyce and she were inches apart. Philippa was half a head taller, even without her trademark high heels; she smiled down with beautiful glowing features. They drew closer until their breasts pressed against each other, and Joyce smiled a multi-layered smile at the contact.

Philippa kissed Joyce tenderly on her lovely smile. Slowly she slipped her tongue out to part Joyce's hot, waiting lips. For a few moments they toyed with each other. Then with a groan as earnest as anything she could muster, Philippa intensified her kiss, pouring her soul into it.

Then backed off. She slowly let her gaze drop down and take in Joyce's whole body. Then her soft, delicate hands also took the same trip. 'Oh, my,' she whispered as her hands gently fondled Joyce's aching breasts. Joyce's nipples still erect seemed to reach out to greet Philippa's touch. Her warm hands then traced Joyce's contours to her hips. Then she carefully took Joyce's hands and placed them on her own full breasts. No encouragement was needed to persuade Joyce to return the exploration.

The tingling sensations were driving Joyce mad with desire and fear and excitement, and when Philippa reached around and cupped Joyce's fleshy buttocks and stretched further to trace between her legs, she thought she could stand no more. She tensed.

That seemed to halt Philippa's dallying, prompting Joyce to ask, 'Can we lie down? It's been a long day.'

'It'll be a longer night,' Philippa promised, her hands drifting to Joyce's wrists and leading her under the mosquito netting surrounding their bed.

They lay facing each other, Philippa letting her hand creep down to Joyce's loins. She seemed to get sort of giddy; Joyce followed suit, closing her eyes and feeling the tingling between her legs. Philippa's hand gently stroked around Joyce's moist labia, touching every wrinkle as if it was the last time she would be there, rather than the first. When she reached the uppermost fold hooding her clitoris, the electricity flashed through Joyce as she writhed and squirmed and moaned under the exquisite, instinctive, yet caring touch of Philippa.

As Joyce's animal noises grew louder and louder, Philippa slipped a hesitant finger inside of Joyce's hot, wet, tight vagina, never leaving that delightful clit as she slid inside. Joyce clutched her, wanted to touch her, love her as she was being loved. Her voice went ragged. 'Let – let me – let me touch –'

Then when Joyce seemed near to the peak of ecstasy, Philippa seemed to finally listen to her, released her probing hand and turned round so that she straddled Joyce and buried her face into Philippa's awaiting folds of pink. Joyce, anticipating this, helped her move and when Philippa had turned completely around she reached up to enfold each firm buttock and pulled herself up until she could tenderly kiss her way slowly up the inside of Philippa's leg to the awaiting sensitive engorged rumple of lusting flesh. Then she, too, immersed her own face in the honey-scented sex poised over her, noting how aroused Philippa already was.

Philippa shivered in Joyce's grasp. Passion and comfort reigned. They each snuggled into the innermost folds of labia until their faces were covered with the love-fluids. Their tongues glided out to probe the swollen fleshy folds, exploring just how aroused and ecstatic they could make each other.

So quickly they'd felt themselves enter the sensuously enchanting world of lovers. The touch of their tongues on each other's sexes made them writhe and twist in a frenzy, and lasciviously their warm tongues continued to invade the other's every fold and recess, bringing hot saliva to moisten and oil, and leaving tingling and hungry.

The sensations were thrilling. They remained silent but for moans and sighs as their warm lips and tongues played games of passion on the other's genitals. All the while they were orally stimulating each other, their hands were not idle. They had crept around to each other's buttocks and were slowly and sensuously stroking them, like caressing the petals of a delicate flower. They didn't miss a contour. The feeling aroused them even more, if that was possible. In unison they moaned, each urging the other on, sending additional shivers of passion down their spines. They each nuzzled deeper into the other.

Philippa took the next step as she ever so gently touched Joyce's clitoris with the very tip of her tongue, sending shudders through both of them. Joyce let out a growling moan into Philippa's pussy.

Then, quickly Joyce followed her lover's lead and let her moist tongue delicately probe until she, too, finally found Philippa's clitoris, which had swollen to visible size and was peeking out from under the protective fold.

Philippa involuntarily arched her back under the urging of Joyce's warm hands still massaging her bum. Sharp cries erupted as an intense flash coursed through her.

The sound was marvellous to Joyce, marvellous and sensual beyond imagination. To be this close to her: the smoothly rising ivory breasts, each crowned with delicious, little pink nipples arrogantly erect; the smooth white legs; the delicate inner thighs; the silky pubic hairs nestled around a passionately heaving mons of flawless contour. And the labia, swollen and ripe and juicy, embracing Joyce's probing, incessant tongue. And the beloved, exquisite clitoris, corpulent and erect, voraciously lusting for an amorous touch . . .

Only when they had reached the very peak did Philippa pause, leaving Joyce standing at the crest of passion. Like in a dream, Philippa backed away from her haven in Joyce's luscious crotch and floated over her lover, sliding over the taut awakened body until once again she was lying full length on Joyce, toe to toe, face to face.

'What is it –' Joyce started, the sensations churning inside her like the contents of a champagne bottle, thoroughly shaken, begging for release.

'I need to kiss you,' she gasped in reply, and pulled Joyce down to her awaiting lips. For a short second they kissed gently, tasting themselves on each other as their hips writhed desperately searching for the other's genitals.

The instant their hands found each other the gentle kiss exploded into one of such intensity that Joyce thought she was dying. Yet she didn't care, for this moment was worth it. Each strained her sex against the other's hand, the pussy lips as intimately engaged as their oral lips. Their hands were soaking. The eruption re-ignited in Joyce's pussy and shot like a bolt of fiery lightning up through her exultant body, radiating intense heat as it travelled. Only when it reached her head did she finally disengage that perfect kiss and erupt in groans of utter agony and utter delight.

Their racked bodies flailed and thrashed in convulsions beyond their control as if they were on the brink of death itself, rather than that other ultimate experience. They heaved and tossed and wailed and screamed and groaned and writhed. The world around them totally and completely forgotten and beyond all caring. Time passed unnoticed.

Finally, as the ecstasy subsided they resumed their kissing and fondling as if they intended to commence that wonderful climb once again. But that was not the intention, for they were as emotionally and physically spent as it was possible to be.

Their eyes were still closed to all else other than each other, and their bodies devoid of any sensation or stimulation beyond the gentle and tender touches, the sensitive fondling of their breasts, the toying and teasing of the nipples, turgid still with passion. They remained locked together, lips to lips, sex to sex, life to life. Together they moaned as they rode the wonderful slow ride down the mountain of perfect joy.

They continued this after-play for more than an hour. Finally, they drifted into sleep, dimly hearing the call of the imam to the faithful, and the cicada chirp from the garden.

TEN

Limbs, pale and soft and alike, snake about each other, the groan of mouths and bedsprings marking the gentle testing. Full eager lips move to heaving breasts, anxious fingers to dark deltas, the urgency for release thick, heavy, like the air before a storm, the drumbeats of anxious hearts machine-gun-rapid. Then one face looks up from the mass of limbs, looks up to see Joyce. 'You never take a chance, do you, Joyce? You never take a risk.'

Joyce bolted to a sitting position, her eyes darting about as if searching for her lost voice. Where was she –

'Joyce?' The voice she found was soft, half-asleep. And not her own. Concern quickly drew Philippa to sit up beside her. 'Are you OK?'

Joyce nodded absently, rubbing at her eyes while her mind found her bearings again. 'A dream. Involving my mother. A time I'd walked in on her, in bed with another woman.'

'Oh, yes.'

'You know about that?'

'Yes.' At the unspoken prompting, Philippa added, 'Your mother told me about it once.'

'I've been having the same dream, more or less, since I learned she'd died.'

'I'm sorry.'

Philippa was naked, her side pressed against Joyce's beneath the sheet that covered them both. It, and their bodies, was dotted with sweat, despite the ceiling fan whirling above them all night, keeping the mosquito net surrounding them in a permanent shimmy. Joyce forced aside such observations to shake her head. 'You've nothing to be sorry about. It's been a momentous few days.'

'Do you want to talk about it?'

Joyce could smell their collective sweat, mingling together, heady and sweet. She shook her head again. 'No thanks.' She nodded towards the meagre light caressing the balcony door windows – or was it a trick of the netting? 'Maybe we can catch a little more sleep before we have to get up?'

But a smile etched on Philippa's lovely face. 'Maybe not.' She bent down and with just the very tip of her tongue teasingly touched just the extreme tip of Joyce's nipple. The electric shock brought a wave over Joyce and she squirmed as Philippa continued her interest in her sensitive nipples; it was as if Joyce had never been satisfied, only hours before!

Last night. Oh, God, last night! What had happened still had not crystallised in Joyce's mind, but her desire to repeat what she perceived as a dream was incredibly strong. And Philippa was more than obliging, reaching out and pulling Joyce down to her.

They kissed passionately, a lingering, deep and loving one that seemed to last for ever, one that seemed to feel like the first time. The sensations in her body made her feel whole. It made her feel heavenly. Philippa's kiss was warm, heartfelt and deeply passionate, and, as it lingered, Philippa gently caressed Joyce's lips with her tongue until Joyce consented and parted them. She explored everywhere, beginning with her lips, then her teeth, and, like someone scouting new territory, didn't miss anything.

They lay there savouring the kiss of love, Joyce trembling in Philippa's arms. Then Philippa let Joyce hold them together as she let her own hands set off to explore Joyce. She reached down and cupped Joyce's delicate trembling breasts in her still-moist hands, caressing the thrillingly sensitive alabaster skin. Philippa's eyes never left Joyce's. For a few moments they lay there comfortably. Then ever so slowly they began meandering along her curves.

Joyce's already erect nipples seemed to struggle to gain their rightful place under Philippa's kind and sensitive fingers. With utmost tenderness the fingers stroked the ruby areola, the sprouting, pouting nipples. Then her loving hands delicately departed the breasts to continue their journey. Philippa's voice was as wispy as the mosquito netting above and around them. 'My God, but you're so beautiful, Joyce.'

As if star-struck, she just sort of stared with her lips slightly parted, slowly absorbing what seemed like Joyce's entire being. It filled Joyce with a love that brought on tears.

Philippa purred like a cat, pulling Joyce close. Joyce reached her legs around Philippa's elegant thighs to ease her concern. She also reached out and gently cupped Philippa's luscious and full breasts in her warm hands. She extended her thumbs and caressed the determinedly stiff nipples. Another slow, fervent kiss exchanged lips.

As they held the kiss long and hard their hands wandered silently over each other, their hands softly and hesitantly meandering among the heavily bedewed hills and valleys. Their nipples stood at rigid attention like lovely, ruby flowers blossoming, and their fingers continued to enjoy their childlike romp.

Philippa stole her hands lower, to Joyce's inner thighs, tenderly stroking the satin-charged skin, then delicately inching towards the rising mound at the apex of Joyce's legs. She ran her fingers carefully around the blossoming labia. Philippa's affectionate hands gently followed Joyce's pliant entrance, slowly tracing the outline, end to end, slowly approaching, slowly sliding in. Joyce's hips began to move.

Before entering, however, Philippa's finger found Joyce's clit, a blood-rich bud, still achingly hard and proudly erect. She rubbed her finger gently back and forth over it, causing little groans of pleasure to bubble from Joyce's lips.

With delicious care and tenderness Philippa surrounded Joyce's exquisitely sensitive bud and caressed every curve. Joyce gave a reflex intake as Philippa reached the tip, her moans surpassing

Philippa's. Philippa dallied with a trembling hand as shivers of passion waved through Joyce's sweat-beaded body, the ensuing moments of pause broken only by Joyce's laborious and loud panting.

She slowly began to let the tip of her finger delve down into Joyce's sex. She used her fingers to draw back the labia like curtains, revealing the succulent pink interior. Then, while using the thumb to keep tender contact on Joyce's clitoris, Philippa slid her forefinger down and began to slide the fingertip inside. Joyce groaned as Philippa's finger rhythmically slid in and out of her hot, wet pussy, stroking, caressing, searching, slowly exciting Joyce more and more.

Joyce flew higher and higher under the gentle lead of Philippa's touching, caressing, embracing, her heart quickened, her breath catching, releasing, swept up in an uncontrollable, sensual whirl-wind. She felt like she was falling, tumbling joyfully over and over into an abyss of soft sensual pleasure. She had never felt this delightful before, and she never wanted it to ever end. It was like no addiction imaginable.

After an eternity, Philippa slowly, as if to not break the spell, turned and moved one leg over the supine Joyce until she straddled her. Lowering herself on the still-sensitive body of her lover, she let her breasts play upon Joyce's own heaving bosom, nipple to erect nipple. Slowly Philippa gyrated, lowering her pelvis on to Joyce's abdomen, pressing into her, slowly rotating in circles. The slightest suggestion of motion at their nipples sent tremors deep into Joyce's flesh.

A gasp escaped Joyce as she felt herself quicken towards that awful and wonderful peak. She reached out to hold Philippa close and let her soft warm hands play on Philippa's back, sidling down to her rotating buttocks, cradling each cheek in her hands. Then she tried to spread her legs so that she could feel the sensuous movement on her sex, but found herself pinned by Philippa's thighs pressed close to her sides.

Not wanting to break the spell, she stopped, but Philippa recognised what Joyce needed. Slowly and with great care she pulled away from her lover and slipped her knees down the bed until she was lying full length on her. Then she snuggled in, forcing Joyce's legs apart until she could move her pussy down and against Joyce's still-moist labia.

Their kiss lengthened and intensified as Joyce instinctively spread her limbs out to enfold the delicate churning hips. Their sexes, both hot and wet touched, aroused and slid over each other, ever moving, never still. The delicately soft and sensitive folds of flesh sent electric tingles every time each contacted the other.

She came in long, rushing, rolling waves of pleasure, wet and writhing, and then Philippa came, too. After an eternity of bliss, Joyce settled back into a pleasant, dreamy state. At least, until the knock on their door from Faith.

The trek was waiting.

The horses were saddled, fed and watered, the supplies checked, rechecked and packed, the team tired, anxious and eager. It was still relatively dark, the sky a deep indigo dotted with stars and strips of cloud, and birds and dogs were the only witnesses.

It was cold, something else Joyce hadn't expected; she tugged at the zipper to her jacket, though it was already up as far as it would go. She watched her horse shake its head, as if she too were complaining about the early rise and the climate. Beside Joyce, Philippa was silent, glancing about the outskirts of the town, waiting, waiting for Ruth, Faith and Kimya to end their private discussions.

Joyce watched, couldn't help but keep glancing at the formidable-looking rifles slung across their backs. She'd accepted the necessity for weapons while on the savannah, for self-protection as much as hunting; they could hardly expect supermarkets along the way, or for Zebaki to capture rabbits or something. But the idea of actually having to use them was another level of realisation entirely.

'Maybe it's been cancelled,' she mused aloud.

Philippa sidled closer – she was so good at handling her black steed – reached out, took Joyce's free hand, and brought it up to her mouth to kiss, squeezing it once before releasing it. 'Such last-minute delays must be expected.'

Joyce couldn't help but smile, more over the overt show of affection than by the placating reassurances. She could quite easily, quite happily, spend the rest of her life with this woman. And yes, she recognised what a cliché that was. But she also knew that this would be different, because *Joyce* would be different.

Then the trio broke up, Faith cantering closer to the others, her slouch hat hanging low on her shaven head. 'Well? Are we ready? Any last-minute trips to the bathroom?'

Joyce and Philippa said nothing. Nearby, Nina, on her own steed, looked half-asleep. At least she kept silent, and away from Joyce; Joyce knew that it was inevitable that she would have to speak with the woman, be near her, and she knew that when that happened, she would behave in a mature fashion. But for now . . .

When no one replied, Faith pointed westward. 'Then let's head 'em up, move 'em out. Rawhide!'

The rising sun thankfully remained at their backs and out of their eyes, as they progressed from the township, into fields and huts, then into the wild. There were no official boundaries as such; before one realised it, signs of human habitation evaporated like dew before the steadily brightening sky.

Cradled by smooth grey mountains appearing more ephemeral than real, the savannah opened before them, rows of hills like gentle waves, irregularly dotted with thorny scrub and trees that appeared flattened by the immensity of the sky overhead. Birdsong serenaded the party throughout the morning, steadily dying away as it grew warmer, and occasionally Joyce reacted to the scuttle of unseen animals in the scrub. There was nothing like the lush tropical jungle that Joyce had always lamely associated with Africa, mainly through films.

'My arse is sore,' Nina informed no one in particular, an hour into the fourteen-day journey. No one responded. Joyce shook her head at Philippa; she felt the same way, of course, but there was no point in mentioning it, especially if it might validate anything Nina had to say at the moment.

'When do we stop for a break?' Nina now asked.

'As discussed already,' Kimya intoned, her voice clear, distinct, 'it's best to cross as much distance as possible in the morning, with the sun still behind us. And times and places will also be dependent upon known water sources along the way.'

'Ah, I see,' Nina replied, deliberately mocking Kimya's accent. 'I must have blinked when that was mentioned.'

Joyce cringed in her saddle, suddenly embarrassed at being part of the same nationality as Nina; how could she have fancied a woman like *her*? She glanced to Philippa, who wore a harsh expression, and was bolstered by their sharing the same thoughts.

As the sun rose higher above the savannah, the colours of the fauna and landscape grew brighter, more vivid. There were no large animals in sight; Kimya had explained that these would not be seen until they moved further inland, perhaps by the end of the second day.

And as it grew warmer, Joyce found herself drawing down the zipper of her jacket more and more, though she didn't remove her jacket entirely, at least not until their first rest stop, an hour later. Kimya had selected a natural grove protected from the occasional huff of dust-coated wind by large, craggy trees. There was grass and a small watering hole for the horses, and an opportunity to top up their canteens, once the water was boiled and purified.

The party stretched and moved about stiffly, even Kimya, more accustomed to life behind the wheel of a Land Rover (not that Joyce would have known until Kimya herself had confessed to it). Only Zebaki seemed a font of energy and excitement at being in the wild again. Joyce rubbed her own backside, working back the circulation to the muscles.

Suddenly she started as something slapped against her, as if to help: Nina. 'Hiya, sport. Need a hand?'

It was as if the woman had never deceived her. Joyce took a deliberate step back from her, her voice as taut as her expression felt. 'No thanks.'

Nina just winked and grinned. 'Maybe later.' She whistled to herself as she moved towards the trees marked as the party's toilet area.

'Don't count on it,' Joyce called after her, consequently feeling several eyes on her back. She ignored the others to move closer to Philippa, who was removing the kettle of readied water from the tiny fire to cool down, before filling up the canteens. Joyce kneeled beside her. 'Do you believe that woman?'

'What, believe that she can act that way? Yes. Yes, I do.'

Philippa seemed a little too unconcerned, too uncaring, for Joyce's liking. She'd hoped for a stronger display from her new lover. 'And it doesn't bother you?'

Philippa's mouth opened as if to reply, then closed again, before she looked to Joyce and proceeded. 'You're an adult. Be firm with her. Tell her in no uncertain terms what you will and won't accept from her. Otherwise, it's going to be a long fortnight. For all of us.'

Joyce stared blankly; it wasn't the reassurance, the support, Joyce had wanted. On the other hand, Philippa *was* right. And what did Joyce expect, that Philippa would come along and fight Nina, like some schoolboy defending her girlfriend from unwanted suitors? She finally nodded and said, 'I'll do that.'

Now Philippa smiled *that* smile – the one that melted Joyce's insides each time it was trained on her – and reached out, squeezing Joyce's thigh through her trousers. 'I can't wait until tonight. I have a surprise for us both.'

Joyce felt herself blushing, without knowing why. And through-out the rest of the day, she couldn't worm from the woman what that surprise was. Philippa proved good at keeping secrets.

And Nina proved good at complaining, once they were under way again. 'Jesus, doesn't this country ever *end*?'

'Doesn't your bitching ever end?' Faith quipped.

But the actress ignored it. 'Maybe we should give the horses more of a break from carrying us? Say, a couple of hours?'

'Yeah, I pity the horse that has to carry *your* fat ass about.'

'I dare say the horses can outlast us all,' Kimya, leading the way, informed them. 'But if you're that concerned, Miss Hoskins, why don't you get off yours and walk alongside her the rest of the way?'

Nina mumbled something, but kept silent for a while longer.

★

It took most of the day before Joyce could notice the change in the appearance of the mountains, an almost imperceptible shift that registered the meagre distance the travellers had crossed that first day. She looked behind her, still expecting to see signs of civilisation. But there was nothing. No buildings, no streetlights, no rubbish on the ground, not even footprints or hoofprints, apart from the ones they themselves made.

Magnificent.

The mosquito coil standing near the campfire continued to smoulder, a spicy aroma that thankfully kept the sextet from having to soak themselves further in the more potent, more pungent insect repellent. Conversation since dinner had dimmed like the capricious breezes, allowing the night life to fill the silence: insects, the whoops of distant hyenas, the whistle-chirps of the closer, friendlier mungos, all hidden in the veil of absolute darkness beyond the campsite.

It was frightening. It was exhilarating. Joyce never realised how much she took streetlights for granted, until this first night on the Mahali savannah. The campfire light seemed to be eaten by the darkness around them, like prey for the predators. Even above her, the night sky, with its countless glittering constellations undiluted by citylight, could not pierce the darkness hanging like mist on the ground.

A shiver ran through her. She still couldn't believe how cool it was in the evenings here: another preconception bites the dust. She'd rise to retrieve her jacket, but she suspected they'd all be going to bed soon anyway.

True to her burgeoning instinct, they decided to call it a night, and packed up their equipment so as not to find it shredded or covered in various animal faeces in the morning. She was rolling up some of the blankets near the horses, when Nina appeared with the leftover food. In the near-total darkness, she seemed more shadow than substance, her voice low and dreamlike. 'Hey, cutie.'

Joyce grew chillier than the night air. 'Stay away from me.'

Now Nina chuckled. 'Oh, come on, girl. It was just a game.'

'Tell that to Ruth.' Joyce felt cold, she felt the saddle sores in her muscles and the sunburn on her face and hands – it was as if Nina had brought all the aches and pains and other unpleasant things along with her – and she turned to go.

Nina snagged her by the elbow. Her voice dropped to a near-whisper, as if imparting a great secret. 'You think you're gonna be better off with that stuck-up bitch? You don't know her as well as you think.'

The warmth of Nina's coffee-flavoured breath reached Joyce's face, and for a moment, the two of them seemed to stand alone at the motionless centre of their own little world. But then someone threw more wood on the fire, in preparation for Ruth taking first watch that night. The sounds of crackling wood, and the sight of disturbed sparks flittering firefly-like into the black night air, broke the spell, and Joyce made a show of pulling out of Nina's grasp, taking a step back. 'Keep your hands to yourself. Keep your opinions to yourself. I should never have let you touch me.'

Nina straightened up casually. 'Sure.' She did not appear offended in voice or manner.

But, of course, the trek had only started.

So had the night. Joyce lay on her side of the dome-shaped tent she shared with Philippa, who moved about, a silhouette in the firelight from outside through the red vinyl tent walls. The sound of the unscrewing of a jar lid was heard. 'I feel so cut off out here. So detached from civilisation.'

'And we're only a day away from Mzuri,' Joyce noted, nodding in the near-darkness. She stretched out on her stomach, nude, feeling only a slight chill.

The chill flared as Philippa soothed the cream, with its rich, roseate fragrance, into Joyce's sore muscles, and began to massage the flesh beaten from a day in the saddle. She was gentle, at least at first, then worked with increasing pressure, the cream warming up as it worked into Joyce's skin, and Joyce could feel its heat penetrating her aching muscles. She moaned and Philippa made a smiling sound. 'Enjoying it?'

'Mmm, yes.' She sounded again as Philippa finished with her

arms and shoulders, and moved to Joyce's thighs and calves. The penetrating heat soothed and relaxed Joyce's lower half.

Philippa started on her back, making Joyce sigh again at the warm, soothing touch of the salve. 'Tell me about your first time.'

'My first?' It seemed a strange question to Joyce. But she obliged, talking about Paddi. And from there, moving on to her last meeting with Rhonda, opening up as she never had to anyone else before. It felt as liberating and soothing to have a sympathetic ear to her troubles, as it did to have sympathetic hands on her flesh.

'I'm done with your back,' Philippa told her. Joyce rolled over, hoping the salve wouldn't stain the sleeping bag she was lying on. Philippa was careful, reverential now, as she smoothed the salve into each breast, her voice lowering. 'My first was with the head girl at boarding school.' She giggled, as if having regressed to that adolescent age again. 'Isn't that so clichéd?'

Joyce made a non-committal noise; the sound seemed distant, even to herself, and she felt both detached and linked to her body, her breasts, now aching, her nipples, now growing hard. It was someone else's thighs that parted, slightly, beneath her. It was someone else's body that was responding to the caress of the woman's touch

'Yes.' Philippa moved on to Joyce's stomach, working in the salve. 'She gave me an appetite for servitude.'

'I wouldn't have considered you the servile type.' Her senses focused on Philippa's hands, as they ventured closer, closer – and Joyce surprised herself with the intensity of her own impatience. The woman's long, slender fingers reached Joyce's pubic thatch, massaging her mound. Joyce parted her thighs instinctively, offering easier access.

'I don't mean servitude for *me*.' Philippa giggled. Seconds later, Philippa entered her throbbing vulva, her fingers descending into the wet tunnel to the limit, creating a painful but pleasurable sensation as they slowly moved around inside, discovering the softness of the smooth velvet walls. Joyce yielded to the touch, her body limp as if bound.

She opened her eyes once when Philippa bent down and pressed her mouth against Joyce's, invading it with her tongue. Then she closed her eyes again, relishing the sensations of Philippa's tongue caressing Joyce's lips with her tongue in a snake-like movement.

Then Philippa withdrew her hand, making Joyce gasp. 'Close your eyes,' she said with a smile.

Joyce's voice was hoarse with arousal. 'What are you doing?'

'It's the surprise I told you about.'

Joyce's imagination ran riot as she heard her lover rummage through bags, followed by the rustle of clothes. Then Philippa said, 'OK.'

Joyce opened her eyes and exclaimed, 'Good Lord!'

Philippa kneeled before her, a silhouette with curves, breasts – and a long, curving shaft jutting from her groin.

Joyce sat up in disbelief, reaching out as if to confirm with her hands what her eyes told her. She touched the shaft, touched the warm rubbery surface, and moved out to the warm leather harness strapped around Philippa's hips with cool metal buckles, around which the crinkly hair of Philippa's pussy could be felt.

'Surprised?' Philippa asked needlessly.

'Yes,' Joyce answered, equally needlessly. Of course she wasn't so naïve as to be ignorant about dildo harnesses. But she'd never seen one in the proverbial flesh – and certainly never wore one, or had a lover who wore one. Tentatively she touched the shaft again. It seemed so massive, curving upwards.

Philippa sounded pleased by Joyce's reaction, her right hand reaching down to stroke the length of the shaft. 'I bought it in Berlin, long ago – but I've never used it with anyone.'

'Then we'll both be virgins at it.' Joyce's hand tenderly crept up the inside of Philippa's thighs. Long, cool and graceful, Joyce's fingers cupped around Philippa's artificial cock, as Philippa moved her own hand away. Her fingers glided up and down the column in light, fleeting strokes; she could almost imagine it jerking and twitching. Joyce grasped the rod tightly, squeezing, as if testing the fatness of its circumference.

'I want to use it on you, Joyce.'

That was obvious, Joyce told herself. She didn't think she had any qualms about it, didn't subscribe to any phallophobic tendencies. Indeed, as she continued to touch it, her already awakened libido cried out for her to find out what it felt like inside her.

With a growing smile on Joyce's lips, she opened her arms to Philippa and the woman drew closer, reclining beside and over her. Philippa's hands were at the sides of her face, tenderly brushing her cheeks and toying with the softness of her hair. In darkness and silence, their eyes spoke the words of their love as they gazed at each other for a few brief moments.

Leaning further down, her lips were on hers in a light, brushing kiss. Waves of gooseflesh rippled over Joyce as her chest was on Philippa's with a warm gentle pressure. The stiff tips of her nipples tingled even harder and stabbed into the woman above her. Just soaking in the feel of her, Joyce's hands roved over Philippa's back, revelling in the smoothness of her skin and the roll of her muscles beneath.

Her lips moved away for an instant, then she was back. Her tongue teased invitingly at her lips until they parted and her tongue entered the hot sweetness of her mouth. Pressing her weight harder against her yielding willingness, her tongue darted around in the sweet harbour it had found. She welcomed her, tightening her arms around her back and using her own tongue to taunt over and around the invader swirling at the roof of Joyce's mouth.

When Philippa finally withdrew, her tongue was flicking its way over Joyce's ear lobe. She worked until she could feel the shivering trembles of Joyce's excitement, then she let her teeth nibble for several moments.

Low moans rolled up from Joyce's throat as Philippa's lips moved down the arch of her neck. Lightly kissing, she took control of Joyce's body, a body she knew and had already learned to arouse to its fullest during their brief time together, controlling and affecting Joyce like no other lover had been able to do. Her mouth drifting with tantalising slowness towards the waiting bulges of Joyce's breasts, she slid down beside Joyce, delighting as she trembled along the length of her body.

Joyce's own hands were far from still. They roamed down Philippa's spine, finding the cheeks of her buttocks. With titillating dexterity, her fingertips taunted at the flesh and the deep crease between the tightening cheeks. Like feathers of loving caress, she played, forcing Philippa's buttocks to draw up hard and ready, and press the phallus against Joyce's thigh.

Philippa's own hands were on Joyce's breasts, sizing up the full circumference of their enticing forms. Around the ample flesh, her fingers circled, exciting in the warmth they found. In spiralling fashion, her palms climbed the sloped curves of Joyce's breasts.

Squirming under Philippa, one of Joyce's hands left the woman's buttocks and grasped the shaft poking at her groin, as if she'd been handling real penises all her life. She giggled despite her arousal.

Suddenly Philippa's mouth dropped down, capturing one of Joyce's stiff little buds, sucking and pulling at the nipple until Joyce moaned and jerked. Then Philippa's teeth bit lightly into the button seized by her lips.

Fire flamed through the aching nipple, when the mouth abruptly retreated and then attacked the nubbin of flesh. Joyce groaned and quivered as her hunger for this woman grew. She was Philippa's! Hers to do with as she pleased!

Harder and harder Philippa's lips sucked at the burning bud of Joyce's breast. Joyce's back arched up, shoving the luxurious pillow of flesh into Philippa's face and licking as she moaned and writhed under her ministrations.

Her whole body jolted as one of Philippa's hands left its firm hold on her breasts and slid down over Joyce's stomach to grasp the thatched mound waiting between her spread thighs. Joyce's lust-inflamed sex twitched and pushed into the woman's palm.

Firmly squeezing the fleshy mound, Philippa easily slid a finger into the wet warmth of her pussy. Joyce twitched and rotated the hungry lips of her pussy, trying to impale herself on the taunting finger – a wish Philippa complied with in a driving plunge that drilled her finger into the caressing entrance of Joyce's pussy. Philippa's finger pumped in and out of the slick channel, while she tickled another fingertip between the pouting cleft of Joyce's outer lips.

Upwards the inquisitive digit taunted along the wet crease of her pussy, to cajole the tiny bud of her clitoris out from under its hood. Joyce groaned and twitched as the dual sensations of her mouth at her breast and her vigorously fucking fingers sent ardent waves of pleasure through her body. Joyce's hips hunched into Philippa's hands, caught in the rhythm of Philippa's fingers. Her control of Joyce was complete. Her whole being begged for her to open her with the thick, swollen rubber shaft now between Philippa's legs.

'Now!' she moaned. 'Now! Please! Give it to me now!' Pulling Philippa's lips from her breast with a wet pop, the woman's mouth once more was hers and her tongue was frantically striving to slither into her throat. Joyce's legs spread even wider, opening to her as Philippa rolled atop her waiting nakedness. Then, in an easy twitch of her pelvis, Philippa slid the shaft into the well-lubricated channel of Joyce's pussy. Deep, sinking to her hilt, she glided into the wet, embracing folds.

Joyce grunted and quivered as she entered. Big, hard, and swollen, the phallus filled Joyce to the brim. 'Fuck me,' she heard herself whisper, heard herself moan, pulling her mouth away. 'Fuck me!' A part of her couldn't believe what she was saying, how bold and lewd she could be.

The penetration drew a sharp cry of delight from her lips, and the tight muscles of her pussy contracted into a sheath of squeezing delight, surrounding the shaft. Philippa's hips jerked upwards, then drew down again, burying the phallus deeper into Joyce's yielding sex. And as Joyce's hands dug into the woman's buttocks, her nails biting her flesh with aroused need, Philippa pumped and poled into her, urged on by Joyce, pulling her hard with each down-stroke of Philippa's groin. Joyce's legs crossed around her, locking the woman to her in the rising desperation of her desire. She groaned and writhed under the unstoppable touch that opened and reopened her, and she begged and pleaded for more.

Harder, the phallus drilled into the warm caressing recesses of her pussy, while Joyce squirmed and quivered under her, her buttocks swishing and hissing over the sleeping bag as her hips took up the rhythm of the fucking. As Philippa lunged down, Joyce's pelvis leaped up and greeted the hard shaft, helping it to move even deeper into the grateful centre of her unignorable lust. She no longer groaned, but grunted with each entry into her eager sex. Her body was jolted time and again, as Philippa pumped the shaft into her with reckless abandon.

She groaned as Philippa drew her closer, closer to orgasm. Her hands anchored firmly into Philippa's buttocks and she pulled even harder as she lunged, as if trying to take the woman fully into her. She twisted and squirmed with soaring pleasure under the battering attack of her loins.

Higher and higher she soared in a fervour of erotic delirium. Joyce's thighs throbbed and pounded with the growing agony of near release. Aching, writhing and groaning, she was caught up in an imploding universe of lust – a lust that consumed her in tidal wave after tidal wave of body-tearing passion, the folds of her pussy contracting sharply about the shaft.

Her desperate, wanton lust expended, she clutched Philippa tightly to her with one hand, the other moving frantically over her clit, her grateful body heaving and trembling in the wake of orgasm. With tender love, their mouths met and kissed in silent thanks and mutual disbelief at the pleasure shared.

'You – you – I have to –' Joyce found herself gasping.

Philippa was grinning against her skin, asking between kisses, 'Have to what?'

'Your – what about –'

'I've had my fun already.' She left the shaft buried inside Joyce. 'Did you enjoy that, darling?'

'Did I!' Joyce gasped. 'Yes! Yes!'

'Then all I want from you is your devotion. Do I have that?'

'Oh God, yes! You own me!'

There was a pause. Then Philippa whispered, 'Say that again.'

'What?'

'What you just said. Say it again.'

'You own me. Oh God, you own me!' Swept up by the sensations within her, Joyce meant every shameless word of it.

ELEVEN

Until she was upon it, Joyce had no idea about the immensity of the savannah, its sheer length and breadth. Maps were inadequate, or so they became, after Joyce consulted hers and saw just how little ground they'd actually covered that first day, having overestimated their overall strength.

It looked very much like it would take at least a fortnight to get to the mountain and back.

But, then she looked across the campsite at Philippa, who was putting out the campfire and helping clean up. And Joyce still felt the echoey afterwaves of her orgasms last night from Philippa's sweet assault – she had to stop every so often and just let it run through her, like a chill from the morning air – making her realise she didn't care about the time. Let them live out here for ever, away from people, away from decree and disapproval!

Nina moved about, clad in trousers and T-shirt and rubbing her bared forearms, and doing nothing else in particular. 'Jesus, it's fucking freezing! What the hell kind of country do you call this?'

Kimya was kneeling by her steed, checking one of its hooves. 'I call it *my* county, Ms Hoskins. And it's not too late for you to turn back if you can't handle it.'

Nina stopped in her tracks and stared in the Mahali woman's direction. 'Hey, I can handle it, girl! Don't worry about *that*!'

'I'm not,' Kimya ended simply.

Nina grunted at that, then looked over at Joyce, caught her gaze – and smiled. 'Hey, Joyride! Maybe you can warm me up somehow, huh?' She chuckled at her own innuendo.

Joyce started to reply, then turned away and finished packing up the tent. There was no point in trading words with the woman, or even telling her to shut up. She'd go away when she realised that Joyce wasn't taking the bait.

But Nina didn't go away; she looked about, as if to see who else was in earshot, before adding, 'You and Philadelphia kept yourselves warm last night, didn't you? They could have heard you back in London!'

Now Joyce shot up again, angry and mortified. Damn it, it never occurred to her until now that she might have been heard! How could she have been so stupid – or at least, so swept up in the passion Philippa fostered in her?

Now Faith stepped forward, wide-brimmed hat pulled down over her eyes to the morning sun – or to Nina. 'Why don't you stop flapping your gums and do something constructive?'

Nina made an exaggerated display of being shot in the heart. 'Ooh! Ahh! Ya got me, pardner!' Once she tired of her own feeble joke, Nina turned and snapped, 'Ruthie! Get me my jacket, pronto!'

Nearby, Ruth silently, sullenly walked over with the jacket from Nina's horse and helped the shorter, broader woman into it, as Joyce secretly stared in wonder. How did Nina get away with it? And from someone as confident and strong as Ruth?

Nina was a head shorter than Ruth. But that didn't stop the woman from reaching up, clasping a thick hand on the taller woman's neck, and drawing her down for a long, wet kiss, a rough gesture, a gesture of possession rather than affection.

Joyce looked away – to see Philippa staring at *her*, the woman's expression unreadable.

The sextet, their mounts and packhorses rode through a patch of arid, dust-strewn ground, dotted with gnarled acacias, rising and falling haphazardly, as if some giant had trailed his fingers through the dirt.

'Gullies,' Kimya explained. 'Soon they'll become rivers and tributaries, with the approaching rains. And all the land around us will turn green, just for the season.'

'What about the trees? Don't they die out when it's not raining?'

'The trees store enough water internally to last the year.'

'So, the trees take to water the way Ruthie's hips take to Italian food?' Nina quipped.

No one laughed. Until Joyce added, in a moment of inspiration, 'Or your mouth takes to verbal bollocks?'

She was pleased at the response until Nina cantered closer to Joyce and asked, 'Hey, Joy-Toy, did you know I also do impressions? Guess who this is.' And then she launched into a set of orgasmic yelps and moans, finishing with, ' "Philippa! Oh God, Philippa! I love you!" '

'Piss off.' Joyce left Nina to her fit of giggles and cantered ahead, to Philippa and Ruth, leading the way. She caught Philippa's eye, tilted her head, looking for words, for an expression, of love, support. Something.

She got something from Philippa. But whatever it was, it certainly wasn't love or support.

The savannah twisted though the surrounding slate-grey mountain walls, leaving behind the arid ground and gullies; within this shelter, Kimya had said, lay a multitude of habitats and some spectacular rock formations.

But though Joyce took pictures with the camera hanging around her neck and marvelled at the sights, her mind wasn't fully on what was without, but rather what was within – Philippa. What had happened between last night and today? Had she, too, been embarrassed by the revelation that the others had heard their lovemaking in the tent? The woman had kept her distance since breakfast, not giving Joyce the opportunity to speak to her in private.

Above them, birds swooped and soared in a near-cloudless sky of hazy blue. The morning chill that had been complained about hours before was now longed for, as jackets were tied about waists and around necks, and canteens were tapped more often.

Before Nina could ask, for a third time at midday, when they were going to stop and rest, Kimya pointed ahead. A cluster of gnarled acacias rose from the yellow grass, dominated by a huge tree, a tree whose size put the others to shame. A tree made to properly reflect the expanse of the savannah.

'There, Ms Hoskins,' Kimya said, though her voice was raised for the benefit of the others. 'There, you can rest your bum – and hopefully your mouth as well.'

'Hey, I'll do the jokes here, girl.'

'Oh yeah?' Faith countered. 'When are you gonna start?'

On closer inspection, the tree showed itself to be nearly three metres in diameter at its base, its massive gnarled roots sinking into the earth like the talons of some great bird gripping its prey, unchecked even by an adjacent man-sized, monolithic rock, jutting from the earth like a fang. The thick, furrowed grey bark was peeling off in places, either from the weather or from animals, revealing a fresh inner surface that appeared bright yellow in the sunlight. Further up in the cat's cradle of branches, there were wigs of dried grasses wedged here and there: the nests of tiny, yellow-black weavers, chittering quietly to themselves like locals gossiping over the new arrivals to their neighbourhood.

Kimya moved to the rock and motioned to the others. 'You might want to see this.'

As they approached, the group saw what she meant: a pair of shallow, crooked initials, chipped into the rocks. The first pair – CW – was instantly recognisable as Constance Wilde's.

It was the second pair – SB – which brought furrows of bemusement to Joyce. 'Who's that? Was it added afterwards?'

She looked to the others, receiving equal mixtures of bewilderment in return – except for Faith, who pretended to be busy, and Kimya, who was now examining patches of ground nearby.

It was the latter's sudden intensity that garnered the group's curiosity, and it took Faith to ask, 'Is there a problem?'

The guide looked from the ground to the horizon, then at the expectant group. 'Probably not.'

A hot, dry smell like tobacco clung to the afternoon as the horses were fed and watered. Joyce had approached Philippa at one point, to have a quiet word with her – she'd be damned if she would continue like this until nightfall!

But Kimya approached them both, carrying the snare kits. 'So, who wants to try catching dinner?'

Joyce repressed her annoyance at the interruption to consider the offer. That they would be supplementing their food supply on game was discussed and agreed upon, and everyone learned how to set the snares. But now, having to do it for real, and to eat what she caught, what had been running around alive and free not an hour before . . . Then she set aside such thoughts; did she ever give much thought to the cow that became her hamburger back home?

As it was, Philippa spoke up for them both, accepting the kits. 'OK, we'll go.'

Kimya nodded, unslinging the rifle from her shoulder and handing it to Joyce. 'Set them up just like I showed you. You can't miss the giant tree, so you're not likely to get lost. But if you get into trouble, fire a shot in the air.' She pointed towards another grove of trees, separated from their current site by an expanse of tall, chest-high grass. 'Try that way.'

'Um, there won't be any animals, will there?'

'If you mean large, dangerous animals, Ms Wilde, no. Not until tomorrow, I should think.'

'Hey, girls,' Nina called after the departing duo, spoiling another moment, 'mine's a bacon double cheeseburger!'

They were silent, apart from the crunch of dry ochre grass beneath their boots and the gentle slap of the leather snare loops against Philippa's side as she strode along, her eyes ahead.

Joyce kept her eyes ahead too, occasionally looking to her companion. 'So how are you finding it today?'

Philippa never looked back; her own face appeared taut. 'Fine.'

'Fine.' Joyce watched as Philippa stopped and set the first trap, just inside the grass, before proceeding. Joyce watched and sighed, hand wrapped around the sling of the rifle across her shoulder. It was something else she was uncomfortable with, the weapon, and she hoped she'd never need to use it. 'Good.'

Philippa set the next trap and continued towards the grove. Joyce followed, breathing in deeply, trying to find a way out of the conversational dead-end Philippa had driven her into. 'I wonder if my mother hunted for game along here as well, years ago.'

'I expect so.'

Now Joyce reached out and clasped Philippa's elbow, stopping them both. 'What's wrong with you? What did I do?'

Philippa shook herself from Joyce's touch. 'I thought it was obvious.'

She continued towards the trees. Joyce had to catch up. 'It's *not*! Why won't you talk to me?'

Philippa never answered. They emerged from the thick, harsh, waist-high grass into the trees, where insects buzzed in the relative shade, out of direct sunlight. Joyce stood and looked about, looked back the way they came; the campsite seemed so far away and, in the haze of the air, it seemed as ephemeral as the far distant mountains.

She watched Philippa enter the grass around the grove in different places, setting more snares. Then she emerged, empty-handed, staring directly at Joyce, as if ready now to discuss matters.

Joyce took the hint, unslinging the rifle and setting it against the trunk of an adjacent tree. 'Please tell me what I've done wrong.'

Philippa absently dusted her hands on the sides of her trousers. 'I saw you. Looking at Nina like that.'

'Like what?'

'Don't play coy with me, Joyce.'

'I don't know what you mean! When was this?'

'This morning! And all day today!'

Joyce's breath quickened. 'I haven't been looking at her! Or talking to her! I've tried avoiding her all along!'

'Who are you trying to fool, Joyce? Me, or yourself? Everyone can see you're leading her on, encouraging her.'

Confusion and alarm rose like bile inside Joyce. What did she mean? It couldn't be true. It just couldn't! 'I'm not! I haven't done anything, Philippa! Believe me, I haven't!'

Philippa's expression was glacial. 'You're a good liar, Joyce. I bet you're even convincing yourself. I should never have opened up to you.'

Joyce drew closer, the tears starting. 'Philippa, *please* – I swear to you I haven't – I *love* you –'

'You have a strange way of showing it.'

'*I love you!*' Joyce cried, reaching out for Philippa.

But the woman pulled back, as if Joyce was some pariah. 'You obviously didn't mean what you said last night, in the tent.'

Joyce had to fight back the choking sobs. 'Mean what? What did I say?'

'You said that you were mine. You repeated it, over and over.'

Philippa filled her mind, filled her dreams, inflamed and invigorated her. And though they'd known each other only a few days, Joyce was willing to give up so much.

Philippa's expression had changed, and Joyce seized upon it, shocked by where she was leading herself in her desperation. 'I did! I *did* mean it! I'm yours! You've – you've possessed me. You possess me now.'

And it was true. Joyce looked into her heart, and found Philippa had filled a gap there Joyce never acknowledged had existed before now. Her thoughts were filled with Philippa, inextricable. It was mad – she didn't even know Philippa existed four days ago!

And yet here was Joyce now, in the wilds of Africa, declaring . . . what? Love? Loyalty?

Submission?

Something must have shown in Joyce's eyes, because Philippa's finger-and-thumb grip on Joyce's chin tightened, along with her expression and subsequent warning. 'Don't just say what you think I want to hear, Joyce. Because I told you in Mzuri, I don't do anything in half-measures. I'm very possessive. I expect full measures of love. Of devotion. Of obedience.'

She exuded command. Sex. Joyce wanted to melt into her arms, wanted to be swallowed up by this magnificent woman and remain inside her, a part of her, for ever. She'd die without her. So, even if she still denied to herself any wrongdoing on her part with Nina, it was hardly a chore for her to murmur, 'Philippa, I'm . . . I'm sorry. For my behaviour. Please forgive me.'

Was it so strange? She loved Philippa. And love seemed to go hand in hand with possession. Will you take this woman to be yours, to have and to hold.

'Philippa, I –' Her voice faltered, returned. 'I belong to you.'

Philippa nodded at this. 'And *are* you sorry for your behaviour?'

Joyce was ready to argue this further – she was certain she'd done nothing to deserve the accusation – but instead she nodded, the tears flowing down her cheeks. 'Yes.'

'And are you ready to do what I say? And to accept the consequences of your doing otherwise?'

'Y-yes.' It was terrifying, this. Defeat, embarrassment ran through Joyce, but suffused with it was an excitement, an arousal she'd expected, though not with such intensity. Was it from her ultimate acknowledgement of Philippa's supreme authority over her? She wasn't so naïve as to not recognise the power game at work here; she was surprised by her reaction. Perhaps Philippa engineered the false accusations all along, to put her in this position.

She should have been angry. She should have bolstered her pride, not swallowed it, not let the desire flow unchecked through her veins.

Philippa stood there, strong and vital and commanding and so self-assured. Then she stepped back, releasing her hold on Joyce, regarding her. 'I believe I'll go easy on you, your first time.'

Joyce half-understood the declaration. Arousal as much as embarrassment made Joyce's face burn as she replied, 'Thank you, Philippa.'

Philippa made no acknowledgement of Joyce's decision, her courage, instead simply saying, 'Strip.'

She said it so casually, Joyce almost didn't respond, as if Philippa may have been talking to someone else. 'What?'

'I said strip.'

Reflexively Joyce looked back the way they had come, to the

camp only a quarter-mile away. If anyone viewed them with binoculars, they'd surely see what was happening.

'So, there *is* a limit to your supposed love,' Philippa mused.

Before she even acknowledged it to herself, Joyce's fingers were moving to obey, undoing the buttons on her shirt, wanting to get this over with quickly, but still glancing back at the camp. This was just a game, she assured herself. Her shirt fell to the ground, followed by the canteen belt around her waist; Philippa's eyes were on her every step of the way, though only the weavers in the trees sounded in the still afternoon air. Joyce's discomfort increased, and her loins reacted with extreme sensuality. She was trembling, as her sweat-stained T-shirt and bra were peeled from her body. She paused, breathed in sharply, her arms wrapped across her chest, as if she was threatened with instant sunburn (which, given the climate and her pale skin, wasn't as unlikely as it sounded), and she turned away from the direction of the camp, expecting all eyes on her now.

'I didn't say you can stop,' Philippa informed her, her own arms across her chest as if mocking Joyce's modesty.

'Isn't this enough for you?'

'Honey, I haven't even *started* yet. The rest, now.'

Joyce swallowed, and kneeled in the dirt beside her cast-off shirt, T-shirt and bra, untying her bootlaces, slipping out of her boots, relishing the freedom of them once again, a freedom she did not feel with the rest of her body. She had to stand to undo her trousers, peel them down the columns of her legs.

'Keep the knickers and socks on,' Philippa offered, as if it was a grand gesture on her part.

'Thanks,' Joyce said absently. The air felt cool and dry on her now exposed skin, and she felt unaccountably locked into a diminishing maze of sexual urgings, all paths leading to the same destination.

'Straighten up. Face me.'

Joyce obeyed, her arms back across her chest. It was difficult not to blush, or to ignore the scent of sex upon her like sweat, the moistness of her gusset, moistness from something other than sweat.

Philippa had a bold look about her, the icy blue eyes staring, and making no apology for so doing. 'You're anxious. You're aroused. This new direction we're taking is like riding a roller-coaster, exhilarating and out of your control. But you still know, deep down, that you're in safe hands with me.'

Joyce frowned, trying to force herself not to like standing out here near-naked. 'What direction?'

'I think you already know. Why did you undress? Why have you agreed to be punished?'

Joyce swallowed, hating to be seen like this before Philippa now. 'To please you –'

'Liar. You want to taste submission. There's no shame in admitting it. Equal partnership between lovers is a myth.'

She made it sound so convincing. Joyce kept glaring at her, until Philippa approached, hands moving up Joyce's bare arms. 'Well? Am I right?' She punctuated her question with a gentle kiss on Joyce's lips.

Joyce swallowed again. 'Yes.'

'And do you want to submit yourself to me?'

That answer came easier. 'Yes.' She wanted to cradle herself in Philippa's arms, let her take care of her. Control her. Give up the heavy burden of her responsibilities, and live to obey another, as long as they were worthy. And Philippa was very, *very* worthy.

Philippa smiled and kissed her again – gently but firmly pulling the arms away from the breasts. The act was enough to sap at Joyce's spirit and make her feel as though her will – and her body – were no longer her own. Strangely enough, the combination in her character of sensuality and the desire to please added an odd thrill to the experience. Even now, with Philippa scrutinising her near-nudity, it was like the first time again, only more so. And Joyce wanted her to do more. A rope seemed to knot in her stomach and a tingling centred in a warm spot between her legs, and she knew she had no choice in the matter.

Philippa's hands lightly travelled along the contours of Joyce's body. 'You *are* beautiful,' she noted, almost whispering with reverence, her fingertips dancing along Joyce's nipples.

'Thank you,' Joyce whispered back, glancing briefly down at

them, noted how they rose to the attention, then looked further down at her dark delta of hair, visible though her panties, waiting, wanting further attention of their own. She remained silent now, but a chilled excitement was sending shivers of apprehension and expectation down her spine and over her skin. So this was what it was like to have another hold power over you; to her own surprise, her body was responding further, as if sensing Joyce no longer had control over it.

'With cheeks ripe for caning,' Philippa added, reaching down and patting Joyce's bum. She took Joyce by the wrists and gently but firmly led her around the nearest tree, to a large fallen trunk, a half-metre in diameter, lying in the dirt at a near-level angle. 'Prepare yourself. Straddle it, the full length. Oh, and remove your knickers.' When Joyce looked at her questioningly, she added, 'I've changed my mind. Do you have a problem with that?'

'No.' Head bowed, Joyce obeyed, turning and sliding her wet panties down her legs, balling them into her hand, refusing to let go of them, a pathetic attempt to maintain some level of autonomy. She was naked now but for her socks, her sex tingling, her heart racing. Carefully she lifted one leg over the trunk, mindful of keeping her balance, before lowering herself upon it. The bark, what was left on it, was striated with narrow furrows, while other parts were smooth, almost a polished yellow; her pussy rested on one of the smooth parts.

Joyce lowered herself further, until her face and the sides of her breasts and thighs rested on the bark, and her cheeks were raised and parted, to the air and Philippa's continued scrutiny. There was a bit of bark pressing into her slit, and she couldn't avoid it no matter how much she moved about.

She was impatient – impatient to get it all over with. But more impatient to get *started*.

Philippa strode about the grove, lifting up small branches, testing them before discarding them. Her deliberate scrutiny told Joyce the woman knew what she was looking for.

Philippa returned, swishing one long, thin branch at her side. Joyce's pulse quickened as Philippa's improvised switch tapped at each cheek; Joyce held her breath and swallowed the moan of delight. A pleasurable response was something she would need to grasp, to keep and use to counteract the stinging bottom she knew was to soon come.

'You've never been punished like this before,' Philippa asked, 'have you?'

'N-no.' It was true; her great-aunt had never been one for corporal punishment, and her past lovers had never raised a hand to her even in loveplay, much less a switch.

Glancing behind her, Joyce could see Philippa standing beside her, eyes feasting on Joyce's naked back and trembling buttocks. Her sex was now open, and Philippa's switch was now lightly grazing, poking at the soft lips and parted cleft, tapping each cheek. Joyce tensed, held her breath. But even knowing what was to happen, she couldn't help but start at the touch of the tip of the switch at her pussy, at the moist acceptance it encountered.

'You're wet already,' Philippa purred unnecessarily.

'Y-yes.' Joyce's voice seemed fragile, detached even from herself.

'However, this isn't supposed to be about your pleasure, is it? It's about your punishment,' Philippa continued. 'You *still* think you should be punished for your behaviour. Don't you?'

Joyce didn't answer, not until she felt the tip of the switch tap against her damp sex. Then she found her voice again. 'Yes.'

The switch tapped at Joyce's sex once more. 'Louder, please.'

'Yes!' Joyce cried, hating her. Loving her.

'Good,' said Philippa slowly. 'Good.' And the switch tapped her sex again before Philippa raised it and levelled a stinging blow across Joyce's buttocks.

Joyce gasped. Her fingers gripped the sides of the trunk, dropping the rolled-up knickers in one hand, and her nipples swelled against the wood beneath them. Her bottom stung and burned with the kiss of the switch. Her pelvis had pushed down with the blow. Her pussy had pressed harder against the knot of wood between her legs, just as expected. She would come, like this. She knew it.

'I will give you only six today,' Philippa announced. 'You will count them as they strike. And each time you miss counting one, or get the count wrong, I will add two more to what you deserve. Are you ready?'

'Yes,' answered Joyce without hesitation, a glow of tingling delight spreading upwards from her willing thighs, though her voice trembled, 'I'm ready.'

'Good,' Philippa purred. 'Then we shall continue.'

The air swished as the switch fell.

'Two!' cried Joyce as her buttocks clenched and stung beneath the blow. The knot firmly kissed her clitoris, and her clitoris kissed back.

'No,' Philippa corrected. 'One.'

'B-but –'

'You surely don't expect that first one to *count*, do you? That was a mere demonstration. Now that's two added to the six deserved.'

The air swished again. The pain shot through her again. Joyce gasped again. 'Two!' Her bottom began to glow.

Again the switch flew through the air. 'Three!' Now she was almost wishing for its stinging caress and for the pelvic movement that accompanied it and pressed her more firmly against the knot.

And just as she had wished, it came again. 'Four!' Her buttocks quivered, warmed beneath its burning touch. 'Five!' she exclaimed, and felt the fires of orgasm spreading through her loins and homing in on that very sensitive spot that was pressed so tightly to the knot.

Joyce had failed to keep her rising need in check, and felt herself moving back against the knot, desperate for release. The switch swung out again – 'Six!' – stopping her, but still drawing her closer; sweat beaded between her naked flesh and the wood, and the knot pushed its hard, rough surface firmly against her clitoris. Her orgasm was rising, nearing like storm clouds. Her bottom quivered; it was redder and warmer now, tingling as much from sexual longing as from the switch.

But the switch was not through with her. It cut the air again, and Joyce moaned again. 'Seven!' Her voice was shaking as the first waves started, quivering through her parted sex and causing her empty, aching pussy to shed its moist fluid so it dripped through her sex and on to the trunk to join her sweat.

The final blow of the switch would come now. She craved it, longed for its burning kiss on her bottom so her sex would thrust one more time – just once more – before the flood of orgasm washed over her.

It came. 'Eight!' she cried, and pressed her clit tightly against the knot, riding it in small sharp spurts until the last eruptions of her orgasm had melted away. It was *glorious*.

Joyce looked up, breathless, exhausted, enquiring – then she remembered. Her skin stuck to the trunk with sweat as she rose weakly, shifting down on to all fours on the ground like an animal in heat, trying to focus her senses.

Philippa was upon her now, rolling with her on the ground, hands and lips over Joyce's near-nude, hot, pliant body. Joyce felt pain as her buttocks touched the ground, but ignored it for the groundswell of dizzying giddiness and acute pangs of arousal. Joyce could never resist the beautiful, demanding Philippa now. Her hot open mouth and the sweet taste of her saliva gave Joyce a resurgence of arousal, as if she was never far from climax. Philippa reached between Joyce's legs, her eyes riveted on Joyce's bush and wet swollen pussy. She was spellbound, her face flushed and very aroused.

A dam broke inside Joyce. She felt a hunger for Philippa deep within her soul, a hunger to make her feel as satisfied as she felt now. She helped Philippa work the zippers and catches on her trousers, undo them as Philippa concentrated on lifting her shirt and T-shirt up from her slim belly. Joyce lowered Philippa's trousers and knickers, feasting her eyes on Philippa's beautiful wet pink pussy, and felt another powerful spasm between her legs that almost made her faint.

She kneeled over Philippa almost reverently as Philippa raised her shirt and T-shirt up, then helped her breasts spill out from the bra. She placed her mouth on Philippa's large soft breasts and licked the hard bumpy pink nipples. Joyce was overwhelmed by a desperate primal need to make Philippa come. She moved down, buried her face in Philippa's sex, and the strong female musk brought on another powerful spasm between her legs.

Philippa reached down and pulled Joyce's face into her, covering Joyce's face with her hot juices. Joyce started to lick her and Philippa gasped when Joyce's tongue reached her large hard clit. She whispered hoarsely, 'That's it, Joyce. That's it, my little slave. Don't stop. I love you. I love you.'

Slave. The word sent hot, hard charges off inside of Joyce — more than the word Love did. She could feel Philippa's hard hot clit against her tongue and licked her with slow steady strokes. She twirled her tongue around Philippa's clit and Philippa responded by spreading her thighs as far as they would go, with her ankles hobbled by her trousers and knickers. Joyce explored Philippa's vaginal lips with trembling fingers and Philippa began breathing in gasps.

She quickly slid her fingers into Philippa's pussy and Philippa's moans became louder and louder. She thrust her fingers in and out and licked Philippa's swollen clit hard and fast. Suddenly Philippa began to come. She cried out as her body was flooded by a powerful torrent of pleasure. Orgasm after orgasm cascaded over her as Joyce made her come, again and again.

She dressed silently, as Philippa disappeared to check on the snares. Joyce felt parched, but waited until her clothes were back on her body before reaching for her canteen. The sweat ran down the sides of her face and off her back, and her skin tingled — though not as much as her bum did.

'I've snared myself a pretty catch today,' Philippa announced as she emerged from the grass.

Joyce looked up to see the woman proudly holding two grey duiken, tiny antelopes almost as small as hares, caught in the snares set earlier.

For a moment, Joyce thought Philippa had been referring to *her*.

But only for a moment.

TWELVE

I t was close, sultry in the tent.
   Joyce didn't really notice.

Philippa and she lay on their sides, facing each other, each woman's face at the other's breasts. They were naked. A meagre light from the tiny hand torch hanging from the top of the tent cast a curtain of yellow and shade over their bodies. They should shut it off, let the darkness of evening blanket them entirely, if for no other reason than not to give Kimya, standing guard over the campsite outside, an erotic shadowplay.

But neither of them moved.

If Joyce thought about it, she could still feel the sting of her birching from Philippa that afternoon. She certainly still felt it when she was on horseback afterwards, not relieved until tonight, when Philippa had gently, lovingly salved her sores.

They lightly stroked each other's breasts, fingertips combing furrows of sensation along supple, animated skin. It made Joyce shiver – and Philippa chuckle. 'You respond well to my hand.'

Joyce chuckled. 'In so many ways.'

'Yes.' From anyone else, it might have sounded arrogant. But Philippa had a casual insouciance about how she dominated Joyce, to which Joyce couldn't help but respond positively. 'Sit up. I have something for you.'

144

Joyce complied, cross-legged, her forearms resting on her thighs, her hands hanging by the entrance to her pussy, as if keeping them warm at the fire of her sex. She couldn't wipe the grin from her face as she watched Philippa rise as well, draw her carrybag over on to her lap and fish through its carefully packed contents.

Then she produced . . . something. Joyce had half-expected another sex toy, like the dildo harness, now sitting beside them like a bizarre alien plant emerging through the tent floor. After a moment, Philippa held up the object of her search: a short, thin strip of black leather, with a hook and latch on either end.

A collar. With Joyce's name on it.

'Rise to your knees.'

Joyce didn't move. 'It looks too short; I won't be able to hide it inside my shirt –'

'But why would you want to *hide* it? If you don't want it –'

'No, it's not that,' Joyce assured her. She sighed.

Philippa held the open ends of the collar between the thumbs and forefingers of each hand. 'I told you to rise to your knees.'

Her voice was silky, nonchalant. But Joyce obeyed, her hands folding by themselves to rest in front of her bush, a vestigial gesture of modesty.

It did not go unnoticed. 'Put your hands at your sides.'

Joyce breathed again, and obeyed. Now Philippa rose to her knees too, shifted closer until their breasts almost touched. Joyce could smell the woman's sweet, irresistible scent as she raised her arms and wrapped the collar around Joyce's throat, clicking it shut. It was taut, but not too constricting, or even uncomfortable. But Joyce could never forget it was there.

Which was, of course, the intention.

'And now,' Philippa continued, leaning back to rest her buttocks on her heels, 'I own you.'

'Yes.'

'Say it.'

She'd said it before, but now Joyce felt an additional weight on her, as if the collar weighed a tonne. 'You own me.' Her pussy throbbed.

Philippa smiled a sweet little smile. 'Do you want me to fuck you?'

Joyce felt a rush, almost imperceptible; it was both disconcerting and acutely arousing to hear such explicit language in that posh accent. 'Yes.'

'Say it. Ask it of me.'

'Fuck me. I want you to fuck me. Please.' To say it out loud was doubly exciting.

Philippa's eyes moved along Joyce's body, stopping as she tilted her head and regarded the collar. 'It suits you.' Then she reached for the dildo. 'As this does me.'

Joyce laughed, almost nervously. Yet her pussy burned at the sight of the dildo, and she could feel the hungry feeling in the pit of her stomach growing more intense.

Philippa held the phallus by the base with one hand, and idly stroked the length with the other. 'Touch your breasts, Joyce.'

It was almost unnecessary, as Joyce was ready to do that very thing, order or not. She rubbed her full breasts with gentle sensuous motions, and her nipples were instantly erect. The tiny pink tips stood up proudly, and she worked them between her fingers, enjoying the sensations it gave her. Her hands were like distant objects, intended only to obey Philippa, stimulate herself and make herself feel good.

'Touch yourself elsewhere.'

The drops of lubricating fluid nestling just within the frilled slit of Joyce's pussy made their presence known, and she rubbed her inner thighs together as she felt the sensitive nerve end of her clitoris respond. Releasing one of her nipples, she ran her hand down over the smooth flesh of her belly until she reached the sparse beginning of the curling triangle of soft pubic hair. It was her pussy she was after and, pointing the way with her middle finger, she slowly worked her hand down over the mound of pink flesh. Joyce's finger drifted naturally into the moistened slit, and she drew it back until it made contact with her already sensitised clit.

Joyce moaned out loud as the bolt of electric pleasure danced through her lust-hungry body. The nerve end was hard, and she played her finger over it, enjoying every sensation that it gave her.

Philippa let the leather straps of the harness snake between her fingers, but her eyes remained bolted on the display before her. 'Make yourself wet, Joyce.'

'I – I'm already wet,' Joyce gasped.

'*Wetter*, then,' Philippa snarled, grinning.

The pit of Joyce's belly was on fire, and the manipulation of her clitoris made the fire burn brighter. Pushing her whole hand down over the mound of her pussy, Joyce parted her thighs further, and she then worked her middle finger around the tight opening of her passage. The trembling crevice was wet and warm, and her finger slipped easily inside herself. It felt silky sweet, but her mind was thinking about the huge dildo in Philippa's hands. The thought of having that phallus fucking her was enough to make her moan aloud, uncaring of who might hear her outside.

She closed her eyes with a rush of blood through her body like a sneeze, and opened them to find Philippa leaning close to her breasts, her mouth open and her eyes staring with lust. In one swift motion, the blonde woman's red lips pulled an erect nipple into the warmth of her mouth, and it so surprised Joyce that she cried out. The sensation of her lover's mouth sucking on her nipple was tremendous, and Joyce reached up and dug her fingers into the soft round breasts that swayed before her, teasing the pink tips into hardness.

For what seemed like an eternity, Joyce writhed in the lewd sensation of Philippa's sucking and nipping of her nipple, and then she felt the blonde-haired woman's hand moving slowly down across the sensitive white skin of her belly. She was moving her fingers towards Joyce's hungry pussy, and Joyce wanted to swallow up those creeping fingers. She knew that it would feel luxurious, and she arched back, her breast still at Philippa's lips, in welcome as the other woman's fingers worked down into the soft flesh in search of her clit.

'Oh fuck!' Joyce hissed when the contact was made, and she squirmed her toes against the sleeping bag beneath her to fully enjoy the sensation from Philippa's touch. Her belly started jerking involuntarily as her lover worked over the sensitive bud again and again.

Philippa pulled back. 'One moment.'

Joyce gasped. 'W-what?'

Philippa rose, drew something from the shadows: a T-shirt? Was she going to cover up Joyce or –

Her question was answered as Philippa kneeled behind her, pulled Joyce's hands behind her, and began tying them at the wrist, making Joyce start, then squirm against her additional bonds. Oh God, that felt so *delicious* . . .

Philippa returned to examine Joyce – naked, collared, bound, and descended once more to Joyce's hardened nipple, pulling it deep inside her mouth. Philippa ran her tongue wetly around the sensitive tip, and then nipped lightly at it with her teeth. Then, after a few moments of playing with Joyce's clitoris, Philippa searched for the sensitive opening to Joyce's sex, and running her finger along the ragged pink flesh of her vagina, she felt the moisture of her lover's passion. For a time, Philippa played her finger over the opening as if undecided whether or not to plunge the seeking finger inside.

Drawing her bum up from her heels, Joyce raised her hips to try to screw her pussy up around Philippa's probing finger. She wanted to have it inside the tight walls of her passage, fucking into her like a narrow hot spit being stuck into a roast. It was maddeningly titillating the way Philippa started to dip her finger inside, then playfully retreated just when Joyce thought it was going all the way. Finally, just at the peak of the balance between arousal and frustration, Philippa sent her extended middle finger up into the warm depths of Joyce's pussy.

Oh God, *yes*! Joyce thought she would climax right then and there, the plunging finger felt so good, and she squeezed her eyes shut and arched her hips up to take it as deep as it would go. Philippa wiggled her finger inside the moist passage until Joyce thought she could climb the tent walls with pleasure, and she wanted more.

But Philippa was not so inclined. Philippa's lips were gone from her nipple, and her finger pulled from the groaning woman's pussy. Joyce opened her eyes to see what had happened just when Philippa kneeled back, the dildo in her hands, and the sight of the phallus made Joyce's belly jerk with excitement. She was going to be fucked by that huge thing again, and her lover was going to do it. The lust-driven woman knew her pleasures would be twice what they had already been with Philippa's finger, and she suddenly lost all momentary annoyance at having her pleasure interrupted.

'Lie down,' Philippa ordered. 'Face down.' Her voice sounded coarse, ragged in the heat. Her head was beside the tent light, and she knocked it slightly, sending the torch spinning on its hook, a whirlpool of light and shadow swirling within the tent. Joyce obeyed, as best she could with her hands bound behind her.

Philippa undid her hands. 'Lift yourself up. Present yourself to me.'

As if in slow motion, but not pausing even to rub at her wrists, Joyce rose to all fours, imagining the pink stripes from her caning still there, perhaps some pointing to the moist, shadowed valley between her cheeks. Stretching her hands out she began to claw at the groundmat, her ass suddenly waving wickedly, inviting Philippa.

Hands moved about the creamy surface of her upturned ass. Philippa parted her thighs further, until Joyce felt her buttocks were fully separated, and the lips of her sex were pouting at her lover, daring her to do her worst – or better yet, her best!

And Philippa was up for the challenge. Kneeling between Joyce's legs, she grasped her hips and lifted her up slightly, making her pussy more receptive. Joyce moaned as she felt the head of the phallus meet the wet folds of her sex, moistening it as it gently but firmly slid its entire length into Joyce. Philippa's body was pressed against Joyce's bottom; sheer bliss shot through Joyce. She was climaxing already!

If Philippa perceived her surging and pulsing reactions, she said nothing, drawing almost fully out of her before plunging back in, then again and again, her hands firm on Joyce's hips, supporting her easily. Joyce braced herself, meeting the driving thrusts, her breasts pendulating, feeling as if her body would eventually split in two. She groaned aloud, savouring the oncoming rush of another orgasm. She sucked the air between her teeth and felt her ass moving, arching back to meet the phallus.

She gasped and whimpered as the heat swelled within her sweaty, aching body. She began to shake like a dog just climbing from a pond, her ass gyrating in a frenzy, pounding back and forth on the object stretching and filling her bubbling sex so sweetly. She was no longer embarrassed, no longer ashamed. She was filled with a boiling ecstasy, fucking as much as being fucked. The moist sounds of her pussy filled the tent and Joyce lifted her head to yelp with pleasure.

The phallus, ramming deep into her gripping sex was setting off a series of sweet, delicious tremors and they increased her wild churning ass-tossing movements. Joyce was yelping as the spasms shot through her, causing her sex to clamp on to the phallus like a scalding vice, sucking and nibbling.

Philippa was slamming the dildo deep and hard into Joyce, slapping her cheeks at the same time. The smacks sent Joyce into a more powerful surge of desire. She slammed her pussy back against Philippa tightly, the urge to push overpowering. Her wet, steaming sex sucked at the length within it, the flexing of it extremely tight. She sprawled forward on to the floor, almost violently feeling the phallus pull from inside her.

Dizziness, confusion. Then Philippa was straddling herself over Joyce's face. The aroma of Philippa's sex, the sweaty, sweet skin of her thighs matched only by the moisture in the mat of hair clasping the entrance to her sex, was overpowering, and greedily Joyce lifted her head and opened her mouth, ignoring the phallus, still in the harness around Philippa's waist.

It wasn't easy, in her current position and with her arms under Philippa's shins, but she managed to use her tongue to pry apart the swollen lips, silky and warm, releasing more succulent perfume, and the taste of Philippa's dew. Joyce was too close to properly see, but felt the rise of her mistress's protruding clit, emerging from its hood above the entrance to her vagina. And once Joyce had a hold of that between her lips, Philippa descended further, until it seemed as if she'd smother Joyce between her thighs. Then she began riding her face, barely giving Joyce enough time to catch her breath. At the same time, Joyce rubbed herself skilfully to orgasm, her fingers soaked from her own wetness.

Then Philippa began riding her with increasing vigour and, pressing her labia against Joyce's face until the latter thought she might suffocate, she let her orgasm free, her tight channel embracing Joyce's weary but happy tongue.

It seemed to take ages, but Philippa finally collapsed beside Joyce, reaching out to clasp Joyce's face, sticky and smelling of her sex. Dimly she felt the collar hugging her neck, the tiny latch binding it to her, an almost imperceptible, but not totally unignorable presence.

Kimya pointed to the next animal appearing in view, her voice low, eager. 'Impala. They keep harems of fifteen and more, some as many as a hundred. Which is very . . . generous of them.'

'Uh-huh.' Joyce smiled and raised her camera again for another shot, peering through the telephoto lens at the deer-like creature with its glossy rufous coat and lyre-shaped horns, and remained amazed that the animal could ignore the approaching party of humans.

'Aren't they the fast-moving ones?' Philippa asked nearby, drinking heavily from her canteen now that they were closing in on another source of water, her interest almost as palpable as Joyce's.

Kimya made an approving sound. 'They can clear ten-metre lengths, and three-metre heights. Faith?'

Beside her, Faith leaned forward in the saddle and made another of her calls, a yipping sound that made the impala at the water look up, then dart off out of sight.

'Hey!' Joyce let the camera rest in her lap. 'You didn't have to scare him off.'

'He'll be back,' Kimya assured her. 'Him, and many more.'

The party arrived at a clearing in the scrub, a clearing widened by past human involvement, to judge from the small metal tower and mechanism, squat like a baobab near the pool-sized watering hole. There was an open area beneath several rusted pipes, and a hand-pump of sorts, like one might find on a farm.

Kimya was off her horse and moving to the pump before the others had time to react. She kneeled, looked about, then up at the party. 'Ruth! Faith!'

The Israeli and American women dismounted and approached, horses in tow, while the three remaining women stayed mounted, watching in bemusement.

'They're gonna hog all the water themselves,' Nina quipped.

Joyce shunned her, looking away.

But that didn't prevent Nina from manoeuvring her steed to face Joyce again. 'Hey, don't fucking ignore me!'

Now Philippa sidled her horse to Nina's other side, leaving the woman flanked by Joyce and herself, a psychological surrounding. 'You don't speak to her without my permission. She's *mine*.'

Hearing Philippa speak aloud of their relationship, especially to Nina, filled Joyce with a mixture of embarrassment and arousal, as well as the expected unease about any confrontation; the collar around her neck seemed to tighten. At least no one had commented on it.

Nina chuckled at Philippa's words, glancing at Joyce like she was regarding a child's attempts at rebellion. 'Boy, have *you* let yourself in for trouble, girl.'

'Not as much as *you'll* have,' Philippa warned, 'if you come near her again.'

Inwardly, Joyce was pleased at her lover's protective stance. But still a part of her didn't want things to escalate out of control. 'Philippa –'

Now the woman shot Joyce a withering glare. 'Don't speak, unless spoken to.'

Before Joyce could voice her indignation at that, Kimya stepped forward. 'Is there a problem, ladies?'

After a heartbeat, Philippa announced, 'None.' Then she looked about. 'Where did Faith and Ruth go?'

Another heartbeat, before Kimya's reply. 'Just looking around for some animals nearby.' Now the woman was all business. 'You know the drill, ladies. Unsaddle and sponge down the horses at the watering hole. Then we can enjoy a midday meal and –' she indicated the pump '– the facilities.'

The sun bore down in an azure sky only bordered by clouds at the horizon, pursuing the party at a leisurely pace.

Having tended to her mare and her stomach, Joyce now sat under the meagre shade of a tree and watched as the others took their turns at the pump, which had a facility for an open shower. Away from the constraints of society, stripping off in front of others and stepping under the water seemed to offer no apprehension. And more . . . Ruth and Nina stepped under the showerhead together, seemingly at the latter's insistence. Nina's body nude was as Joyce remembered, back on the beach at Mzuri: stocky, pale with recent sun-tanned patches.

Ruth's was taller, more lithesome, her limbs more muscular, her breasts smaller, her skin swarthier. She also had . . . tattoos? Yes, that's what they were, on various parts of her body, though Joyce was too far away to discern them properly. Her body was pressed against Nina's, as the smaller woman vigorously rubbed her hands over Ruth's back and buttocks, as if to wipe the fatigue of the last few days off the other woman's body.

Joyce looked away as Philippa approached, already unbuttoning her shirt. 'Our turn next.'

Joyce blanched. 'I, um, I think I'll wait till later.'

Philippa cast off her shirt, exposing her upper body and white bra to the sun. 'We won't be here later. Get undressed.' Now she grinned devilishly as she kneeled to work at her bootlaces. 'Or I'll undress you myself.'

Joyce paused to examine the reasons for her apprehension, and found them wanting. Was it a residual umbrage at how Philippa had treated her in front of Nina? Enough contemplation. She leaned forward to remove her own boots . . .

The water was warm, as expected, but a divine caress, and a reminder of how many days it had been since the last time they could indulge with so much water.

She was startled from her repose by a pair of hands encircling her waist from behind. Closer now, Philippa's face appeared at Joyce's shoulder, her smile broad once more. 'Hi.'

'Hi yourself.' The woman's breasts, her nipples, pressed against Joyce's back, both their bodies slick and smooth from the water; the intimate contact was most welcome. Joyce looked out at the campsite, saw the others tending to various tasks, none staring at what was going on, but could see if they looked up.

But then, so what? It was no secret that Philippa and she were lovers. It was a small thing indeed now to be naked (apart from her collar), only a slightly greater step to be openly affectionate in front of them. Despite her moments of hesitancy, she knew she was now enjoying a freedom she never could in the real world.

Philippa pushed closer, as if deliberately pressing her matted pubic mound against Joyce's right buttock, and brought her lips closer to Joyce's right ear, her voice barely audible over the shower raining down on them. 'I have guard duty tonight, first watch. But I'll want you ready for when I return. OK?'

Joyce's pussy twinged with desire, and she pushed her bum back against Philippa's body. 'Of course. Whatever you want.'

'"Whatever I want". I like your philosophy.' Philippa chuckled at her own words, darting her tongue out to lick the outer rim of Joyce's ear, sending electric tingles through the other woman, before withdrawing from the shower and padding back to her clothes and towel, more conscious about the hot sand beneath her feet than her nudity.

It was another several hours before they settled again, this time for the evening. Around the dinner of more snared topi, Kimya announced, 'I'm cutting down the watches at night from four to three hours each time.'

'Any particular reason,' Nina asked, 'or just to piss us off?'

'I wonder if there is anything that *wouldn't* annoy you, Ms Hoskins. As it is, we're venturing into wilder country, with a greater chance at encountering animals bold enough to approach camp. Shorter watch times mean greater alertness.'

'Just keep the lions away,' Nina joked.

'The lions and the tigers,' Faith added.

'And bears, oh my.'

The last few days had served to help Joyce discard all her preconceptions about Africa like so much other inappropriate belongings. Gone were images of dense jungle, in favour of flattened rocky hills and termite mounds, dotted by islands of trees and watering holes. And the 'traditional' animals were nowhere to be seen; instead, myriad species of antelope seemed to dominate this land, from the hare-like dik-dik to the bovine eland. Exotic animal names leaped about unbound in her head – bushbucks, gerenuks, hartbeets, topis – making her feel like an explorer on an alien world rather than her own.

A world which seemed to truly come alive only in the twilight hours, when so many of the animals emerged to drink at the infrequent watering holes, such as the one near where the party had camped; it was amazing how they ignored the torch lights occasionally shone upon them. And the initial tension among the party seemed to have lessened; even Nina had reduced her grousing and regaled the others – though not Joyce – with her stories and jokes.

But Faith was the real surprise, with her remarkably effective animal calls, able to fool the most cunning animals on the savannah.

'You do that well,' Joyce had to admit to the woman. 'For a New Yorker.'

Faith looked ready with a quick comeback, then realised Joyce was being sincere. 'Oh. Thanks. Uh, a little prayer to St Francis of Assisi does wonders. I –' Then she seemed to catch herself being equally sincere, and looked away. Joyce relished, in a cursory, immature way, snaring the other woman out like that.

When Philippa had said that she wanted Joyce 'ready' for her upon her return from the watch, she had no idea just how far the woman would take it.

And finding herself lying in their tent, stripped to her bra and knickers, gagged, wrists bound over her head with soft nylon utility rope to the main tentpole, could certainly qualify as 'far'.

Not that it kept her pussy, untouched and untouchable, from being stimulated enough to cry out for attention. In fact, she wasn't really bound anyway; she could pull the tentpole out of the ground easily if she had to, even if the resulting collapsing tent did alert the others, and spit out the knickers half in her mouth. But it was a test, Philippa had said. A test of devotion. Another test. She listened once more to the sounds outside, the animal noises, and the air in the enclosed tent heavy on her body. How much time had passed?

Feeling bold, deliciously bold, Joyce parted her thighs in the darkness, then slapped them together. If she lifted and crossed one leg over the other, her pussy was squeezed, and she could feel the wiry hairs of her bush, now damp with varying types of moisture, could imagine feeling the pink, wrinkled folds of her sex, dripping with the milky colour of its own dew. Her clit was there, but untouchable. Images and sensations danced and flirted and tantalised before her mind's eye, like the twisting, turning colours in a kaleidoscope. Philippa, birching her in the wilderness. Going down on each other. Receiving her collar –

'Joyce?'

Philippa's voice, soft, barely audible, outside the zipped door to the tent. Instinctively Joyce pushed her thighs together; thank God, Philippa's watch was over! At this rate, Joyce felt she'd have to make herself come just from wringing her own muscles!

The zipper of the tent door was slowly drawn up. Joyce's heart quickened further, as desire and excitement ran helter-skelter in her mind, not sure which choice would be preferable. Blind in the darkness, she listened as the figure half-crawled inside, breathing lightly, as the flap of the door was left to hang closed if unzipped, as if to let her make a quick getaway if the need arose. What was wrong? Was Philippa still on duty, perhaps, and couldn't wait! If so, she couldn't be any more impatient than Joyce felt now!

'Joyce,' she breathed again, her tone teasing. Hands reached out, slapped Joyce's shins to part them. A pair of lips suddenly enclosed around the big toe of Joyce's left foot, the tongue swirling around the base and up to the nail, the teeth nibbling, the mouth suckling. It sent thrilling little shivers running up Joyce's legs and making her gasp, then writhe as the mouth moved on to the other toes on the foot, the smaller the toe, the more sensitive it seemed. It was all she could do to keep from moaning aloud. When she did so, Philippa shushed her.

As Philippa's mouth reached Joyce's smallest toes, her hands were already scouting ahead, along the shins, towards the knees, drawing along sweat. Joyce shivered, regardless of the heat. Philippa's mouth followed, dropping ant trails of kisses and nibbles, even as Joyce parted her legs, her thighs, exposing her pussy, harsh and demanding, as if to spread her musk deeper into the tent.

But even as she did this, possessed as she was by mounting passion, Joyce realised that the head now worshipping her lower half was topped, not with a mane of silky hair, but by a short crop of sturdier hair. And the chin beneath those luscious lips on her legs was not sharp and narrow, but broad.

'Nina?' she mouthed from within her impromptu gag.

No answer.

No need.

Alarm rose within Joyce – oh, God, she was bound here, helpless! Well, perhaps not *helpless*. But if she made any noise, any attempt to resist, Philippa would be alerted in the darkness outside. Oh God, Nina, don't –

She considered kicking out, but huge hands were restraining her legs. She felt rather than saw the smile against her skin. The mouth travelled higher and higher; Joyce's clitoris began throbbing as the other woman reached the upper thighs.

Come on, come on, Joyce silently urged, get it over with and leave. Nina paused, smiling in the darkness, a cat toying with its prey, and began gently nibbling away, teasingly, tantalisingly close to Joyce's aching pussy, knowing what Joyce was waiting for. Joyce pushed her pussy up against the face. There would be time for recrimination later. Joyce could even pretend she didn't even realise it was Nina, if they were caught.

Nina parted Joyce's thighs further, shifted in place to drop a brief kiss on her woolly delta, and trailed her tongue along her clitoris. Joyce sighed with immense satisfaction and mounting longing. Exquisite! *Exquisite!* Nina's tongue continued its long, teasing course, painting the outline of Joyce's open, throbbing sex.

Joyce was very aware of her dew trickling from her pussy to

cover Nina's face. She imagined the taste of herself on Nina's lips, and felt dizzy from the sheer pleasure. The world beyond Nina's tongue and her own sensations seemed both a distant, ignorable thing, yet also acutely perceptible, her senses hyper-charged.

Nina's face pushed further into the space at the top of Joyce's thighs; Joyce could feel the once-more-familiar bumps of the woman's ears, her warm, bony cheeks and chin, the stumpiness of her nose, the heat of her breath. Then suddenly, Nina's tongue teased no longer, entering Joyce's slippery, receptive vagina, the penetration making Joyce bite her lip to keep from crying out even inside her gag. Nina's nose nuzzled at Joyce's clitoris, tormenting it simultaneously.

Joyce's mouth had dried, and her breathing became ragged, staccato through her nostrils, punctuated with muffled gasps, as Nina's tongue expertly moved in time to the throbs its ministrations produced in its prey. On and on, unrelenting, Joyce's buttocks rising from the sleeping bag, rising and falling to the rhythm of the thrusting tongue.

The woman brought her to a shuddering climax, making Joyce tighten her sweaty thighs around the woman's head, refusing release, wanting to keep her there for ever.

And Nina seemed ready, willing and able to oblige, continuing around, drawing together the afterwaves of orgasm to form another. Then another. Somewhere along the way, Joyce lost all feeling in her lower half, and let her legs collapse.

She closed her eyes and felt her mouth curl into a smile of supreme contentment. And with that, a sobering awareness of what had just happened.

Movement at her feet – Nina was manoeuvring about: leaving.

Suddenly, the moment of rapture curdled.

THIRTEEN

Philippa returned to the tent an eternity later, drawing the knickers from Joyce's mouth, kissing her and whispering lovely things to Joyce. Joyce barely heard, so suffused was she by shame at having given in to Nina's seduction. Shame . . . and still-mounting desire, sated yet insatiable.

It was agreed from the start of the trek that consequent watches would be taken up by tentmates, to minimise disruption. But Philippa made no immediate attempt to untie Joyce's wrists, lying down clothed beside her and kissing, long and deep, chewing Joyce's lips, sucking her tongue, relishing her mouth, delighting in the taste of her.

Joyce didn't want to feel so wonderful again, didn't believe she deserved it after her surrender, not that long ago, to that bitch Nina. But still she found herself breathless, kissing back with equal fervour, feeling Philippa's hot body against her cooler, near-naked one, feeling Philippa smiling into her mouth.

Her hand snaked down, brushing agonisingly over Joyce's breasts while the other slid under Joyce's lower back, as if she might escape her clutches. Joyce's head arched back into the by now dishevelled sleeping bag under her in anticipation of Philippa touching her breasts some more. But the woman moved straight to her pussy, searching Joyce's mound with strong movements.

For a cold heartbeat Joyce thought that somehow, however irrationally, there would be physical evidence of her earlier infidelity.

But if there was, Philippa made no reaction. Joyce gasped with pleasure as Philippa's fingers moved into her soaking pussy, gripping on to Joyce as she plunged them into the bound woman. Joyce almost came with that first thrust, she was that close. It was so electric, a slow electric burning building as Philippa's fingers moved within her. She gripped Joyce tightly, sapping any meagre control Joyce might have had left as she was steadily, relentlessly pleasured.

Her guilt was now comatose; she concentrated on prolonging the sensation, prolonging the pleasure. She tried; she really tried. But the intensity was too immense, and she began to shake and cry out. Philippa clamped her mouth on to Joyce's to keep the noise to a minimum and possibly alert the others needlessly. Joyce exploded, one orgasm following another, Philippa clinging to her as they crashed over Joyce in rapid succession, her fingers never ceasing, wringing more and more from her captive lover.

Joyce thought she lost consciousness. She certainly lost awareness, so numbed was she in body and mind, not feeling Philippa lying silently beside her, stroking her hair, untying her wrists – perhaps even helping her dress for her overdue watch.

The sky outside was like a canvas of deep black, broken only by the small fire near the camp centre, flaring only with the odd hush of breeze and spitting sparks into the dark. The air was filled with sounds: animals and insects and rustlings that would certainly keep her awake. Joyce sat cross-legged close to it, the rifle cradled on her lap, and fed sticks into the fire, staring into it like some shaman seeking divine guidance. Zebaki sat nearby, ever-faithful, ever-attentive; she doubted if she could survive out there without this handsome dog nearby.

She had sworn to be faithful to Philippa. She hadn't been. Never mind her earlier, libido-fuelled excuses about the pitiful bonds and gag, about not wanting to alert the others by making a noise. Never mind any mealy-mouthed attempts at blaming Philippa for leaving Joyce in such a state for so long.

But now what?

The answer came surprisingly easily to her: say and do nothing. It was too late anyway, and time would make such an admission all the more difficult. And any claims Nina might make in the morning would be dismissed as hot air. Yes, she had the expected problems covered.

She amazed herself by her capacity for practical duplicity.

'I'm gonna make my own film,' Nina was announcing again around breakfast. 'Or set up my own theatre group, with lots of nubile young actresses looking for personal instruction.' She chuckled to herself, then pointed to Faith. 'And what are you gonna do with *your* share?'

It was an old game by now, but it was still played, albeit some with a boredom that made them change their previous answers.

Such as Faith. 'I'm gonna give all mine to the local KKK. But only if they make me their Grand High Exalted Poobah.'

Philippa shrugged, staring at Joyce. 'There's a Monet I've had my eye on for quite a while.'

Kimya cradled her canteen, stared into it. 'I have nieces and nephews. I'm going to give them the best.'

Ruth nodded at Kimya's serious, unchanging response. 'I'm returning to university. Archaeology was my first love –'

'Oh?' Nina crooned. 'That's not what you told me.'

Ruth ignored her. 'I spent a summer going over an excavation site west of Dimona, back in Israel, when I was a teenager. I never got over that.' She smiled to herself. 'I guess I'm most looking forward to seeing the Hidden City on Baridi. I know it's already been checked out, but to walk on the ancient pavements –'

'*Boring*,' Nina crooned, able to spoil any moment with a minimum of effort. 'What about you, Joyful?'

'I don't know.' Joyce tried to catch Ruth's eye, tried to share with her some empathy with the woman. But all she got back was coldness.

They found themselves in an area of the savannah where domed, striped bitumen mountains and soft rust hills sprouting tufts of white flowers and hardy green grass dominated the view in all directions. Stripes of wispy white draped high in the sky like jet trails, auguring thicker, lower, darker clouds following behind.

'The storms,' Kimya noted that morning around the dying campfire, 'are almost upon us.'

'Good,' Nina huffed, rising and stretching. 'Could do with a break from the heat.' Then she chuckled. 'Of course, the nights are cold. It's good to have someone with you, isn't it, Joy-Joy?'

Joyce ignored her. Faith was joking privately with Kimya now as they gathered the breakfast rubbish, and Philippa was checking one of her horse's hooves. And Ruth –

Ruth was staring intently at Joyce, much of her expression unreadable.

But of course, it would have been most unlikely that Nina could have disappeared from Ruth's and her tent to visit Joyce, without Ruth knowing about it. Perhaps Nina even boasted about it.

Joyce recalled the casual way that the Israeli woman dealt with those huge drunken men at the Stomping Grounds club in London. Recalled how Ruth managed to knock down all the tin cups with her rifle, from a hundred metres away without wasting a shot, during the practice at Mzuri before starting the trek.

And now the confidence she'd bolstered herself with from last night seemed to evaporate.

It hadn't taken Joyce long to conclude that even after independence for Mahali, dust would still be king here. Without grass and undergrowth woven into the ground, dust devils swirled at the slightest breeze. Joyce made it a habit to keep her lip balm and skin moisturiser close at hand in her jacket.

Dust and deception were its queen. She kept up a positive face with Philippa, chatting and joking as best she could. Sometimes, she even forgot to ignore Nina, forgot to ignore Ruth, riding behind her, forgot to keep checking to see if the other woman was staring at her again.

When they stopped for midday meal and rest, in a shallow gully surrounded by small slopes that blocked the view all around,

Kimya made a perch on top of one of the slopes, scanning the area with her field glasses. No one spoke about her increased alertness, no doubt borne of natural, reasonable caution the further they rode from civilisation.

She skirted down the slope to join the others. 'Ruth, I want you to scout ahead, north, through those gullies we saw before stopping.' Ruth nodded silently and moved to her horse as Kimya continued, 'And I want someone with you as well.'

Faith nodded and rose from her squatting position. 'I'll go –'

'No,' Ruth interrupted coolly. 'Joyce will come with me.'

No one said anything. Then, 'What, let you two go off alone?' Nina teased, sidling over to Joyce and putting an arm around her. 'Can you two be trusted?'

Joyce pulled out of the shorter woman's grasp, as Philippa snapped, 'What did I tell you before? She doesn't want you touching her!'

'Oh, I wouldn't be so sure about that.'

Now Faith stepped to the centre of the group. 'Would you three stop with the fricking dyke soap-opera theatrics? It's getting on my tits!'

But Nina continued, looking at Joyce again while speaking to Philippa. 'She didn't say anything last night while you were on guard –'

'*Enough!*'

It was Ruth, astride her horse, one hand on the reins, the other clutching the sling of the rifle across one shoulder. It was the loudest Joyce could remember the woman ever speaking, and the single word was sharp and unexpected enough to make the others give pause, to forget the heat and riding and exhaustion and disturbed sleep of the last four days.

Kimya stepped in, taking advantage of the moment. 'Joyce, get going with Ruth; I want you both back in an hour. The rest of you can get lunch ready.' Then she turned and ascended the slope again.

Nina and Faith walked away, in separate directions. Joyce turned to go, but Philippa caught her arm, stared silently, intensely at her, the question not asked with words.

Joyce felt Philippa's collar around her neck tighten somehow, and her reply was almost a whisper. 'No. She's lying.'

Philippa held on to her a moment longer, then nodded slightly and released her, her expression lightened. A little. 'Fine, then.'

The gullies were like a maze, with the flanking slopes sometimes smooth and shallow, other times steep and rocky. Occasionally the women would guide their horses to the top of one slope, to regain their bearings, but mostly Ruth kept them in the gullies, as if to ensure they weren't seen.

It was hot; Ruth didn't complain, though. Perhaps she survived on the same chilly reception she was now giving Joyce.

But perhaps Joyce was being overly sensitive, because of her guilt; the woman was focused on scouting. Maybe, just maybe, her silent glare ahead and tense arms bound by muscle and will to the rein and the sling of the rifle had nothing to do with what had happened between Joyce and Nina the night before. Ruth might not even know about it.

Yeah, right, as Faith might say.

Joyce glanced behind them, wondering what this gully would look like during the rainy season; how far would the water rise?

'Something wrong?' It was the first direct thing Ruth had said to her since they started out.

'What? Oh, no.'

Ruth never took her eyes off the gully ahead. 'You seem afraid for some reason.'

'I'm not,' Joyce lied.

Silence.

Joyce hated the silence now; perhaps Ruth had been looking to break the tension with that question? 'So . . . you were a body-guard in Hollywood before all this. That must be an exciting life.'

No reply.

'Any interesting stories?'

'No.'

So much for breaking the tension.

'Did you enjoy last night?' Ruth asked.

Joyce's voice failed her.

After a moment, Ruth added, 'I don't mind.'

She wasn't very convincing. Joyce's mind and stomach were helter-skeltering, as if she'd been kicked out of her saddle. She looked around her, watching as they found the gully they were in joined by another to form a wider, deeper ravine.

She felt trapped here, alone. 'So, it really doesn't bother you?'

A pause. 'I didn't say that.'

Birds flew overhead, uncaring.

Ruth muttered, 'Forgive her.'

Joyce looked to her. 'Pardon?'

Ruth was breathing heavily; was she fighting back tears? 'She's funny, talented, warm, loving. I'm lucky she gives me the time of day, let alone . . . It's easy to forgive her when she . . . teases.'

Not so easy, Joyce thought. 'Can you forgive *me*?'

Ruth straightened up in the saddle. 'Yes. For your mother's sake. For what she did.'

'My mother? What did she do?'

'Nina and she met in California, not long after the American network cancelled Nina's show and bought out her contract. She –' Ruth's face grew even more taut, like a bandage immobilising a broken limb, and every breath now sounded almost painful, every word emerging sharpened by the memories. 'Do you know how close Nina had been to suicide, in those days?'

Gutted that such a question could be asked about a jocund character as Nina Hoskins, Joyce could only shake her head No.

Ruth's rifle was in her hands more quickly than Joyce could have imagined, the barrel pointing up and near Ruth's head, the finger never far from the trigger. '*This* close.'

Joyce's breath quickened, though paradoxically her heart seemed to have stopped. She didn't know what alarmed her more, the sight of the gun in Ruth's hands, next to her, after all the hurt Joyce had caused her, however inadvertently, or the idea that the gun could have been a tool of suicide for someone she knew. She decided it was the latter; if someone with a seemingly endless font of merriment as Nina could fall that far into despair, could anyone else feel secure about themselves? 'And my mother talked her out of it?'

Ruth lowered the rifle barrel to point at the ground, measurably calming Joyce down. 'I don't know what was said – Nina's not ready to talk about it to me yet, if she ever will be ready – but whatever it was, it was enough. She inspired Nina to work the comedy circuit in Europe, Australia, arranged auditions. She saved the woman's life.'

The tautness in her voice and expression had lessened further, relaxing Joyce as well; nothing untoward would happen now between them, she was certain. It gave her the courage to comment, 'She may have had a rough time in the past, Ruth, but you're still bothered by what she . . . does. You owe it to both of you to bring it out into the open.'

'I serve Nina. As you serve Philippa.'

'I don't –'

Cracks, sharp and distant. Ruth wheeled her horse to face the way they came, rifle cradled in both hands. Then, the sound of thunder.

'A storm,' Joyce guessed.

'No. Gunshots. And . . .' The thunder was steady. Growing like an approaching wave.

Now Ruth whirled back. 'Get riding, quickly! Out of the gully!'

'What –'

'*Do it!*' And she was off. After a moment, Joyce brought Shohan into a gallop to catch up with the other woman.

It wasn't until she was almost beside Ruth that she looked behind them again, and saw the stampede: scores of twist-horned antelopes, chestnut-hued as if having sprung from the ground itself to attack the trespassers on this land. They were tightly packed, snorting with exertion and panic, their hundreds of beating hooves the turbulent storm she'd heard before. They kept pace in the winding, deep gully with the women on horseback.

Or not on horseback, in Joyce's case, from the way she was bouncing about in the saddle, desperate for something more substantial to hang on to than the stirrups around her feet or the reins in her hands. Stopping was out of the question; the antelopes were smaller than horses, at Joyce's height with the horns. But so many of them would still quite easily trample over both women. And while they might manage to climb the slopes on either side of them now, they were still steep enough to force them to slow down . . . and if they fell off their horses . . .

Ruth shouted something at her, but Joyce didn't hear it, too absorbed was she by so much else, including the pounding of the herd – and her heart. Then she saw the woman pointing to a slope on their right ahead, a slope low and easy, and certainly better as an escape route than anything they'd seen so far.

Suddenly (as if such a word had any more meaning, things had moved so quickly and unexpectedly in the last minute or two) Joyce felt Shohan taking her up that very slope alongside Ruth, without being guided by Joyce, at least, not consciously.

Something took her out of the saddle to stumble first to her feet, then hands and knees, as the stampede continued, sounding so loud she feared they would follow the herd instinct up the low slope. When she wasn't trampled to death, she assumed they were continuing on their way.

Ruth was at her side now, arms around her. 'Are you OK?'

Joyce gasped. 'I hurt in places I never knew I had.'

'Good. At least we're both alive to hurt.' She coughed in the cloud of dust rising from the gully.

'So,' Joyce panted, the rush of excitement only now being felt after the fear, 'I guess I did have reason to be afraid back there!'

Ruth stared at her for a moment. And then she began to giggle. And laugh. Joyce followed, exhilaration at their near-miss with death making her feel more alive than she had in days. Her nipples were hard, pointed, inside her bra: amazing.

Ruth struggled to control her laughter, forcing out, 'Damn! Missed my chance to make it look like an accident!'

The joke sent Joyce into another fit of laughter – stopped only when Ruth drew close and kissed her. Their lips met; it took only a heartbeat for Joyce to begin pressing back, opening, tongues entwining. Ruth reached around and clutched one of Joyce's cheeks through her trousers, squeezing roughly.

Their bodies carried them to the ground, a patch of long, dry, carpety grass that looked soft but felt rough – not that it mattered.

Joyce reached up between them and kneaded Ruth's breasts through her dirty, dust-covered T-shirt. Ruth, her mouth still glued to Joyce's, moaned almost painfully at the contact, slowly grinding her pelvis on to Joyce's thigh, her bootheels digging into one of Joyce's shins, as Joyce reached up and drew Ruth's shirt up over her head, their mouths parting to accommodate the action.

Ruth sat up on Joyce; Joyce gripped her by her sides, staring hungrily up at her. The woman's sleek, lithe appearance was betrayed by her round, ample breasts, but Joyce was more drawn to the gallery of skinwork around them. Closer now, Joyce caught better glimpses of them: Celtic chains and Hebrew letters unwrapping themselves from her arms to the outer sides of her breasts, the butterfly on the right breast itself, perched on her nipple.

Joyce couldn't help but stare; her fingers couldn't help but work at the tab to Ruth's trousers, either. After a moment's silent agreement, Ruth rolled off her to help remove their clothing, with almost frantic motions, casting them about like shreds of a blanket. Once they were naked, Ruth was on top of her again, her gaze fixed, like a cobra's, her hand snaking down to Joyce's pubic mound, probing between the labia. Joyce shuddered and cried out, squirming beneath Ruth as the woman found the source of Joyce's desire, massaging it further before she withdrew her fingers, taking with her webstrands of dew, unmistakable signs of lust.

Ruth practically collapsed on to Joyce once more as their mouths fought with each other, Ruth digging her nails into Joyce's back, shoulders and breasts, enjoying the reaction she invoked in the woman beneath her. Joyce's breath caught as the other woman's eyes and hands roamed over her, cupping one of her breasts, squeezing appreciatively, before bowing and engulfing the nipple, sucking gently, then fiercely biting. Joyce moaned, biting her lip under the attendance.

Then Ruth chuckled softly. 'Are you gonna be selfish?'

Joyce couldn't speak, but knew what was expected, and with her excitement mounting, shook her head weakly. Ruth quickly flipped over and on top of Joyce, her thighs on either side of her head. Then Ruth's tongue continued where her fingers had started, and Joyce's ecstasy multiplied. Joyce opened her eyes and looked up at Ruth's bush, and beneath it, the sex, open for her: a delicious pocket of sculpted skin with a deep pink inner lining, moist with milky dew, her clit protruding from the folds of flesh encasing it.

Drinking in the musky aroma, Joyce reached up and eagerly spread the fleshy pink outer labia further, then the darker inner fold of flesh, exposing more of the hard bud of her clitoris and the deep, dark, moist channel of her vagina. And when Joyce's tongue snaked into that tight, velvety burrow, finding a sweet, succulent taste – a contrast to the harsh, salty demeanour Ruth tried to exude – Ruth clamped on to the sides of Joyce's head with her sweat-beaded thighs, demanding more.

And Joyce obliged, relishing the writhing and moaning that overcame Ruth as Joyce's veneration grew bolder, more frantic, Ruth's juices covering her face, mixing with the dust and sweat already there. Finally Ruth was bucking on to Joyce's face, and Joyce could feel the woman's muscles contract against her, again and again, her breath escaping in short, sharp yelps, between her own treatment of Joyce. They both squirmed and sighed into each other as their climaxes finally arrived, the circuit complete. They were alive, had cheated death, feeling the adrenalin rush through their bodies like desire – and now that had to be expelled from them.

Afterwards, they lay clasped in each other's arms, raining strings of kisses over each other, tasting themselves and each other. Finally Ruth rose and reached for her clothes. 'We have to get out of here; the sun'll bake us.'

'The sun. And the others; they'll be expecting us back by now.' She sat up, gathering her strength once more, feeling parched. 'What're we going to do? Say?'

Ruth slipped into her boots. 'Tell them the truth: someone was shooting on the savannah, and set those antelope on a stampede.'

'Shooting?'

'Of course.' Ruth buttoned up her shirt. 'I heard the rifle reports beforehand.'

Joyce paused, breathed in deeply. 'Who?'

'Poachers, probably. They'll most likely want to avoid us. On the other hand, they may think six women on their own could be an easy target for . . . robbery.'

There was more, but it was left unsaid.

FOURTEEN

The oryx stood on the hot, dry lakebed, patient and immobile, as if mad. Or petrified, like the strange, alien bicarbonate spires around it, spires designating dead springs, like grave markers. The oryx was a large, scimitar-horned antelope of striped face, dun body and black underbelly. And, according to Kimya, ideally suited to the current weather, the last gasp of heat before the rains: other creatures' brains would have boiled by now, but the oryx had a special network of fine blood vessels in its nostrils, cooling the blood before it reached the brain.

Lucky bugger.

The party was in a strip of barren land that didn't seem to make even a pretence at being lush. The heat was near-unbearable, the air even worse when the frequent wind whipped the loose feather-brown dust from the ground into devils to persecute the travellers and their horses. And the insects . . .

A slap, and then a muffled, 'Goddamn bugs!'

The party lay flat on an incline overlooking the lakebed. The slap and curse inevitably came naturally from Nina. The response inevitably came from Kimya. 'Shush. They can hear us.'

'Don't tell me to fricking shush!' Nina snarled. But she did keep low and quiet, not wishing to miss what the African woman promised them, what all considered worth lying out here to see.

And they weren't disappointed. The lionesses attacked again, the oryx suddenly breaking from his inert stance to dodge and weave away from them. The pride moved in uncanny organisation, but they seemed unsure, or weak, or something. Or were they just playing with the oryx, the way a domestic cat will toy with a caught bird or mouse – before killing it?

Joyce didn't feel like asking why. She'd kept silent since Ruth and she returned to the others that afternoon, hoping their infidelity didn't show on them. Fortunately, the business with the poachers occupied everyone for most of midday, though they never saw or heard from them again. And then they came upon this sight. Magnificent. Frightening.

Beside her, Philippa reached out and squeezed one of Joyce's cheeks through her trousers. Joyce once more felt the miasma of emotions rise within her: desire, guilt, anger, anxiety. Philippa demanded – and deserved, Joyce guiltily admitted to herself – loyalty as well as subservience in her lovers. And she was perceptive; how long would it be before she divined what had happened today between Joyce and Ruth?

'Such *mishigas*,' Ruth whispered. 'How long will they keep that up?'

'Until nightfall,' Kimya replied, shifting as if to glance over her shoulder at the setting sun. 'Under moonlight, the pride will bring her down. By midday tomorrow, the pride will have taken its fill of the carcass, leaving what's left for the rest of the animals: vultures, hyenas . . .'

The oryx made a plaintive cry, as if protesting in vain at how its life was soon to end, or perhaps even a plea to the women on the hill. A part of Joyce wanted to help, of course, as she'd wanted to help in similar situations she'd witnessed since the start of this trek. But she understood: some things must run their natural course.

She twisted and crawled her way back down the incline towards their camp, no longer wishing to witness the natural course.

The camp was in an area at the edge of the dry lakebed, with the ubiquitous baobob surrounding four round, whitewashed, thatch-capped huts, sandblasted but still habitable for nomads. Any nomads.

The fire in the centre of camp cast a dense pall in the surrounding area. And stank as a fire made out of cattle dung is wont to do. But it would protect them from the tireless assaults of the mosquitoes far more effectively than their dwindling supply of sprays. Kimya noted that the locals would also coat themselves with ash from such pungent fires.

But Joyce couldn't see herself going that far.

In fact, in Philippa's and her chosen hut for the evening, cut off from the outside with the makeshift blanket door, Joyce couldn't see much of anything. The blindfold over her eyes – her own panties from today – cut her off from any remaining light.

But her other senses were sharp, focused: the feel of the ground beneath her shins and feet as she kneeled there, naked, her wrists bound behind her. The touch of the still, heavy air on her body, a blanket rather than the more-welcome cooling caress of a breeze from her outdoor adventures. The smell of the fire outside, and the closer, more intimate scent of her own sex from her panties. The taste of the air on her lips, her desire on her tongue. The sound of Philippa's boots on the dirt floor as she slowly circled Joyce.

And the voice . . . oh, that woman's voice, like the honey from her own pussy, slow and deliberate and oh-so-delicious. 'Ah, my little slave . . . how luscious you appear to me like this. Bound, submissive, ready to serve my every need.' A pause, also slow and deliberate and oh-so-delicious. 'You *are* ready to serve my every need, aren't you?'

Joyce tried to speak, found her mouth had dried with anticipation, then wet her lips. 'Y–yes, Ms Sheringham.'

'I hope so. Are you wet, then?'

Joyce felt the sweat bead down the curves of her breasts, slow-motion rivulets arcing away from her nipples at the last minute, as if responding to her quickened pulse. 'Yes, Ms Sheringham.'

'Then say it. Say it in colourful, graphic detail. Use the rudest words you can imagine.'

Joyce breathed again, closed her eyes behind her makeshift

blindfold. 'M–my . . . cunt is wet . . . it's throbbing . . . my clit feels full, standing up from the top of my pussy –'

'Part your knees further.'

Joyce breathed in once more and obeyed, shifting in place; her knees had already been separate, but this further separation opened her pussy to the still air even more now; her pussy lips smacked open with sweat and lubrication. Her head spun, and for a moment, she thought she might topple over.

Philippa was behind her again; the hairs on the back of Joyce's neck rose. 'I didn't say stop talking.'

'No, Ms Sheringham. Sorry, Ms Sheringham.' Joyce swallowed again, sought more words. But it was so difficult – and so revealing, to have to voice it all. 'I – I so want to come. My cunt is hungry, hungry for your fingers, for your tongue and lips –'

'For my cock, too?' Philippa teased.

Joyce shuddered, recalling the dildo her mistress and lover used so well on her. 'Yes, Ms Sheringham.'

'Tell me more about it, about what you want from it.'

Joyce's head spun again, as if unable to keep up with Philippa's constant orbit of her. 'I want your cock to fill up my cunt. I want your cock to pump into my cunt until I come.' A part of her detached itself and listened, marvelling at how colourful she had become. And she enjoyed it, too. Oh God, how she enjoyed describing aloud how she felt!

And from Philippa's chuckling, the other woman seemed to relish it, too. 'Dirty bitch. Are you *really* that wet?'

Joyce's head nodded of its own accord, and her voice seemed likewise independent. 'Y–yes, Ms Sheringham, yes!'

Suddenly Philippa was kneeling behind her, pressing her clothed body up against Joyce's naked back and bound arms, and she hissed in the other woman's ear, '*Prove it to me!*'

And without waiting for Joyce to ask how, Philippa's arms snaked around to Joyce's front, one hand rising up to cup one of Joyce's breasts, the other to snake down into Joyce's bush, through the matted pubic hairs to her sensitive mound.

Joyce moaned.

'Quiet,' Philippa hissed in her ear, punctuating her order with a lick of Joyce's outer lobe.

Joyce shuddered at her Mistress's touch, how it boldly, lewdly traced along her tortured, sensitive outline. She pushed back, her bound hands feverishly trying to clasp on to Philippa, wanting to touch her, caress her, even hurt her, just to give the woman a taste of the intensity that Joyce was feeling now.

Philippa's middle finger extended, slid just beneath the surface of Joyce's pussy lips, to glide along the slick inner surface. Joyce drew in sharp breaths, her head tilting this way and that. God, her whole body was pulsing and throbbing!

Philippa clutched on to her tightly now, pushing her finger further and further inside: squirming, probing. Joyce arched her head back and let her mouth saucer, as she rocked to the other woman's touch.

Philippa's hiss had become a low growl. 'You like my finger inside your cunt, don't you?'

'Oh God – Oh God –'

'She can't help you out here. Only I can.'

And with that, Philippa withdrew her finger, her arms, her very presence, as quickly as she had produced it.

The absence left Joyce reeling, her head spinning, her pussy screaming for relief. She was close, so *close*! How could Philippa, how could any woman, do that to her? Low moaning sounds escaped her lips, and she only half-heard Philippa rise and step before her, only half-heard the woman approach again and breathe, 'You need to come. Here's your chance.'

Joyce frowned beneath her blindfold, wondered what Philippa meant. Then she felt Philippa's boot, her trousered shin, slide in between Joyce's parted legs.

Joyce understood. Understood how degrading it would look. And how exciting. And with an ease that would surprise her later, she manoeuvred herself on to Philippa's boot, clasping the rough leather and bootlace between her legs, and clamped her thighs about the leg.

And she began to hump Philippa's leg. She began to hump her

Mistress's leg like the devoted bitch in heat that she was. It was scant relief for Joyce's aching sex, but it would suffice for now.

'That's it,' Philippa was saying above her. 'That's it, my little slave. My little, *unfaithful* slave.'

Amazing: even in the throes of an approaching orgasm, how one word could still make her pause, and look up (pointlessly, given the blindfold). 'W-what –'

'You heard,' Philippa said simply. 'Did you think I wouldn't find out somehow?'

'I – I don't –'

'Don't try denying it. She could hardly keep her mouth shut about it when we talked.'

Her mind still reeling, Joyce fought to regain some mental balance. 'I – uh, Philippa . . . we were swept up, from the stampede . . .'

'*What?*'

Joyce blinked as the blindfold was removed. It was dark in the hut, bare but for their equipment and supplies. Philippa stood there, her outer shirt removed to reveal her breasts in their immaculate white bra, her tanned roseate arms and shoulders and stomach. And her face, redder now. 'Ruth? You fucked *Ruth* as well as *Nina*?'

Joyce's stomach plummeted like a lift severed from its cables. Philippa had been talking about the incident in the tent the other night with Nina, not about today's incident with Ruth. And now Joyce had inadvertently given the game away about the latter. 'Philippa –'

'You *slut*! So not only do you betray my trust in you with Nina, but you have her toy, as well?'

Panic welled up like a geyser inside Joyce, and she slid herself away from the trembling Philippa. It was desperation that made her blurt out, 'It's not true! Nina was lying to you again!'

'I doubt it. She was able to describe how I'd left you, how you were tied up. So, either you told her all that the next day – which is unlikely – or she *was* with you. And you fucked her.'

'I didn't – she took advantage of me –'

'Those weren't manacles on you, or iron gags! You could have resisted. *If* you wanted to, that is!'

Joyce started to deny this, then held back. Because the woman was absolutely right. There was no real excuse to be had. She sank deeper into herself, her bound, naked, submissive posture somehow accentuated with her defeat. 'Philippa, I'm – I'm sorry –'

'You've been very, very bad. I'm never going to be able to forgive you.'

The declaration, even if spoken in righteous anger, nevertheless somehow galvanised Joyce's dwindling self-respect, making her recall Rhonda's words from a lifetime ago in London: *I'm sorry. But I'm not that sorry.* 'Look, Philippa, I'm sorry –'

'You're more than sorry. You're sad. A sad, pathetic creature, unworthy of my life, my love.'

'Now *look* –'

Then Philippa moved towards her, and for a brief, panicky moment, Joyce thought the woman would physically attack her. Instead she was untying Joyce's hands from behind her. 'Your mother had her faults. But at least she remained faithful to her lovers. You obviously didn't inherit her maturity.'

Joyce pulled her arms before her, rubbing her wrists, trying to suppress the tingling sensations running through her arms. 'That's not fair –'

But Philippa turned away, began lifting up bags. Joyce's bags. And flinging them through the curtain door to the outside. 'Get out.'

'What?'

'Get out. I won't have you sleeping near me tonight.'

The absurdity of the notion nearly drew an inappropriate burst of laughter from Joyce. 'This isn't London or Berlin! Where do you expect me to go?'

'That's your problem, not mine!' And with that, she threw out Joyce's clothes, the ones she'd removed not long ago, then threw out her sleeping bag. And once that was done, she held open the curtain door – for Joyce to walk through.

Absurdity turned to anger. Yes, Philippa had a right to be furious. But this was beyond the pale! 'You can't do this –'

'Was my love too much to handle for you? Like all other challenges life has thrown you?'

That stung. Joyce swallowed, and that's where her anger got the better of her. For a moment, her mouth went taut. Then, with agonising slowness, she breathed, 'Go to hell.'

Philippa shook the parted curtain against her outstretched arm. 'You first.'

After another agonising moment, Joyce reached up, removed the collar, flung it to the ground at Philippa's feet, and stormed naked out into the open and sought out her discarded clothes. It was twilight, and everyone was in their huts, ready to get an early start tomorrow, in order to make the old army camp in twenty-four hours' time. The air stank and she tasted ash in her mouth – or was that just the result of her argument?

Joyce had dropped to the ground to put on her boots, when she realised that Faith, on first sentry duty with Zebaki, was sitting by the fire – having watched the scene, watched Joyce dress herself. She squatted on a fallen baobob log, cigarette dangling between two fingers on one hand.

Joyce glared at her – then felt her glare dissolve, as if melted away by the fire. Once her boots were back on her feet, she lifted up her other bags and carried them over to the fire, trying to ignore the heat and the smell.

Faith stared into the flames, the rifle resting on her lap, her face glistening, in the fire's reflected light. She offered the smoke to Joyce, who almost declined. But then reconsidered. Faith could just as easily have offered whisky or cocaine or hemlock or a tattoo; Joyce just needed something to take her mind off what had just happened. She held the hand-made smoke between thumb and forefinger, dragged on it – and began choking.

Faith retrieved it, as if afraid Joyce might drop it in the fire. 'Sorry, should have warned you. Thought you realised though.'

'It –' She coughed, then coughed again. 'It tastes –'

'It's not all tobacco.' She was clad in stone trousers, dust-covered boots and a black sleeveless vest that displayed sturdy, muscular arms. She took another drag, tilted her head, as if to listen to the crackling of the fire or the animal sounds in the distance.

Joyce stopped trying to talk further, just focused on letting her lungs clear as best they could under the circumstances, then settled forward, like Faith, both staring into the fire like a pair of cavemen.

The silence between them, like the smoke and smell, was uncomfortable. Then Faith said, 'You can bunk with me tonight. Kimya takes over after me, and she can sleep with Philippa.' She grunted. 'I mean, sleep in the same hut as Philippa –'

'I know what you mean.' Joyce's voice was more harsh than she would have preferred, despite the chagrin she was feeling, and she quickly added, 'Sorry.'

Faith shrugged. Then, after a while, she leaned back, as if to fight an ache in her spine, yawned and smacked her lips. 'It's not easy, is it?'

'What?'

'It's not easy, giving your heart over to someone. Someone who might throw it away, or squeeze it so hard it breaks.'

Joyce stared at the younger woman, waiting for the inevitable quip, the smirk, the display of contempt she obviously felt for the submissive role Joyce had played in her relationship with Philippa.

But none was forthcoming. Faith was merely making an observation. Perhaps she was even trying to show some appreciation of Joyce's difficulties. 'No. It's not easy.'

'Definitely a risk,' Faith agreed, taking another slow drag. 'Take the word of a professional risk-taker.' Perhaps it was whatever was in the smoke, but now the woman seemed to take on a contemplative, almost philosophical look in her expression. 'I know *I* couldn't take it.' Then she chuckled, as if at a private joke.

Joyce stared at her. 'No? What about you and my mother?'

Faith's expression grew taut now, more melancholy. 'That was . . . different.'

'How so?'

Faith stared back, her eyes narrowing, as if having trouble seeing Joyce in the dwindling light of the sky and the fire. 'Are you happy?'

'Happy?'

179

Faith nodded towards Philippa's hut. 'Happy being – her plaything?'

Joyce wasn't so naïve as to have not noticed Faith avoiding the subject of Constance and herself. And while she almost reflexively protested Faith's use of the term 'plaything', she had to admit – at least, to herself – that it was true. Well, partly true, anyway.

Mostly true. 'Maybe I am. Why?'

Faith shrugged. 'You didn't strike me as the submissive type. Now, I *know* Ruth. She's tough, smart, fearless – but she enjoys abandoning the burden of responsibility for being all that, for a few hours of letting someone else call the shots. That, and being submissive makes her come like a jackhammer.'

'Really?' Joyce quipped dryly, recalling what the Israeli woman was like today on the dry riverbed. But was that an aberration for her, a genuine response to the near-death experience?

'Oh, yeah. You forget, we've known each other for years, through Constance.'

Joyce nodded to herself; she lifted the canteen resting at Faith's right foot, uncapping and drinking lightly from it, wondering just how well the woman had known the others. 'And you think you know what *I* like after knowing me only a few days?'

Faith made a pouty face of comical, exaggerated concession. 'Maybe you're right. I've been wrong about you a couple of times already; why not about this, too?'

Now Joyce smiled, a genuine, warm smile. 'The incomparable Faith Ballard, admitting she's wrong . . . Whatever next?'

On cue, Faith pointed towards the sky. 'Look, a pig!'

Both women laughed, leaving themselves in a silence, but an easier, more companionable silence this time.

Sometime during the night, Joyce awoke in a cold sweat. Her breathing was loud in her ears, so loud it should have woken her hutmate Faith. But the woman lay curled beneath her sleeping bag top, sleeping the sleep of the just, with none of her cocky, dynamic energy discernible.

Joyce tried to remember what her dream had been about. After all, there had to have been a dream, right? You don't bolt out of a dead sleep after a day's horseback ride and emotional upheaval, unless you've been dreaming something pretty bad.

But for the life of her, she couldn't remember it. She closed her eyes and tried to conjure an image out of the enforced darkness. Nothing happened.

Sighing, she lowered herself down again, acutely aware of how alone she was, Faith's presence notwithstanding. Go to sleep again, you silly bitch, she insisted silently. You have another long day ahead of you. Philippa can't be here now to hold you, keep you close.

Philippa. She missed Philippa. Missed the woman's eyes, her hair, her smell. Missed her voice, her laugh. Missed the touch of her hands on Joyce's body. Missed her sweet, potent domination.

Oh God . . .

A sensation as cruel as a trickle of ice water made its horribly cold and deliberate journey down the middle of her back. What had she done? What had she thrown away? She felt the rise of fear and anguish at the thought of never again being with Philippa, never again touching her . . . fucking her . . . rise from the pit of her stomach to her throat, constricting it, before slamming down again into her gut like the hammer of doom.

Oh God . . .

She lay back and let her hands sink into the material of her sleeping bag, let her hands twist into talons until she thought they would snap like twigs. And she let the anguish spill silently out of her, the tears run freely, the sobs wrack her body.

She wasn't strong, she knew. She wasn't Faith, able to fuck many women but still keep them at a distance. Joyce threw herself fully and completely into a lover's being as easily as she did into her arms. She'd been wrong to be unfaithful, and dishonest. She felt dirty, unworthy.

But still, she had to win Philippa back . . .

She emerged into the night. The sky was an indigo dome of a million, million stars, but she ignored them. The fire was smaller than before, and Zebaki lay nearby, lifting his head up once at her appearance. She ignored him, too.

The woman by the fire was another story. Philippa sat, cradling the rifle, occasionally reaching to the pile of dried dung beside her to feed the fire, or lifting her canteen to splash water on her face. She never looked up at Joyce's approach, though Joyce knew the woman couldn't help but have noticed her.

In the veil of darkness surrounding the camp, the night was filled with sounds of life, life that stayed hidden and watching during the day. They formed an audience, an audience to Joyce's surrender, surrender to the overpowering sensations this other woman shaped and drew out of her. 'Philippa, I – I'm sorry. I'm so dreadfully sorry. Please – please forgive me.'

Philippa gave away no visible, discernible reaction to Joyce's apology, let alone Joyce's presence. Damn the woman!

But it only made Joyce want her more. And made Joyce understand what Ruth had meant, yesterday, before the stampede. Hurt pride was like a slap across the face, but one recovered from that. But the pang of loneliness was like a stab in the heart, much sharper, much more painful. And the arousal, or at least the promise of it, made a very soothing balm indeed.

Joyce walked around to Philippa's other side, closer to her and the fire. Then Joyce kneeled on the ground, resting her hands flat on her knees, letting her head drop but her eyes still fixed upon Philippa, waiting, then adding, 'I'll take whatever punishment you deem fit, Ms Sheringham. Please, just . . .'

It took all of Joyce's willpower not to react when Philippa reacted, turning her head to stare at the prone figure beside her. Turning to appraise the woman, and not with much compassion, either. 'That's assuming I even consider you worthy of my attentions any more.'

Joyce's breath caught in her throat – not of fear that Philippa would reject her, but of her own submissive stance, physically and otherwise, of Philippa's voice, her eyes. Inside her knickers, her pussy twinged and pulsed with life.

A pulsing that quickened when Philippa added, 'Perhaps you'd better remind me of the qualities that first attracted me to you. Take off your clothes.'

Joyce's breath caught again, more so when, as she started to rise to obey Philippa's command, Philippa corrected, 'No, no – remain on your knees while you do that.'

Like when they were in the tent; that she still did that, out in the open night with the dog watching, filled Joyce with greater arousal than ever before. Arousal, and fear.

Clothes were cast aside along with pride.

Philippa dropped something at Joyce's knees: the collar.

'Put on your collar,' Philippa sneered. 'Acknowledge your place again.'

Joyce obeyed, her hands trembling.

Philippa circled her like a predator now, more so than in the tent the night before, snarling, 'Oh, yes, you little bitch, you may think everything's fine now. But you'll think differently before I'm through. Get on all fours!'

Joyce did so, watching Philippa kick dust ahead of her. She had something in her hand – it took another pass by her eyes before Joyce could identify it as the dildo, minus the harness. She twisted it in her grasp, held it like a weapon in Joyce's direction. Joyce's stomach was now doing somersaults inside her with the instant awareness as to what would now happen, breath and pulse quickening as she watched Philippa saunter around to her rear, could feel her hovering like a cat toying with its half-dead, doomed prey.

Then she felt Philippa kneel behind her, shifting Joyce's ankles, then her knees and thighs, apart. Joyce gasped, as the cool air touched her now exposed, now aroused lips of her sex. She could feel some remnants of her modesty cringe as Philippa's hands, strong and powerful and cold, now ran down Joyce's back and over her tensed buttocks.

Joyce shivered, trying desperately to keep still, as Philippa's hands ran to Joyce's sides, gripping her there and playfully pushing forward, gyrating her pubic mound against Joyce's cheeks. 'It's going to take a great deal of hard work on your part, to get me to trust and love you. You know that, don't you?'

Joyce's mouth had dried. 'Y-yes, Ms Sheringham –'

'Yes. A great deal of hard work.' Her hands moved back to Joyce's cheeks, parting them and baring the deep cleft of her bottom. 'And sacrifice.'

Now one of Philippa's fingers touched the puckered opening of Joyce's anus, making Joyce squirm and break protocol. 'What are you doing –'

'Now you don't really need to ask that, do you?' Philippa continued, reaching for Joyce's open, moist sex, stirring up the dew she found there, then ignoring Joyce's moans of delight at the contact as Philippa brought the now moist finger back to Joyce's anus, gently but firmly inserting it, working it back and forth, wordlessly inviting Joyce to open further.

And it was doing so! Joyce stared out into the fire, eyes wide as saucers, gasping as much from the shock of her response as from the stimulation itself. Never before had anyone touched her inside *there*. And her reactions to it, beyond the fear and humiliation, were *amazing*!

And apparent, to judge from Philippa's consequent words. 'Nice to find some virgin part of you. But I'm not doing this to give you pleasure, am I, dear?'

Joyce continued to shudder at the woman's touch as she answered, 'N-no, Ms Sheringham.'

'That's right. I'm doing this for *my* pleasure, not yours. So, you'd better not come, not without my permission.' Philippa's finger quickly withdrew from Joyce – and was just as quickly replaced by something harder, wider, cooler: the dildo.

Joyce cried out, feeling as if she was being split in half. Her breath quickened like a trapped bird's, and she thought Philippa was inserting the entire length of it into her. But she held her ground, refusing to collapse, willing herself to relax, to ignore the mounting climax within her pussy, to accommodate far more than she could have imagined, while Philippa continued, finally stopping and removing herself from Joyce's proximity. 'You should see yourself, girl.'

Joyce took that as an order/invitation, and looked behind her, but could barely glimpse the phallus firmly embedded in the wrinkled hole between her taut, hot cheeks. But she didn't have to see it; she could certainly feel it, and it made her sex wet, throbbing, impatient for release.

Philippa stood back and stared coolly, as if admiring some museum artwork. 'Yes. Very pleasing to the eye. Now . . . crawl.'

'What?'

'Crawl. Crawl around the fire.' After a pause she snapped, '*Now!*'

Joyce's hands and knees felt as if they were being abraded by the dirt as she crawled. But Joyce was ignoring this, drawn as she was by how her thighs rubbed together as she crawled, how the object inside her was stimulating her further. She quivered, the motion of her crawling working their magic like a lover's hands, wringing forth not only more of her juices to run down her legs, but a heat that overpowered the cool air around her. She stopped, put a hesitant hand between her legs, just for a second. She wasn't really touching herself. Not really. A heat that rekindled the sparks that had been building up inside her since appearing to apologise to Philippa. Building, flaring like a star about to explode –

Her climax came more quickly than even she was ready for, and she collapsed with a loud, unmistakable moan of delight. Her muscles forced out the dildo.

Above her, Philippa made a sound that could have been disappointment, or pleasure. 'You didn't make it. But then, you weren't meant to. It's not meant to be fair. Remember that. I'm not in an equitable frame of mind now.'

Joyce would remember that, long after these overpowering sensations of pain and pleasure had ebbed.

FIFTEEN

The lakebed was a particularly harsh and unforgiving patch of the savannah, and Joyce for one was glad to leave it behind her for relatively greener pastures – along with her memories here.

If only she could leave the memory of Philippa's punishment, and her words, behind as well. But they were carried with the rest of the party, with the dismissive manner Philippa took with Joyce, no matter what the subject. With the way the woman now inexplicably stayed closer to Nina, as if to torment Joyce further in some fashion.

She was thankful that they were only a day away from Mount Baridi and its surrounding greenlands. The mountain was a flat-topped structure, striped with varying shades of green and the grey of mist, more ephemeral than real; through her binoculars, Joyce could see the bands of green in richer detail.

'Wicked bad sight, eh?'

Joyce glanced from behind her binoculars at Faith, who had sidled up beside her without Joyce discerning her approach. She couldn't help but smile and share in the younger woman's awe. 'It's eerie, too. All this arid land, and there that sits, like it's hogged all the life and water and such from the surrounding areas.'

Faith grinned. 'That's what the local legends say about Baridi. That he was a fat, greedy demon who couldn't be bothered to

186

move from that spot, even when the grass and trees started growing around him. Occasionally you're supposed to hear his stomach growling from indigestion; but then, it *is* an extinct volcano, but with underground hot springs.'

Joyce nodded and smiled back at the story. 'I wonder why there's different coloured growth at different levels?'

'I asked Kimya about that. She says –'

'Joyce!'

Both women turned at the sharp sound of Philippa approaching, with Nina and Ruth a few lengths behind. The blonde woman's face was sharp beneath her sunhat, and her tone like that of a mother scolding an unruly child. 'When you're *quite* through wasting time, I have a list of work for you when we make camp.'

'But that's not until this afternoon –'

'Did I say you could speak back? *Did I?*'

Joyce reined in her anger, swallowed it and replied, 'I'm sorry.'

Faith, however, was under no obligation to remain silent. 'Jeez, Philippa, give it a rest, willya? It's too hot for that shit.'

Philippa's glare transferred to the younger woman. 'Stay out of this.'

'Fuck off –'

But Joyce held up a hand in Faith's direction. 'It's OK. Really.'

Faith looked to her, but it was Philippa who retorted, 'See, Faith? It's OK. Really.'

Faith ignored Philippa, staring at Joyce a moment longer, offering – what? Derision? No. Empathy? Yes. Support? Perhaps. Like at the campfire last night.

Then she was riding off towards the advancing Kimya, leaving Philippa to point at the ground behind her. 'From now on, stay behind me, stay close, stay silent. Understood?'

A part of Joyce suddenly hated Philippa.

Just as a part of her surged with excitement at her dominance over Joyce.

It was that latter part – with a direct line to her libido – that made her say, 'Yes, Ms Sheringham.' And guide her horse to remain behind Philippa for the rest of the day.

★

Clouds, billowy and dark and ominous, clung to the horizon behind the travellers, like a pack of predatory animals, in pursuit but seemingly not willing to attack – yet.

Around them, the trees of the savannah grew more plentiful, the grass higher, thicker, the wildlife more plentiful. Animal sounds filled more and more of the air, as did the buzz of the ubiquitous insects.

Before she realised it, Joyce found they had arrived at the camp, set almost at the foot of Baridi. A tall fence, part rusted wire mesh, part lumber (both types interwoven with vegetation, and looking as if the vegetation was what was keeping it up) surrounded an overgrown area protecting several large prefabricated Quonset huts, some water storage tanks and pumps, and a rickety-looking observation tower.

'Not exactly the Holiday Inn,' Nina quipped.

'It serves its purpose,' Kimya explained, without sounding defensive. 'It was a valuable position during the border wars with Bahaska in the Eighties and early Nineties, but it's been left for wardens like myself to use now. Ironically, now with peace in the area, there's fewer patrols and military stations out here, and thus more chances for poachers to come across the border.' She dropped from her horse and fished for the key to the lock on the front gate – a purely symbolic gesture, Joyce thought; anyone could climb some vulnerable part of the fence, or even shoot out the lock.

Inside the camp, there were open spaces between the huts, perhaps for trucks or troops; these spaces were now overgrown with grasses, and dark buzzing clouds of insects performed intricate displays about each other. A rich, pungent smell clung to the still air, and like the buzzing it added to everyone's general sense of discomfiture and enervation.

Kimya pointed to a water tank and pump mechanism, with a trough made out of metal barrels cut open. 'It's just like the one on the savannah, three days ago. The water here should be all right, but drop a few tablets into it before the horses or yourselves drink.'

Joyce wasn't even off her horse completely before Philippa

thrust the reins of her horse into Joyce's hands. 'Take care of him. Then bring my things inside.'

Joyce swallowed. 'Yes, Ms Sheringham.' It was easier now, easier to behave the way Philippa wanted.

But then Philippa remained a moment longer, then leaned closer. 'You've done well today. So I have a special treat for you tonight.'

And that hint of better treatment, that meagre crumb of affection, was for Joyce like a feast. And any resentment or annoyance at her ill treatment suddenly evaporated, and she smiled dumbly. 'Thank you.'

Afterwards, she kicked herself for her reaction. But she couldn't deny the pulsing inside her pussy.

The thunder grew closer, sharper, but not by much; there were flashes of lightning through the dirty windows of the one hut the travellers had marked for their own use. Not that it was the nicest, so much as it was the least filthy and insect-blown than the others, as well as containing the skeletons of old bunk beds that could hold sleeping bags as makeshift mattresses.

After a while, Faith appeared inside, looked around, then offered the two women an expression of sympathy. 'Listen, anyone up for a game?'

Joyce looked up. 'A game?'

Faith grinned and held up a football. 'Look what I found outside. Had to fight a lion and tiger for it, too.'

'Aye, right.'

She grinned more broadly now, unrepentant. 'Well?'

Joyce smiled. 'Why not?'

Ruth agreed. And for the better part of an hour, they kicked a battered-looking, half-deflated football back and forth over a weed-strewn patch of ground, losing it half the time, while the sun beat down mercilessly.

Joyce hadn't had so much fun in a long time.

Thunder remained with the clouds on the horizon at twilight, but each clap still made the windows of the hut rattle, as if by a passing train or plane. There was a small generator in a tiny shed adjacent to the hut, and provided power to the naked bulbs hanging from the low, web-canopied rafters overhead. The light was weak, as if unable to wade through the close air within.

Philippa sat at the hut's rickety wooden table, ignoring the years of carvings and graffiti in its surface with a serene fold of her hands, as Nina sat opposite, withdrawing from her shirt pocket a deck of cards. 'Ruthie! Ass over here, now.'

Almost simultaneously, Philippa barely glanced over her shoulder as she motioned, more graciously, saying, 'Joyce, come here, darling.'

Joyce and Ruth sat or lay on separate bunks in the far end of the hut near Faith, who was squatting, searching for her cigarettes. She looked up as she found them and caught Joyce staring at her. Something unspoken, ineffable, exchanged between them. Then Joyce rose and followed Ruth over to the table.

The women at the table never looked up from the sight of Nina shuffling the cards, but Philippa spoke. 'We're going to play poker. Strip poker.'

Joyce glanced at Ruth, who'd adopted a stoic expression, before declaring, 'Philippa, I don't know how to play –'

Philippa sighed with world-weariness. 'I never said *you* were going to play. Just stand there like Ruth, and do as you're told.'

Faith drew closer, lighting up. 'Anyone want to go for a walk around the compound? Joyce? Ruth?'

The Israeli woman didn't pause as she replied, 'Thank you, Faith, but no.'

Joyce was less quick in replying, drawing a glare from Philippa. But then she added, 'No thanks, Faith.'

'You heard Ruthless and Joy-Ride,' Nina quipped. 'Go keep company with Kimcorder in the tower, if you want.'

'Your act's gotten real stale, girl.' Faith blew grey smoke in the woman's direction, before exiting to the greeting sounds of Zebaki outside.

'Bitch,' Nina muttered, barely under her breath. She dealt the cards to Philippa and herself, as Joyce and Ruth stood by their respective mistresses, glanced at each other furtively. For a moment, there was only the sound of cards slapping on to the table and the odd rattle of the windows and door. Joyce watched the interplay of cards, saw Philippa's hand, but didn't know whether it was good or bad.

It turned out to be good, as Nina cursed and thumbed at Ruth, who immediately began unbuttoning her shirt.

Joyce was too stunned to do more than gape as the Israeli woman drew the shirt from her body and cast it aside, standing there in her white sports bra hugging her bosom, where the butterfly was barely visible on her right breast. So that was what they were there to do, pay the forfeit for their mistresses. Humiliating. But she couldn't look away, couldn't raise any defiance; tremors of lust ran through her like thunder, at what was further to come. Literally.

Another hand; Nina lost again, and Ruth kneeled to remove her boots and socks; Joyce watched, watched Ruth flex her toes against the unpolished, wooden-slatted floor as she straightened up again.

Another hand: Philippa lost this time, and she never even looked up as Joyce removed her shirt, as if not expecting Joyce to even hesitate, let alone defy her. Joyce didn't expect it, either, and that frightened as much as it excited her. The air was like another layer of clothes on her body, but she still shivered as if from cold, rather than the excitement of standing there in her bra, with Nina – and Ruth – gazing at her.

Another hand, then another: Philippa lost both times, and Joyce removed her boots and socks, then her trousers (she didn't know whether she was expected to remove those, or her bra; then she realised it didn't really matter). She stood there in her bra and knickers, hands trembling as they clasped together before her. It was cooler on her body, out of her sweat-drenched clothes. She wanted to break and run, to dress again, but something held her rooted to the spot beside Philippa.

Nina whistled, deliberately exacerbating Joyce's chagrin. 'I forgot what a nice body Joy-Joy had.' Then she indicated Ruth. 'Curvier than *this* slab of beef.'

Joyce's breath caught in her throat at the insult, and averted her eyes so as not to catch Ruth's gaze.

'Oh, I don't know,' Philippa noted idly, glancing up from her cards at Ruth. 'Yours isn't without charms of her own. I'll enjoy her.'

Joyce started at that. 'What?'

Philippa looked up, then set her cards face down on the table and rose to stand before Joyce, reaching out to hold Joyce by her waist; her hands were hot, clammy, gripping. She stared deeply, magnetically, into Joyce's eyes, her voice husky. 'I might have her. As you had. The difference being that, unlike you, I'm being open about it.' Her hands moved up to Joyce's breasts, teasing her nipples through her bra, softly pinching them, rolling them between her long, graceful fingers, tugging them outwards to make them stand behind the material. 'Unless you wish to play the hypocrite, and try to deny me?'

'Try to' deny her. As if Joyce had a hope in hell of stopping Philippa. She swallowed, and her arms felt leaden at her sides, even as her pussy twinged inside her knickers. She was melting.

Behind her, Nina threw down her own cards and rose to her feet. 'Enough of this crap! Let's get it on!'

Before Joyce could react, Philippa smiled and drew her hands away, turning to face Ruth, even as Nina took her place before Joyce, reaching up to draw the woman into a kiss. Joyce gasped, felt a twitch of her limbs exhibit vestigial defiance, before her body betrayed her, and she opened her mouth to let the smaller woman thrust her tongue inside, even as her hands explored Joyce's body once again.

Joyce felt herself leaning against Nina for support, as if feeling prostrate from just the heat without, instead of within, dimly aware of Nina undressing herself. Then the woman pulled back enough to snarl, 'Get the rest of your clothes off, slut.'

Anger. Humiliation. Desire. The first two made Joyce's hands shake as she reached behind herself to unhook her bra, but the last powered her muscles to do it anyway, powered her hands to descend to the waistband of her knickers, peeling the wet crotch from between her legs, even as she watched Nina cast aside her own clothes. The woman's breasts were as she remembered them: full and round and heavy, the nipples large sturdy buds, dimpled at the tips, surrounded by large aureole. Joyce had the inane urge to touch those heavy, warm masses, to measure their firmness and weight again, to feast upon them with her lips and tongue. Her head buzzed from the heat and desire, and she thought of nothing, of what was happening and what was going to happen to her.

Nina's hips were as she remembered, as was her bush, dark and brown, thick and curling, nestled between strong, alabaster thighs. But Nina caught Joyce's eyes again, seeing the surrender in them.

Joyce closed her eyes submissively again to the kiss, Nina's bared breasts pressing against Joyce's chest, Nina's hands reaching around to clutch Joyce's cheeks, digging her nails into them.

Joyce swooned against the woman – then pulled back as she felt Nina reaching up and taking a fistful of Joyce's hair, gently but firmly pulling Joyce back. Nina's eyes were ablaze, but the passion in them was mingling with a tart malice and made Joyce swallow involuntarily again. 'On all fours, slut.'

Joyce gasped, struggled to find some strength, some inner resolve. There was none. She sank to her hands and knees, the floor harsh on her shins and palms, the ache of today's ride still in her thighs and calves. She stared at Nina's feet, could smell her own desire between her legs down here.

Nina clung on to her hair, her words like venom. 'You kept quiet about my visit to you in the tent the other night. I think that's insulting.'

Joyce found her breasts heavy beneath her, found her breath racing, from fear, from excitement, from lust. 'I – I didn't want Philippa to know –'

Nina chuckled. 'Stupid cunt, she *knew*. She knew all along! You think I could have snuck in that night, with her on guard a few feet away with the dog? You think she and I could be so pally with each other all this time, if she'd *really* been upset?'

Joyce tried to look up, at her, or over at Philippa, but Nina held her head in place. Philippa knew all along? She just played at being anguished at the betrayal and deception?

Now Joyce felt betrayal. Betrayal and humiliation, throughout her, unchecked. All of Philippa's words about loyalty and devotion and possession replayed in Joyce's head, mocking her flooding again and again. She was used. Used and abused, and only now could she admit to it.

And do something about it. 'Let me go –'

Or at least, *try* to do something. Someone approached, an extra set of hands manipulated her. The hands were Philippa's, drawing Joyce up to a kneeling position, drawing Joyce's hands in front of and over her head. Joyce stared, angry and confused, at Nina's bush, smelled her. 'What the hell –'

Something went into Joyce's mouth, wrapped around her face: cloth, some clothing. Panic welled up as she was raised to her feet, and she began struggling, to no avail. Almost before she realised it, she felt her hands being drawn up to the ceiling; her wrists were bound with a long nylon rope, part of their survival gear, as Philippa flung it over the rafter overhead, securing it only when Joyce was forced to straighten out her body like a cliff diver, almost on the balls of her feet: uncomfortable, but not threatening to cause serious damage in any way.

Joyce fought to contain her panic, seeing Ruth standing nearby, naked, her hands self-consciously in front of her, her face a canvas of conflicting emotions. Finally the Israeli spoke. 'Nina, she doesn't –'

Nina stabbed a finger in her direction. 'Shut the fuck up! She loves it, like you do!'

Then Philippa appeared in view before Joyce, as the other woman continued to undress herself. She laughed – a velvet-gloved, iron-fisted laugh that no one around her seemed to like the sound of much – and reached out, her touch electric against Joyce's skin.

'Your eyes look hesitant,' she teased, her fingers descending between Joyce's legs, nestling in her bush. For a terrifying moment, Joyce thought the woman might pull a fistful of hair out at the roots. Instead, her varnished fingertips grazed the lips of Joyce's pussy. 'But the rest of you can't lie to me.' She dipped into Joyce's vagina, finding it wet, hot. Joyce whimpered, then groaned at those fingers that slid all too easily into her; the effect was spectacular, making Joyce quiver.

Philippa moved even closer, until her breasts pushed against

Joyce's. She could feel the heat from Philippa's mouth, as the woman almost whispered, 'And now, your punishment continues, my little slave.'

The words sent a mortifying, uncontrollable pulse to Joyce's pussy, contracting it around Philippa's fingers. Joyce gasped and nodded her head, while still fighting her bonds, fighting her own body.

Philippa made a noise that fell somewhere between a laugh and a sigh. 'See? You are enjoying it, my little slave.' She withdrew her fingers, bringing them to her mouth to smell and taste Joyce's juices, before turning back to Nina and Ruth. 'Let's draw the sleeping bags on to the floor here in front of her, make sure she can see everything.'

And they did. Tugging helplessly at her bonds, Joyce watched as Philippa drew the two women with her to the makeshift bed on the floor. Philippa closed her eyes and stretched out as if on white silk sheets, languishing as Nina began touching, stroking her, laughing and murmuring, growing mercurially harsh when she saw Ruth just lying there, looking as mortified as Joyce felt. 'Get to work! Now!'

Ruth couldn't look up at Joyce, instead moved up and kissed Philippa; Joyce could see her opening her mouth wider, imagined her tongue slipping into Philippa's mouth. She watched Philippa open her eyes again to stare up at Joyce, sending her own tongue in reply, even as Nina was running strong, confident hands along Philippa's nude body.

Joyce's legs, her whole body was quivering, and her arms tingled as the blood rushed down from them, collecting with the rest of her blood in her pussy, engorging it, unable to understand that Joyce could not heed its call for satisfaction. Her mouth had gone dry; she could collect no saliva for it, as if all her energy had been directed towards observing the erotic, tantalising, terrible tableau before her.

On the sleeping bags, Philippa swiftly guided Ruth beneath her, trailing kisses over her warm, round breasts, down her stomach to the soft, deep-pink folds of her labia, parting them with her fingertips and drinking in the released perfume. A pause, and

Philippa pierced her with her fingers. Another pause, and Philippa replaced her fingers with her tongue, lapping up the nectar and teasing the engorged clitoris. She was no novice to the pleasures of the female flesh, as Joyce well knew.

Beneath her, Ruth moaned and thumped her head back against the covers, crying out. And somehow, Philippa remembered to look to Joyce at regular intervals, perhaps gauging the reactions on her bound slave's face and body, perhaps only to silently crow – probably both.

Before them, Joyce was wriggling impotently in place, eddies of pleasure churning unwanted upwards in greater intensity as she rubbed her thighs together, feeling them moisten with sweat, with her own juices. She could not control the dark sensuality that had risen from within her since coming here, and now was no exception. She could imagine herself being touched, as Ruth was being touched, giving pleasure, receiving it. If she concentrated hard enough, she could almost feel the touch of skin on her own, caressing, demanding. It seemed so real, and it was all so unfair! So *unfair!*

Nina did not remain inactive among the threesome, moving behind Philippa's half-crouched position, reaching between her parted thighs and delving deep inside her with expert fingers, cooling her obviously hot inner flesh. Her mouth still planted on Ruth's vulva, Philippa groaned aloud, bucking against her quick, hard thrusts.

Joyce twisted, as if she could unscrew herself – no pun intended – from her bonds. Her pussy felt velvety, tight, as wet as she had ever known, pulsing with moist, eager passion. It cried out to her, shamelessly uncaring of the humiliation she also felt. She wanted to close her eyes, her ears, her mind to it all, but tortured herself with the knowledge that even if she could shut down her senses, she wouldn't. Philippa had been right, damn her!

Philippa lay back, looking upside down at Joyce now, as two pairs of hands, lips, bodies worshipped her own. Nina worked her way to her vulva again, drinking in her copious juices, as Ruth worked on her tender nipples. But Philippa never looked to see who did what, irrelevant as it was to her. Her lovers were there for a greater reason than just to provide pleasure.

Joyce's nerve endings were on fire, her legs trembling more; only her fear of being suspended by her arms alone kept her steady enough. Her breath left her body in staccato jumps, her feeble attempts at a dignified defiance cast aside, like everything else, in a tidal pool of emotion, churned further as she watched Nina mount Philippa, pumping into the woman's engorged sex with her hand, while Ruth rivalled her own mistress's penetration with her tongue into Philippa's mouth again. And still, Philippa continued to stare at Joyce, refusing to let the woman go, giving no quarter in the battle of wills.

Joyce was consumed, her mind and body spiralling upwards into a ferocious, undeniable climax, just as the lovers on the bed seemed to speed up, too. She watched Nina, the blur her hand had become as it drove in and out of Philippa, flesh slapping rapid-fire on flesh, applause for her performance. Philippa, her mouth still covered by Ruth's as her breasts were covered by Ruth's hands, moaned aloud.

And that was it, for Joyce. Raptures of orgasm jerked her hips, making her whole body quiver, and she cried out, losing all self-control as her climax washed over her in unrelenting waves, her hips jerking as if in disgust at the pee which now ran down between her thighs and over the tops of her feet. Only then did her eyes squeeze shut, in rapture if not shame, and her teeth bit down on her lower lip, until she thought she could taste blood.

The blood was rushing through Joyce's ears, so she started when she felt the ropes holding her arms up give way, providing slack. She collapsed to her knees, as much from surprise and exhaustion as from the afterwaves of her climax, the strength and will long since drained from her like water from a sponge. Someone took her, held her – Philippa? Ruth?

'What the fuck is *wrong* with you people?'

Faith.

Hands worked to release Joyce's wrists, to release the gag from her mouth, as she looked up into Faith's concerned, angry expression. The younger woman's voice turned tender. 'Are you OK?'

Joyce worked her tongue, sought moisture, settling on silently nodding.

Then Faith looked to the three women on the bags, her words as sharp as her grimace. 'You people are pathetic! I've got nothing against SM, but this is hardly what I'd call responsible erotic behaviour. She could have passed out in this heat, dislocated a shoulder!'

Ruth rose and reached for her clothes, as did Nina, albeit more slowly. But Philippa remained where she was, then rolled over on to her stomach and sat up on her elbows, resting her chin on her hands, letting one foot rise and fall behind her like she was posing. '*She* didn't seem to mind.'

'Bull*shit*!' Faith glared angrily at the others. 'You and Nina, I expect it from. But *you*, Ruth . . .'

The Israeli woman looked away, unable to meet either Faith's or Joyce's eyes.

Now Faith returned to Joyce, gathering her clothes up. 'Come on, you can stay in the next hut with me tonight.'

'She's not going anywhere with you,' Philippa informed her.

But Faith stabbed an incensed, shaking finger at the woman. 'Don't even *think* about starting up with me now, Philippa! I'll hit you that many times, you'll swear you're fucking surrounded!'

Philippa remained nonchalant. 'Such support from you . . . considering the circumstances between yourselves and Constance. Why not ask the woman in question?'

Faith drew closer to Joyce, drawing some of Joyce's discarded clothes over her back. 'Can you walk out of here tonight with me?'

Joyce looked to Philippa, the woman who'd snared her heart, who'd talked of devotion and possession, then casually twisted it into something bitter and nasty. She looked so confident, confident that she still held Joyce under her domination.

Joyce was sick of it. She spoke through parched lips. 'I'll bloody well crawl out of here if I have to.'

SIXTEEN

Joyce was thankful that her mind seemed not to remember the subsequent hours, seemed not to remember Faith taking and dressing her in an adjacent hut, leaving for their possessions, the inevitable resurgence of arguments and threats, the explanations to a baffled Kimya. She did remember Faith removing the collar and tucking her in like a child, holding her, when Joyce began to weep again, not at the pain of her humiliation, for she had enjoyed that, ultimately, at Philippa's hands, but at the thought of never being intimate with Philippa again. Eventually, her tears slowed. It was dark in the hut; the electricity wasn't set up here, and the air was musty, the night broken only by the odd clap of thunder and subsequent bark from Zebaki.

She wondered for a time what would happen during the rest of the trek. The party had seemingly split in half, and because of her. She had messed up from the start.

And she was damned if she could figure out how to repair the rift. If it *could* be repaired.

Grey light seeped in through the dust-curtained windows of the hut when Joyce remembered waking again, watching a silhouette move quietly about, then exit the door; only then did she recognise the figure as Faith, dressed. Careful not to awaken

199

Kimya nearby, Joyce rose, wrapping her sleeping bag around herself in the cool morning air to follow Faith outside.

The air was misty, and buzzing with insects; her watch told her it was just after dawn, though the sky above remained a milky grey. Joyce frowned as she watched Faith stride over to the temporary corral near the water tower, and she cast off her sleeping bag to trot up behind her. 'Hey –'

Faith had already turned at the approaching footfalls on the grass, and held out her hand in a palm-down, lower-your-voice mode. 'Something wrong?'

'I don't know, you tell me.'

Faith unslung the rifle around her shoulder and fitted it into her saddle. 'I'm starting out to begin the search for the wreckage. The sooner we find the diaries, the sooner we can start back.'

'What about the others?'

'Kimya pulled a double shift last night, so she's catching some extra Zs. The others won't be willing to head out without her, so I thought I'd get away from them for a while.'

'It'd be stupid to go out on your own. Give me ten minutes to get ready.'

Faith frowned. 'Are you sure you're up to it?'

Joyce smiled. 'Try and stop me.'

At Faith's returning smile, she turned and rushed back to the hut, pleased at the strength she now found within herself. Despite her willing subordination the night before, she was beginning to suspect that her nature was not that of a true submissive: she enjoyed the giving-in, that was true, but Joyce was also aware that she relished self-sufficiency.

The mountain dominated the area ahead of them, an intense green-banded castle amidst a forest of acacias and baobob, and others. Once or twice, Joyce had to duck in the saddle to keep a low branch from smacking into her. Beneath the hooves of Shohan, the ground crunched like broken glass.

'Obsidian,' Faith explained, ahead of her. 'Shards of volcanic rock, used by locals to forge the first tools and spearheads.' As they emerged into a clearing, getting a full view of the mountain, Faith stopped and raised the binoculars hanging around her neck; Joyce followed suit with her own. 'Notice the different layers? The terrain changes at different altitudes. The first thousand metres is all forest, like this, only thicker. Another thousand, and you're at a belt of bamboo, with some stalks twelve metres high. Another five hundred, and there's thick grass and heather. The last thousand metres is moorland – what you can see of it through all that mist. And there's different flora and fauna on each level.'

'Somebody's done her homework,' Joyce quipped.

Faith grinned as she lowered her binoculars. 'I didn't spend *all* my high-school days snogging Debra Connolly in the girls' bathroom.'

'Where's the plane crash supposed to be?'

Faith's grin dimmed, but didn't disappear entirely. 'At the foot of the mountain, on the right side; I've seen the aerial photos taken after the crash by the army.' Her features grew even more sober. 'We don't have much time out here. I'd hate to run into an army patrol out here after our travel permits ran out.'

'Or poachers,' Joyce added, remembering how they'd dogged their trail for a couple of days. Still, she wasn't worried now, certain they'd got their fill of game with the wildebeests and such in the savannah.

As they proceeded, the lighter, thinner, more sparse acacia and baobab yielded to the thicker, greener, almost closed-canopy forest of giant camphor, vines and ferns. The ground rose into the foothills of Baridi, and tiny, shallow streams gurgled through the trees. For a while, Joyce believed they were simply making their way through the forest, rather than following any sort of trail.

That belief was dispelled as they emerged at a narrow, metre-wide footbridge of battered wood and rusted iron slats and supports, stretching over a twelve-metre-wide, three-metre-deep gorge seemingly carved by the shallow river now running at the bottom.

Joyce had to raise her voice over the sound of the water. 'Hardly seems worthwhile building a bridge over something like that.'

'Say that again when the rainy season starts,' Faith countered, descending from her horse and taking his reins in hand. She looked to Joyce, adding, 'Wait until I get across, before coming over, OK?'

Joyce dropped to her feet. 'OK. Be careful.'

Faith grinned. 'What, *me* take risks?' She turned and started across the bridge, pausing with each creak and groan of protest. Joyce winced, drew closer with Shohan to the end of the bridge, peered past Faith's horse to see Faith grin back at her –

Then fall through a rotten slat with a sickening crack.

Joyce never hesitated, and many times afterwards would marvel at her own response: dropping Shohan's reins from her hand, she charged ahead, shouting at Faith's horse to proceed ahead, heedless of any further danger the horse might find on the rest of the bridge, or for that matter any further danger on the bridge for herself. The horse proceeded over the suspended form of Faith, half-hanging between broken slats, face screwed up in pain or anger, trying to help herself back up, while her boots almost touched the water below; part of the side rail had broken away, too, floating off down the river.

Joyce kneeled and helped the woman back up on to the bridge, where both sat there, facing each other, trying to catch their breath. Joyce ran a forearm across her head, acknowledging it was the heat and sudden fright, rather than any exertion on her part, that had induced the outbreak of sweat. She unclipped the canteen from her belt and passed it over to a grinning Faith. 'Thanks. I had a quick, all-purpose prayer to Saints Aldegun, Barbara, Cecilia, Agrippina and a few others, promising to give up my life of drink and debauchery if I could be saved.'

Joyce smirked. 'Knowing how much you enjoy those, I'm almost sorry you were saved.'

Faith burst into laughter, spitting out the water she was drinking, before trying again. 'Ugh, water's no good without whisky.' Then she added, 'I mean it – thanks. You took a chance.'

'Not really. Most of the bridge seems sturdy enough.' She tapped at an adjacent slat, then thought better of it, not wishing to tempt fate.

'Yeah, well, *you* didn't know that at the time. You didn't think about your own danger.'

'I didn't think at all.'

Now Faith playfully kicked her boot. 'Hey, I'm not this thankful very often; enjoy it while it lasts.'

Both women laughed, and in that moment, Joyce took a measure of the excitement of the last moment, the thrill of danger she couldn't properly enjoy until now – and the joy of the camaraderie she now felt with this young woman.

The morning sun rose, as did the ground, but the sun was held back by the high leaves and branches of the trees, filtering through only as rafters of ochre, barely caressing the dark, mossy ground and lichen-painted rocks. An abundance of life thrived here, undergrowth so luxuriant in places that small trees had taken root in the moss which festooned the larger trees, and trapped soil in the tangled roots became flowerpots for the ferns, the brighter begonias and the shy orchids scrabbling for the shifting rafters of light.

It was the sweltering height of day now, and the jungle was blaring with the white noise of insects and birds, all the raw wild life in the jungle terrain screaming without reason. Further distant, yet still close-seeming, primates like Colobus monkeys and vervets scampered and chittered like squirrels.

It was the closest Joyce had come so far to the traditional Hollywood image of an African jungle, yet it still held surprises for her.

Some, she cared not to encounter. 'Are there any larger animals in here we should be wary of?'

Faith had dismounted a while back, and was guiding them through the forest with her compass and map. 'Girl, there ain't an animal on this continent I'm not wary of already.' She paused, looked ahead, her smile dropping. 'We're here.'

Joyce followed her gaze. At first, she saw nothing but more trees and boulders, with the odd clearing. Then she focused on one clearing.

And there it was; the twisted blue-white corpse of a twin-prop cargo plane, small by modern standards, but up close it looked like the carcass of a great dinosaur that had given up the ghost in this primeval lair. In fact, the adjective 'twisted' didn't do justice to the appearance of it, with its nose shoved into the ground, its fuselage broken in several places, resting on trees torn and splintered by the impact. Much of the metal was burned to ash as thin as paper. Debris was scattered here and there.

Joyce shuddered, fought to control it. It was like all those images of wrecked cars she'd ever seen, visible proof that the machines of man, the machines she so often relied upon, were not indestructible, would not protect her from all harm.

That this was the site where her mother had died, did not escape her awareness, either.

Faith broke the uneasy silence. 'It was quick, I was told.'

'No survivors?'

'No.' Perhaps as if in answer to her own unspoken fears, she added, 'All of the bodies were accounted for.'

'Hmm.'

'And soon, all this will be swallowed up.'

'What?'

Faith indicated the fallen trees. 'With these cleared out by the crash, secondary vegetation – thick grass and bamboo shoots – will grow, unfettered, and make this clearing inaccessible. The jungle takes care of its own.'

'Y'know, if you're not careful, I might start thinking you're quite sane.'

'Yeah, well, we can't have that, can we?' She sighed. 'It's an olive-drab canvas shoulder bag, with her initials on the side.'

Joyce wrapped Shohan's reins around an adjacent tree branch. 'Let's get to work, shall we?'

And they did, both women determined to set aside the emotional backdrop to this, and treat it as a simple investigation, a search for lost goods.

For all the good it did them. Over the course of several hours, not counting the midday break, they found scores of items of equipment, emptied cargo containers and crates, unidentifiable mechanical pieces, contorted pieces of metal . . . seats . . . some small personal items . . .

But no luggage. No diaries.

'I don't understand,' Joyce declared wearily, planting herself on a fallen log and tugging the sweaty clothes from her body. 'Could they have been stolen? Maybe before she even left the airport?'

Faith sat nearby, hunched over, staring at the ground; the air was thick here and their exertions taxing. 'This wasn't an ordinary passenger flight. Constance hopped on the nearest available plane to get her to where she was going; she would have carried her belongings with her.'

'Then someone must have stolen her luggage after the bodies were transported to Patricksburg – someone who knew how valuable the diaries were –'

'Like whom?'

Joyce couldn't answer that, recognising that she was clutching at straws. The diaries were around here, and they had to be found. But not for the money, because to Joyce they were far more valuable as sources of information about her mother, a woman she wanted to know better now, after her death. She owed it to Constance, as well as herself –

'Shit!'

Joyce looked up, started to speak, then caught herself at Faith's expression, open and alert and looking in the direction of the camp. It was probably the others, finally arriving, though the day was mostly over.

And yet, when Faith shot to her feet and scrambled for the surrounding trees, almost frantically signalling for Joyce to follow, Joyce unhesitatingly did so, her heart racing, her mind juggling a dozen questions about what was going on. Questions she wasn't ready to voice until she crouched with Faith behind another log, barely in view of the clearing now. Her voice was a squeak. 'Faith –'

The younger woman winced. 'Shush. Company. Bad company.' She nodded in the direction of the clearing.

Joyce followed the nod. Figures appeared, began poking around the wreckage. Men. 'The poachers?'

Faith's face grew taut. 'Bandits. They weren't poachers. They've been following us all this time.'

'Why?'

205

Faith breathed in, then rose, stood behind a tree. 'We have to go, get away from here. They'll know we're nearby.'

Joyce wondered how, then kicked herself mentally: of course, their horses, still in the clearing! With nearly all of their supplies, too! 'We have to get back to camp.'

'Yes, but not tonight – it's almost dark, and I don't fancy running into those bastards tonight. I know a place we can go, and spend the night.'

'But Kimya, Ruth, the others – they'll be worried –'

'Kim knows better than to try and search at night.' Thunder loomed above the verdant canopy. 'Come on, they're gonna start searching the area.'

Joyce rose, began following Faith as she led her upwards along a barely perceptible animal path, fighting to keep her heart under control. 'You didn't say –'

Faith barely glanced over her shoulder. 'Say what?'

'Why they might be after us.'

'Didn't I? Oh.'

She left it at that.

So did Joyce. At any rate, she was feeling . . . excited. Inexplicably excited, and worse, she was enjoying it. An adrenalin junkie?

The noises about them increased with the darkness, and more than once Joyce tripped over a root or had a branch slap in her face. And more than once, she felt herself panic into believing Faith didn't really know where she was leading them.

However, she'd been most knowledgeable so far. Far more knowledgeable than she would have expected of a brassy New Yorker. She must have visited here before with Constance –

She bumped into Faith, who turned and whispered unnecessarily, 'There it is.'

Joyce didn't understand.

Then she opened her eyes.

The Hidden City was indeed almost completely hidden by centuries of undergrowth; in fact, if someone on their way further up the slopes wasn't looking for it, they could easily miss it. Only the churn of the stream running through it might have attracted attention, but there was plenty of those running down the mountain. It was no more than a series of buildings, columns, pillar tombs and courtyards, all of surprisingly well-preserved grey coral limestone, though perhaps the moss and creepers running through the structures like blisters and veins were all that was holding them together.

Joyce didn't want to speak, such was her awe of the ancient place; she hadn't felt this way since those school trips to cathedrals back home. But curiosity bade her ask, '*This* is the place Constance wanted to visit?'

She thought for a moment she hadn't been heard over the water, but Faith eventually nodded. 'It was discovered in 1956. It didn't exactly fill the international headlines then – the Suez Canal crisis took that place – but Mahali knew about it. And when Constance heard about a lost city, she had to see for herself.'

'And they still don't know who built it?'

'Or why; a thousand years ago, people built settlements nearer the sea, for trade and shipping, not inland, halfway up a mountain. For that matter, why did they abandon it two hundred years later?'

Around them, the sounds of the forest filled the intervening silences, as if a constant reminder of what outlasted the builders of this place. Joyce drank from her canteen again, then passed it to Faith, when she didn't see the woman's own. 'You left your water behind?'

Faith shrugged. 'We've got water. It won't be pleasant, but it'll be drinkable.'

'Where?'

'The fountain.'

It wasn't a proper fountain, but more an aqueduct fed by a large and beautiful waterfall ten metres high. The water appeared from the tops of the trees covering an almost vertical slope, cascading with mist and swirl into a large oval pool bordered by fitted limestone bricks. The pool fed the water into a narrow aqueduct that ran down what must have been the city's main street, before disappearing into the forest of the lower slopes.

'Remarkable,' Joyce breathed, feeling stupid.

'And hot, too,' added Faith, kneeling and cupping water in her hand. She drank, grimaced, then drank again. 'One of the hot springs. Hot enough from the mountain, and fast enough coming down the hill, to minimise parasites.'

Joyce sat beside her, facing the rest of the city, and reached down to splash water on her face. 'Will they still be after us?'

Faith reached behind herself and pressed into her lower back. 'Nah. They'll have headed back to their own camp . . . with our horses and supplies.'

Joyce cursed; she'd miss Shohan.

The fountain water was foul, as Faith had promised, and the shared sparse meal of a fruit bar Joyce had on her person didn't dispel the pangs of hunger. Wind whipped through the surrounding trees, and birds continued their song, pausing only for thunderclaps. It would rain soon, and with a vengeance.

The women had chosen an empty domicile for their shelter, small but facing the direction they had travelled from the plane wreckage, and with an exit in the rear.

The heat was oppressive; when it was dark enough, with only the moon shining down above the surrounding wall of trees and mountain, they'd stripped off and cooled down under the fountain. Faith's nude body looked eerie, spectral, in the pale light. And lithe and graceful and beautiful.

They sat facing each other in the domicile, backs pressed against the walls. Joyce looked around her, wondered at the people who had built this place, a thousand or more years ago. 'Who were they? What did they think? What did they feel?'

'They were like us,' Faith replied, obviously knowing what Joyce was asking. 'With thoughts and feelings little different from our own.' She paused and cleared her throat. And when she spoke again, it was with a depth of lyrical feeling Joyce hadn't heard from her since the younger woman's concert in London.

'I want to stand in the verdant grass of the savannah, and let my soft, glad laughter carry in the waiting, windless dark. With no regrets.

I want to climb the steps of Green Mother, to touch

yesterday, kiss today, and lay my head to rest upon tomorrow. With no regrets.

I want to race with the beasts in the harshest of lands, and howl at the moon with them, in quintessential joy at living to see another day. With no regrets.

I want to weep to the midnight whalesong on an ocean embracing half the world. With no regrets.

I want to love and laugh, embrace and wrestle, betray, and be betrayed. With no regrets.

I am presented with a feast called life, and told to make of it what I wish, for I do not know when I will be called away from the table. I want to indulge myself to the fullest.

With no regrets.'

The air hung for a handful of heartbeats after that. The poem sounded strangely familiar to Joyce, prompting her to ask, 'Constance's?'

Faith nodded. 'A poem she wrote at school when she was sixteen. And received a bad mark for, because of its "espousal of hedonism and decadence". That summer, they went out to this place. The army was called in on the search, Constance got into a shitload of trouble –'

' "They" went out?'

Faith paused; Joyce couldn't see her expression in the darkness. 'There was a girl in her class, a girl named Saraid. They'd fallen in love; Constance said *that* was her First Great Adventure. Coming here was almost just an afterthought in comparison.' She looked outside, at the waterfall now. 'When they were alone, they'd sworn their undying love to each other over there, even performed a traditional Baridi binding ceremony.'

So that was it, Joyce concluded, with some satisfaction at seeing the truth now fully divined. 'And she was coming back here to finish her book, where it all started?'

Faith nodded. 'Ironically, landing close to the site of her First Great Adventure.'

'So what happened with Saraid when they got back?'

Faith grunted. 'Saraid was Muslim. She was betrothed by her

parents to marry a local man. Your mother couldn't stand to stay here after that.'

Joyce nodded, almost pitying what her mother had undergone, recalling her own moments of teenage anguish at what she'd later see as minor nadirs in her own pathetic adolescent love life of unspoken crushes. She also found herself grateful to Faith – who had been most intimate with Constance in the final years – for the information. 'Thank you.'

Faith rose and moved over, closer to Joyce. 'Any time.'

There is an expectant pause in Nature here just before a storm, when the collective breath of the animals, birds and insects is held, after they've scurried for cover to await the inevitable rain.

Time had lost meaning, the passing of the hours marked only by the disappearing light and progressive heat within the building, rising with the approaching storm.

They lay there, their outer clothes meagre protection against the harsh stone floor. Sweat beaded down Joyce's body; she'd long since stopped trying to wipe it from herself; her hands were damp, too. And that wasn't all; as the erotic pain of her time with Philippa had subsided into memory, and the aches and fatigue of the day settled within her like water soaked like a sponge, she couldn't help but feel an ache in her pussy. Philippa – this whole adventure – had awakened and stimulated her libido to new heights, new hungers.

She almost didn't realise what she was doing as her hand ventured between her thighs.

But Faith was here, little more than a metre away. She couldn't do anything now. Perhaps later, when she was sure the other woman was asleep.

There was silence, apart from the cicada chirp outside. Then Faith's voice sounded, throaty and unused for hours. 'I'm horny.'

Joyce laughed, more amused and relieved than embarrassed. 'Me, too.'

'Quite a storm building up outside.' As if on cue, lightning brought the girl's soft, dark features briefly to light, the pursuing thunder animating it with a boom that rattled the very foundations of the millennia-old building.

'Yes.' They sat closer together. 'Faith, I'm – I'm sorry.'

'For what?'

'For being a bitch to you.'

Faith chuckled. 'Isn't that supposed to be *my* line?'

Outside, the lightning and thunder continued erratically, like an air raid in some old war film. Faith lay cuddled up to her, leg twining around hers, arm thrown loosely across, starting whenever there was a closer thunderclap.

They faced each other. Feeling a hot wave pass through her, Joyce's eyes drifted down, catching at a moment of lightning her friend's groin, encased like her own in damp knickers. Joyce remembered how she looked, under the waterfall, at the water tower, in the London club, and Joyce felt her own dew escape, quickly gather in the gusset of her knickers. The air, and the tension soaked within it, hung heavily between them. They both knew where this could lead, and in fact hoped for it.

A particularly close thunderclap made even the thick, millennia-old walls rattle – while Faith shrieked and nearly climbed on top of Joyce. They held each other close, Joyce suddenly aware of her nipples growing taut, erect beneath Faith's body.

The next moment, as Faith's lips pressed against her own, Joyce's thoughts ceased. She felt her stomach do somersaults as Faith's tongue caressed Joyce's lips in a snake-like movement, deep and urgent. She reached around to clasp Faith to her, drawing her even closer until their breasts were squashed together.

One of Faith's hands slipped down, very gently between them, to tentatively stroke the mound inside Joyce's pants. Then two fingers dipped under the legband, vanished into Joyce's throbbing, waiting channel, while her thumb flicked over her equally expect-ant clit. Her breasts fell swollen, the nipples strong and pert; Faith pulled her mouth away from Joyce's to engulf one of Joyce's nipples.

Joyce gasped, nearly bucked. Pleased at the reaction, Faith stopped, helped Joyce remove her damp knickers, then her own, and returned to Joyce's waiting, wanting pussy. Her fingers moved in practised dives and circles, occasionally teasing with a nip or two. Joyce felt like melted butter; she was hot and moist, Faith's fingers sliding easily inside her, drawing out more droplets of dew.

Joyce's back arched as Faith lay on her side as her hand continued its ministrations. Joyce, her eyes clamped shut, gritted her teeth as she let her hands reach up to squeeze and knead Faith's breasts, full and firm. Waves of exquisite pleasure ran through her, as Faith stopped teasing and, thumb still placed firmly on Joyce's clit, began pistoning the fore- and middle fingers of her hand in and out of Joyce, who parted her thighs further, gasping and shuddering, a puppet beneath Faith's touch.

Joyce's climax had been as expectant as the rain outside, and now her pleasure overflowed, her climax long and strong and driving. Joyce moaned softly as her head fell on Faith's shoulder, her tears running on to the other woman's bare skin.

'There, there,' Faith said as she gently withdrew her hand and held Joyce's face, planting kisses all over it. It wasn't the thrilling, dominating attitude of Philippa, but one that was caring, loving. 'Now lie down.'

'Like hell.' Joyce gathered her remaining strength and twisted in place, driving forward and grinding a hot, open, demanding kiss on the other woman's lips. Even as she did this, she pushed Faith back until their positions had reversed. Her hand invaded the thin dark strip of Faith's pussy hair, and pierced the deep cleft of her target with her fingers, a target so like her own.

Faith yelped in delight, and she ended up clutching her new lover as Joyce's ministrations continued. Joyce felt Faith's labia, already wet, begin to slide further with the warm fluids she produced under the work of her fingers, and Faith gyrated frantically against Joyce's hand. Meanwhile, Joyce clasped the other woman's shin between her own thighs, and began to stimulate herself, ready to come again, her pace agitated, impatient, her body having been commandeered by her sex.

Not that Joyce cared, drawing up the eddies of pleasure from her loins with each grind of her pussy against Faith's leg, even as Faith moaned in sublime ecstasy, soft rushes of breath escaping through clenched teeth. It was a moment of ineffable rapport.

'Fuck – oh fuck –' Faith was gasping, cursing through clenched teeth. She had a powerful feral aura about her, something which stimulated Joyce tremendously. Her soaking sex sought out faster, harder stimulation from Joyce's fingers, stimulation Joyce readily provided. She bucked on to Joyce's aching hand, cursing the darkness and pleasing Joyce immensely. Then she came, like herself a wanton, shameless bitch in heat, her body pressing harder against Joyce's. The bold animal reactions startled and excited Joyce, and before she realised it, she wanted to do it again. And again. And again.

Finally, Joyce shuddered and twitched as her own second climax washed over her, sending her hips jerking in time to the crest of each wave, her swollen bud yielding to the force of Faith's hard shin against it. It came quickly and easily, lifting her up until she no longer rested on the floor. Her body tightened as the first wave swallowed her, then the second, and she was gasping for breath. She felt as if she were floating in space, and she let her senses revel in it, until she came back down to earth again.

They lay entwined, hot, sweat binding their limbs together like epoxy, their faces nuzzling, their nostrils filled with their own and each other's scents.

Then Faith started giggling, kept doing so until Joyce was prompted to ask, 'Are you OK?'

Faith had to calm down somewhat before she could reply. 'I'm . . . I'm glad to see . . . we've worked out our differences. '

Joyce sighed and reclined back, smiling. 'So am I.'

SEVENTEEN

They reclined naked, the heat in the morning air thick, the sweat on their bodies beading; perhaps later they'd risk meeting snakes and spiders again for another dip under the waterfall. Joyce's nipples were erect again, sending little flares of sensation downwards to her receptive, approving groin, as she stared into Faith's dreamy eyes.

She reached up warily, lightly drawing her fingers along the outline of Faith's smooth, round shoulders, as if to confirm that the woman was real. Despite the heat, Faith shivered, stopping when Joyce's hands rested on her jawline, cradling her head as past lovers had done to Joyce (like Philippa – No! No comparisons!), pressing their mouths together, hot, spent, but still lively. It was so bizarre, doing this with *Faith* . . .

Now Joyce descended, slowly, dramatically, trailing kisses along Faith's throat, tasting sweet sweat, sliding to her full, round breasts, the nipples hard and begging for attention – and receiving it – then past the woman's navel, stopping at her abdomen.

Closer now, Joyce could see fine hairs on Faith's chocolate-brown mound, grass-like stubble reappearing around the mahogany strip of pubic hair; the woman would need to shave again soon, a part of her thought with detachment. Perhaps Joyce could do it for her? Then maybe get her own done in the same way? A laugh was forced down, leaking only into a smile. She could feel her own body, hot and excited, consumed by a desire to become intimate with this woman.

Faith parted her thighs. Joyce was entranced by the sight of the woman's open, waiting sex, an oval shape of delicately sculpted skin that gasped at Joyce's touch. The inner sex was deep pink, shadowed only by the secret folds leading to the vagina, moist with milky dew, and now Joyce could drink in the sweet and heady fragrance, so much like her own. She even thought, or at least imagined, she could see it pulse with desire, as her own was doing again now.

As she peered closer at this wet treasure, she could see the head of Faith's clit, protruding from the folds of flesh encasing it, tasting the air outside. She could feel the heat radiating from within Faith's body as she drew closer, finally burying her face into the other woman.

Faith moaned and clutched Joyce's head, as Joyce sought out the tiny shaft she'd found, her lips wrapping around its throbbing length, sending waves of delight strumming like guitar strings through the woman. Her hands reached under to clasp the fleshy buttocks, which wavered between anticipated tautness and supple submission to the bliss flowing through her.

Joyce felt her own vulva react sharply as her lips left Faith's clitoris, and her tongue drove a trail down to sample the sweet dew, her taste buds awakening as her nose had to these fresh delights, before entering the hot, wet, waiting channel she found. Faith thrashed about in place.

Ignoring her own frantic need for relief, Joyce returned to Faith's hard little nub and began greedily sucking on it, no longer content with gentle exploration. Faith spasmed, the gasps from her inarticulate pleas and demands for Joyce to stop and continue and stop, her fingernails digging into the sides of Joyce's head.

Suddenly Joyce could feel Faith's muscles contracting sharply against her face, indeed her whole body shaking with release; she tried to re-enter her vagina, finding a climax-induced resistance. Joyce sighed against her with a deep satisfaction, stroking the smooth flesh of her thighs, but now with little strength to put aside the clamours of her own needs.

Joyce parted slightly from Faith's crotch to look up at her, feeling Faith's juices on her face, hoping Faith could see them, too. Faith looked down, her hands running through her scalp, before lying back, looking exhausted, looking satisfied. Yes, Joyce had done a good job indeed. She'd wanted to.

But with that need, that want, came doubt. Was she simply on the rebound, from her time with Philippa? Oh God, it had to be.

She sat up. Faith sat up too, crossed her legs and faced Joyce. 'You OK?'

Joyce touched her wet face, didn't want to be seen to be wiping off Faith's come. She nodded. 'Yeah. It's light: we should be heading back. They'll be worried sick.'

Faith nodded at that, and they began dressing. Halfway readying herself, Faith turned and started, 'Joyce, I have to – I have to tell you –'

Joyce stopped. 'What?'

The younger woman seemed to struggle with something within her. Then her face resolved. 'Never mind. It can wait.'

Their stomachs grumbled; the fountain water didn't help. Their pace was inevitably slowed by their increased vigil regarding the bandits.

But in doing so, Joyce found her senses alert to the sheer vivacity and beauty of the jungle. Bedewed ferns beckoned lazily above a carpet of pulpy undergrowth. Morning mist veiled the verdant canopy above, diffusing its light through vaulting branches of trees whose wide trunks were shamrock green from sky to roots with velvety moss and lichens. The air was also woven with the whistle of birds and the skitter of animals in the darkening branches, an endless pastoral. Then there was the smell of the place, raising the scent of a constant stir-fry, eternally moist on their cheeks, uncomfortable in their clothes.

A sound came floating, a low, coughing grumble that made the hair stand up on the back of Joyce's neck. Then some underbrush caught her instep, and she fell forward, cursing, hating herself, hating showing even a moment of weakness in front of Faith –

Then forgot all about it. For without that moment, she would never have seen Constance's luggage.

It hung there from its strap, four metres up in a tree, almost obscured by its dark colours, its soft canvas material, and the surrounding flora.

Joyce and Faith sat or kneeled there for a moment, just staring at it, as if it was some mirage, or some trap. But then, they were still near the plane wreckage.

'It can't be,' Joyce found herself breathing.

'Let's find out.' Faith decided.

It wasn't easy; the tree was virtually unscalable, and they lacked the equipment to properly climb or retrieve the bag; Faith reluctantly ended up using the rifle and its sling to snag the luggage strap.

As Faith worked away, Joyce stood back, fighting to control her excitement. It was not necessarily Constance's bag; it could just as easily be someone else's from the plane.

Except, of course, nearly all the cargo and bags were accounted for.

The bag fell with a thud on to the jungle floor, and Joyce and Faith nearly bumped into each other in their eagerness to examine it further. The olive-drab canvas was damp, thick with moisture, and speckled with bird and animal guano.

But the CW stencilled in black military lettering on one side was intelligible enough. And unequivocal enough.

'Oh shit,' Faith whispered. She started to work at the flap buckles, then paused, thought better of it, and released the bag, glancing at Joyce. 'You're *her* daughter. You should do it.'

Joyce wanted to say something. Instead, she forced her fingers to work properly, wiping moisture from the buckles and straps. The smell of mildew assailed her nostrils as she opened the flap of the bag, and Faith and she found themselves laughing as they both reached in and removed the clothing within, setting them aside.

Had they not smelled so much, Joyce might have taken time out to examine them, items of her late mother's clothing, to see what she was wearing in her final days – judging from their colour and feel, they were rough travelling clothes, similar to her own. Even the yellowed, dog-eared paperback novels – erotic ones, Joyce couldn't help but notice with a smile –

'Hah!' Faith gasped with a manic grin.

There they were.

Five red or black diaries, each one slightly larger than a woman's foot, each other thicker than Joyce's thumb, each one numbered One to Five.

And each one wrapped in protective plastic. Perfectly preserved.

'Oh God,' Joyce found herself breathing, cloaked in awe. Here they were, *finally*, after so long, after so much hardship . . .

Like a mother unwrapping a sleeping infant's swaddling, Joyce uncovered the first of the diaries, set the plastic close by to wrap them up again once they were on the move back to camp; no sense finding them preserved now, only to lose them if they fell into that river again. She opened the front page, recognised at once the familiar swirls of Constance's handwriting, and read aloud. ' "For Saraid. For Joyce. For Faith." '

Faith, squatting there at the foot of the tree, listened, and slumped down, looking both relieved and overcome. She stared away, towards the direction of the wreckage.

Joyce felt the weight on the younger woman, and kept silent. Joyce stared at the words, an obvious dedication for the memoirs. Constance's first lover, her daughter, and her last lover. Well, why not? She thumbed through some of the pages. 'I can't wait to read these in full –'

But then Faith gathered up the other diaries. 'We'd better head back to the city, and then return to camp, before Kimya and Ruth start to have kittens.'

Joyce stared for a moment, then acquiesced, her stomach grumbling. Even hare or topi kebabs would be welcome now.

Moving downhill was of course far easier for them, even with Constance's knapsack slapping against Joyce's back as they followed their way back, across the rickety bridge, and through the thinning forest. 'How are we going to get back to Mzuri without our horses?'

'We'll use two of the pack horses, redistribute the supplies, dump some of the gear.'

'Can we afford to "dump" anything?' She remembered the talks from Kimya about limiting their possessions while on trek to the absolute minimum.

'Most of our remaining pre-fab food. Maybe one of the tents; we'll have to share with others.'

Others. Philippa and Nina, she meant. The reminder of them fell upon her shoulders once more like a snake falling from the higher branches; as if on cue, thunder cracked above and made the life about them shriek or scamper in alarm. Joyce didn't know what was worse: the humiliation she'd undergone these last few days and nights, or the fact that it had so acutely aroused her then – and now.

Her consternation must have been *so* transparent to Faith, who paused, rifle in hand, and smiled affably, sincerely. 'We'll work something out. Stand By Me.' Then, on a cue of her own, she launched into the song of the same title, not stopping with the thunder that silenced the other songbirds many times more on their journey back to the camp.

The gate was open; that should have been the first sign of danger. But the two women, after a night and two days of roughing it far more than they had before, of minimal food and suspect water, of the emotional peaks of making love and finding the diaries, had left them exhausted and distracted.

Seeing Nina up in the search tower, waving towards the huts on their entry but only nodding at them silently, should have been the second sign of danger, as was Zebaki, tied up at the foot of the tower, barking madly. But for Joyce's part, any contact with the abrasive woman was unwelcome, and she could stay up there until Doomsday for all Joyce cared. As for the dog, he was probably just reacting to the imminent storm.

Seeing no one leave the main hut on their approach should have been the third sign; where was Kimya, at least, come to see where they'd been? Unless she was out in the jungle, looking for them right now –

The door burst open; dark-skinned men in full military camouflage outfits and brandishing rifles emerged, aiming their weapons at Joyce and Faith, shouting and snapping in rapid-fire local patois. Joyce froze alongside Faith, unable to understand them, but getting the message when Faith dropped her rifle and raised her hands. Joyce followed suit, too stunned to be afraid. Yet.

The men circled them, grabbed them by their collars and half-pushed, half-dragged them inside the hut.

Kimya and Ruth sat on the floor of the hut, their backs against a wall, their knees drawn up to their chests, their wrists bound, as armed men stood on either side of them; the women looked ragged, exhausted, and Ruth's face sported dried blood.

Philippa sat at the card table, cradling a battered tin cup in her hands, her face unreadable. She sat beside a large, broad-faced, broad-shouldered, bearded man with skin the colour of dark chocolate, and weather-worn fatigues and boots.

Joyce couldn't help but feel the pang of emotion on seeing the woman, even in the rising fear and confusion over the armed strangers. 'Philippa, what's –'

The bearded man barked something in the local language, but was understandable enough for Joyce to stop speaking. He rose from his seat and approached, his attention seemingly focused on Joyce alone, but still keeping a defensive posture around the equally tense Faith. He orbited them, smelling of sweat and cigars and alcohol.

Then there were the hands, huge and callused. And invasive. The hairs on Joyce's neck rose, and she shuddered and stiffened, half-expecting them on her, but still fighting to control herself, to keep from fighting back at the invasion. The smells, the touch lingered after he returned to stand beside Philippa, his words now in fractured English. 'You were right: fit *and* beautiful.'

Philippa lifted her cup closer to her mouth, but didn't drink. 'They'd hardly have made it this far if they *hadn't* been fit, Achebe. And they *are* beautiful, just like in the photos I sent you from Patricksburg.'

'And will they respond?'

Philippa smiled. 'Faith will need breaking in. Joyce . . . was born to servitude.'

Joyce was chomping at the bit for answers; she could almost feel the same from Faith. Outside, the thunder clapped again, making the very walls rattle.

She caught Philippa's gaze again, and the woman almost looked ready to avert her gaze, but instead ordered, 'Put the bag on the table, Joyce.' She drank from her cup and added, 'And don't expect me to explain things all over again. Let the others fill you in.'

Joyce didn't move until the bearded man barked at her again, and the rickety table nearly collapsed from the impact of the bag. Then Philippa reached out of view and lifted up something familiar: the collar. 'You keep losing this, my dear. I thought I taught you better.' It dropped to the table. 'Put it on again. Show Captain Achebe how obedient you are.'

Joyce remained still, fighting to sort out the miasma of emotions within her. 'Philippa –'

'If you don't put it on, I'll have one of the captain's men shoot Zebaki.'

Grinding her teeth in confusion and agitation, Joyce obeyed. Then she found Faith and herself pushed towards Ruth and Kimya, made to sit down on the floor in front of them.

Joyce ran her hand lightly over her body, as if to wipe the memory of that man Achebe's hands from it, and listened to Philippa opening the bag behind them, as Faith leaned forward towards the other two women and whispered, 'What the fuck –'

'They're slavers,' Kimya uttered simply.

Faith just cursed and blessed herself. Joyce wasn't sure she heard correctly. '*What?*'

Ruth looked as if she'd been up all night. Or had they . . . hurt her? 'They're slavers from across the border. They abduct people, carry them across a border or two, and sell them.'

'That doesn't happen nowadays!' Joyce blurted out, suddenly feeling foolish for the denial, for the reactions from the others. She hadn't felt so naïve in so long a time. After all, wasn't Philippa working for an organisation investigating modern slavery here? Her voice and pride lowered, she asked, 'What is she doing with them? Negotiating for our release?'

Ruth's expression darkened into a frightening enmity. 'That *khazer* is negotiating, all right. But not for our release. For our sale.'

Joyce's stomach twisted into knots. She fought to keep from looking behind her. Before she could ask the inevitable, Kimya continued, 'Nina and she arranged for them to capture us here.'

Joyce's breath quickened now. 'But . . . *why*?'

'The tontine,' Ruth explained wearily. 'The publishing contract. It's worth millions even if all of us are there to sign the final papers. But for two survivors of an "accident" while in Africa, it'll be worth far more.'

Money. Philippa and Nina were selling out her friends, her . . . for *money*? Joyce gripped her hands together; Faith reached out and clasped a hand over Joyce's, adding, 'There were men around the wreckage. Achebe's men.'

Kimya nodded. 'They're the "poachers" who have been running parallel to us all this time. Keeping an eye on us. They went to find you yesterday morning after you went missing.'

'Why didn't they take us before we even reached the camp?' Faith asked.

'Partly so Philippa and Nina could find the diaries first. Then I think Achebe panicked when you two disappeared. Also, sometimes army patrols will appear and stop travellers in the savannah, check their credentials. If they'd stopped Achebe and his men, they would have seen fake papers claiming they were our "escorts", keeping a fair distance from us to give us "girls" a sense of privacy and independence, as if we were doing it on our own.'

'But we *were*!'

'Tell that to some pig-headed army officer.'

'Now Philippa and Nina will return to Mzuri,' Ruth continued blankly. 'Telling a tale of tragedy, of our bodies being washed away in the coming –' outside, the thunder cracked again, and a torrent of rain began pelting down on the hut, a billion tiny drumbeats '– storm. The bodies won't be expected to be found;

222

the jungle leaves very little behind for forensics. It will be a grim end to the story of Constance's life.'

'Maybe they'll make a book on its own about it,' Faith quipped sardonically, having to raise her voice over the downpour outside.

'And what will happen to us?' Joyce had to ask, though she feared the answer.

Kimya sighed. 'Any number of fates, in any number of countries. None of them attractive.'

There was a chilling finality to the woman's words; living here, she was obviously more knowledgeable about this abhorrent trade than the rest of them. And Philippa's earlier words, about Joyce being 'born to servitude' . . . all the episodes of sexual submission . . . Had she been *training* Joyce? Testing her reactions to being under the authority of another? Surely one could enjoy being dominated without playing out a servile role in *real* life?

Had she anything substantial in her stomach, Joyce would have brought it up by now.

'I take it you've found the diaries?' Ruth asked bleakly. 'Then we'll be leaving soon.'

Now, for the first time since arriving, something like a smile of hope – or desperation – crept on to Faith's face, and she glanced at Joyce. 'Oh, I wouldn't say that just yet.'

And suddenly, Joyce felt the same way.

EIGHTEEN

Philippa's face was quite the picture of wrath. '*Where are the diaries?*'

Faith glanced up, as if just asked for the time. 'What? The *dairies*? Go find your own fricking cows . . .'

The woman strode from the table, uncaring about knocking over Constance's bag and its belongings to the floor, boiling with rage. 'What did you do with them?'

Joyce kept her face neutral, the moment of triumph at having seen Philippa's reaction already passing. She'd contemplated denying that they had even found the diaries – better that they never see the light of day again, rather than let this bitch profit by them – but then realised that without the diaries, they had nothing left to bargain with.

Only now did Joyce figure out why Faith had been adamant about not bringing the diaries back to camp straight away. A stance which turned out to be most justified, under the circumstances.

With an abrupt snarl Philippa grabbed Joyce by the collar and half-dragged her to her feet, spinning her in place and practically shrieking, '*Where are they?*'

The utter lack of control on the superior Philippa's part triggered a half-nervous, half-pleased smirk on Joyce's part. A smirk wiped away when Philippa struck her face with the back of her hand.

And with an abrupt snarl of her own, Joyce struck back, delivering a roundhouse across Philippa's jaw.

The women fell to the floor, struggling, cursing and scratching, while Joyce dimly heard the cries of her friends and fellow captives, and the laughter and shouts from their captors.

Somebody stepped in, pulled the two women apart and back on their feet. It was the man Achebe, grasping their shirts in his huge fists, extending his long arms to keep them as far apart as possible. His laughter boomed like the thunder outside. 'No, no – can't have the new women damaged!'

Joyce's struggles ended at that, at the reminder of how this man viewed her, as property, as commodity. It was almost inconceivable.

Almost, but not enough for her not to want to do something about it.

And Faith picked up the ball and carried it, twisting in place on the floor and rising to an almost-predatory crouch, facing Philippa, her face flushed with a rage of her own. 'Aww, is poor little Philippa gonna lose out on all those millions? My heart bleeds for ya, skank.'

'Not yet, it doesn't,' Philippa snapped, moving towards Faith now, but still restrained in Achebe's grip. 'Let me go!'

Achebe grinned Cheshire. 'Not to harm her, either.'

'The deal isn't over yet! You have them, but I don't have the diaries.'

'That's not my problem,' the man replied simply, looking only slightly amused at Philippa's loss.

Philippa stopped struggling and looked at him. Joyce, her face tingling from where Philippa had struck her, closed her now-torn shirt and watched them both, unsure. They were still in the same dilemma as before, when they considered denying finding the diaries. What if they tried bargaining –

Joyce's mind paused at the sight of Philippa's face, watched her posture soften and melt before the huge man. Her hands glided along his arms to his shoulders, then his face, stroking him gently, like a cat. Only it was her voice which purred. 'Captain, love, I really, really *need* those diaries. Can't you make them talk? If you could, I would be *so* grateful.'

She performed so well, Joyce almost believed her.

And when Philippa's hands moved down Achebe's chest, to his belt, to his trousers, stroking him through the ever-tightening material, Joyce forced her gaze to remain on the man's face, to see his reaction. He was aroused, interested, and then, perhaps in realising how vulnerable and manipulated he might seem right now, adopted a harsh, stony countenance, more to scare Joyce than out of any genuine rancour, pushing Philippa away to focus on Joyce. 'Tell where the books are, now!'

'Go to hell.' Joyce had no idea where that came from. Was it her own mouth? No, she wasn't *that* brave.

He backhanded her across the face; she surprised herself, again, by remaining standing.

Achebe withdrew from the leather holster at his right hip a vicious-looking black revolver with a long barrel. He pointed it to the ceiling, moving his hand gently as if it were a rattle and he was trying to attract a baby's quicksilver attentions. 'You see, I don't wear this for fashion. I *use* it.' Now he pointed it at her forehead. 'And I can use it on *you*.'

Joyce tried to focus on the man's eyes, on the throbbing lower lip, on anything rather than the long black barrel, just inches from her skull. She fought the urge to release her bladder then and there – more than enough time to do that if he shoots you, she mindlessly quipped – and to keep from hyperventilating.

And it worked.

'Last chance.' He cocked the hammer back, with a click she felt more than heard, while the storm raged outside, like an audience desperate for an exciting conclusion to the play.

Within herself, Joyce sought the fear in order to control it – only to find none. Yes, her life could end, here and now, in an anonymous hut in the middle of Africa, half a world away from the one she thought was enough for her.

But it didn't matter.

She'd been offered a feast called life . . .

'I said last chance,' Achebe muttered with a death's head grin.

Now she focused on his eyes deliberately. 'And *I* said go to hell.'

She'd already lived more than she could ever have hoped, had done things – both good and bad – that had been the stuff of dreams beforehand. If now was the time the feast would end, then so be it.

But it wasn't. He dropped his gun arm, and dropped her, half-falling into Faith's arms below, while he started arguing with Philippa. Joyce half-lay there in Faith's lap, while the younger woman embraced her, murmuring, 'Pretty brave, girl. Pret-ty brave.'

Joyce felt herself grinning, felt herself melting to the woman's touch, her scent. 'Yes, it *was* brave, wasn't it?'

Now Faith's smile became a smirk. 'Of course, he *was* bluffing, you know. You're too valuable to kill, just for Philippa.'

Joyce stuck a defiant tongue at her.

Beside them, Kimya finally spoke up, in the local language, directed at Achebe. He paused and looked over at the captives, first looking to silence the guide, then listening.

Then laughing, and replying, gesturing at Philippa, before returning to the woman's attention.

Kimya cursed under her breath, as Ruth asked, 'What was that?'

'I was tempting Achebe with taking *six* captives across the border, rather than just us four.'

'Oh. I take it he didn't buy it?'

The woman shook her head. 'If all six disappear, the army will be out in force and tighten the border patrols. If just us four "accidentally" drown in the nearest river, our bodies lost, but our deaths verified by Philippa and Nina –'

'It's simply marked as a tragedy.' Joyce nodded. 'And international pressure doesn't fall on the government to track our kidnappers.' She breathed through her nose. 'I suppose we'll not be able to summon help wherever . . . '

Faith finished the query for her. 'Wherever we're sold?' A cold but not unsympathetic smirk creased her features. 'Those sorts of brothels don't usually feature a lot of outside communications for their . . . workers.' She hissed. 'Fuck it!' Then she turned in place to glare at Philippa. 'Hey, bitch! You want the diaries? Then we deal!'

Philippa turned, throwing back a look that chilled Joyce to her bones. It was not an angry look, not a desperate look. It was a look of someone who suddenly finds themselves at a high stakes power game, with a winning hand. She took the revolver from Achebe and approached, unable – and unwilling – to restrain the gleam in her eyes. 'Yes. We deal.' She raised the revolver in their direction. 'You tell me where they are, or one of you dies.'

Joyce tensed, but Faith rested her head on one fist in her lap and grinned. 'That's already been tried, sweetheart. We're too valuable to kill –'

'I just bought one of you,' Philippa declared simply.

Now all the captives tensed as one.

'My investment in this undertaking has grown considerably,' she continued. 'But it will *still* be well worth it, once I have the diaries, once the deal is signed in Manhattan.' She struggled slightly with the hammer on the large revolver, but managed to cock it back. 'Now,' she concluded, 'I'm not going to say which of you I've bought. But I *will* say it's not you, Joyce. You'll live to see another day – but are you willing to just sit there and watch one of your friends die?'

Even if Joyce wanted to give another answer, which she didn't, her expression to Faith already gave away her true feelings.

And Philippa saw, as well, lowering the revolver. 'Good. You'd better get up and get your raingear. Wouldn't want you catching flu.'

Africa, Joyce had concluded a lifetime ago, did nothing in small measures: life, beauty, expanse, heat, cold, tranquillity, danger.

And now rain.

It had indeed opened up like the Apocalypse, and it was only the beginning. The rain beat upon their ponchos with a million tiny assaults, merging into a hypnotic drone that kept them marching along through the forest.

Well, that, and the two men with guns close behind them.

The ground was quickly turning into mud, even under the relative shelter of the trees, and Joyce had to struggle to keep her boots from sinking and remaining. Beside her, tied to her own wrist, Faith was grunting. Exhaustion, hunger, fear; it looked to be an effort for her to just keep her head up.

Joyce understood that. She tugged at the rope, catching her attention. Faith's face was barely visible past the hood of her poncho; she looked like some sort of monk or *Star Wars* character.

Joyce's mouthed question was plain: *what are we going to do?*

They couldn't fight the two armed men escorting them to the diaries. They couldn't bring the diaries back. There was no cavalry over the hills, ready to rescue them.

Faith gasped, then deliberately looked ahead, nodding. Joyce's gaze followed: the footbridge.

Joyce looked to her again; should they run across it, surprise the men, or –

Oh no.

And yet, despite the pangs of renewed terror, Joyce nodded too, and proceeded, hoping Faith could swim as well as herself. She was glad they had convinced Philippa that only the both of them could find the hiding place for the diaries.

The bridge was creaking, with little wonder; the stream they had seen only hours before had grown into a torrent, a loud torrent of water that rushed and swirled down the ravine, occasionally carrying dead branches and other things with it, or perhaps it was just Joyce's imagination.

A moment's hesitation as they stepped on to the bridge, together, but they continued, Joyce feeling herself grow more resolute, more focused. She could do this. She could do this. Her mother could have done it. So can Joyce.

They reached the open spot, where part of the railing and path had broken away yesterday, leaving it open for anyone clumsy or unlucky enough to fall into the water.

Or anyone wanting to jump in.

Taking a deep breath, she reached out, took Faith by the hand, and pulled them both over the edge.

They hung in the air – for a heartbeat. Joyce would swear later that she heard the call of the men behind them, still on the bridge, obviously shocked by the act of obvious suicide.

Then they hit the water, warm, violent water that dragged them under, catching their ponchos like wind in sails. She had caught a good breath, and she knew how long she could hold it – under normal circumstances. Tumbling along the bottom of these rapids, she rapidly lost nearly all her lungful in moments, but refused to surface.

She forced her eyes open; the river was not really deep, but it was dark, the dirt whipped into a froth by the water's churn. Seeing stars flashing against the blackness of her vision, she pumped for some anchor, yet also dimly aware that they couldn't stop too soon, or the men would see them and track them down. Drums beat and roared in her ears – my pulse, she wondered, or the water? Whichever. Either way, it sounded as if it would burst the sides of her head in a moment.

The river threw them with a vicious slam into a gnarled, hidden tree root. She wrapped an arm around it, feeling it wrench as she hung on to Faith as well.

Joyce's lungs were heaving after that. It took every iota of will not to open her mouth and suck in river water. With faltering strength, she helped Faith and herself to the surface.

The first gasp of air tasted sweeter than honey. The second, third, fourth and fifth calmed her nerves. By the twelfth, she was aware enough to wonder whether Achebe's men would swiftly pluck them out of the flow and haul them, streaming water, back to the camp.

Head whirling, vision blurred as if drugged, she teetered for a few agonising seconds in the swift churning river around her. Her clothes were getting heavier, even in their now tattered state, and her skin felt cut and bruised in several places. She struggled to stay afloat, but the task was nearly impossible between the roar of the water and the weight of their soaked boots and clothing. As she clung, fighting the force of the water, she removed the rope connecting them together, wrapping her legs about Faith's middle, then began stripping off, modesty be damned, helping a near-unconscious Faith to do likewise.

In barely nothing at all, Joyce now inched them both along the root towards shore – then lost her grip, as they were pulled underwater again, helpless as babies, bound at the wrist. Joyce rolled under the surface of the thundering force, somehow finding the strength or luck to propel both of them to the surface again, just in time to take a feeble breath. She was nearly finished, but the air was sweet again, and she felt a grip under her feet, a grip of mud.

Joyce pitched forward into grey muck, dragging Faith along and turning her on to her back, dimly thinking to check the younger woman. Faith was coughing and spluttering, spitting up water – but at least she was still breathing.

Joyce lay back beside her, letting the rain pelt their mud-stained, near-nude bodies. She felt delirious – and excited. Exhilarated, as she had when Ruth and she were nearly killed in that stampede. Even when they were being pursued in the jungle by Achebe's men yesterday.

Madness.

'You – you –'

Joyce turned her head and blinked at Faith through glazed eyes, wondering if the woman was trying to speak. She reached out and patted her weakly, comfortingly on the shoulder. 'It's . . . all right. We . . . made it.'

'You – you –' Faith rose up on to her elbows, coughed again, and looked at Joyce. '*You crazy bitch*! Why'd . . . you pull us into –' she coughed '– the fucking river like that?'

Baffled and dazed, Joyce tried shaking the wet matted hair from her forehead, found she had to comb it back weakly with her fingers. 'But – but that's what you were signalling, on the path! That we should make a break in the river –'

'No I didn't! I was –' she coughed again '– I was signalling that we should . . . should keep going, and wait until we get back to the plane wreck!'

'You nodded once!'

'I was flicking the water from my face!'

'That's what your fucking hand is for!'

They paused, breathing heavily, glaring at each other – and

began giggling. That was all they could do, at their present energy levels.

The following minutes – hours? – were lost in a struggle to work their way through the jungle, uphill, staggering and enduring more cuts and scratches on their bare feet, their bare skins. Above them, the assault of the rain was partly eased by the thicker tree cover, the endless patter easing the silence between them, the silence brought about by a need to conserve their strength.

They found the diaries, where they'd hidden them, in the room of the hidden city, the room where they'd spent the night – and made love.

The sky above was milk and slate, and continued to weep as they sought dry twigs and kindling for a meagre fire. Faith helped Joyce off with her collar, tried striking the metal studs on it against the stone floor to generate sparks, even as Joyce pondered what else could be used as fuel. Their bras and knickers were soaked; what about – no, not the diaries. Unless there were some blank pages –

'Dammit!' Faith cried out, hurling the collar to the far corner of the room. She kneeled by the twigs and leaves, wrapping her arms about herself, lifting her breasts up as she began shivering, her teeth chattering. 'Where are the saints when you need them the most?'

Joyce sat there, with her back against the wall. And began stripping. 'Get those things off.'

Faith shuddered from the chill, looked up; her face was wet, though whether from the rain or from tears, Joyce couldn't tell. 'What?'

Joyce slid her bra down from her arms, wiping one forearm across and under her breasts, then reached for the waistband of her knickers. 'Do it! Get undressed! We have to get warm again.'

Faith kneeled there, nodding absently, and began reaching behind her. When she didn't move quickly enough, a naked Joyce crawled over to her and helped, concerned about the clammy feel of Faith's skin. She rubbed the skin vigorously, even as Faith tried the same.

'It's OK,' Joyce was saying, aware, even in her need to keep them warm, how they kneeled facing each other closely, how their breasts pressed against each other, how like a mirror it seemed, even with the difference in skin colour.

'H-hold me,' Faith whispered. 'Please.'

A sudden eclipse of invulnerability. Quickly, readily, Joyce took Faith in her arms, embracing her, squeezing strongly, confidently, rocking in pace gently.

Joyce gratefully hugged her back – but wanted more. She wanted to make love to Faith again. She wanted intimacy, the comfort of a living body next to hers. She wanted a reaffirmation of her own vitality, her own continued existence. She wanted a distraction from her exhaustion, from their situation. She wanted all that, and more.

And when Joyce pulled back enough to press her lips against Faith's, and Faith responded positively, Joyce knew instinctively that Faith wanted the same.

It was a strange, frantic ballet of theirs, a dance of lips and tongues and limbs, of kisses and embraces as they lay down upon the harsh stone floor.

The meagre grey light from the outside lent Faith's dark skin a delicate sheen, and Joyce stroked her lovingly, inhaling the distinctive warm aroma of her intimate parts. Invigorated now, they explored the nooks and crannies of their bodies, lying voluptuously on one another, rubbing their nipples against each other's velvety, charged skin, thrusting their pelvises and loins together so that their mounds met, sensitive vulvas touching, to be replaced by fingers and lips and tongues seeking the inner places.

Joyce bent over her lover, relishing the smell and taste of her, erotic and enticing, admiring her huge dark eyes, her skin, her nose, slightly flattened so that the nostrils flared, her dazzling white teeth and beautiful, rapacious lips. Eagerly she passed her hands over the dark breasts, and sucked those hard nipples into her mouth. Faith lay on her back and spread her legs, lifting her pelvis so Joyce could see every one of her female secrets, could see things she couldn't in the dark.

She could see Faith's lovely brown-pink pussy. She could see

Faith's clit: large and swollen with excitement, the head fiery – unspeakably beautiful.

She came very quickly against Joyce's tongue, her juices running copiously, wetting her lover's mouth. Instantly she twisted, agile as a cat, and her own tongue fastened on Joyce's clit, sucking and licking till she, too, spiralled into a mind-blowing climax.

Time had no meaning. They lay entwined about each other, absently stroking each other's arms, neither wanting to make the first move towards working out what they were going to do.

'We have to get moving,' Joyce announced finally.

'Not yet,' Faith breathed.

'We shouldn't delay. We have to plan, to –'

'I mean, I have something to say. In case something . . . happens later.' She shifted in place, reached out and stroked Joyce's face. 'Something I should have told you before. It's about Constance.'

Joyce sighed. 'Faith, you don't have to say anything about Constance. She was my mother; she had responsibility for my welfare, that's all.'

'She had responsibility for my welfare, too.'

Faith's words and their implication didn't sink in right away. When they did, Joyce twisted slowly to face Faith, her reply unsure, tenuous. 'Pardon? You're my . . . *sister?*' Joyce felt her head shake in utter disbelief. She disentangled herself from Faith and paced naked about the room, her hands moving together as if trying to juggle all this revelation being thrown to her. This was too much.

'Not exactly – and certainly not biologically. I was born in Mahali. My natural mother was Saraid Bizaro . . . Constance's first love. The man she married later was my father; he died soon after. Saraid lived and worked on her own in Patricksburg, had lost touch with Constance – but never forgot her.'

Faith rose to her feet as well. It looked bizarre – two nude women, former adversaries, walking about an ancient African city room, sharing life stories after making love – but bizarrely appropriate, as they could no longer hide anything of themselves, within or without. 'After Constance was forced out of Britain, she returned to Mahali, somehow found Saraid. I was six at the time, but still remember this strange white woman coming to live with us, all laughter and songs and stories from the Big World. They had only a year together, before Saraid died.'

Pain gripped Joyce's bosom. 'I'm sorry.'

'Me, too.' Faith paused, breathed in deeply, continued. 'Saraid left me in Constance's custody, and Constance arranged for me to leave Mahali and go to New York. I didn't see her often, but I grew up there, and I got an education – boarding school, believe it or not – and an attitude.' She smirked. 'I even had Constance change my surname to the more Anglicised "Ballard", 'cos I didn't want to be called Miss "Bizarro"; did you know it means "bald"?' She ran a hand quickly over her scalp and made a laughing sound. 'Much later, when I was an adult, we became friends. I left school and we travelled, and talked. About you, among many other things.'

Joyce couldn't help but smile, even a bittersweet one. 'You became the daughter she wanted *me* to be, sharing her life, her adventure. No wonder you hated me so much.'

Faith's expression grew grave, and she moved closer to Joyce, taking the woman's hands in her own. 'That was wrong of me, arrogant. My relationship with Constance was not that of a mother and daughter. We were lovers, as adults. Still, I'm sorry.'

'But why didn't you tell me about this before?'

Faith swallowed, looking more guilty than ever. 'I asked the others not to say anything; I was angry, and jealous. The tontine gave you another opportunity to be a part of her life, even after her death. An opportunity I didn't think you deserved.' She shook her head. 'Man, in the history of stupid things, that's got to be in the Top Ten.'

Faith grinned, drew Joyce into an embrace. Joyce hugged her back, still needing that closeness, that comfort. She'd lost a mother, but found a lover.

NINETEEN

There wasn't much time. No doubt Achebe's men would have returned with news of the women's escape and/or death. Which would mean one of several possibilities: Philippa arranging for the men to continue the search, no matter how futile, for the diaries; Achebe searching for the missing women, in the belief that they might not be dead; or Achebe cutting his losses and departing with his 'property', leaving Philippa and Nina high and dry to do the searching.

Whatever the outcome, Joyce and Faith had to get back, reconnoitre, see about freeing Ruth and Kimya. As to how they were going to take on half a dozen armed men . . .

The rain had let up a little, and Joyce knelt by a patch of mud, digging her hands into the muck to coat her body. It went against her instincts to get deliberately dirty, but it made for good camouflage. She was wearing her bra and knickers again, and she had to keep her mind focused away from her relative state of undress.

Nearby, Faith was using a sharp-edged stone to frantically carve points on to the ends of thick, sturdy, relatively straight-looking branches, forming makeshift spears. She wore only her knickers; her bra lay in near tatters beside her, following an unsuccessful attempt to make a sling of sorts. But it might still come in useful, she'd promised Joyce.

Joyce nodded at that, more interested in the way Faith's breasts hung on the younger woman, the curves of them and the dark nipples. Faith was so beautiful, in a way Joyce couldn't have appreciated a fortnight before. Her 'sister'. Even in the midst of their tribulations, Joyce couldn't help but grin madly at the very notion.

'There,' Faith said, stabbing the last of the makeshift spears into the earth between them. 'Best I can do, on short notice and without proper tools.' She breathed heavily. 'Robinson Crusoe, I'm not.'

'They'll do,' Joyce assured her, coating her arms in more mud, then her breasts. The unanswered question was whether or not the women could actually *use* such things on another human being. Even slavers.

Well, they'd soon find out, wouldn't they?

Faith rose, looking in Joyce's direction and moved to kneel behind her. 'You've missed a few places, White Girl.' Chuckling, she scooped up handfuls of mud and slapped it on to Joyce's cambered back, smearing it about while chuckling further at Joyce's yelp. 'Hey, no pain, no gain.'

'Bollocks.' Then Joyce paused as Faith's hands moved over Joyce's backside, over her knickers. 'Hey –'

'Hey yourself; we've got to muddy these, too. Unless you want to go back without them?'

Joyce braced herself as Faith's hand moved between Joyce's cheeks, between her legs, stroking her crotch from behind. The touch of the woman was electrifying. 'No, don't –'

'Don't you like it?' Faith teased.

'Yes – but now's not the time –'

'Later?'

'Yes, later!'

'Promise?'

Reluctantly – *very* reluctantly – Joyce pulled away from the younger woman's touch and turned to face her. 'Yes, I promise! OK?'

Faith nodded, but she couldn't keep the anxiety from her

expression. 'Good. That promise will keep you safe. You wouldn't dare go to the afterlife beholden to me, now will you?'

Then Joyce understood, understood how afraid Faith really was. It was a fear Joyce shared. But it was also coupled with an exhilaration, a sense of purpose and resolution. She'd never felt so alive.

La Vida Loca.

And it was within the space of just a few quickened heartbeats, but Joyce felt a sudden, profound elation, one which brought tears to her eyes. She'd travelled far, seen and heard and felt and tasted so much, experienced so much, more in the last fortnight than in all the rest of her life beforehand. If she died, here and now, her only regret would be that she hadn't done it all before. It was an immense, complete satisfaction with herself an ineffable rush of joy at being who she was, where she was, when she was. She felt so very much *alive* now.

Was this how her mother felt all the time, she wondered idly, already knowing the answer.

She pulled Faith into a kiss, a hard, grinding, passion-soaked kiss that appeared to take Faith's breath away. Joyce was taking risks, chancing it, just as those women in her dreams had encouraged her to. She had more in common with her mother than she had thought. Then Joyce pulled back and slapped Faith on the thigh. 'Right, let's get to work.'

And they did, tramping back down from the Hidden City, steering clear of the original trails, ignoring the cuts and bruises on their bare feet. Even with the rain, most of it kept from them by the canopy of green above, it was warm, humid, but at least it kept Joyce's mud camouflage fresh.

Her senses were on alert, always scanning about her, while carrying several spears in her grip. She'd never felt so primal, so prehistoric, an animal in search of prey. Already before leaving they'd caught a snake, killed and eaten it raw; their initial aversion had been overruled by hunger, their need for sustenance to keep them going if they were to be any good to the others.

Behind her, Faith bounced along. Both women had remained

silent, alert, conscious of saving their energy. Around them, the jungle abided, oblivious to the coming struggle, or at least not acknowledging it as being any more significant than the million other grapples for survival which occurred here every day and night.

That didn't make Joyce feel insignificant, however. On the contrary, she felt such an integral part of things . . . even in her current state, without clothes, without modern weapons, she felt strong.

Of course, if some body armour and machine-guns were to drop from the skies about now, she would not be ungrateful.

The camp was a flurry of activity, even in the rain; the gates were open and Achebe's men moved about a large, battered-looking truck with military olive-drab colours, including the dirty canvas stretched over a high covering frame in the back.

Behind some trees, Joyce had to ask, 'Is it the army? Have they come to rescue us?' Despite her hopeful voice, a part of her felt . . . disappointed at the prospect, at not being able to handle things themselves, sort out their own destinies.

But Faith's reply made it academic. 'It's Achebe's. They must have kept it hidden when we showed up this morning, so as not to put us on the alert.' She slumped against the tree. 'Jesus, Joyce, what the hell were we thinking? Two naked women, armed with fricking spears, against *them*?'

'It's not about gender, or strength, or numbers,' Joyce found herself saying – and believing. 'It's about being sneaky. And ruthless –' She paused, watching as figures emerged from one of the huts, flanked by armed men. 'Ruth! Kim!'

'Yeah!' Now Faith frowned. 'But who're . . .'

Her words trailed off, having answered her own question, and Joyce's own unspoken one. Because more than just Ruth and Kimya were being led along, bound by the hands on a single linking rope – Philippa and Nina were attached to it too, both looking the worse for wear.

Faith couldn't help but smirk. 'Looks like Achebe's made up for his loss of the pair of us.'

Joyce grunted, tightened her grip on her spear. Yes, there *was* satisfaction at seeing Philippa hoisted by her own petard. But there was also the bare bones of a plan. 'The guards are all wearing ponchos, leaving the women exposed to the rain.'

'Yeah, bastards –'

'No, listen: those hoods hang low. They can barely see ahead of them, remember?'

Something like a smile stretched Faith's lips in both direction. 'Yeah. Keep your head low, watch your step, don't trip in the mud.'

Joyce fed the line of reasoning further. 'And what do they have to look up for anyway? Their prisoners are tied up in front of them.'

'The rain, and Zebaki's barking, can cover our approach,' Faith added, liking the idea more and more. 'Come on.'

Joyce nodded, before she had time to think too much about it.

They darted from tree to tree as they approached the front gate. Away from the softer earth beneath in the forest, it was more difficult on the feet, but they grit their teeth and bore it, glancing up at the search tower: no one there. Joyce's heart was pounding like a rabbit's; she looked down to see her knuckles white around the thick, pointed spear.

She was going to kill someone today.

Now.

Ahead of her, she saw her friends – and enemies – roped together, being led to fates that were surely, to coin a cliché, worse than death. No one else could save them.

The man turned, facing her, suddenly making her moral quandary academic.

As did Ruth, suddenly charging him from behind even as Joyce used her spear as a club, smacking him across the side of his head, sending him sprawling.

Joyce looked away, not knowing what Ruth might be doing to him, not wanting to know, and poked the second man in the gut with the blunt end of her spear, even as Faith, and then Kimya, brought him down.

'Joyce, help with this!'

Joyce forced herself to look back, saw Ruth holding an appro-
priated knife in her bound hands. She was all decision, all action.
'Joyce, now!'

Joyce didn't have to be told a third time. Frantically, with hands
shaking, Joyce worked at the nylon ropes, watching the frays
appear one after the other, blossoming –

Sounds from the hut, a door opening – more swiftly than Joyce
could have imagined, Ruth spun in her squatted position, snapped
the remains of the ropes the rest of the way, pointed the man's
rifle and fired several rounds behind her. Joyce looked up to see
an open door, hear the sting of bullets strike the tin frame around
the doorway. She saw no bodies; either Achebe and his men were
swift enough to duck back inside, or –

'In the truck!' Ruth was barking. 'All of you!'

Joyce returned to the immediate, saw Kimya and Faith scavenge
a knife, gun and ammunition from the other man – Joyce didn't
look too closely to see if he was still alive – and cut Kimya's bonds.

Leaving Philippa and Nina bound together. Joyce shot Philippa
a wrathful glare, one which had the effect of making the other
woman wince. What did she see in Joyce now, besides a near-
naked, mud-stained, wild-eyed woman?

No victim any more, that was for certain.

And what did Joyce see in Philippa?

Nothing repeatable.

Nina, however, was acting as if she'd done nothing to deserve
her fate, holding up her bound hands as if in supplication. 'Hey!
Lemme help!'

'You wanna help?' Faith sneered, grabbing one end of the rope
holding the women together. 'Become a fricking human shield!'

'Faith! Kim! Get the truck started!' Ruth repeated, flattening
fully on to the ground and firing another couple of rounds. Inside
the hut, there were shouts and curses, and Joyce understood her
urgency: they'd soon be firing back.

As if on cue, shots cracked the air from the hut, and bullets
stung the ground and the canopy covering the truck, like mosquitoes braving the rain. Joyce took action, pointing her spear/
club at Philippa and Nina. 'In the back! *Now!*'

They didn't have to be told again. As she climbed in after them, staying low behind some crates and supplies the slavers kept back there, she wondered why she didn't just leave the two of them to a well-deserved fate. Probably for the same reason she chose not to kill that man, no matter how much he may have deserved it: having just learned to fully appreciate life, she could hardly take it away from even the most execrable human beings.

More shots, and the sounds of struggle. The three women crouched low in the back, Joyce's eyes darting between the open rear of the truck and the women.

Nina rubbed her bound hands together as if cold (not too improbably, given they were all drenched). 'Nice outfit, Joy-Joy. Very Sheena, Queen of the Jungle –'

Joyce sneered. 'You can impress the Mahali courts with your patter. Both of you.'

But the woman, her wet platinum blonde hair clinging to her head, merely stared back blankly. 'I'm not going to jail.'

Something about the way she said that made Joyce grip her spear even tighter.

Philippa leaned forward, eyes open and unblinking. 'Untie us, Joyce. We can do a deal, the three of us. Collect the tontine –'

'Spare me,' Joyce interrupted. 'I wouldn't trust you to tell me the sky was blue.' Next to her, she saw a crumpled man's shirt in swirling olive-drab camouflage colours. It wasn't the cleanest of items of wear, but she slipped into it, feeling a chill from the rain and the adrenalin. The canopy behind Philippa and Nina suddenly sprouted several holes as bullets thudded against and through it, and they dived face down together on to a pile of assorted equipment.

Joyce smirked, then started at the roar of the truck engine and the consequent rumble of the chassis, like thunder. It began to move with protests to its gears and the bad traction in the mud, and she crawled to the open rear, looked out to see Ruth, still on the ground! '*Ruth!*'

The woman wasn't there! Had she jumped into the front of the truck or had she been captured, or – Then the slim, muscular figure appeared from the opposite periphery of Joyce's vision, carrying the rifle in both hands and pounding double-time towards the rear of the truck, alongside a now-freed Zebaki!

Joyce almost called out to the front, to get them to slow down. But inertia and the bumpy road surface took care of that already, and in short notice the dog was leaping up, then Ruth was flinging, first the rifle, then herself into the back of the truck, with a helping hand from Joyce. The Israeli spun about, rifle back in hand, pointing it towards the hut and the men, now appearing and disappearing, as the truck drove out of the gates.

Ruth relaxed, and fell back on to her bum from the bouncing of the truck, and rested the rifle in her lap. She looked up at Joyce, sitting opposite, looking weary but grateful. 'That was – that was good work – and very, very brave – Thanks –'

Joyce nodded – there were other things, regrets, apologies, resolutions, none of which could be spoken now – and laughed as Zebaki licked her face. She found other clothes and slipped into a pair of oversized trousers and boots. Towards the deep end of the truck, Philippa and Nina stayed face down, which was probably the best thing for them; Joyce might not have had the stomach to hurt them for their betrayal, but she doubted if Ruth would be as merciful. 'So what now?'

Ruth glanced outside; Kimya and Faith, whichever one was driving, was taking them along the edge of the forest. 'We can drive around the mountain, find an army patrol in the borderlands and call for assistance.' She sighed. 'Pity. I'd hoped to be able to see the Hidden City.'

Joyce nodded in understanding, having seen it herself – then leaped up with alarm so quickly she almost tumbled out. 'You still might. *Faith!*'

It was risky, stopping so near the camp as they were; Achebe and his men still had the horses and might take the chance that something could happen to the truck.

Which wasn't that improbable, to hear Faith cursing and pleading for St Margaret of Antioch's help – 'for women, and for escaping from devils', she explained – once they'd stopped in a clearing; to the north, the borderlands stretched out, a wasteland of trenches and pillars of basalt like some lunar landscape. But at least she was now dressed in fatigues similar to Joyce's, and Zebaki watched their new prisoners while Joyce and Ruth trekked up the mountains, and Kimya kept an eye on the possibility of Achebe in hot pursuit.

Joyce led the way, feeling like she now knew this tiny bit of Africa like the back of her hand, even if they were climbing it from the other side of the mountain. She now moved with a power and purpose and aplomb that, quite frankly and proudly, she liked. She had faced demons within and without, and prevailed over both.

They reached the city. Ruth quietly admired it – Joyce's gift to her – while Joyce retrieved the hidden diaries. Afterwards, she hated to have to remind Ruth of the need to return to the truck; the look on the other woman's face was as much a treasure as the city.

'We'll come back someday,' Joyce promised her. 'All of us.'

The rain had stopped for a while. It was a silent trek back down the hill, emerging –

Into an ambush. 'Drop the gun, Ruthie!'

Nina's voice.

Joyce and Ruth froze in place, eyes darting about the truck. There was no one in sight.

The woman shouted again; the voice came from the behind the truck, or within it. 'I'm watching you! And we've got Faith and Kim here! I won't ask again!'

Joyce looked to Ruth as she called back, 'Let us see them!'

After a moment, four women appeared from behind, Faith and Kimya in front, their hands on their heads, with an armed Nina pointing the rifle at them and Philippa leading the rear, sporting a satisfied look. Now she spoke. 'You heard my colleague, Ruth. Drop the weapon. No, wait, give it to Joyce, and she'll give it to me; I've seen how quickly you can recover from adversity.'

Muttering under her breath, Ruth complied, her face taut. 'How'd you escape?'

'You'd be surprised what those slavers kept hidden in the back of their truck: knives to cut ropes, even a bloody stungun to deal with angry dogs. Now stand with the others. Not you, Joyce. Follow me. Nina, like we planned.'

The other woman nodded and grinned, motioning to her captives. 'OK, girls, over by those trees.'

Joyce held the bag of diaries at her side, staring at Philippa. 'What are you going to do to us?'

Philippa slid her hands into her trouser pockets, affecting a casual air as she gestured for Joyce to follow her to the cab of the truck. 'I *should* kill you all. What do you think?' She smiled cruelly. 'What would you be willing to do to save your life, and the lives of the others?'

Joyce glanced to her side, saw Zebaki, lying in the bush, still but breathing. She stopped and glared back with cold ire. 'You don't fool me any more. Or intimidate me. I know you won't kill us. You can't have bodies being found out here.'

'True enough. I've settled on employing a variation on my old plan. Achebe and his men will be along shortly; they have to come this way if they wish to cross back over the border. And you four will be here, tied up like gifts and waiting.' She took the rifle from Joyce, flung it into the cab.

'How could you do this? I mean, your job –'

'– My job doesn't pay for Renoirs and Monets,' Philippa replied simply, as if that made all the difference in her reasoning. 'And there'll always be men like Achebe in the world.' She leaned in closer, whispered in mock-conspiratorial fashion. 'We don't always get the luxury of liking the people we work with. Nina, for example – if I thought I could trust Achebe and his men, I'd have turned her over to them along with the rest of you.' Her brow furrowed. 'Be thankful you'll still be alive, somewhere, Joyce.' She opened the bag, peering inside, smiling to herself as she withdrew one of the plastic-bound diaries. 'Excellent. And extremely valuable.'

'Is that all my mother meant to you? All that talk in Berlin about how she helped you open your eyes to the problems of others –'

'And she did.' Philippa looked up, appearing sincere. 'And I'm grateful to her for making me appreciate all the more how wonderful it is to be rich, and not one of the peasants.' She kissed the diary and returned it to the bag, flinging it inside the truck cab and climbing in beside it, behind the steering wheel, starting up the engine. 'Joyce, our time together has been memorable; when this is over, I shall drink a toast to your continued health and well-being in New York.'

'Philippa?'

The woman glanced down at her.

'This is all *far* from over.'

Philippa paused, as if gauging the expression and tone of voice on Joyce. Then she slammed the cab door shut. 'Do us a favour, Joyce.' She shifted gears as the truck began to roll. 'Tell Nina I took the bullets out of her rifle before I gave it to her.'

Joyce stood and watched her depart, as further up the clearing, Nina, watching the scene, suddenly called out and took off towards her. She raised the rifle and pointed it in the direction of the truck – or Joyce – but nothing happened; Philippa had not been lying about her eventual betrayal of Nina. Joyce paused, checked out Zebaki – he was starting to shake off the stun he'd received – and she was confident that the others would deal with Nina.

Then Faith trotted over to her. 'Is he –'

'Fine.'

'Are you –'

'Fine, too.' She embraced the younger woman, squeezing her tightly. 'We have to get moving. Achebe's men could be here any minute now.'

'Yeah.' Still holding on to Joyce, Faith pulled back and looked into her eyes. 'Sorry.'

'For what?'

'For letting those two bitches get the drop on me.'

'You're not alone. They've done the same to all of us.' She nodded, more to herself than to Faith. 'We'd better start making plans. I have a promise to keep.'

TWENTY

Philippa leaned back in the plush leather chair in the conference room, letting her newly manicured fingernails dance lightly over the wineglass cradled between her hands. Her trek fatigues were discarded, burned, half a world away, and she wore an immaculate white Ralph Lauren hand-tailored skirt suit and matching Manolo Blahnik shoes.

She was *gorgeous* once again: nails, hair, skin – she'd treated herself well on her return to Berlin, determined to wipe away all traces of Africa and the unpleasantness she'd left there. She'd washed her hands of it and jetted to New York to sign the papers.

The publishers, of course, were shocked at the news of the tragedy; it even made a minor footnote in the news, though the connection with Constance Wilde was never publicly made, labelling the lost party 'tourists'. Philippa displayed suitable shock and grief at her loss, kept hidden her impatience at getting the tontine completed and the publishing contract signed over to her fully, while they performed the necessary legal investigations. They even stayed open today, on Thanksgiving Day, a public holiday. Just for her.

She'd kept herself amused this week in Manhattan's shops, noting her dwindling currency – she'd have had to start selling her art collection at this rate, if she hadn't signed the contracts – and by mentally counting the money she was about to earn.

And she *did* earn it. It wasn't easy, leaving Joyce and the others to lives of slavery. Really. Her work had given her an insight into where they might end up: brothels, sweatshops. But at least they'd be alive, somewhere.

Especially Joyce. Philippa owed it to Constance's daughter.

If only Joyce had known that a teenaged Philippa Sheringham had once lost her virginity to an older woman who was her university lecturer. A woman who subsequently spurned Philippa, something Philippa had never forgotten and never forgiven, even if she appeared all smiles afterwards. A woman named Constance Wilde.

Of course, if *that* was bad, what would Joyce and the others have thought about Philippa's involvement with the 'accident' with Constance's plane?

But no one had figured that out. And nothing had been heard about Joyce or the others. For the first time in the weeks since leaving Mahali, Philippa had begun to truly relax. Soon, she would return to Europe, ten million dollars richer. Then she'd holiday somewhere. Somewhere civilised. And cold. With champagne. And caviar.

She kept staring out the window, enjoying Manhattan's cityscape, imagining she could hear the Thanksgiving Day parade below. Then the doors opened behind her; the publisher's attorneys had some final papers for her to sign before the business was concluded. Then she would go out and find some impressionable young thing to make kneel before her –

'Hello, Philippa.'

Philippa froze, nearly let the glass tumble from her tenuous grasp and spill over the mahogany table. Her heart leaped into her throat; she forced it down with a swallow, fought the impulse to react, to rise, to look behind her. 'Good morning, Joyce. I . . . wasn't expecting you.'

'I told you, the last time we were together, that it was all far from over.'

'So you did.' She raised her glass to her lips, ignoring her trembling hand. 'How did you . . .'

'Survive?' Joyce stepped into view. She was dressed in simple black T-shirt underneath a beige windbreaker, jeans and boots; her eyes were hidden behind dark aviator glasses. She rested her bum against the table near Philippa's chair and folded her arms under her chest. 'It's a long story and not an easy one to recount, let alone live through. You'll have to read the additional chapters they're going to put in Constance's book to find out.'

'*My* book,' Philippa corrected, though even she knew better by now, if Joyce was here. 'I've signed the papers.'

'You signed nothing of importance. We'd been in touch with the publishers for over a week now, and they've been very good, keeping you distracted while Faith, Ruth and myself made the proper arrangements.'

Philippa cradled her glass between steepled fingers again. 'And Kimya? And Nina?'

'Kimya's offering testimony on our behalf at Nina's trial in Mahali. And the rest of us will be doing the same for yours.'

Philippa smirked, barely able to suppress her alarm. 'If you expect me to return to that hot, primitive country –'

'You don't understand. Men are outside those doors, with extradition papers. Mahali takes a very dim view of anyone conspiring with slavers. And kidnapping. And assault.'

'Are you really willing to detail every sordid little aspect of what I did to you, Joyce? For the courts?'

'Yes.' Joyce removed her glasses and leaned a little closer, noting how Philippa sank back into her chair, unable to look away, a mouse caught in a cobra's gaze. 'Because I've seen their prison cells. Hot, squalid, smaller than your walk-in closets. Flies and mosquitoes, slopping out, chain-gang labour . . . no museums, no health clubs, no after-dinner brandy . . . Still, a pretty thing like you will make friends quickly enough –'

Philippa hurled the glass across the room, smashing it against the window; red dew like blood dripped down as the doors opened, and a man's voice asked, 'Is everything –'

'Yes. I'm done with her. She's yours.'

Joyce watched silently as the suited men read out the extradition warrant, as uniformed officers cuffed Philippa's hands behind her. The woman never took her disbelieving eyes off Joyce, her mouth opening and closing like a fish gasping for breath. Finally, she seemed to find it. 'I'll get the best lawyers – my paintings – I'll sell them –'

Joyce nodded, content to say nothing about what Faith had done to Philippa's collection on their return to Berlin. She remained there, watching the party depart into the outer offices, leaving bewildered secretaries and executives, and Faith and Ruth, dressed like Joyce. Joyce approached them as Ruth nodded. 'I'll go along with Philippa for the ride.' She smiled. 'Sweet, wasn't it?'

Joyce smiled back. 'Very.'

Faith leaned against a wall, grinning. Joyce wanted to embrace her, kiss her – but they were no longer on the savannah. They were back in the real world, the world where she had been so timid herself, the het world that disapproved of such things –

Fuck it.

She pulled Faith into an embrace, their lips pressing together until she thought they'd burst. Dimly, Joyce heard the murmurs from those around her. And didn't care.

She left Faith breathless, eyes wide in disbelief, or at least awe at Joyce's boldness. 'Uh, can we get going?'

Joyce grinned and lifted up their backpack. 'You bet.'

They avoided the lift, entering a stairwell and ascending, though they were already on the top floor of the building and the final set of stairs. Faith tried the door they found awaiting them, then removed a set of keys – or key-like objects – from her pocket and began working them into the lock. 'So, you never told me what you'd planned to do with yourself now.'

'Didn't I?' Joyce teased. The truth was, she didn't know. Her old life would be so . . . boring now. Still, she had the rest of her life to worry about that. 'Yourself?'

With a click, the door opened on to the building's roof, with a bright midday sky, fresh and vivid and windswept. 'I thought I'd put together another band, maybe do some recording in LA.'

Joyce watched her rise to her feet again. 'I've always wanted to see LA. Can we drive cross-country?'

Faith grinned Cheshire. 'Yeah.' They kissed again, but Faith pulled back. 'Come on, the parade's waiting for us.'

With a playful laugh Joyce chased her out on to the roof of the building, bare apart from some squat air filters, whining air-conditioning units and scaffolding. The steel and glass spires of Manhattan surrounded them like the walls of some giant's castle in the sky, some buildings taller than the one they were on now. People dotted many of the windows, no doubt watching the parade below. She wasn't worried about their witnessing Faith and herself on the roof; for all they knew, they could be fellow parade spectators.

Joyce looked up at the nearest building, felt a mischievous grin break across her face. Then she reached out and grabbed Faith by the front of her T-shirt, pulling her closer into a heavy clinch, squeezing her breast through her shirt.

'What are you doing?' Faith breathed, overcome by the abruptness, the potency of Joyce's actions.

'Don't you know? I'd hoped *one* of us would know.' Joyce kissed her, thrusting her tongue deep into the woman's mouth, tasting her. Faith started, but then quickly relaxed. Joyce dropped her hands, pressed them to the woman's body, and slid them up under her arms, under the silk inner lining of Faith's jacket. Zips jangled, and she cupped Faith's heavy breasts in her palms.

Faith breathed heavily into Joyce's ear as she nuzzled it, bit the lobes. 'You like an audience? Maybe I should get you in the band?'

'Maybe we should forget the music and I just fuck you on stage?'

'Works for me.'

She pulled Faith tight in towards her body, breasts, bellies, thighs, all pressed close together through thin cloth. The wind up there whipped the legs of their trousers and the sleeves of their jackets, and as they twisted in place, Joyce glanced up, wondering how many people were watching them now instead of the parade.

They collapsed on to the roof, Joyce impatiently and noisily opening Faith's jeans. Half-lying on top of the younger woman, she let her hair dangle over Faith's giggling face as Joyce's hand dived inside, sliding under the elastic waistband of Faith's knickers, touching naked flesh, crinkly hair, and wet, puffy sweetness.

Joyce's pussy grew hotter, pulsed for attention; hungrily she began stripping Faith and herself, kicking off boots, jeans, jackets, T-shirts, bras, knickers . . . Joyce's eyes widened. She *loved* the sight of a dishevelled-looking Faith, sweaty brown skin, breasts heaving, curly black tuft of hair at the full crotch – and the wide eyes staring up at Joyce somewhere between arousal and admiration. Their clothes served as an impromptu blanket against the harsh, knobbly surface coating of the roof.

Joyce descended, pushing Faith's thighs apart. Closer now, the warm, damp smell of her pussy hit Joyce's nostrils. Breathless, unable and unwilling to wait, she dipped her head between the younger woman's cool thighs. She licked one delicate wet stroke across Faith's clit, making the body throb and the girl cry out.

Joyce's hands dug into Faith's thighs, and she felt and heard rather than saw the woman's hands slap her own stomach in frustration at the sheer bliss she was receiving. Joyce buried her face into Faith's pussy, hot and wet and eager as Joyce felt, and her head spun as she inhaled the strong, musky woman scent. She let her tongue indulge itself along the outer lips, before plunging it hard and deep and mercilessly into the inner folds. Faith's hands clamped now on to Joyce's head, tugging and weaving hair between her fingers, but Joyce remained relentless, flickering slowly, then quickly, driving her tongue deep inside Faith.

Balanced between the throbbing wetness between her own legs, and the delicious thrill of making love with another woman on a New York City skyscraper roof, she knew she could afford to take risks with Faith. Maybe at some point even play around with the games in which Philippa had so excelled, who knew? It would be all right, Joyce knew, because she trusted Faith. Trusted her with her life. Joyce rubbed her bare, heavy-feeling crotch against Faith's leg, still thrusting her tongue into Faith's pussy. Faith's body jerked and her hands pulled Joyce's hair hard, before Faith's lithe, muscular thighs suddenly tightened and released, then again. Feeling that orgasm made Joyce's own thighs clamp about Faith's leg, rubbing harder, humping, pressing harder, a bitch in heat. She, too, exploded, feeling the juices seeping from her to mark Faith as her own.

They lay curled about each other, only now hearing the distant sounds of the parade below. Faith's eyes were wide. 'What a beast you've become!'

Joyce growled and laughed.

Then security men burst through the rooftop door.

'Shit!' Faith cursed, rising and grabbing items of clothing, while Joyce grabbed the backpack and harness, and they rushed around the corner – leaving clothes behind. Most of their clothes, in fact, except for their underwear and boots.

They dressed quickly, Joyce ignoring the chill on her skin, delighted and excited. Then Faith fitted the harness on herself, attaching Joyce to the front. 'Are you sure about this, girl?'

'Yah!' Joyce's answer was unequivocal.

'OK – just like I taught you.'

Security men appeared in view, calling for them.

Faith wrapped her legs around Joyce. And Joyce began to run to the edge, an open area of scaffolding.

She was afraid. Terrified. But that was fine. Fear made her heart beat faster, made it beat louder. Reminded her how alive she was, how every precious moment meant more than all the wealth poor Philippa could possibly have hoped to gain from her deceptions.

The roof became scaffolding, with nothing underneath it, narrow and treacherous. And ending, very, very quickly –

They were in the air.

Air above, around and below them.

Down below, crowds and Thanksgiving parade floats, like ants and children's toys.

To the sides, people gawking at windows, disbelieving their eyes.

New York was never meant to be seen from *this* angle, surely!

Joyce wanted to pee, but Faith had wisely advised her to empty her bladder that morning – and not eat.

Her stomach *did* jump into her throat, and she tasted bile; the wind screamed around her ears and slapped against her body like a million hot dry flannels. In fact, she thought the wind was strong enough to lift them both up again.

But it was the parafoil, opening from Faith's backpack. Joyce found she was gripping the harness keeping her to Faith, a literal lifeline, and she turned to see Faith's wide grin, her hands gripping the directional lines. Above her, the parafoil looked like a red aeroplane wing, with cords running down to Faith's hands; the leading edge was curved and puffy, the rear edge thin, fluttering in the wind.

And suddenly, Joyce became aware of how slow they were travelling as they descended. And she found comfort in that slowness. It was so peaceful.

'Yo, girl!' Faith was shouting and laughing.

Joyce just laughed in reply, and let her arms extend like wings.

They twisted through the air, keeping a steady course between the buildings, following the path of the parade below. It was drawing closer, steadily closer. Where had she got the mad idea that they were drifting gently downwards?

They were bare metres over the balloons and floats, and close enough to hear the cheers and cries from the thousands of spectators lined along the pavements. They rose, and dropped, and rose again.

'Get ready!' Faith was shouting now.

Joyce found herself making some noise of acknowledgement, as Faith released her legs from around Joyce's thighs. There was the head of the parade, a clearing that was being made wider by quick-thinking cops. Joyce felt her lips were sore, realised that her mouth was open, her teeth clenched in a mad grin.

She hit the ground running, supporting Faith's lithe body to keep their legs from getting tangled up and tumbling over each other. Her boots pounded the street pavement, sending shocks through her leg muscles. She slowed to a sprint, then a walk, then finally a stop, the cheers of the crowds filling her ears as the parafoil collapsed upon them, as if aiding in hiding their state of undress from the media.

She was laughing hysterically, never feeling Faith unharness them. But she *did* feel Faith pull her into a kiss and embrace, before the police apprehended them.

Joyce was presented with a feast called life, and told to make of it what she wished, for she didn't know when she'd be called away from the table. She wanted to indulge herself to the fullest.

With no regrets.

www.sapphire-books.co.uk

SAPPHIRE NEW BOOKS

ICE QUEEN

Published in August 2000   Suzanne Blaylock

Which of these women is really the Ice Queen: a horny out-of-work actress with her eye on the main chance? A beautiful, successful author whose appetite for female lovers is a famous open secret? An eccentric butch dyke with an uncompromising attitude and a sardonic sense of humour? Drawn together by an accident of time and circumstance, a disparate group of women all hide behind masks of cool deception – but when their paths cross the ice soon melts in a furnace of passion.

£8.99   ISBN 0 352 33517 3

SHEELA-NA-GIG

Published in October 2000   Bridget Doyle

Jane Claremont, a not-so-innocent 19th century English novice, is just about to be ordained a nun when she begins to experience sensual visions – and ones that have the knack of becoming true. This news reaches Lady Elaine, a benefactress of the convent, and she entices Jane away with the promise of a better life. While Jane is greatly attracted by Elaine's beauty, she starts to feel there is a more sinister reason for the other woman's interest.

£8.99   ISBN 0 352 33545 9

IN HOT PURSUIT

Published in December 2000   Della Shannon

Late evening: young American adventuress Faith Ballard makes a reckless and illegal parachute jump off a tall building. Meanwhile in London, gay but reserved charity clerk Joyce Wilde awakens and pleasures herself in the afterwaves of a bizarre erotic dream. *In Hot Pursuit* takes both women to the savannahs and jungles of Africa – and to danger, intrigue and the raunchiest sex imaginable.

£8.99   ISBN 0 352 33553 X

ALSO IN PRINT

RIKA'S JEWEL
Astrid Fox

Norway, AD 1066. A group of female Viking warriors – Ingrid's Crew – have set sail to fight the Saxons in Britain, and Ingrid's young lover Rika is determined to follow them. But, urged on by dark-haired oarswoman Pia, Rika soon penetrates Ingrid's secret erotic cult back home in Norway. Will Rika overcome Ingrid's psychic hold, or will she succumb to the intoxicating rituals of the cult? Thrilling sword-and-sorcery in the style of Xena and Red Sonja!

£6.99   ISBN 0 352 33367 7

'Splendid stuff' – *Diva Magazine*
'★★★★!' – *SFX Magazine*

ALL THAT GLITTERS
Franca Nera

Marta Broderick: beautiful, successful art dealer; London lesbian. Marta inherits an art empire from the man who managed to spirit her out of East Berlin in the 1960s, Manny Schweitz. She's intent on completing Manny's unfinished business: recovering pieces of art stolen by the Nazis. Meanwhile, she's met the gorgeous but mysterious Judith Compton, and Marta's dark sexual addiction to Judith – along with her quest to return the treasures to the rightful owners – is taking her to dangerous places.

£6.99   ISBN 0 352 33426 6

'Never again will I be able to look at an ice cube or a tube of Wintergreen without breaking into a sweat! As for champagne . . . it's too good to just drink!' – *Libertas!*

HIGH ART
Tanya Dolan

Tinisha – a gorgeous, non-monogamous painter – is queen when it comes to the high art of seduction. If only the beautiful women of Cornwall would stop throwing themselves at her, she might be able to get some portraits done, as well.

£8.99   ISBN 0 352 33513 0

'Just the book to relax those sun-warmed bones after a day on the beach' – *Libertas!*

I MARRIED MADAM
Daphne Adams

Anna has a blast making the rounds of North London dyke pubs with her best friend Joan, but it's no cure for the rut she's fallen into with her girlfriend Vicky. Still, life gets more exciting when she meets enigmatic Marlene: a tall dark German who wears silk suits, smokes long expensive cigarettes and is, in short, a Dietrich-dream come true. A funny, bittersweet and very sexy tale about what *really* happens when opposites attract.

£8.99   ISBN 0 352 33514 2

— — — — — — — ✂ — — — — — — — — — — — — — — — — — —

Please send me the books I have ticked above.

Name ....

Address ....

....

....

.... Post Code ....

Send to: **Cash Sales, Sapphire Books, Thames Wharf Studios, Rainville Road, London W6 9HA.**

US customers: for prices and details of how to order books for delivery by mail, call 1-800-805-1083.

Please enclose a cheque or postal order, made payable to **Virgin Publishing Ltd**, to the value of the books you have ordered plus postage and packing costs as follows:

UK and BFPO – £1.00 for the first book, 50p for each subsequent book.

Overseas (including Republic of Ireland) – £2.00 for the first book, £1.00 for each subsequent book.

We accept all major credit cards, including VISA, ACCESS/MASTER-CARD, DINERS CLUB, AMEX and SWITCH.

Please write your card number and expiry date here:

....

Please allow up to 28 days for delivery.

Signature ....

— — — — — — — ✂ — — — — — — — — — — — — — — — — — —

WE NEED YOUR HELP . . .

to plan the future of Sapphire books –

Yours are the only opinions that matter. Sapphire is a new and exciting venture: the first British series of books devoted to lesbian erotic fiction written by and for women.

We're going to do our best to provide the sexiest books you can buy. And we'd like you to help in these early stages. Tell us what you want to read. Send your completed questionnaire to Sapphire Books, Virgin Publishing, Thames Wharf Studios, Rainville Road, London W6 9HA.

THE SAPPHIRE QUESTIONNAIRE

SECTION ONE: ABOUT YOU

1.1   Sex (*we presume you are female, but just in case*)
      Are you?
      Female   ☐
      Male   ☐

1.2   Age
      under 21   ☐   21–30   ☐
      31–40   ☐   41–50   ☐
      51–60   ☐   over 60   ☐

1.3   At what age did you leave full-time education?
      still in education   ☐   16 or younger   ☐
      17–19   ☐   20 or older   ☐

1.4   Occupation _____

1.5   Annual household income _____

1.6 We are perfectly happy for you to remain anonymous; but if you would like us to send you a free booklist of Sapphire books, please insert your name and address

_____

_____

_____

_____

SECTION TWO: ABOUT BUYING SAPPHIRE BOOKS

2.1 Where did you get this copy of *In Hot Pursuit*?
    Bought at chain book shop ☐
    Bought at independent book shop ☐
    Bought at supermarket ☐
    Bought at book exchange or used book shop ☐
    I borrowed it/found it ☐
    My partner bought it ☐

2.2 How did you find out about Sapphire books?
    I saw them in a shop ☐
    I saw them advertised in a magazine ☐
    A friend told me about them ☐
    I read about them in _____ ☐
    Other _____

2.3 Please tick the following statements you agree with:
    I would be less embarrassed about buying Sapphire
    books if the cover pictures were less explicit ☐
    I think that in general the pictures on Sapphire
    books are about right ☐
    I think Sapphire cover pictures should be as
    explicit as possible ☐

2.4 Would you read a Sapphire book in a public place – on a train for instance?
    Yes ☐   No ☐

SECTION THREE: ABOUT THIS SAPPHIRE BOOK

3.1 Do you think the sex content in this book is:
    Too much ☐   About right ☐
    Not enough ☐

3.2 Do you think the writing style in this book is:

      Too unreal/escapist ☐   About right ☐

      Too down to earth ☐

3.3 Do you think the story in this book is:

      Too complicated ☐   About right ☐

      Too boring/simple ☐

3.4 Do you think the cover of this book is:

      Too explicit ☐   About right ☐

      Not explicit enough ☐

Here's a space for any other comments:

SECTION FOUR: ABOUT OTHER SAPPHIRE BOOKS

4.1 How many Sapphire books have you read?

4.2 If more than one, which one did you prefer?

4.3 Why?

SECTION FIVE: ABOUT YOUR IDEAL EROTIC NOVEL

We want to publish the books you want to read – so this is your chance to tell us exactly what your ideal erotic novel would be like.

5.1 Using a scale of 1 to 5 (1 = no interest at all, 5 = your ideal), please rate the following possible settings for an erotic novel:

      Roman/Ancient World ☐

      Medieval/barbarian/sword 'n' sorcery ☐

      Renaissance/Elizabethan/Restoration ☐

      Victorian/Edwardian ☐

      1920s & 1930s ☐

      Present day ☐

      Future/Science Fiction ☐

5.2 Using the same scale of 1 to 5, please rate the following themes you may find in an erotic novel:

Bondage/fetishism ☐
Romantic love ☐
SM/corporal punishment ☐
Bisexuality ☐
Gay male sex ☐
Group sex ☐
Watersports ☐
Rent/sex for money ☐

5.3 Using the same scale of 1 to 5, please rate the following styles in which an erotic novel could be written:

Gritty realism, down to earth ☐
Set in real life but ignoring its more unpleasant aspects ☐
Escapist fantasy, but just about believable ☐
Complete escapism, totally unrealistic ☐

5.4 In a book that features power differentials or sexual initiation, would you prefer the writing to be from the viewpoint of the dominant/experienced or submissive/inexperienced characters:

Dominant/Experienced ☐
Submissive/Inexperienced ☐
Both ☐

5.5 We'd like to include characters close to your ideal lover. What characteristics would your ideal lover have? Tick as many as you want:

Dominant	☐	Cruel	☐
Slim	☐	Young	☐
Big	☐	Naïve	☐
Voluptuous	☐	Caring	☐
Extroverted	☐	Rugged	☐
Bisexual	☐	Romantic	☐
Working Class	☐	Old	☐
Introverted	☐	Intellectual	☐
Butch	☐	Professional	☐
Femme	☐	Pervy	☐
Androgynous	☐	Ordinary	☐
Submissive	☐	Muscular	☐

Anything else? _____